Thief of Hope

Thief of Hope

Cindy Young-Turner

Gray Corbie Press

Thief of Hope
Cindy Young-Turner

Copyright © 2014 Cindy Young-Turner

ISBN: 978-0-692-32094-5

Second Edition
Cover Design: Taria Reed

For Audrey

Because children really do bring hope to their parents

Prologue

The bell jangled over the low murmur of conversation and wisps of laughter. His face obscured by a hooded cloak, Oryn stepped across the worn threshold of the crowded tavern. The patrons spared him a glance before returning to their ale and concerns about the Guild's offer to the inhabitants of Last Hope, uninterested in an old man wearing a shabby cloak, leaning on a gnarled walking stick. A fleeting smile touched Oryn's lips. He shuffled toward the back corner.

Only the man seated at the back table took notice. A guttering tallow candle illuminated his tight-lipped expression. One hand rested on the dagger in his belt. Tense. Ready to bolt. The quarry of a relentless hunter.

Oryn approached him. The candle flickered, sending shadows skittering across the low ceiling blackened with the smoke of many years. He wrinkled his nose. The stench of strong ale and stale sweat was heightened by the pungent undercurrent of poverty and desperation clinging to the crowd, and even more strongly to the man seated across from him.

"May I join you?" Without waiting for a response, Oryn sat. He lowered his hood and brushed the shaggy white hair from his face.

The man's hazel eyes widened. He exhaled slowly, his body uncoiling. With a slight tremor, he reached for his brimming tankard of ale. "How did you find me?"

Oryn pushed up the sleeves of his worn cloak and set his elbows on the table. "Have you forgotten who I am, Edgar? Finding you has been the least of my problems in these dark days."

Edgar grunted, raising the tankard to his lips. "I've tried to forget a lot of things."

"You may try to forget, but you cannot deny what's happening." Oryn's voice dropped to a whisper. "You've seen what will befall the people of Last Hope if the Guild takes control of the town. They already control nearly all the merchant and craft guilds throughout the land. Their false promises of prosperity and independence are a yoke squeezing the necks of the commoners. Someone must challenge them."

"Like the poor soul they hanged in the square this morning?" Edgar shook his head. "I'm done with challenging the Guild."

"I recall not long ago you dubbed someone who uttered those words a coward."

"Times have changed. Being a coward has kept me alive. Unlike a lot of good people. Besides, I've taken an interest in other matters these days."

Oryn's gaze shifted to the five-year-old girl perched on a barstool. She spoke earnestly to one of the barmaids. Her pale face was smudged with dirt, her brown hair unruly. Her ragged clothes revealed skinned knees and elbows. Others saw no more than a barefoot waif, but Oryn glimpsed the gossamer threads of fate entwining the girl named Sydney, visible only to his wizard's eyes. The interweaving strands of possibility formed a constantly shifting tapestry, easily unraveled by the slightest alteration.

"It's not easy, raising a child in a place like Last Hope. Is this the sort of life you want for her?"

Edgar leaned forward. "How do you know about Sydney? She's no concern of yours."

"I'm afraid she is. Her future concerns me. Unless you

change your present course and fight for what you believe in, she'll have no future."

"I won't let Sydney be a pawn in one of your schemes. I've seen what happens when your kind meddles in the affairs of mortals. Leave her alone."

"Wizards have been trying to preserve what good still exists in this world." Oryn studied Sydney again and turned back to Edgar. "Tell me, Edgar, whose child is she? Is she even yours?"

Edgar clutched the handle of the tankard, his knuckles turning white. "She's not my blood, but she is *my* child," he said, his voice low and intense. "I found her abandoned on the street and fostered her when no one else wanted her. I won't let you take her, old man."

Oryn stroked his beard, pleased by Edgar's reaction. "It isn't my intention to take her from you."

"Then what do you want?"

"Edgar?" A feather-soft voice spoke before Oryn could reply. They turned to see Sydney standing beside them. She tugged Edgar's sleeve, a determined crease in her forehead. "Edgar, I gotta show you something."

"Not now, Sydney," Edgar said with a weary smile. He gave her a gentle push.

Her green eyes fixed on Oryn. He sensed a momentary spark of recognition, as if she realized what he was. *Impossible. She isn't a wizard. Perhaps I've overlooked something.*

Sydney thrust out her lower lip. "But I have something for you."

Edgar pinched the bridge of his nose. "All right. What?"

Her face brightened. Her scrawny arm thrust a handful of string at him. "For you."

He carefully untangled the knotted mass. The string looped through a hole in the center of a copper coin. "What is it?"

"Don't you see?" Sydney jabbed a grimy finger at the coin. "My first take! Pinched it this morning, like ya taught me. It'll bring luck. Do ya like it?"

A smile crossed Edgar's face, easing the haggard lines. "Of course I do," he said, patting her head. "I'll keep it with me always. For luck."

She grinned. "We need all the luck we can get. Like you always say."

"That we do, Sydney." He brushed the hair from her forehead. "Now you'd best be getting to bed. I'll be up soon."

Sydney embraced him before darting back into the crowd. The barmaid she'd been talking to earlier caught her hand and led her to a staircase across the room.

Edgar faced Oryn. "If Sydney's so important, why should I risk being hanged?"

"Every parent makes sacrifices for his child." For an instant, he faltered under Edgar's fierce stare. "To give Sydney a better life, you must teach her to do what is right. Make your life an example for her to follow." From within the folds of his cloak, he drew forth a leather purse and placed it beside the empty tankard.

Edgar grasped the purse and loosened the drawstring, his eyes widening. To someone in his present circumstances, the silver coins were a fortune. "Why are you giving this to me?"

"Use it to give hope to those who have none. Use it to help others fight—"

"Bribery? You must be desperate if you'd stoop to bribing me, old man." Edgar tugged on his stained shirt, frayed at the seams, and rubbed the stubble on his chin. He stared at Oryn a long moment. "And if I refuse?"

"You've always been so damn stubborn." Oryn expelled a long breath. "Do you really want the Guild to win? Do you—"

"If...now if I do what you ask...I'd expect you'd be in my debt." Edgar placed his hand on the purse, fingers clenching the soft leather.

"Indebted? To you? Really, Edgar." Oryn curtailed a sharp laugh and leaned back in his chair.

"I've never asked you for anything before." Edgar's eyes glinted in the flickering candlelight. "Promise, you'll look after her…if something should happen to me."

"Please, don't ask me that. Anything but that."

"Keep her out of harm's way. That's all I ask." Edgar reached across the table, seized his hand, and squeezed it, startling the old wizard. His voice caught in his throat, full of resignation. "You owe me, Oryn. Promise me this one thing."

Oryn knew such a promise would be impossible to keep. Sydney represented a single thread in the tapestry. Many others also required his attention. "I'll do what I can, but I can make no such promise."

Edgar glanced at the purse, his jaw tightening. He released Oryn's hand and looped the purse under his belt. "I'll do what I can, too, and we'll call it even."

Oryn stood and put a hand on Edgar's shoulder. "I'll count on you. Be well, Edgar." He moved toward the door, his mind a jumble. *Much remains to be done.* He tarried in the doorway to glance back and saw Edgar press Sydney's coin to his lips.

Raising his hood, Oryn stepped into the muddy cobblestone street and dodged a puddle. Light rain beaded on his wool cloak. He leaned on his staff, his shoulders sagging. He'd just committed a man to certain death. A good man, who deserved more hope than he could offer.

In these dark times, the Kingdom of Thanumor desperately needed hope. Not long ago, when the world was young and the veil between the realms of human and faery was whisper thin, enchantment and magic had inspired the kingdom and its people. Now, magic was looked upon with distrust, even heresy.

Hope was a fragile creature. Oryn had held it, fluttering, diaphanous, a delicate heartbeat thrumming beneath his fingertips. Grip it too tightly, and hope would be crushed, forever lost. Let it go, and hope might grow and expand to many who needed it.

A light flared in one of the second-story windows, and a child's face pressed to the glass. She fixed him with her stare, her green eyes luminous in the darkness. This time, Oryn *knew* her. The realization rattled his weary bones. He turned, his staff tapping in time with his quick footsteps, his knowledge wrapping him in a cloak of apprehension.

Without the proper guidance, hope might also grow wild and untamed, a creature transformed, all nails and teeth and harsh angles. A creature to be feared.

Chapter One

Nineteen-year-old Sydney stared out the narrow window at the darkened street below, tossing a silver coin from one hand to the other. The man in the bed grunted and turned over. She froze. Motionless, she waited for his breathing to grow steady. Her pulse beat faster. She crept closer to the straw pallet on the flimsy wooden frame to be certain he was still asleep. Standing over him, she watched his chest rise and fall in a peaceful rhythm. A spindle of saliva pooled in one corner of his lips.

She moved to the brown velvet tunic and shiny black leather boots beside the bed. With practiced fingers, she extracted two silver coins, a third of what he carried, from the purse tucked into his boot. Though tempted to take it all, she dared not be too greedy. He was a Guild official, and she was already risking much by stealing from his purse. He'd likely blame the loss of a few coins on carelessness; losing his entire purse would be a different matter.

Loud voices, punctuated by raucous laughter, drifted up from the tavern on the first floor. A soft snore drew her attention to the man in bed. She had to hurry. She gripped the coins in her sweaty fist. This would buy bread and ale for a week if she were careful.

The stout man had actually bragged about his position in

the Guild when he'd opened his fat purse and offered to buy her a pint earlier this evening. As if to impress her. Now she fought the temptation to spit in his face.

She'd spent the evening listening to his stories and watching him drink. She'd flirted while she sipped her ale, and once he was glassy eyed and slurring his words, she'd suggested they get a room upstairs. A silver coin paid in advance, another pint of ale, more tales of the Guild's glorious future, and finally, mercifully, he'd passed out.

A frigid breeze rattled the ill-fitted windowpane. The oil lamp on the floor flickered, sending shadows skimming across the walls. The floorboards creaked loudly beneath her worn, knee-high calfskin boots. Her stomach dropped, her leg muscles tightening. Retrieving her knife from beneath the straw pallet, she slid the blade into the sheath strapped to her boot and moved soundlessly to the door. The man began to snore, and she blew out a breath.

She slipped out and closed the door behind her, walking toward the rickety staircase. Downstairs, smoky candles sputtered on the long center table. A group of men clustered near the crackling fire in the hearth, woolen cloaks draped across chairs, tankards in hand. Most were working folk, dressed in dark homespun clothes, half of them still in the garments of their trade, a leather apron or a stained tunic. Sydney let her shoulders relax, inhaling the odors of spilled ale, roasted meat, and unwashed bodies.

"Syd, I was starting to worry 'bout you." Kat rushed to her side and wrapped her arm around Sydney's waist, steering her toward the bar. "Have any luck?"

Sydney forced a smile. "Enough."

Although Kat was in her early twenties, the dark circles under her eyes left harsh angles on her sallow face. Her long, amber hair was styled in a braid looping on top of her head with loose tendrils curling down her neck. She sat on a stool and arranged her ragged black shawl. The man next to her grinned. Kat gave him a wide smile, leaning forward to offer him a glimpse of her ample cleavage.

Turning back to Sydney, she tucked her hair behind her ears and adjusted her tattered red dress, a patchwork of muslin and lace frayed at the edges. "Still think you'd have better luck if you'd worn a dress like I told you. I coulda loaned you something to wear."

Sydney smoothed the wrinkles from her threadbare shirt and breeches, glad she hadn't taken Kat up on her offer. *Dresses were so impractical.* Her close-cropped hair and slender build enabled her to pass for a boy, at times a necessary deception when forced to live on the streets.

"Sometimes it doesn't matter what you're wearing," she told Kat, fishing out one of the silver coins. "How about a drink?"

Kat caught the bartender's attention. "Two ales."

Sydney placed the coin on the bar when the bartender returned with two wooden tankards. The bartender plunked down five copper coins, studying her longer than Sydney thought necessary. "Less the ale and the use of the room." Sydney drew in a long breath but didn't protest. She scooped the remaining coppers into her pouch.

He leaned closer, still staring into her face. "You look familiar."

"I don't think so." Her pulse quickened, and her hands worried at the hem of her shirt.

"I've seen you here before," he said, rubbing his unshaven chin. "I'm sure of it."

"Not likely. You must be thinking of someone else." She took a long swallow of the watered-down ale.

"I remember now." An unfriendly smile crossed his face. "It was years ago. You was here with Edgar."

Her heart skipped a beat. Sydney's hand gripped the tankard tightly. She struggled to keep her expression neutral. "Never heard of him." She downed the rest of the ale and touched Kat's arm. "Gotta go."

"You take after him, don't ya?" The bartender laughed. "Screwing the Guild, eh?"

His laughter followed her as she pushed her way outside. The cool night air offered a soothing counterpoint to the stifling tavern. The moon cast a faint glow on the nearby thatch-roofed houses and shops crowding the narrow lanes. The tavern door opened, spilling light onto the rutted street and revealing Kat's gaunt figure.

Kat straightened her shawl and hurried over to her. "You coulda waited until I finished my ale. Who's Edgar?"

Sydney turned from Kat's questioning stare. The mention of Edgar's name brought back the all too familiar constriction in her throat. Tears formed, and she angrily rubbed her eyes. "No one you'd know."

Kat squeezed her shoulder. "You think too much. This'll help." She reached between her breasts and withdrew a glass vial, the size of Sydney's little finger, and handed it to her. "Go ahead, take it. I don't need it tonight."

Sydney eyed the multicolored pills. Fantasia. The powerful drug transported the person who used it to fantastical realms, where all troubles ceased to exist. She was well acquainted with it.

She gave the vial back to Kat. "You keep it. I'm done with it."

"Suit yourself." Kat tucked the vial back between her breasts. "How about you find Zared? He'll take your mind off whatever you're worrying about."

"I'll think about it. You, uh, seen him tonight?"

"Earlier. He left while you was upstairs." She gave Sydney a gap-toothed smile. "Don't worry, I won't tell him what you was up to. And don't give him any of your coin. This time, it's all yours."

"Get back to work, Kat. Be careful, will ya?"

"Always am, luv." Kat smoothed her hair and walked to the

tavern door, but it banged open before she could grasp the handle.

The Guild official Sydney had robbed had awakened and dressed in his fine velvet tunic. His face red, eyes bulging, he jabbed a finger at her. Two burly men appeared in the doorway behind him. "There's the wench who stole my money!"

Sydney tensed, and her heart hammered against her ribcage. *Too many to fight alone.*

She glanced at Kat, who hung her head and averted her eyes. The three men moved out of the doorway, and Kat ducked inside, leaving Sydney to fend for herself.

Sydney whirled and ran. Her boots smacked the dirt street. Footsteps pounded behind her, punctuated by shouts of *"Don't lose her!"* and *"Stop, wench!"* Fear of imprisonment, torture, or even hanging spurred her faster.

Not daring to glance back, she zigzagged from one narrow street to the next. The footsteps chasing her kept a steady pace. A light bobbed ahead. The night watch.

Bloody hell.

She turned a corner and skidded to a stop. She stumbled, falling on her hands and knees, and stifled a cry. Pebbles cut into her palms. She forced herself up on shaky legs and ducked down a familiar shortcut. An overhang concealed her. Footsteps ran past, and the shouts quickly receded.

Running along the lane in the opposite direction, her heartbeat thundered in her ears. Her breath came ragged and quick. Clouds shadowed the moon, which barely illuminated the maze of pathways. Finally she staggered, doubled over, hands on her knees, lungs bursting. When she'd caught her breath, she backtracked and scanned the surrounding streets. No sign of her pursuers. Unlikely they'd continue searching for her in this part of town.

Too hungry. Too desperate. Should've known better than to steal from a Guild official.

A distant bell tolled across the town. Eight chimes. Curfew.

The taverns would be emptying, and most law-abiding folk would return to their homes. The wind gusted, bringing with it a chill and the stink of sewage. She drew her shabby cloak close and stuck her hands in her armpits for warmth. Cautiously, she eyed the shadows. A scuttling sent her pulse racing. Just a rat.

She needed a safe place to hide. *Zared.* He'd help. He'd hidden her from the Guild before.

Sydney hastened to a dilapidated, two-story boarding house, watching the shadowy alcoves for movement. Like many of Last Hope's workers employed by the merchants or master craftsmen in various trades, Zared rented a room in this part of town, although he usually avoided legitimate employment. Most people could barely afford meals and lodging after paying the Guild's dues. Often several families crammed into a single, squalid room.

She climbed the staircase and knocked softly, hoping to find him alone. No answer. She knocked louder. "Zared, it's Syd," she called softly through the door.

The bolt slid back, and the door opened. Zared's dark hair hung loose over his shoulders, framing his handsome, angular face.

She took in the room behind him. A flickering candle on a table provided a dim light, revealing a straw pallet on the floor and blankets and clothes piled beside it. Better than many of the rooms they'd shared, filthy hovels with rats gnawing in the walls.

"I wasn't expecting you."

She fidgeted and ran a hand through her hair. "Had some, uh, trouble. Can I come in?"

He stepped back and motioned her inside, bolting the door behind her. He folded his arms. His untucked shirt was rumpled. Tall and lean, he liked to dress well and somehow could always afford tailor-made clothes, which allowed him to make connections with people who had power and influence in

Last Hope.

"Trouble with the Guild," she added.

"I ain't surprised. Kat mentioned a Guild official. Did she put you up to it?"

"What I do is *my* business. Not yours."

"It's my business if you come here in the middle of the night asking for help."

Her fingers trembled as she retrieved a silver coin from her neck pouch. "He owed me."

"Not bad." Zared held out his hand.

He acts like he helped earn it. She hesitated, and then dropped the coin into his palm. *No reason to tell him about the other one.*

"You hungry?" He grabbed a bundle from the table and handed it to her.

Unwrapping the bread and cheese, she sat on the straw pallet to eat. He sat in the chair next to the table, his dark eyes watching her. When she finished, he tossed her a silver flask.

"You should've come to me first. Kat doesn't care who she sleeps with. I'll make sure you're safe."

Sydney took a long swallow of the potent liquor and handed the flask back to him. "You think I'd sleep with a Guild official?"

His mouth, at times either sensuous or cruel, twisted into a frown. "Did you?"

"Does it matter?"

He sat beside her on the makeshift bed and snaked his arm around her waist. "I think if you did, you'd have a handful of silver."

She pushed him away. "It ain't worth it."

"What're you gonna do when picking pockets isn't enough? You'd rather starve?"

She hugged her knees to her chest. Selling her body wasn't as easy as he made it seem. She often fooled herself into thinking Zared understood her. He didn't. He didn't understand the principles Edgar had instilled in her. Principles she desperately wanted to uphold but lacked the willpower to.

"The bartender said he'd seen me there before. With Edgar. What if he tells someone?"

"He won't. He's got no reason to. In a day or two, they'll forget what you did tonight. Like I told you before, don't make trouble, and they'll leave you alone."

She clenched her fists on her knees. "I should make trouble for them. I shoulda done more. Like Edgar did…."

"He's dead. You survived. Ain't that enough for you?"

It wasn't. Surviving would never be enough.

"Syd, you didn't actually come here just to talk about Edgar or the Guild, did you?" He traced the line of her jaw. Heat danced across her flesh. His lips brushed her neck, and his mouth caressed her skin.

"I've missed you." His breath warmed her cheek. The candlelight reflected the need burning in his eyes. "We've gotta take care of each other, remember?"

He captured her hand and brought it down his chest, muscles tensing at her touch. Her fingers settled over the evidence of his need. With a groan, he pressed against her. His body warm, hard, solid. She fumbled with the laces of his breeches, feeling his pulse beat with heat and pleasure. *Want and need.* She covered his mouth with hers. His lips tasted of the heady liquor.

He pulled her shirt over her head and leaned her back on the bed, tugging off her breeches. Her body quivered at his gentle strokes, aching for more, needing him to ease her pain, to banish the loneliness from her heart. She drew him close, enflamed by the desire in his eyes.

"We love each other, don't we?" she breathed.

He shed his clothes, and she searched his face for the elusive closeness she so desperately craved. He pressed his lips to hers, hard, yearning, and lay over her slender body, parting her legs with his. When he entered her, she clung to him and tangled her fingers in his hair. They moved together in a fierce, familiar rhythm. He gripped her hips, whispering her name until they both reached a fiery climax.

Yet afterward, lying beside him, listening to his heartbeat, Sydney had never felt more alone.

———

A pounding jolted Sydney awake. She shivered under a thin blanket. Cold. Alone. Muffled voices. A slice of daylight crept into the gloomy room through a gap beneath the door.

"Open up in there!" a voice shouted.

Dammit. How did they find me? Where the hell is Zared?

She snatched her clothes and struggled into them, her hands shaking.

Fear coursed through her. She couldn't move. Couldn't think. The hammering on the wooden door grew louder, rattling it in its frame. Desperately she scanned the room. No windows. No means of escape.

The door burst open. Two men wearing the brown uniforms of the town guard rushed inside. In the doorway stood the Guild official from the night before.

"Grab her!" he yelled.

"Get your bloody hands off me!" She kicked at them. One guard punched her in the stomach. She doubled over, groaning and gasping for breath. He wrenched her arms behind her back and bound her hands. The other guard took her knife and jerked the pouch containing her hard-earned coins from her neck.

"The money belongs to me." The Guild official swaggered into the room, holding out his hand. Reluctantly the guard handed over the pouch.

Circling her like a hunter cornering his prey, he leered at her. "Thought you'd get away with stealing from me, eh, wench?" His stubby fingers reached out and grasped the front of her shirt, pulling her upright, bringing her close.

She gagged on his foul breath.

"I know who you are." His whisper held a sinister promise. "You're Edgar's child. Who would've thought a cheap whore could turn out to be such a prize?"

Sydney's breath came in gasps. Someone turned her in. Not Zared. *Please, not Zared.* Kat was a more likely choice.

"You're wrong. I ain't no one important."

He lifted a chubby hand and slapped her. Hard. She staggered back. Her ears rang, and spots appeared before her eyes. Her cheek swelled and stung with pain. He backhanded her again, driving her to her knees, and kicked her in the ribs. Pain spiked her side, and blood filled her mouth.

He straightened his tunic and waved a hand at the guards. "Take her to the gaol. I'll speak with the captain to arrange for the execution."

The Guild has already destroyed my life. Time to start fighting back. If I'm not too late.

Before the guards dragged her outside, she managed to spit on the Guild official's dirty boots, earning another slap across the face. At the sight of the waiting gaoler's cart, her defiance faded, leaving her breathless and limp. The ropes around her wrists tightened, digging into her skin. Like a noose.

Chapter Two

A chill enveloped Sydney, more penetrating than the biting wind. She turned from the empty market square to the two guards who had escorted her from her cell. One leaned against the wooden platform, arms crossed. The younger man, not much older than Sydney, paced, fingers tapping the hilt of the sword belted at his waist. His brown coat and trousers were rumpled, and the bits of straw clinging to his clothes suggested he'd been roused from sleep.

The tall, wooden scaffold gleamed in the early morning light. The crimson-streaked sky and crisp autumn air, with its scent of wood smoke, offered Sydney a taste of freedom. But only a taste. Coarse ropes dug into her wrists. Anxiety churned in her stomach. Her muscles ached from a restless night sleeping in the damp, fetid cell in the gaol located beneath the Guild Hall. Dried blood crusted her face and spattered her shirt. Swaying in the gusty breeze, the hangman's noose appeared to beckon her to her fate.

"Please." Sydney held out her bound hands, supplicating. Her voice cracked. "I-I ain't done nothing worth being hanged for."

The younger guard stopped pacing. He moved toward her, eyes narrowing to slits, and spat at her feet. "Filthy wench. Should've left you down in the hole for a bit. Let you think on what happens when you defy the Guild."

"She'll be dead soon enough," said the older guard. "Besides, if we left her down there too long, you'd not be able to bear the stink of her." The two men laughed.

Sydney focused on the deserted square, fighting back tears. The stench of the gaol lingered on her clothes, seeping into her skin, worming away her dignity.

Early dawn shadowed the thatch-roofed merchant shops bordering the market, alighting on the Guild Hall at the other end of the square. At this hour, no one stirred. A night in the gaol, and no one to stand up for her. Part of her still believed Zared would get her out of this. She clung to the hope he hadn't betrayed her. Especially not to the Guild.

"Early for a hanging, isn't it?" asked the young guard as he stretched.

"Captain said to bring her out now. Probably has something special planned for her. Remember when we nailed that bloke's ear to the post last week?" The guard chuckled. "Got a good turnout."

"Chopping off a hand might be better. She's a thief, isn't she?"

"True. She might scream louder, too. The screams always draw a crowd."

Sydney's empty stomach churned. Her body shook. She couldn't breathe. Her gaze was drawn to the tall wooden post on the other side of the scaffold. The blood of countless prisoners who'd been tormented before their executions stained the weathered wood. She flexed her fingers. Thin and delicate, despite the grime encrusting her fingernails. Her livelihood.

The last pink hues of dawn had given way to daylight when the captain of the guard finally arrived on horseback, leading two mounts. "Change of plans. We're not hanging this one."

"But she's an enemy of the Guild. Edgar's girl, is what I heard."

"Last time we hanged one of Edgar's conspirators, people

rioted in the square. We'll take care of her quietly. She goes out to the Wizard Tree."

The older guard muttered an oath, and Sydney's heart began to pound. She'd never heard of the Wizard Tree before.

The young guard's mouth turned down, defiant. "Master Conrad was insistent she be hanged. Guild's orders."

"Are you questioning my decision?" The captain's commanding voice and carriage, and the streaks of gray in his dark hair and beard, gave him an air of authority.

"No-no, sir."

"Then let's go."

The younger man tied a lead rope to Sydney's bonds and looped the other end into his left stirrup. His smile mocked her. "Try to keep up."

The two guards mounted. The horses began to trot, and the rope grew taught, jerking her forward. She hobbled after them, stumbling, clenching her teeth.

A wagon passed carrying produce for the market, wheels clattering over the cobblestones. Goats and cows grazed in the fenced-off pasture. Last Hope's main thoroughfare took them to the town gate, the only entrance through the wooden wall surrounding the town. Sydney drew in a deep, shuddering breath when they passed through the solid, iron-reinforced gate.

The guards and their captain took the road winding past the cultivated fields outlining the town. The sun shone brightly, but its warmth eluded Sydney. She shuffled along the dirt road, avoiding the muddy furrows, pushing her bruised body to keep pace, lest she be pulled off her feet and dragged behind the horse.

They crested a hill and halted at a crossroads. An arrow on a stone marker pointed toward Lord Aldric's keep, more than half a day's journey to the west. Though Last Hope fell under Aldric's domain, the Guild had usurped their lord's authority over the town. Sydney glanced back at the smoke rising from the chimneys of the homes within the walled town. She'd lived there all her life. Built on the edge of the Kingdom of Thanumor, nestled near the ancient forest and the desolate Wastes, Last Hope struggled to provide a semblance of civilization in a land where the Guild controlled the gamut of life.

Tears filled Sydney's eyes. With a pang, she realized she was leaving the only home she'd known for the last time. The raucous cries of the crows circling a nearby field mocked her.

The captain raised a hand toward the eastern road, the one leading into the forest. The rope pulled Sydney forward, and her stomach lurched. A haze of danger and malevolence cloaked the ancient forest. Few people dared to enter the dark wood for fear of the strange creatures inhabiting it. Woodsmen often returned to Last Hope bearing tales of fighting off fierce and hungry wolves, and late in the evening, after pints of ale, they'd share foreboding tales of the Tuatha, the faery folk.

The faery folk had once lived in the desolate Wastes beyond the forest. Now they hid within the shadows of the tall trees, waiting to spirit away any poor soul who stumbled into their sylvan domain.

Only stories, nothing more. Sydney shuddered, trying not to imagine these enthralling and terrifying creatures watching them.

She didn't believe in the Tuatha any more than she believed in the all-powerful god who the church claimed offered salvation and a paradise after death. Magic and miracles weren't so different. Neither had ever offered her any comfort.

After several hours, the road grew narrower, and the guards dismounted. The younger guard stayed behind to tend the horses, and the older guard took the rope binding her and accompanied the captain along an overgrown path. Sydney's hair was plastered to her head, and sweat pooled between her shoulders. Thorny branches tore her clothes. Traversing the thick undergrowth sapped her remaining strength. Acorns littered the ground, crunching beneath the guards' heavy boots. The chance of escape receded with each step deeper into the forest. Exhaustion, pain, and fear became her reality.

They entered the clearing at midday. Shadows hung like curtains from the towering oaks ringing an open expanse littered with leaves and tree limbs. The air had a suffocating stillness, and the pungent aroma of wildflowers and damp earth wafted around them. An enormous oak dwarfed the other trees. Rotting ropes encircled the base of its massive trunk, and its skeletal branches twisted overhead to form a dense canopy.

The guard spoke in a hushed voice. "What manner of place is this?"

"Wizards were once executed here." The captain matched his tone.

"Wizards?"

"Years ago. Now it's the perfect place to execute certain criminals. No one will ever find her here."

With a burst of renewed energy, Sydney struggled as they dragged her to the tree and tethered her to it with heavy rope.

"You can't do this to me! It's a mistake! I ain't done anything!"

"You don't need me to stay, do you?" The guard glanced nervously into the forest.

The captain withdrew a dagger from his belt. "Go wait by the horses. This won't take long."

"Please," her voice cracked. Her legs gave way, but the ropes held her upright. "I'll do anything."

He wiped the sweat from his forehead with the back of his hand and regarded her for a long moment. "Edgar was a good man. Too bad you didn't live up to his name. Just a no good thief."

Her throat constricted. "You don't know anything about me. Or Edgar."

"I know enough. He convinced people to support each

other when the Guild blacklisted them. He helped them hide when they needed to and made sure their families were safe. He was close to overthrowing the Guild." A muscle twitched in his cheek. "Until Schrammig came."

Schrammig. Sydney tensed and bit her lip. Schrammig was one of the Guild's most terrifying enforcers, known and feared throughout Thanumor for hunting down the Guild's enemies. The man responsible for Edgar's execution. She'd had nightmares about Schrammig even before she'd seen his face.

The captain lowered his voice, "Schrammig is on his way to Last Hope. If he knew you'd been arrested, he'd show you no mercy." He ran his thumb along the hilt of his dagger. "If I let you go, I risk my position. My life. But I made a promise to a dying man. It was the only thing I could do for him."

Her eyes widened. "For Edgar?"

"He asked me to spare your life," the captain said with a curt nod. "He said I was to bring you here, to the Wizard Tree, instead of the gallows. An unusual request. Why would he ask such a thing?"

"I-I don't know."

The breeze gusted, swirling the leaves near her feet. A strange whispering drifted on the eddy. The captain's brow furrowed, and he scanned the clearing. The fluttering tones grew louder, raising the hair on Sydney's arms.

The captain took a step back. "What are you doing?"

"Nothing."

Inky shapes flitted among the trees.

He moved toward the tree line, taking slow, cautious steps, sweat beading on his forehead. "Is someone there? Show yourself!"

Not someone. *Something.* The whispers roared in Sydney's ears. Shadows coalesced. A sinuous fear rippled across her skin, a primal terror of things unknown and powers beyond comprehension.

The captain's mouth opened and closed, an expression of

terror contorting his features. He turned and fled back the way they'd come without another word.

"Wait! Don't leave me here! Not like this!"

Chapter Three

The shuffling footsteps faded, and the whispers trailed away, replaced by the chirping of crickets. Sydney scanned the tall trees. The captain had said wizards had been executed here. Somehow she knew an unknown and sinister presence remained in this accursed place.

She yanked on the ropes binding her until her wrists were raw and bleeding. Her heart pounded in her ears, and a bone-chilling stillness spread across the forest. She looked up at the bare limbs above her.

I can't die like this.

Her breath grew shallow, and tears blurred her vision. She turned her head, the tree bark rough against her cheek. The reek of decomposing leaves now permeated the air. The stench of death.

Shadows lengthened in the fading sunlight. Orange and violet streaked the sky. The air grew colder. Her stomach ached, and her tongue felt thick in her mouth. Defeated, she slumped against the tree, unable to contemplate a slow and painful death by starvation, thirst, and exposure.

Dusk arrived too quickly. A howl sounded through the woods. Her head snapped up, all her senses alert. The beasts would be hungrier this time of year. Not for a girl all skin and bones, she hoped. Terror seized her. In desperation, she strained against the blood-slicked ropes.

Her aching muscles tensed at the soft rustle of leaves. In the deepening shadows, a four-legged shape moved back and forth inside the tree line. When the beast crouched, a pair of bright yellow eyes gleamed from the shadows.

At least Edgar had died for his beliefs. If only she could have done things differently. If only she'd been strong enough to follow his example. Edgar had taught her never to cry, and now his voice echoed in her mind: *"You must be strong to survive in this world, Sydney. I have faith you'll make the right choices."*

"You were wrong, Edgar," she whispered. "I couldn't be what you wanted."

Warm tears slid over her cheeks. The rustling grew louder. She closed her eyes, hoping for a quick end.

"You're in quite a predicament, aren't you?"

Sydney's eyes flew open. An elderly man stood at the edge of the tree line. He wore a dark blue cloak, mud-splattered and frayed at the edges. His shoulder-length white hair and unkempt beard were matted with sticks and leaves. Bright blue eyes and a thin nose lent grace to his craggy countenance.

"It's hardly polite to stare with one's mouth open," he said. His smile broadened, and he winked at her. "It also invites flies."

Her gaze darted to where the wolf had been. It was gone. She wiped the tears from her face on her shoulder. "Who the hell are you?" Her voice was as raw as her wrists.

The lines on his face furrowed. He moved closer. "I had hoped for a more welcoming greeting from you, Sydney."

"How'd you know my name?"

"I know many things. Knowing how to find you is among them, although I would have preferred that we meet under different circumstances."

Sydney studied him. *The face, the eyes....* Something familiar, but she couldn't figure out why. "How'd you get here?"

He chuckled and leaned on a long wooden staff. "We have much to discuss, my dear, but the forest is no place for conversation." He crooked a finger in her direction. The ropes binding her dropped to the ground. She kicked at them with her feet. *Magic.* It had to be. The stranger moved, reaching for her.

"Don't touch me." She slid to the ground. Setting her teeth against the pain in her cramped legs, she rubbed her calves through the thin fabric of her breeches.

She fingered the ropes at the base of the tree. Her muscles tensed. "*What* are you?"

"Why must I be anything? Perhaps I am merely an old man who has taken an interest in your welfare and saved you from certain death."

A wizard.

"Now come, we must make haste." He began to walk away.

Sydney slowly got to her feet, wiping her face on a dirty sleeve. She searched the shadows for wolves.

"Wait," she called. "I ain't going anywhere with you until you answer me. Who *are* you? Why're you helping me?"

He glanced over his shoulder. "I'm not going to hurt you. Not when I've just saved your life." He faced her, stroking his beard with gnarled fingers and added, "However, I'd be telling a falsehood if I said I was acting solely out of kindness."

Sydney folded her arms, not surprised.

"If you don't come with me, where else will you go? Back to Last Hope? To a death sentence? You lack provisions, and you'll find no refuge in the forest. You'd be dead within days. I can offer you shelter, a hot meal, and a bath."

Her stomach rumbled at the mention of food. She kept her arms crossed, eyeing him suspiciously. "What do you want from me?"

He leaned on his staff and let out a breath. "Apparently Edgar has bequeathed you his stubbornness as well as his chosen profession."

"Edgar? You knew Edgar?" Her arms fell to her sides, her eyes wide.

"My knowledge extends to many things, dear Sydney, but this is neither the time nor the place to discuss them. Come now, will you accept my offer? Or would you rather wait for the wolves?"

She relaxed her stance. Most people couldn't be relied on. Yet, the old man's gruff kindness encouraged her to trust him. His familiarity with Edgar aroused her curiosity. And he was a wizard. Not to mention, his words rang true. She'd never make it to the next town on her own.

"All right." She took a step forward. "First you gotta tell me your name."

"You may call me Oryn."

When she stumbled, he offered his hand. Sydney waved him away and put a hand on the sturdy tree trunk. "Gimme a minute."

After kneading her tight muscles, she limped after him. He left the clearing and approached a wagon hitched to a gray nag. The horse whinnied, and Oryn rubbed its nose. A lantern hanging from the wagon illuminated a dirt road. Trees crowded along the edge of the path, tall and menacing.

Sydney didn't remember seeing a road when the guards had brought her to this place. Roads simply didn't appear where they hadn't been before. Unless it was magic. The hair prickled on the back of her neck. "Where are we going?"

"My home isn't far. You'll be safe there."

"You live in the forest?"

Oryn seated himself in the wagon. "You'll see. Come along."

Sydney climbed in. The wagon jerked forward. In the stillness, a faint whisper echoed. The same whisper she'd heard earlier. Oryn focused on the road ahead and whistled under his breath to the nag.

"Is it true wizards were…executed here?"

The lines on his face deepened. "No, not wizards. The Tuatha."

Her eyes widened. "The Tuatha? They ain't…real."

"They are indeed as real as you or I. And the correct phrase is 'aren't real,' Sydney. Surely Edgar must've taught you to speak properly."

She slumped on the seat. "Yeah, I guess he did. But Edgar's been gone a while now."

"Yes, he has. And I'm sorry for it. However, his death is no reason to conduct yourself like a common street urchin. I'm certain Edgar taught you better."

She opened her mouth to say she was indeed a common street urchin, but his intense gaze silenced her. His azure eyes drew her into their unfathomable depths. As if she could see into his soul. Power the likes of which she had never experienced emanated from him. Her breath quickened, and an exhilarating tremor pulsed in her veins. Images flashed before her, of unfamiliar people and places, and joy and sorrow and fear and loneliness.

Oryn touched her arm, breaking the spell.

Sydney jerked back. "You *are* a wizard."

"You, my dear, see things most people do not."

A shiver jolted up her spine. "What sort of things?"

He withdrew a half loaf of bread and a skin of water from a leather pouch on the seat between them and handed them to her. "I expect you're hungry. No more talk. Eat."

She mumbled a *thank you* and took long, gulping swallows before stuffing bread into her mouth. While she ate, she scrutinized the pouch from the corner of her eye. The curious object was no larger than her hand, far too small to contain the things Oryn had removed from it.

He focused on the path, apparently not paying any attention to her. She knew how to snatch purses without anyone taking notice. Her hand inched across the wooden seat, fingers nearing the drawstring.

In a swift motion, he whisked the pouch away, hiding it within the folds of his cloak. He smiled. "Curiosity can be dangerous, especially when magic is involved."

Chastened, she clasped her hands in her lap and watched the tall trees pass. "How far to your home?"

"Not far. Would you like to sleep until we arrive?"

Weariness enveloped her. She yawned. Sleep beckoned, but she dared not succumb. "I ain't…I mean, I'm not tired."

"As you wish."

Sydney's eyelids drooped. She struggled to keep her wits about her. With a start, she realized she didn't hear the horse's hooves or the creak of the wheels. Though the ground was uneven and rocky, the ride was smooth, without a single bump. An unsettling manner of magic. A strange whisper resonated within her mind, hinting of a dangerous power. The trees blurred, and the lantern light swam before her eyes. She held the seat, swaying. Her thoughts muddled.

"Sydney?" Oryn's hand took hers and squeezed. "This will be more difficult for you than I expected. Hold on. We'll cross over quickly, I promise."

The darkness shifted. The air grew heavy, shrouding Sydney with an unseen veil. She tensed and choked back her rising panic, fighting the urge to flee. Her hands gripped the wooden seat. She shrank against Oryn. His arm went around her shoulders, solid and comforting. The warmth of his body sheltered her from the frigid, shadowy swells crashing over them.

A pinpoint of light sparked on the horizon. Oryn steered them out of the sable night, away from the grasping shadows and their icy tendrils. The wagon jolted and at last halted. The vast sky, an opaque canopy lit by the quarter moon, had never seemed quite so ominous or so close. A desolate panorama of sand and rock stretched to the horizon. Silence swept over them, a hush full of promise. Of power. And foreboding.

Sydney swallowed hard and clutched her hands between her knees. Oryn had brought her into the Wastes.

Chapter Four

The wagon rolled over the rugged wasteland, so still and silent that Sydney's heart beat loudly in her ears. A pinprick of light winked in the dark landscape, as if a star had fallen to earth.

Oryn's face crinkled into a smile. "Welcome to my home."

A massive structure materialized on the barren plain. Several times taller than any building in Last Hope, the circular tower stood alone, unattached to a castle or keep. In the moonlight, the white stone tower took on a luminous hue. Dark windows resembled the eyes of an unearthly creature.

Oryn alighted from the wagon. "Stay close. Things out here are far more dangerous than wizards. Don't dawdle, lest my magic be unable to protect you." He walked toward the tower, waving her to follow. "Come, I promised you a hot meal, remember?"

Sydney rubbed her arms to ward off more than the chill air and hurried after Oryn.

The figure of a woman emerged from the shadows near the base of the tower. She ran to Oryn and caught him in an embrace. "Where have you been? I was beginning to worry."

Her alabaster skin gave her an ethereal appearance, and her chestnut hair cascaded over her shoulders in soft waves. A braided golden belt tied around her slender waist, cinching her coral gown.

Oryn embraced her. "Vadnae, you shouldn't have waited out here in the cold."

"I haven't been waiting long." Vadnae squinted in Sydney's direction. "Did you find the one you sought?"

He beckoned to Sydney. She approached cautiously. Vadnae's perfumed hair and rustling silk dress complemented an air of grace, but she surveyed Sydney with condescension. Fidgeting, Sydney ran a hand through her tangled hair and brushed the dirt and leaves from her worn shirt and breeches.

"Sydney, this is my granddaughter, Vadnae."

The corners of Vadnae's delicate mouth turned downward. "Wherever did you find her? Roaming the alleys of Last Hope?"

"Actually, he found me in the forest." Sydney met Vadnae's stare without flinching.

"Under unfortunate circumstances." Oryn winked at Sydney. "Despite her penchant for picking pockets, I believe she has great potential."

"Picking pockets?" Vadnae asked. "Surely you don't trust a thief. What can she offer us?"

Sydney balled her hands into fists. "You'd be surprised at what I can do."

Vadnae's nostrils flared, and she wrinkled her nose. "You've brought a wild one this time."

Oryn patted her shoulder. "Vadnae, the hour is late. Take Sydney inside while I tend to the horse. You did prepare a room for her, didn't you?"

Vadnae's hand flew to her mouth. "Yes, I did what you asked, but I assumed…I mean, the other guests are men, so I was certain…." She fiddled with the ends of her belt. "You never said you'd be coming back with a woman. The room I prepared is entirely inappropriate. We can't just put *her* anywhere, can we?"

"My dear, you act like Sydney might murder us in our sleep." He chuckled, but Vadnae's eyes widened. "Put her in your room for now. We'll sort it out later."

"Can't we—"

"Vadnae, do as I say. I'll be in once I've seen to the horse."

She lowered her head. "Yes, Grandfather." With resignation in her voice, she turned and said, "Follow me, Sydney."

Oryn touched Sydney's arm and spoke in a gentle voice, "Go on. Don't worry, Vadnae will make you comfortable. We'll talk on the morrow, after you've had a good night's sleep."

She followed Vadnae, whose tall and graceful frame made Sydney wish she were more statuesque. When they stood before the stone structure, Sydney gaped at the high walls. No door or any other means of entrance was visible.

Vadnae mumbled several unintelligible words. A pinpoint of light appeared near the base of the wall, shifting and elongating until the glowing outline of a door appeared.

Sydney's eyes grew wide. What she wouldn't give to learn how to do such things. "Did he teach you magic?"

"Of course." A smug smile touched the corners of Vadnae's mouth. "*You'd* be surprised at what *I* can do."

Sydney grimaced to hear her words thrown back at her. She sniffed. Vadnae could create doors out of solid stone, but Sydney doubted she'd survive one night on the streets of Last Hope. Especially not in that pretty gown.

Once they entered, the magic doorway disappeared. A short hallway lit by beeswax candles in silver sconces opened into a large banquet hall, a flagstone hearth at one end and a winding staircase at the other. A crystal chandelier hung above a long, rectangular wooden table and ornately carved high-backed chairs. Flickering candlelight caused the crystals to throw rainbows dancing across the walls and floor.

Awestruck by the opulence, Sydney lingered near one of the many tapestries adorning the walls. In this one, the image of a woman seated in a field of flowers had been woven into the geometric design. The brilliant blue of the sky matched the blue of the woman's eyes, and the candlelight glinted in her red-gold hair. Drawn in by the lifelike colors, Sydney reached out a hand to touch the tapestry.

"Don't!"

She jumped back, startled by the anger in Vadnae's voice.

"Grandfather is very particular about his things. Besides, you're filthy. Follow me. And *don't* touch anything."

Sydney stuck her hands in her pockets, reluctant to incur the wrath of a wizard.

Their footsteps on the flagstone floor resounded in the cavernous room. Vadnae waited at the foot of the staircase, gesturing for Sydney to ascend first.

Keeping her eye on me. Afraid I'll pinch one of their pretty trinkets.

Another tapestry graced the alcove at the foot of the stairs, depicting a similar image of the woman in the field. The woman's gaze appeared to follow her.

Not possible. Or was it?

The staircase encircled the inside wall of the stone tower. At the second floor, Vadnae touched her sleeve, directing her down a hallway. The stairs spiraled above them.

"How high does it go?"

"There are seven floors. We shall remain on the second." Vadnae pushed open a heavy oak door on the left with an iron handle carved into a flowering vine. "This is my room."

With a wave of her hand, the silver sconces embellished with the same flowering vine pattern lit themselves. Positioned on the opposite wall stood a four-poster bed piled high with thick blankets and pillows. Arranged on a side table near the bed were several tiny glass bottles and a silver comb and brush. A tall oak wardrobe and a roll-top desk littered with papers and a stack of books stood on either side of the door. *Vadnae must be a scholar and a wizard.* Most people Sydney knew, including herself, couldn't read. Vadnae walked to the bed and righted a stuffed toy on the pillow, which resembled a miniature wolf.

Sydney shivered, remembering the wolf in the forest.

"First, you need a bath," Vadnae said.

You'd need a bath, too, if you'd been sent to the gaol and sentenced to die.

Accustomed to washing with cold and often dirty water from a bucket, Sydney gaped when Vadnae ushered her into a private bath. The white tiled floor and claw foot tub gleamed. The soothing scent of lavender and the anticipation of getting truly clean began to ease her tension. Vadnae uttered a strange word Sydney didn't understand, and the tub instantly filled with water. She pointed to two glass jars containing red and blue stones on a shelf above the tub.

"The stones control the water temperature. I'm sure you can figure it out. Meanwhile, I'll find you some…." Vadnae examined her, and a flicker of sympathy crossed her face. "Some clean clothes. Then food if you're hungry."

Sydney nodded. Soaking in a tub of warm water would be an indulgence.

Vadnae lifted a green block of soap from the shelf and handed it to Sydney. "This is the soap. Use lots. You certainly need it."

"Like I've never heard of soap," Sydney muttered after Vadnae closed the door. She stripped off her clothes and dipped a cautious toe in the water. Cold. She took the glass jars and gathered a handful of stones from each. Smooth and round, the stones resembled ordinary pebbles. The red and blue colors varied in hue, from dark to light. She tossed a light red one into the water. The stone sank to the bottom of the tub. Slightly warmer. A dark red stone, and three light blue ones, and finally, she eased herself into the tub. She lathered away the dirt and grime, gingerly touching the purplish bruises from her beating and the welts from the ropes. Dunking her head, she scrubbed her hair until it squeaked. Even the dirt beneath her fingernails washed away.

The fragrant soap reminded Sydney of the sweet, earthy

perfume Zared had once given her. She remembered Edgar saying only whores wore those scents. She slid into the water.

Some things didn't wash away so easily.

She sat in the tub until her skin began to wrinkle and Vadnae called, "Are you finished yet?"

"Coming." She stepped out of the tub and used a large blue linen cloth hanging from a hook to dry herself. She wrapped the cloth around her slim frame and opened the door, holding her filthy clothes. "You got something I can wear?"

Vadnae stifled a gasp. "Did someone beat you?"

Sydney hugged her arms to her chest. "It's nothing. Don't hurt much—doesn't hurt, I mean."

"I see." Vadnae quickly opened the wardrobe and rifled the garments hanging inside. Tiered racks within the oak cabinet displayed dozens of dresses in a variety of colors and fabrics.

Sydney clutched her tattered clothes, patched with rags and bits of cloth she'd scrounged.

"You can wear this for now." Vadnae held out a white linen robe and turned away while Sydney put it on.

The soft material caressed her skin. Sydney tossed her grimy shirt and breeches on the bed. "Here. Burn them if you want."

"Don't put them there." Vadnae snatched them up, wrinkling her nose. "I must go check the other guests."

"Guests?"

"Two others are also enjoying our hospitality. Wait here. I'll come back with dinner for you." Vadnae considered her a moment and rolled her eyes. "What Grandfather was thinking, I can't imagine. I won't be long. Then we'll decide where you'll sleep. Perhaps Grandfather can help prepare another room."

The door closed behind her, leaving Sydney alone in a room full of treasures. She scanned the room. *I won't bother anything. Not too much.* She opened the wardrobe and ran her hands over the dresses, marveling at the soft velvet and silk. In a bottom drawer, she found frilly white undergarments with laces and stays. Proper attire for a lady, but she couldn't imagine how women managed to wear such things. A long-sleeved blue silk gown caught her eye. She carefully removed it and stood before a full-length mirror propped in a corner, holding the dress in front of her.

The exquisite dress didn't match her gaunt face. Dark circles shadowed her eyes, and scratches marred her pale cheeks. Her lip was cracked and swollen. She curled a strand of her damp brown hair around her finger, thinking of Vadnae's lustrous tresses. For a moment, she imagined herself properly dressed. She was no lady like Vadnae, but Zared had often complimented her wide green eyes and high cheekbones, claiming they made her alluring. And at the same time, vulnerable. Men paid extra for those qualities, he'd said.

With trembling hands, she shoved the dress back into the wardrobe. *Damn his charming smile and seductive words.*

Seeking a distraction, she turned her attention to the stack of books on the desk. Colorful, detailed pictures appeared opposite pages of neat black lettering. One book contained pictures of people who reminded her of the woman from the tapestry in the great hall. The slender figures danced in the moonlight in a ring of tall stones. They wore garments spun from golden silk, and garlands wreathed their hair. The faery folk. The Tuatha.

A faint whisper raised the hair on her arms. She set the book aside.

Anxiously she paced. Vadnae's room grew less comfortable. The gnawing in her stomach reminded her of the food yet to arrive. She sat on the bed, and her elbow bumped Vadnae's stuffed animal. Leaning over the bed, she grabbed the wolf by a velvet paw. Probably a gift from Oryn.

Enticed by the downy featherbed and thick blankets, she rested her head on the pillow. Her thoughts jumbled and circled back to the most important question. *What could a wizard possibly want with me?*

A whisper called from the shadows. Her heart raced. She slid off the bed and peered into the dark corners.

Oryn had said she could see things others could not. Surely he didn't mean unearthly things. Until now, she'd led an unremarkable life. Uneasiness pricked her mind. She paced, unable to sit still. The lamplight flickered, and baleful shapes leaped across the walls. As if trying to free themselves.

Until now.

Chapter Five

The mob in the public square jostled for a glimpse of the man on the scaffold. As the crowd roared in her ears, Sydney elbowed through the throng. She could save Edgar, if she could reach him. The hangman placed the noose around his neck. She emerged at the front of the crowd as the hangman gave the signal. The trap door banged. A silent scream welled within her. Removing his hood, the hangman revealed the scar marking his face from forehead to chin. He smirked at her. Hands gripped her shoulders, holding her back when she lunged for him.

"Sydney?"

"Dammit, let me go." She pushed the hand from her shoulder.

The hand shook her again. "Sydney, wake up."

Her eyes snapped open. Sunlight streamed into the room, refracting a multitude of colors from the glass bottles on the bedside table. Vadnae's bed. The tower. Oryn. Sydney pressed her cheek to the feather pillow and let out the breath she'd been holding.

"Are you all right?" Vadnae stood beside the bed, head cocked to one side.

Sydney sat and hugged her knees to her chest. "I'm fine. Just a dream."

She breathed deeply. The dream had haunted her for the

past four years. Every vivid detail seared her mind—the cloudless blue sky, the hollow thud of Edgar's boots when he crossed the platform to stand before the noose, the creak of the rope swaying back and forth.

"I came to wake you for breakfast." Vadnae's voice brought Sydney back to the present. Her skirts rustled when she bent to retrieve a blanket from the floor. "You were asleep by the time I returned with food last night."

Sydney brushed her fingertips over the rumpled bed sheets. "I slept here all night?"

"Grandfather advised me not to wake you, so yes, you slept here, in my bed."

Sydney had a vague memory of someone coming in the room and tucking a blanket around her. Vadnae or Oryn? Vadnae folded the blanket and set it gently at the foot of the bed. Her emerald dress brought out the green of her hazel eyes.

"Thanks. Been a long time since I slept in a real bed."

"I suspected as much." A hint of compassion entered Vadnae's tone.

Sydney pushed her hands inside the sleeves of the soft robe, covering the welts on her wrists. She didn't want Vadnae's pity. "Where'd you sleep?"

"There are other rooms. I simply made do for the night. I'm used to making do when necessary."

A flash of the same power Sydney had sensed in Oryn flickered in Vadnae's face.

"Grandfather thinks a great deal of you, Sydney. I hope you're worthy of his attention." Her words were sharp but her expression placid.

"He ain't told me what he wants yet."

"You'll find out soon." Vadnae placed her hand on a small bundle on the dressing table. "Grandfather asked me to give these to you. New clothes, although he forgot shoes. For now, your old ones will have to do. Once you're dressed, join us downstairs. The other guests are already waiting, and we have much to discuss. Later, we'll find you a room."

Vadnae left, closing the door behind her.

Curious, Sydney hopped out of bed and picked up the bundle. She unfolded a pair of gray woolen breeches, wool socks, and a cream-colored tunic. Green and gold embroidery embellished the neckline, cuffs of the tapered sleeves, and hem of the short tunic. She touched the fine embroidery as she laid the clothes and a leather belt on the bed. New clothes, especially of this quality, were an unfamiliar luxury. They fit her perfectly, as if they'd been made to her measurement. Likely more of Oryn's magic.

She peeked in the mirror and ran her fingers through her hair. A step up from a street urchin, but no match for Vadnae's sophistication. With a snort, she turned from the mirror and located her boots on the floor. Being sophisticated ran counter to her struggle to survive.

Her boots had been cleaned, with new laces tucked neatly inside. When she'd desperately needed a new pair of shoes, Edgar had saved every coin for weeks, sometimes going without meals, until he finally presented her with the finest pair of boots she'd ever seen. She pulled them on and blinked away a tear. Cracked soles and years of hard wear didn't matter. They couldn't be replaced.

After lacing up her boots, she hurried into the hallway and down the staircase. The mouthwatering aromas of sausage, eggs, and buttered toast pervaded the hall. At the foot of the stairs, the tapestry she'd seen the night before drew her attention. The image had changed. Startled, she stopped to peer at it. The scene of the woman in the field was gone. In her place, two armies marched toward each other. Hundreds of soldiers, perhaps thousands. Smoke rose on the horizon, and the sun glinted off the soldiers' shields and spears.

Tapestries couldn't change overnight. Someone must have replaced it, or she'd been so tired she wasn't remembering right. Or the tapestry was magic. She backed away, restraining her curiosity.

The murmur of voices shifted her attention to the table, where Vadnae sat with two men. The table had also changed, now only half the size of the one she remembered. Moving closer, she was stunned by the abundance of food. Silver serving dishes held toast, cheeses, colorful fruits she didn't recognize, crispy bacon and sausage, steaming porridge, and fried eggs. It was enough food to feed several families for days. The four of them couldn't possibly finish it all.

"Please join us." One of the men stood and pulled out the empty chair beside him. His face was weathered and tanned, his dark blond hair gray at the temples and cut above his ears in an unusually short style.

Startled by his act of chivalry, she awkwardly took her seat. "Thanks."

"Allow me to introduce you to Sydney," Vadnae said. "As I was telling you, she arrived with Grandfather late last night. Sydney, this is Gregor." She gestured to the man who'd pulled out her chair.

"Very pleased to meet you, Sydney." The lines at the corners of Gregor's blue-gray eyes crinkled when he smiled. His woolen shirt, worn and frayed, revealed the broad shoulders and muscular physique of someone who perhaps earned his living by the sword.

Despite his kind demeanor, Sydney eyed him warily. Her recent experiences with the guard had been harrowing. She gave Gregor a brief smile and folded her hands in her lap, feigning calm.

"This is Brother Erik." Vadnae gestured to the man who sat across from Sydney.

A portly man dressed in the coarse brown robes of a monk, Brother Erik's dark eyes, wide nose, and dour mouth gave him an unpleasant expression. He nodded to her and touched the symbol he wore around his neck, two small pieces of wood tied together in the shape of a cross. The monks from the abbey in Last Hope wore similar crosses. The church condemned people like Sydney for their sin and wickedness. She cared for the monks as little as they cared for her. They preached charity but sometimes declined to help those who were most in need.

"So glad you could join us, Sydney," Erik said. "Especially since Vadnae tells us you've come upon difficult times."

She was unable to read anything in Vadnae's neutral expression and unsure how much they all knew of her difficult times. Meeting Erik's gaze, she maintained a half smile.

"Erik, the Guild has made life a living hell for many of us." Gregor kept his voice low. "Why don't you let the poor girl eat before you begin lecturing her on the kingdom's decline?"

"Grandfather will be joining us soon, but we should start without him," Vadnae said as she handed a plate of toast to Erik.

"Good idea," the monk agreed. "Last time he kept us waiting so long the sausages grew cold."

"He does things in his own time."

"Believe me, Vadnae, I understand, but it's no reason to keep a man from his breakfast."

Erik was the least likely of them to need nourishment, Sydney thought. His plump fingers reached for two pieces of toast, and he proceeded to fill the rest of his plate. Vadnae and Gregor served themselves sparingly. Sydney decided to follow Erik's example and helped herself to a portion of each item. At once, she began to eat, savoring each bite of toast dipped in egg yolk and hot creamy porridge, chunks of sweet fruit and tangy cheese, and crispy bacon and sausage.

Vadnae picked up a fork and held it between her fingers, her smile strained. "I'm sure you'll excuse Sydney's manners. She arrived too late for dinner last night."

Sydney's face flamed. She stopped a handful of food halfway to her mouth and set it back on her plate. Picking up her fork, she jabbed it into a piece of pale yellow fruit and knocked several other pieces into her lap. She quickly stuffed the fruit from her lap into her mouth and wiped away the juice with her hand. Vadnae shook her head.

Erik dabbed his mouth with a cloth napkin. "Tell me, Sydney, how did you meet the mysterious Oryn?"

Her fork scraped the plate. She laid the utensil aside and caught herself before wiping her mouth on her sleeve. Her napkin, however, was missing. She peeked under her plate.

Gregor gently touched her arm and retrieved her napkin from the floor. A faint scar from a knife or perhaps a sword extended across the knuckles of his right hand. His kind expression reminded her of Edgar, and she wondered if she'd judged him too quickly. She offered him a grateful smile.

She blotted her mouth on the napkin. "Like I told Vadnae, I met Oryn in the forest beyond Last Hope."

Erik sniffed. "Last Hope has proved quite a challenge for our abbey there. Pickpockets on every corner and all manner of immoral activities."

She took a long swallow from a silver goblet. The sweet, fruity liquid was a combination of apples and berries. Mustering her most innocent smile, she said to Erik, "Keep a close eye on your purse if you ever go to Last Hope. Sometimes pickpockets pinch from the monks. At least that way some of the church's money goes to the poor."

"How dare you." Erik's face reddened, and he heaved himself to his feet. "I'll not sit here and be insulted by this-this heathen street urchin."

Sydney caught the grin flickering across Gregor's face. Vadnae scowled at her.

"Please." Vadnae laid a hand on Erik's sleeve. "No one means to insult you."

"She certainly does." He glared at Sydney.

"He insulted me first. There's plenty of decent people in Last Hope."

"You said you'd never been there before, Erik," Gregor interjected. "Hard to judge unless you've seen it yourself. Many people throughout the kingdom have been forced into activities they would otherwise abhor, simply to survive."

"Don't encourage her. There are always alternatives to a life of thievery."

Vadnae's palm slapped the table, causing the dishes to jump. Porridge sloshed over the edge of a bowl, and a piece of toast flew off a plate. "Enough, all of you. No wonder the kingdom is in such a state, if this is what Grandfather has to work with. Erik, sit down. Sydney…" She pinched the bridge of her nose and drew in a long breath. "There will be no talk of stealing. Let's all try to make this a tolerable meal."

"Very well." Erik smoothed his robe and returned to his seat. "I won't insult your generosity."

Feeling Vadnae's stare, Sydney bowed her head. They continued the meal in silence. Only two pieces of fruit remained on Sydney's plate when a blue-cloaked figure descended the stairs. Oryn inspected the tapestry that had changed and shook his head.

Gregor stood when Oryn approached them.

"Don't trouble yourself, Gregor. We aren't at court here." Oryn walked around the table and bent his head to Sydney's ear. "Did you sleep well, my dear?" She nodded, and he added, "I'm glad the clothes fit."

Suddenly shy, she fingered the hem of her tunic and stared at her plate. "Thanks."

Oryn took the empty seat at the head of the table. "I trust you've all had a pleasant stay so far?"

"You and your granddaughter are very generous hosts," Gregor replied. Erik added his agreement.

Across the room, a door opened near the hearth. Sydney didn't remember seeing it before. At first, the strange figure entering the room appeared to be a normal man, but when he moved, the light from the chandelier passed through him.

Wheeling a cart, he swiftly and silently cleared the table. He left without making a sound on the stone floor.

Oryn chuckled. "Surely you didn't think Vadnae and I keep up this place all by ourselves?" His voice grew somber. "We don't receive many guests here. There are unfortunately too many who persecute wizards, and few who can be trusted to keep our secrets."

"Many would welcome your return," Gregor said. "We need you in this fight."

"Perhaps, but wizards are not all-powerful. Which is why you are here." He gestured to each of them in turn. "Gregor, the dishonored knight whose sense of honor leads him to take up the cause of our rightful king. Erik, who dares question the church elders and seeks to bring change to his order. Vadnae, who is among the last of our kind and has been cast out of society due to her aptitude for magic. Sydney, the thief with no hope for her future, whose leadership and desire to fight for her beliefs will bring hope to many. You are all here because your actions will shape the future of our kingdom."

The others watched Oryn with rapt attention. Sydney sat back in her chair. "What's all this got to do with me?"

Oryn's sky-blue eyes seemed to probe her mind. "You, dear Sydney, will play an important role in the Kingdom of Thanumor, whether you accept it or not."

"Me?" She stifled a laugh. "What can I do? I'm a thief. A pickpocket. With no hope for the future, remember?"

He pursed his lips. "Is being a pickpocket all you can aspire to? I've watched you for some time. I regret you've experienced hardship over the years, but the trials you've endured give you the courage and strength of spirit to survive. You now stand at the knife's edge. Live the rest of your days in fear and regret, or take this opportunity to embrace Edgar's cause."

The image of Edgar on the scaffold crossed her mind. The bang of the trapdoor echoed in her head. Her throat tightened, and a surge of anger welled within her. "You know so much about me, do you? Did you know what was gonna happen to Edgar?"

Oryn's shoulders sagged. "I'm sorry, Sydney. There was nothing I could do. Edgar's sacrifice was necessary."

"Necessary?" She jumped to her feet, her voice rising. The others stared at her, mouths agape. She ignored them, fixing her outrage on the old man and his immense power. Power she'd sensed herself. "You're a wizard. You could've done something to save him."

"Edgar made his choices. He accepted the consequences of his actions."

"That ain't true." Sydney clenched her fists and struggled to keep her voice from breaking. "He-he never wanted to die."

"I'm offering you the opportunity to finish what Edgar started. Please, don't throw away a second chance to make something of your life. Edgar wouldn't want you to. At least listen to what I have to say."

Gregor touched her hand. "We've all been given another chance. Don't judge Oryn's actions before you hear him out."

Many nights Edgar had been out late, long after dark. Perhaps he'd met people like those who sat here and talked of the future of Thanumor.

Her chest heaved, and she took a few long, slow breaths. *Gregor's right. I need a second chance.* She sat down, still clenching her fists. "I'll listen."

"Thank you, Sydney." Oryn stroked his beard, and he glanced over the group. "I've concerned myself with the fate of our kingdom for more than a hundred years, advising kings and nobles before they turned on the wizards and banished us. I watched the Guild come to power. At first, the Guild held promise, a means for the commoners to support their interests when the nobility would not. Over the years, however, the Guild has succumbed to the same lust for power as the ruling class. The death of King Lor has spurred them to seek complete control over the kingdom."

The king's death several weeks earlier had been announced in Last Hope's public square. People had expected a festival in honor of the new king's coronation, but King Lor had no heir, and several possible successors had come forward to fight for the throne. Sydney had paid little attention to the politics of the realm. One king was much like another, in her mind. She glanced around the table. "Are we here because there's a new king?"

"If only it were that simple," Oryn said. "The issue of succession has plunged our land into war, and soon the effects will be felt even in this remote part of the kingdom."

"Lord Pendolf is cousin to King Lor and claims the throne should be his," Gregor explained to Sydney. "He's also been named head of the Guild. If he takes the crown, the Guild will take the kingdom. The only thing standing in his way is Willem, the king's bastard son, who has come forward to make his own claim to the throne."

"We all understand what will happen if the Guild gains control of Thanumor," Oryn said. "Willem is our best hope—perhaps our only hope—of stopping the Guild."

"And returning magic to our world," added Vadnae.

"Indeed, dear Vadnae. Unlike the most recent kings, Willem believes magic and wizards have a place in the world. I am certain he will be the one to persuade the Tuatha to break their seclusion and return to our realm."

"Many people think the Tuatha brought a great evil into the world." Erik again touched the wooden cross around his neck.

"Unfortunately, anyone can be corrupted by greed and the lust for power. But magic is not evil. Nor are wizards and the faery folk."

Oryn spoke of so many things Sydney didn't understand. "There's no magic in Last Hope. Why should I care about magic or the Tuatha?"

"Magic binds the fabric of our world," Vadnae said before

Oryn could respond. "You may not be aware of its presence, but without magic, life would be very bleak indeed."

"All of us here at this table are bound to magic, as well as to Thanumor's future, in one way or another," Oryn continued. "The Tuatha, who are far more powerful than Vadnae or I could ever become, remain a vital element of our world. More than a century has passed since they declared that some rulers—and some wizards—were misusing the knowledge they had shared. They grew angry and left our realm, taking most of their knowledge with them. For years they have waited for the right time to return and the right leader to be their champion."

"You're certain Willem is the leader they seek?" Erik asked, his skepticism obvious.

"I am indeed. He is the king we've been waiting for."

"But how can he defeat the Guild? The Council of Nobles will never allow a bastard to take the throne. And I'm sorry to say the church will not defy the council. The church depends too heavily on the support of many among the nobility."

"Many of the nobles already support Willem rather than Pendolf," Gregor said. "Willem has proven himself a strong leader. He also has Lord Stephan's backing. Stephan has considerable resources—men, weapons, supplies, land, influence. Willem stands a good chance."

"Taking the throne by force will taint his rule," countered Erik. "Unless he plans to install a new council to back him."

Gregor shrugged. "It's been done before. King Hilden, Lor's grandfather, stole the throne from the legitimate heir, did he not?"

Their talk of politics, kings, and magic made Sydney uneasy. Last Hope lay at the kingdom's farthest edge, hardly a point of significance. "What do you expect me...." She faltered, looking at the others. "I mean, what do you expect us to do?"

"Willem will succeed by uniting the Guild's enemies and gaining the support of the people," Oryn said, meeting her stare. "The nobles, the church, the commoners—all possess a stake in the outcome. Even wizards. Lord Aldric's lands may be poor, but not so long ago they were a symbol of resistance. Rekindling that resistance here will spark Willem's campaign."

The enormity of his words made Sydney's head spin. He expected them to rally resistance in opposition to the Guild and help put a bastard king on the throne of Thanumor. To finish what Edgar had started.

"A messenger from Willem is on his way here. His news will shape our next course of action. Until he arrives, I hope you will remain here in my home as my guests. However, you are free to go if you choose."

Not much of a choice. "We're in the Wastes. Where're we supposed to go?"

"If any of you do not wish to be a part of this, I will take you to one of the towns under Lord Stephan's domain. Please consider your choice carefully."

Gregor lowered his head. "I will do whatever I can to help Willem."

Erik grimaced. "I disagree with some of your opinions, wizard, but we are on the same side. The Guild is an abomination and must be stopped. I'll also do what I can."

"Thank you, Erik. I appreciate your honesty." Oryn regarded Sydney expectantly.

He'd offered her safe passage to a new town, new opportunities she'd only dreamed of—a new life. A life still under the yoke of the Guild, if they gained control of the kingdom. Overthrowing the Guild in Last Hope, and facing Schrammig, would be a daunting task. But perhaps joining Oryn's fight could atone for the things she'd done since Edgar's death.

She bit her lip. "I'll help."

"I'm glad to hear that. We will need your help, Sydney." He got to his feet, uttering a groan. "These bones are getting older every day. But I've no time to rest. I must leave my more than capable granddaughter in my place, for other urgent matters require my attention."

Vadnae stood and moved to his side, reaching out to clasp his hand. "Grandfather, you just got back."

"I'm sorry, Vadnae, but I have no choice. I suggest you use this time to prepare for what lies ahead. Both body and spirit must be strong." He embraced Vadnae, bowed to the others, and crossed the room.

"Remember, one day each of your lives may depend on the others in this room." A moment later the door slammed, the sound reverberating through the hall.

Vadnae brushed crumbs off the table. Her eyes glistened. She fussed with the folds of her gown. "I hope he doesn't stay away too long."

Erik snorted. "Let's hope he doesn't bring back any more guests."

Chapter Six

"Will this be adequate, Sydney?" Vadnae opened a door down the hall from her bedroom.

Sydney entered the sparsely furnished room. A wooden frame bed, a chair, and a plain oak chest occupied most of the space. A narrow window overlooked the barren landscape, a bleak reminder there was nowhere else for her to go. Despite the view, the room was more than adequate. She'd never had her own space before.

"The room's fine."

Vadnae opened the chest. She removed a soft down pillow and thick blanket and placed them on the bed. "Perhaps these will help make you more comfortable. Grandfather should be back in a day or two. Willem's messenger may be here sooner. My duties will keep me occupied, so you'll be on your own."

"Where did Oryn go? Why did he leave, if what we're supposed to do is so important?"

"He often leaves to attend to matters elsewhere," Vadnae said, turning away. "His work is important for the welfare of the kingdom."

The edge in her tone warned Sydney not to ask any more questions concerning Oryn's whereabouts. She wondered what Vadnae's life must be like if she spent most of her time by herself in the enormous tower. Surely it was a lonely existence.

"You can go anywhere you like on the first three floors, but the others are forbidden. You must be careful. The tower can be dangerous if you venture where you don't belong. Some rooms are rarely found in the same place twice, and some are never found more than once."

"How will I find my way around?"

"You'll manage, as long as you stay on the first three floors. Gregor spends many hours in the third-floor library, if you care to join him there. I'll expect to see you downstairs when you hear the bell for dinner. Don't be late. Otherwise, keep yourself out of trouble." Vadnae hurried out.

Sydney trailed her into the hall. "What am I supposed to do?"

"Find a way to amuse yourself without lifting the silver. You could try, but you'd never get it out of the tower. Now, I really must go. I'll see you at dinner." Vadnae ascended the staircase without a backward glance, probably to one of the forbidden floors.

Sydney sniffed. Vadnae underestimated her skills. She'd already considered slipping one of the silver spoons into her sleeve. The silverware alone would be worth a fortune in Last Hope.

I'm not in Last Hope any more, she reminded herself. In a few hours, the bell would call her to dinner. She needn't be concerned about picking enough pockets to pay for a meager meal or a room for the night, or being forced to depend on Zared's charity to avoid sleeping on the streets.

Unused to having idle time, she decided to explore the other areas of the tower, which quickly confounded her. The dimly lit hallways took impossible twists and turns. A long, straight hallway suddenly shifted at a sharp angle, then curved again in the opposite direction. Doors appeared where they hadn't been a moment ago and disappeared once she passed them. Considering Vadnae's warning about displaced rooms, Sydney decided not to open any of the closed doors.

After losing her way several times, she unraveled the secret to navigating the bewildering tower. It was similar to the mysterious tunnels stretching beneath Last Hope, where notches had been carved into the walls at set intervals, like a coded map for the mysterious labyrinth. Edgar and other members of the resistance had often used the tunnels, and he'd taught her how to recognize the patterns and their meanings. She spotted the same notches on the tower walls. People in Last Hope claimed the tunnels had been made by magic. The corresponding markings seemed to indicate they were right.

Armed with this awareness, Sydney ventured to the third floor. She traversed the hallway, carefully noting the carved markings. A strange whispering filled the stone corridor. She started. It was the same sound she'd heard in the forest, before the captain fled. A cold chill rippled across her skin, and yet she followed the sound, as if gripped by an unknown force. The whispers led her to a door that was slightly ajar and wide enough for her to slip inside.

Cobwebs covered the furniture. A musty odor assailed her, tinged with a sweet, floral scent. On a table, a glass marble glowed, untouched by the layers of dust. She moved toward it, hand outstretched. Then she hesitated. The whispers resonated within her, compelling her. Her fingertips stroked the marble's smooth surface. Her hand closed around it.

The whispers grew louder, like they had in the forest. The floor tilted beneath her feet. Stumbling, she grabbed a chair to brace herself. The other side of the room shifted to a misty, gray landscape. A cry for help caught in her throat. She ran for the door. It had closed behind her, and her hand fumbled with the latch. *Dammit, open!* She dared not turn around to see what lay behind her. With a final yank, the door flew open. She dashed out and slammed the door shut.

The whispers ceased abruptly. Still clutched in her fist, the marble had stopped glowing. Magic. It had to be magic. Heart pounding, she realized the door had vanished. She leaned against the wall, staring at the marble.

Despite her agitation, she was loath to get rid of it. For whatever reason, the marble had sought her out. She stuck it in her pocket. Perhaps Vadnae could give her an explanation. Vadnae might also think she'd stolen it. When Oryn returned, she'd ask him about what she'd experienced. Oryn was the one who'd insisted she was bound to magic.

Her footsteps echoed on the flagstones. After her unsettling experience, the solitude unnerved her. Craving companionship, she again inspected the notches on the walls. The markings directing her toward knowledge led her to the library.

The wizard's library was like nothing she had ever seen before. Floor to ceiling, shelves crammed with books lined the walls of the enormous room. Stacks of books on the floor came to her waist. A spiraling metal staircase led to a narrow walkway circling a second level.

She breathed in the strong scent of musty leather. Gently she ran her fingers over the ancient, cracked spines and traced the ornately embossed gilded lettering. There was so much she didn't understand, and the knowledge contained in those books was inaccessible to her. She pulled a slim volume from the shelves, searching for pictures, wishing the magic in the tower could help her decipher these mysteries.

In the silent room, the creak of the door opening startled her, and she stumbled into a pile of books.

"Is someone there?"

She peered around the stacks. Gregor stood in the doorway. Some of her tension drained at the sight of him. "Only me—Sydney." She stepped into view.

He smiled. "Glad to see you. This is one of my favorite rooms. It's a good place to hide from Erik's lecturing for a while. He'd rather not be in the same room as so many blasphemous books."

She returned his smile. "Are they blasphemous?"

"Perhaps some are, but those are the most interesting." He

chuckled, making himself comfortable in one of two overstuffed chairs in the center of the room. He picked up a book from the stack beside him.

"Can you read these?" She waved a hand at the many books and perched on the arm of the other chair.

"Some. Not as many as I'd like. Oryn has an amazing collection." He gave her a curious look. "Can you read?"

She fingered the cuffs of her sleeves. "Never learned."

"I suppose Last Hope didn't provide many opportunities for you."

"Not really." She didn't sense anything judgmental in his tone, so she decided to ask, "Where're you from?"

"A fair question. I was raised in the north, but I spent more than a decade in Pyredon, the capital, as a knight in the king's honor guard. Few are chosen for the position, usually not more than a half dozen at a time." He fell silent, and a shadow crossed his face.

"What happened?"

"Did you receive much news of King Lor in Last Hope?"

"New taxes and the like. Most people didn't care for the king. Don't care much for Lord Aldric, either."

"Living near the edge of the kingdom has its advantages. You've avoided the unease slowly building in Pyredon over the king's decline. I shouldn't speak ill of the dead, but I truly believe he went mad. Some people took advantage of his lack of judgment. He refused to heed his advisors' warnings about the Guild, enabling them to quickly gain power. Nevertheless, I swore an oath to my king. I was bound to obey him, even when I disagreed with him." His shoulders sagged.

Edgar had often told her a man's word was the most important thing he had to give. She'd heard tales of the knights' bravery and loyalty. "How...." She hesitated. "How'd you lose your knighthood?"

"When the Guild started openly challenging our authority, the authority of the knights, I refused to keep silent." Gregor returned the book to the stack, his eyes focused elsewhere. "They insisted their champions be invited to the king's tournament and cheated in order to win. I called them out. I questioned King Lor's judgment in naming the winner. He was furious. He rescinded my knighthood, and I was forced to leave in disgrace."

A hint of bitterness in his voice bespoke the pain he must have felt. Unexpectedly touched by his story, Sydney put a hand on his arm. "I'm sorry."

He patted her hand and smiled, his warm blue eyes offering something she hadn't been offered in a long while—friendship. Flustered, she picked up the book Gregor had set aside, opening it and flipping the pages.

"Life in Last Hope has been difficult, hasn't it?"

She shrugged. "Did what I had to do. People who speak out against the Guild end up swinging from the end of a rope. I-I just tried to survive."

"You shouldn't be ashamed of your actions. Sometimes surviving is all we can do."

Gregor's sympathetic expression indicated he understood. He reminded her so much of Edgar. She quickly blinked back tears.

"Willem offers hope to all of us, nobles and commoners alike. He'll fight for all of us."

"What if Willem can't defeat the Guild? Then what?"

Gregor's smile turned grim. "If we fail, we'll go to our graves knowing at least we strived to do something good and worthwhile."

———

Unable to sleep, Sydney pondered Gregor's comment. Edgar used to talk with Anaria, his long-time companion, about doing what was "good and worthwhile." He had meant fighting the Guild and helping others to do the same. To Sydney's shame, the only things good and worthwhile in her life lately had been finding food and shelter without having to sell her body on the streets.

She curled up in her soft bed, cursing the quiet. Dammit, she hated being alone. She longed for Zared's touch, the heat of his skin stroking hers.

She got up, paced to the window, and opened the shutters. The night air cooled her face. She hated the longing he stirred within her. He'd used her, like she'd used him, and he'd convinced her she needed him so often she couldn't stop believing it.

Edgar had once told her, "People are often prisoners of their minds." Hers was a harsh gaoler indeed.

A knock startled her. "Sydney?" The latch rattled.

"I'm coming." She pulled back the chair from where she had jammed it beneath the latch.

Vadnae stood in the hallway, wearing a green satin robe over her bedclothes. She frowned from the chair to Sydney. "There's no reason to bar the door."

"I like to feel safe."

The frown deepened. "There's no danger here, Sydney. I came to tell you the emissary from Willem has arrived. Grandfather delivered him and then had to leave, but the man has news we should hear. Now."

They hurried down the winding staircase. The candle sconces glimmered faintly, flaring when they passed to light their way. Sydney doubted the news was good, if it couldn't wait until morning. She brushed the wrinkles from her clothes and stifled a yawn.

Gregor and Erik, a bit bleary-eyed, stood by the hearth with a man dressed more like a common soldier than a royal messenger. A worn, dusty red coat and trousers outfitted his muscular frame, and auburn hair flowed over his shoulders.

"Rolf the Red, they call me," he said with a bow after Vadnae made the introductions.

They moved to the table. The ghostly servant brought Rolf a steaming plate of eggs, sausages, and biscuits with gravy. Though Sydney had eaten more than her share of roasted game hen and savory root vegetables at dinner, her stomach growled.

Rolf held up a biscuit. "Hungry?"

"I can't imagine why the little glutton would be hungry," Erik said.

Sydney glowered at him. He hadn't passed up a second helping at dinner, either.

Rolf grinned, green eyes flashing, and tossed her a biscuit from his plate. His slightly crooked nose, as if it had been broken one too many times, and unshaven face added to his rakish appearance. So did his appraising stare. She left the biscuit on the table and narrowed her eyes at him. His grin broadened.

"What news do you bring to us?" Vadnae asked.

Rolf sopped up gravy with the biscuit. "It's not good, but what we expected. The Council of Nobles named Lord Pendolf heir to the throne, in the absence of what they consider any legitimate claims."

"I told you they'd never name Willem as king," Erik said.

"There was never much of a chance, but Willem wanted to avoid war if he could. Lord Stephan—he's my uncle—renounced his position on the council in protest, along with half the other lords. Looks like our fight is finally beginning." Rolf wiped his mouth on his sleeve and looked at Vadnae. "One more thing. Pendolf now claims magic was involved in the king's death."

"You don't mean he's accused the wizards of being involved?" Vadnae paled. "How dare he make such a false accusation?"

"Pendolf's no fool. He suspects Willem's enlisted your assistance, so he's trying to sway public opinion against you—and Willem—and remind people how dangerous wizards can be."

"What of Willem?" Gregor asked. "Is the Guild moving against him?"

"Pendolf didn't waste any time. We're outnumbered, but Willem seems confident. Part of his plan involves coming here. He's marching to Aldric's keep with a small force while Stephan rallies our allies. I suppose personally enlisting the service of a wizard is worthwhile if it will give us the advantage we need to win." Rolf paused and glanced around the table. "Is there any news of the Guild here?"

Sydney hesitated. "Schrammig," she said quietly. "He's coming to these parts."

"Are you certain? Where did you hear that?"

"I heard it in Last Hope. From the captain of the guard, right before he was going to execute me."

"You have a death sentence on your head?" gasped Erik. "See, Gregor, I warned you about her."

"For stealing from a Guild official," Sydney snapped. "Isn't fighting for Willem worse, in their eyes?"

"She does have a point," Gregor said, and Rolf chuckled.

"Who's Schrammig?" Vadnae asked. "Grandfather has told me about many of the lords, but not Schrammig."

"He isn't nobility." Rolf took a long swallow from his goblet. "Brute of a man. Long scar down the middle of his face. He handles the Guild's important interrogations, executions, those sorts of things."

"He was behind the Guild's first assault on the nobility, about twenty years back," Gregor said. "He became known then for his brutality. Entire families were slaughtered, either by his hand or on his orders."

Sydney clenched her hands in her lap. "Schrammig had Edgar arrested and hanged. He likes to torture his prisoners before he kills them."

Vadnae gaped in horror. "I'm so sorry."

"Willem should be informed of this," Rolf said. "What can you tell me about the Guild officials in Last Hope, Syd? How well do you know them?"

Not the sort of details you'd want to hear. She stared at the uneaten biscuit on the table, her appetite lost. "Their names, but not much else."

Rolf rubbed the stubble on his chin. "I've heard some high-ranking Guild members in Last Hope are sympathetic to Willem's cause."

"You'd trust them?" Erik let out a sharp breath. "You've never been to Last Hope, have you, Rolf? It's a town of thieves who'd stab you in the back for a round of ale."

"I'd trust a town of thieves as much as I'd trust the church. Your brothers continue to deny Willem's claim, don't they?"

Erik shifted uncomfortably in his chair. "They typically back the decisions of the council, but times are changing. Many of the church elders support Willem."

Rolf snorted. "As I suspected." He inclined his head to Vadnae. "Willem values your counsel, milady. He could use your advice on how best to proceed."

"I'm sure Willem wants Grandfather's counsel, not mine. He should be back soon. You'll stay until he returns, won't you?"

Rolf pushed back his chair. "I can stay one day. I'm not one to pass up a roof over my head when it's offered. Now if I can prevail upon your hospitality, I could use a wash and spare bed, if you've got one."

Vadnae rose to her feet. "Of course. You are a welcomed guest. We'll discuss our plans further when Grandfather returns." She crooked a finger at the servant, who glided up the stairs ahead of them.

Back in her bed, Sydney stared into the darkness, unable to sleep. Kings, princes, wizards, and the Guild—what the hell kind of storm was she walking into? After tossing and turning for what felt like an hour or two, she finally gave up and crept out of her room.

The sconces in the hallway glowed faintly when she passed,

providing enough light for her to make her way back downstairs. She stopped to examine the tapestry at the foot of the staircase. The dim light muted the colors. Now the two armies stood facing each other, and hundreds of soldiers stared one another eye to eye. Within seconds, the battle would rage. She turned away from the image, unwilling to witness the ensuing scene of carnage.

Death. The whisper slipped into her mind, raising the hair on her arms. Shadows flitted, dark shapes within the tapestry, shifting, changing, pooling into rivers of black blood.

Sydney fled back up the stairs, back to the safety of her room.

The whispers pursued her, chanting of death. Her future. Willem's legacy.

Oryn did not return the next day. The following morning, Vadnae arrived late to breakfast. She wore a plain brown dress and a green surcoat, much simpler than the gowns she'd worn on previous days. Her hair hung down her back in a single braid.

"I'm afraid Grandfather has been delayed," she announced. "I'm not sure when he'll be back."

"I can't wait any longer," Rolf said. "Willem and Aldric are expecting me."

Vadnae waved away Gregor's offering of food. She considered each of them. "We will accompany you, Rolf. I'm sure Grandfather would want us to. He asked me to act in his place. We must do what we can while there is still time."

Sydney glanced toward the tapestry by the staircase. Going with Rolf meant accepting her role in the overwhelming changes Oryn had described. Returning to Last Hope. Facing Schrammig. Even death. She stared at the table and jammed her fingernails into her palms.

"When can we leave?" Rolf asked.

"This morning. First, we'll gather provisions for the journey. It will take us several days to travel across the Wastes."

"Days?" Sydney's head snapped up. She and Oryn had traveled to the tower in less than a single night, albeit in a disturbing manner.

"I can't use my magic to transport us as Grandfather did to get you here, but there is a safe path through the Wastes. I will guide us."

"The Wastes hold untold horrors," said Erik. "Magic even Oryn said he couldn't control."

"There is a safe path, Erik. We will be fine."

"Won't your god protect you from the evil lurking there?" Rolf's grin mocked him.

"I trust Vadnae will guide us safely," Gregor added.

"Very well, since I'm outvoted." Erik sniffed and pushed back his chair. "Now if you will excuse me, I will attend to my prayers before we leave."

Vadnae directed Gregor and Rolf to the storerooms. Then she asked Sydney to join her upstairs to pack their personal belongings.

Vadnae had already set out two well-worn canvas rucksacks on her bed. "We'll take only what we can carry." She opened the wardrobe, pursing her lips. "I doubt any of my clothes will fit you."

"What's wrong with these clothes? They're new."

"They're not suitable for meeting our future king. You're not a thief any more, Sydney."

"I'm not gonna wear a dress. Who do I have to impress?"

Vadnae raised an eyebrow. "You'd be surprised by how well people treat you if you dress properly."

She picked out several dresses and handed one to Sydney, suggesting they find a tailor to alter it to fit. Sydney fingered the luxurious blue silk gown she'd admired the night she'd slept in Vadnae's room.

"I suppose these will be more practical for you." Vadnae placed a shirt and a pair of breeches on top of the gown in Sydney's arms. She crossed the room to gather two of the bottles from her dressing table and an enormous leather-bound book from her desk.

"What's the book for?"

"It's something I often consult." Vadnae spent a moment arranging the items in her rucksack, taking some out and putting them back in. The rucksack bulged at the sides when she finally buckled it shut, but she lifted it easily, as if the bag were empty.

It must be magic.

"By the way, hold onto the marble you found."

"How'd you know? I was gonna put it back—"

"It was a dangerous thing you did, taking it. But since you did, keep it with you."

"Is it magic?"

"Yes. It once belonged to the Tuatha. For whatever reason, it was drawn to you. Grandfather told me magic might be drawn to you while you were here."

"He did?" Sydney shivered and rubbed her arms. "Why? Strange things keep happening. The marble. Whispers. Shadows. What the hell do they mean?"

Vadnae placed a comforting hand on her shoulder. "I'm not sure yet. We'll find the answers, Sydney. We're all going to be tested by what's to come. Now leave the dress with me so I can pack it properly and go gather your things. We should depart as soon as we can."

Sydney went to her room and retrieved the marble from under her pillow. She carefully wrapped it within the extra clothes in her rucksack.

They carried their belongings downstairs, where Rolf and Gregor had laid out their supplies: cook pots, canvas cloth, water skins, blankets, several coils of rope, two daggers and three knives, a hatchet, and two large sacks of dried meat, cheese, bread, and fruit. They divided the provisions among the five of them.

Erik staggered under the weight of the rucksack Rolf thrust at him. "You can't expect us to carry all of this."

"Would you rather fend for yourself in the Wastes?"

Gregor took Sydney aside and offered her one of the knives, which had a beautiful hilt inlaid with a silver leaf design. "Can you use this?" She nodded, and he handed the knife to her. "Good. I'm sure you'll need it."

"I'll be right with you," Vadnae said when they were ready. "I must leave Grandfather a message."

Sydney slid the knife into her boot sheath. Hoisting her rucksack, she exited the massive wooden door and squinted in the bright sunlight. Vadnae finally joined them, facing the tower and speaking the words of magic. Stone by stone, the wall engulfed the door. Sydney glanced over her shoulder when they started down a narrow path winding between rocky dunes. The tower appeared to shimmer in the distance. The farther they walked, the fainter it became, until the tower was no longer there at all.

"True magic can never be destroyed," Vadnae said. She explained that parts of the Wastes contained powerful enchantments where the Tuatha had once lived. "There are places here where Grandfather would not venture. I respect the Wastes, but I do not fear them. Stay on the path, and you shall be safe."

Sydney turned to the blighted landscape surrounding them. Strange shapes swirling in the distance filled her with dread. *Stay on the path.*

Chapter Seven

The sun blazed. Sydney wiped the sweat from her forehead. Her back ached from the heavy rucksack, and her feet were blistered and sore from hours of steady hiking in the rocky hills of the Wastes. Unlike Erik, however, she kept the pace and hadn't complained.

At dusk, they stopped for the night, straying only slightly from the safe path. A heavy darkness settled across the land. Vadnae walked the perimeter of their camp, invoking an enchantment to protect them during the night. Gregor and Rolf used the canvas tarps they had brought from the tower to set up makeshift shelters. Sydney and Vadnae shared one, the men the other.

Erik sat near the shelter, wrapped in his cloak. "There isn't enough wood in these wretched Wastes for a fire. The heat is unbearable during the day, and now we're freezing."

Sydney doubted the plump monk had ever deprived himself of anything, let alone encountered hardship before. She caught Rolf rolling his eyes at Gregor.

"We needn't feel so miserable, Erik," Vadnae said. She then asked Gregor to cut an armful of branches from one of the nearby scrub bushes. After he had done so, she set them on the ground and stood over them, murmuring softly. A moment later, the branches burst into flame.

Rolf whistled through his teeth. "Now there's some magic I

can appreciate." A crackling fire engulfed the branches. He stepped closer and rubbed his hands over the flames. "How long will the fire last?"

"Until morning. It needs no tending. Yet, I suggest we take turns keeping watch throughout the night…as a precaution."

Sydney peered at the darkness around them. She shivered. *What are we keeping watch for?*

They huddled around the fire and ate the dried meat and fruit they had packed for the journey. The meal didn't compare with the feasts in the tower, but Sydney was too tired to care.

Erik claimed the first spot beneath the shelter, saying he needed to recite his evening prayers. Soon they could hear his snores.

Rolf grunted. "I'd have left him behind hours ago if I were in charge."

Vadnae raised her head from the large, leather-bound book she had packed in her rucksack. "Erik is not always the most pleasant person, but he has a role to play in the events to come. There is a reason Grandfather wanted him to join us."

"If you say so, though I might be tempted to gag him before we reach Aldric's keep. You said about two more days before we're out of the Wastes?" Vadnae nodded. Rolf grunted and slapped the sand from his thighs. "Then maybe two more days to get to the keep. Willem should be there waiting for us."

During the first day of their journey, Rolf told them about the state of affairs in other parts of the kingdom and informed them which lords had decided to join Willem. Lord Aldric was apparently one of the least powerful men in court, with Last Hope the only town under his rule, but Rolf said Willem considered him an important ally.

Sydney remained skeptical. "He never did anything to stop the Guild before. At least not in Last Hope."

"The nobility are realizing they can't sit this one out. Before they were afraid to oppose the Guild openly. Now Willem has given them a reason to fight."

Sydney shuddered. Willem's arrival might well bring war to their doorstep.

"A few hours each keeping watch will get us to morning," Rolf said as they prepared to settle in. "I'll go first. I can't sleep anyway. The magic out here might turn us all into toads while we're not paying attention. Syd, you take the second, then Vadnae and Erik. Gregor can take the last watch."

"Some of us might be more pleasant as toads," Sydney muttered as she joined Vadnae in their tent. She eyed the book Vadnae had carefully laid across her rucksack. "Could you turn someone into a toad?"

Vadnae unwound her braid. "Why would I want to do such a thing? I know I shouldn't be surprised by misconceptions about magic, but sometimes I am. No wonder people are afraid of us."

Sydney recalled the stories she'd heard about wizards and the Tuatha, of children stolen from their beds, livestock dying, and people succumbing to mysterious illnesses. In those tales, magic was often used to harm and punish, very different from the magic she'd seen used by Oryn and Vadnae.

She dared ask, "What else can wizards do besides light candles and fires and create doors?"

Vadnae brushed her hair and tied it back with a ribbon. In a quiet voice, she said, "Magic is not evil, as some people may think. Dangerous, yes, especially when it's misused. Our enchantments should be used for good, to better our lives and the world around us. I hope Willem will give us the chance to finally do that."

"How do they work?"

Vadnae studied her thoughtfully. "I'll tell you how Grandfather first explained it to me." She pulled the ribbon from her hair and laid it across her palm. "Wizards view the world differently. For example, you see an ordinary green ribbon, while I see all the possibilities of the ribbon. I see all the different forms it could take."

In amazement, Sydney watched the ribbon change to a mass of string, a blanket, and a handful of dust.

"I concentrate on what a thing could be, and then I can make it happen. Certain changes require more concentration and practice than others. This one was easy. So is lighting fires."

The dust became a ribbon once more, and Vadnae retied it in her hair.

"And the words you chant? What do they do?"

"The incantations, you mean? They help me focus. Grandfather doesn't use them most of the time. In fact, he's skilled enough to discern possibilities in people. His type of magic is the most difficult of all, for it involves so many factors." Vadnae smiled. "I hope I've explained why I couldn't turn someone into a toad."

Turning someone into a toad would be a useful trick. Apparently, magic wasn't about tricks. "You have. Thanks for telling me."

"These things aren't secrets, but as I said, people are afraid of us. Usually they don't want to hear the truth. They think we're all-powerful, but there are limits to magic. For example, it cannot be used directly to take the life of another living creature. Some wizards attempted to do this, and in the process they destroyed themselves." A shadow crossed her face. "I can't imagine why someone would even want to try such a thing."

"For power. Wizards aren't much different from the rest of us, right?"

"Yes, I suppose we possess the same faults as everyone else." Vadnae unfurled the blankets. "Tomorrow will be another long day. Why don't we get some sleep? I confess I'm not used to sleeping outdoors." She wrapped a blanket around herself and fidgeted.

"It ain't so bad." Sydney had often slept in alleys and on doorsteps. Here, they at least had some shelter and warmth.

Wincing, she gingerly removed her boots and socks.

Vadnae gasped at her blistered and bleeding feet. "However did you manage walking all day today? I knew Grandfather should have given you a new pair of boots." She sat up and opened her rucksack, pulling out a jar and clean cloths and handing them to Sydney. "This will help."

Sydney opened the jar and sniffed at the white paste it contained. The fragrant scent reminded her of Vadnae's soap. "Is it magic?"

Vadnae smiled. "Not completely. Just herbs for healing, along with a tiny bit of magic. Use it, and you'll have an easier time walking tomorrow."

"Thanks." The small gesture meant a lot. Sydney applied the salve and wrapped the cloths around her feet. Immediately, the pain began to lessen.

After a while, Vadnae's breathing slowed. Shadows from the fire flitted on the sides of the tent, distracting Sydney from sleep. She huddled under her blanket, keenly aware of the faint noises outside. Scratching, footsteps, and whispers echoed in her head.

She jumped when someone patted the side of the tent.

"Your turn on watch."

She pulled on her boots and stumbled out. Rolf put a hand on her shoulder, his voice low. "Stay awake and call out if you see anything."

Moving as close to the fire as possible, she stared at the darkness. Shadows appeared to hover beyond the light, whispering her name. *It's all in my mind. Shadows can't hurt me. Or can they?* Vadnae hadn't told them what kind of magic remained in the Wastes. Sydney wrapped her cloak around her. She stuck her hands in her pockets, surprised to find the marble from the tower. She didn't remember taking it out of her rucksack. Curling her fingers around it, as if the object somehow offered a measure of protection, she struggled to keep her mind from the shadows.

Unbidden, the memory of a night when she was about seven years old surfaced. For what had felt like hours, she had lain in bed alone, blankets pulled over her head, paralyzed by a nameless terror. Finally, she had gathered the courage to find Edgar or Anaria. From the top of the staircase, she had spied them sitting together in the barroom, talking softly.

"Dammit, haven't you been listening to anything I've said?" Edgar's voice was harsh.

Sydney stopped, unnoticed, halfway down the stairs. The wooden boards were rough against her bare feet. From where she stood, she could see Anaria's face clearly. Anaria, who was always able to handle anything, was tightlipped and pale. Sydney knew better than to interrupt to seek comfort for her insignificant fears. She sneaked to the bottom step, out of sight, straining to hear their voices, which had grown softer.

"This is our chance," Edgar said. "This is what we've been waiting for."

"It'll never work." Anaria's voice was firm. "What if you're caught?"

"How can you ask me to stand by and do nothing? What kind of man would I be?"

"You'd be alive."

"I'm doing it for Sydney. Don't you understand? I want her to have a better life."

"I suppose you expect me to explain your dreams of a better life to her after you've been hanged?"

At seven years old, Sydney had understood. She'd been to hangings. That night began her dread of losing Edgar.

Unable to sit still, she stood and walked around the perimeter of camp. Nebulous silhouettes coalesced in the darkness. Whispers hummed in her ears. The same whispers she'd heard in the strange room in the tower. Instinctively, she gripped the marble.

The whispers grew louder.

She dared not take her eyes off the darkness, afraid

something might come after her. "Vadnae?" Her heart thudded in her chest. "Rolf? Dammit, something's out here!"

Gregor and Rolf scrambled out of their tent, swords drawn. Vadnae was right behind them. They hurried to Sydney, who raised her hand toward the darkness. "I heard something."

The wailing began. A woman's voice. The keening cut Sydney to the core.

"Don't leave the circle." Vadnae touched Gregor and Rolf on the arm to motion them back. "Stay in here and you will be safe."

"What's out there?" Erik huffed up behind them, eyes wide.

"Grandfather said there was a battle here once, centuries ago. The Tuatha fought among themselves. The Wastes resulted from the destruction."

The shapes Sydney had seen coalesced into distinct forms. They became a writhing mass of bodies, men hacking at each other with swords, sending blood spraying and limbs flying. Magic encircled them. The power beckoned to her, an entwining embrace offering the promise of knowledge. Knowledge of things buried within her. She took a step forward.

Gregor put his arm out to stop her. "Stay in the circle, Sydney."

"I see them. The Tuatha. Fighting."

"Are you sure?" Vadnae squinted into the vast expanse surrounding them. "I see nothing."

Sydney shrugged, remembering Oryn had told her she saw things most people could not. "They're there."

They all stood silent, watching, until Rolf grunted and sheathed his sword. "Let's double up on the watches. I'll stay with Syd and then with Vadnae. Gregor, you do the same with Erik."

Gregor also returned his sword to its scabbard. "Call out if you need us," he told Sydney, laying his strong hand on her shoulder. He, Vadnae, and Erik returned to the tents to get what sleep they could.

Rolf sat by the fire, and Sydney joined him, keeping an eye on the darkness. The battle of long past still raged. If she focused too closely, she saw the sun shining overhead and the mud and gore thick upon the ground. The screams of the warriors echoed in her head.

"You still seeing them?"

"Yeah. Have you been in any battles?"

"Skirmishes mostly. The kingdom hasn't been at war in a while, not counting the petty quarrels between lords. Until now. War is a brutal undertaking, Syd, but sometimes you don't have a choice."

Sydney shivered. There was no reason to be afraid of whatever lay in the darkness. Those things had been real once, but they weren't any more. Real fear was the hangman's noose, the dank gaol, an empty bed. Fear was being alone. Fear was failing Edgar again.

Chapter Eight

In the afternoon of their third day in the Wastes, they crested the top of a hill and saw a welcome sight: the forest marking the eastern border of Aldric's lands.

Erik sighed in relief. "At last. Civilization. We would do well to visit my brethren for the night." He took a long swallow from his waterskin. "Their farm will be an excellent stopping point on the way to Aldric's keep."

"The monks are generous in their hospitality," said Gregor.

"They would even welcome criminals, if shelter was requested."

Sydney ignored Erik's comment. After three days in the Wastes, the prospect of shelter and a meal was tempting, regardless of who provided it.

Rolf swept a grimy lock of hair from his face. "Are you familiar with any of the monks who live there? Do many strangers pass by? We don't want to attract attention."

"I assure you they can be trusted."

Sydney snorted. "Sure, and the church has always opposed the Guild in Last Hope."

"My order has risked much in the name of our faith." Erik puffed out his chest. Though short in stature, his girth added bulk to his figure. "We've often helped those fighting the Guild, defying our elders, risking our lives. They will give us whatever help they can."

"Then we should avail ourselves of their hospitality." Vadnae's tone left no room for further disagreement.

"We will be breaking bread with them by nightfall."

The cool shade of the forest provided a welcome respite from the harsh Wastes. Sydney began imagining a cheery farmhouse with a welcoming fire, warm food, and a soft bed.

"Will the monks provide a place where we can wash?" Vadnae shook the dirt and sand from the hem of her dress.

Sydney stamped the dirt from her boots. After three days, the sand had settled everywhere, in her hair, in her clothes, between her teeth.

"Of course. There are guest quarters for both men and women. Don't worry, the brothers will attend to our needs."

Near the edge of the forest, the bare tree limbs above revealed unusual clouds, gray tinged with brown. An acrid smell wafted on the breeze. Smoke. Not the pleasant odor of hearth smoke. Sydney's pulse quickened.

"Fire." Gregor spoke the word aloud.

"What could be burning out here? We're not far from...." The blood drained from Erik's face. "Dear God, no."

He broke into a run, his rucksack slapping against his back. They sprinted after him. Fear coursed through Sydney, and she pumped her weary legs to keep up. The forest gave way to scorched earth. Smoke drifted above the fields. The crops had been trampled and burned, and animal carcasses lay close to the dirt road leading to the farm. Ahead, the blackened shell of a large building still smoldered.

"This cannot be!" Erik picked up speed, racing toward the remains of the farmhouse.

"Erik, wait!" Gregor called, but the monk didn't stop.

"Gregor, look at this." Rolf pointed to the hoof prints covering the dirt lane. He put a hand on the hilt of his sword. "The monks wouldn't have many horses."

Gregor drew his weapon. He and Rolf moved forward. "Stay behind us," he said to Vadnae and Sydney.

Sydney bent to pull the blade from her boot. Who would attack a group of peaceful monks and farmers?

They approached the remains of the farmhouse. Erik had joined several men and robed monks, some lugging buckets from a nearby well, others searching among the debris. Two smaller buildings also lay in ruins. "Here," a man struggled to move a large piece of timber. The others hurried to help him. One of the monks gave an anguished cry at their discovery and fell to his knees.

Sydney blinked as the smoke stung her eyes. "Who'd do something like this?"

Gregor shook his head. "I can't imagine. But we must do whatever we can to help."

Sydney hesitated when the others moved forward. She doubted any of the monks or townsfolk would recognize her. Nor was it likely they were in league with the Guild. But the Guild had spies everywhere.

"Hey! You there!"

The voice came from behind her. She whirled around. A man ran toward her, carrying a child, stumbling across the uneven field. Sydney's stomach lurched. Of course, children lived here. A number of families probably lived on the farm to help tend the land.

"Hurry! There are others back here!"

Gregor was right. They had to help. She stuck her knife back into her boot sheath and hurried to the man. Soot blackened his face and clothes. He thrust the child at her. "Take her. I'm going back to see if anyone else still lives."

She staggered under the unexpected weight. Blood soaked the front of the girl's dress and matted her hair. Two or three years old, her delicate face was ashen, her limbs heavy. Her breath rattled in her chest.

So much blood. Sydney had seen people die before, but she'd never held death this close. She cradled the child to her chest. *Breathe. Don't give up.* She sprinted toward the others, hoping someone could save her.

Her breath came in gasps when she finally caught up with them. Gregor took the child from her arms and laid her beside several blackened bodies. The stench of burning flesh churned Sydney's stomach.

Gregor stepped away. She grabbed his arm. "Ain't you gonna do something? You can't leave her there to die."

He shook his head. She glanced at the girl. The small chest had ceased to move. Tears filled her eyes. Gregor squeezed her shoulder. "Come, Sydney. There's nothing more we can do."

She let him lead her away from the ruins to where Vadnae stood alone. Tears streaked Vadnae's soot-stained cheeks, but her eyes were dry. "What good is magic if I can't save them? Why couldn't I prevent this?"

"None of us could have prevented this," Gregor said to her.

Rolf soon joined them. His auburn hair stood out in the soot smeared across his face. "They found more bodies in the woods. Poor bastards must've attempted to make a run for it. One boy survived, but he didn't see anything. We've gotta get to Aldric as soon as possible."

"Of course, Rolf," Vadnae said. She retrieved a lace handkerchief from her sleeve and wiped the dirt from her face. "We should leave at once. Where's Erik?"

"He's coming."

Another monk accompanied Erik and introduced himself as Brother Francis. "I just returned from the market in Last Hope." Tears welled in his eyes, and he clutched the charred remains of a book to his chest. "Now they're all gone. Brother Peter, Brother John, Brother Michael.... If I'd known this was going to happen...."

Erik slumped, his face stricken. "If you had been here, you, too, would have been lost."

"We are all saddened by the loss of your brothers," Vadnae said.

"Thank you for your aid." Francis wiped the tears from his eyes. "Strangers are rarely willing to help those in need. I'll assist you, or Willem, in any way I can. You'll find me in the abbey in Last Hope."

Rolf swiveled from Erik to Francis. "Who spoke to you of Willem?"

"Brother Erik said—"

"I told you not to say anything."

"Please, don't be angry with Erik. We are on the same side. Willem and his men stopped here a few days ago. They were on their way to Lord Aldric's keep."

"This must be the Guild's doing," Rolf said. "Retribution for helping Willem."

"The Guild?" Francis took a step back, fingers tightening on the burned book. "We are peaceful men of the cloth. We merely offered shelter to those who requested it. The church has not taken any official position on the matter of Willem's claim to the throne."

"Perhaps it is time we do so," Erik said in a quiet voice. "You see what the Guild is capable of, Brother Francis."

"Before today, I would not have believed it." Francis embraced Erik and bowed to the others. "Godspeed on your journey. I hope we meet again under different circumstances."

The sun had sunk low in the sky when they left the ravaged farm. Rolf insisted they stay off the road. Lighting a single lantern to illuminate their way, they plodded through the thick undergrowth. The tall trees cast eerie shadows, blocking out what little daylight remained. Strange noises echoed in the forest. Sydney kept stumbling from exhaustion, and thorny branches scratched her skin and tore her blood-stained clothes.

A rustling stopped them. Sydney tensed and pulled her knife, expecting a wolf. A lone figure emerged from behind a bush. Rolf drew his sword and sprang forward.

"Wait." Gregor pulled him back. "Who's there? Show yourself!"

The cloaked figure came closer. "Why can't I ever get a welcoming greeting?"

"Grandfather!" Vadnae pushed Gregor and Rolf aside and ran to the old man. She threw her arms around his neck.

"You've done well, my dear, but your journey is just beginning." Oryn stepped back to address the rest of them. He wore the same frayed blue cloak he had worn when he freed Sydney from the tree. Now the lines on his distinguished face appeared more pronounced, as if he had aged ten years in a few days. "Here is a message for you to deliver to Willem." Bony fingers fumbled at the belt around his waist. He pulled out his magic pouch and stuck his arm in up to his armpit, much further than should have been possible. After a few moments, he retrieved a leather scroll case and presented it to Rolf. One end was sealed in wax. "For his highness."

The white-haired wizard fixed his stare on each of them in turn. "From this moment on, you will be on your own. It may take all of my efforts to keep our enemies occupied with other matters."

A tremor crossed Vadnae's face. "We will see you again, won't we?"

He put his arm around her and led her a short distance away where they talked quietly. Soon they returned, Vadnae's delicate mouth set in a determined line.

Next Oryn spoke alone with Gregor, Erik, and finally Sydney. Steering her away from the others, Oryn put a gentle hand on her shoulder. "There are things I must tell you, Sydney, things perhaps I should have told you years ago. Now, more than ever, you should be aware of the truth about Edgar. I wish he'd made this easier for me—for both of us."

He paused, shaking his head. "That's a story for another time, however. What I want to tell you now is that Edgar's family was among the first of the nobility to be destroyed by the Guild, a lesson to anyone who dared to speak out in opposition of the Guild's practices. Only Edgar survived, and he gave up his name and privileges and went into hiding. In Last Hope."

Sydney was speechless. She couldn't imagine the unassuming man who had raised her had once been a wealthy nobleman. There had to be a mistake.

"Many dangers await you in Last Hope. The trials you will undergo will be more difficult than your previous experiences. You must find the strength to do what is right, rather than what is easy, just as Edgar did. This time, others are also depending on you."

Sydney heard his words, but they were meaningless. His revelation threw her entire life into question. Edgar had always stood up for the commoners. Hell, he'd always acted like a commoner.

"He should've told me." Oryn squeezed her shoulder, and she drew back. "How could he let me believe a lie?"

"Knowing the truth about Edgar doesn't change who he was. You meant so much to him. You may question why he kept his past from you, but never question his love for you."

The lines around his mouth softened. "Vadnae said you needed a new pair of boots, but I thought you'd rather keep your old ones."

He gestured to her feet. A tingling sensation began in her toes, spreading to her ankles, up to her knees. The dirt and grime fell away from her boots, dissipating into the air. The leather renewed itself before her eyes, stretching to fill in the cracks. Sydney bent down to touch the soft calfskin, amazed. The boots were like new.

His understanding brought tears to her eyes. "Thank you."

He nodded. "Be well, Sydney. And if I might ask, would you also look out for Vadnae? There is a lot you could learn from her, but I think you can teach her a few things as well."

Sydney forced a smile. "You want me to make sure no one picks her pocket?"

He winked at her. "I would expect nothing less."

They rejoined the others. Oryn embraced Vadnae and shook hands firmly with the rest of them. "Good luck. I hope we will meet again, if the fates are willing."

He gave a little wave and disappeared among the trees.

Chapter Nine

They broke camp before sunrise and continued on. A driving rain had begun during the night and showed no sign of abating. Mud caked their boots and clothes, and the rain soaked them all to the skin. Sydney struggled to focus on the washed-out road, putting one foot in front of the other, but she was haunted by the images of the dead child and the bodies of the monks. Despite a clean shirt, the reek of death shadowed her, like an evil vapor.

"How are you doing, Sydney?" Gregor slowed his pace to match hers.

With a shrug, she pushed back the drooping hood of her cloak. "I keep seeing the people who were killed."

"It's not an easy thing to get past. I've seen too much senseless death in my life."

"How do you get it out of your mind?"

"You don't. Those things remind us why we're here, which is to make sure they never happen again."

Sydney hoped Lord Aldric and Willem shared Gregor's opinion.

Cultivated fields bordered Lord Aldric's keep. Seeing the neatly baled hay and stubble fields of wheat and barley helped ease Sydney's anxiety. The keep and the land around it remained untouched.

Rolf hitched up his rucksack when they approached the

twin towers flanking the entrance in the outer wall of the stone fortress. "Let me do the talking."

A sentry emerged from one of the towers. "State your business."

Rolf bowed slightly. "I've come as an emissary from Lord Stephan, here to see Lord Aldric."

The sentry's eyes swept over them. "Are you all emissaries?"

We don't look like emissaries. Vadnae, of course, still carried herself like a lady, holding her head high, as if attired in an elegant gown rather than a mud-stained dress. Somehow, her dress appeared dry. Sydney's water-logged clothes weighed her down, and her wet hair dripped into her eyes. Her even wetter cloak sapped the warmth from her.

"They're with me." Rolf set down his pack. He withdrew a scroll case, smaller than the one Oryn had given him, and handed it to the sentry. "This is for Lord Aldric. Once he's read it, I'm sure he'll want to see us."

"Very well. All of you, come with me."

Opening the gate, the sentry escorted them into a muddy courtyard that lay between the outer wall and a smaller inner wall. To their left stood several wooden buildings from which rose the murmur of voices.

The sentry guided them to a sheltered overhang. "Wait here while I inform his Lordship you seek an audience with him." He approached two others guarding the entrance to the second wall.

Erik set his rucksack on the ground with a grunt and pushed back the hood of his cloak. "Are you sure Willem is here?"

"We'll find out soon. At the very least, Aldric should offer us lodging and a hot meal."

Sydney took in the courtyard. A stack of barrels marked where she'd listened to the storytellers during the harvest festival. During the annual festival, the open gate would welcome Aldric's subjects, along with the peddlers who'd come from distant towns and performers who danced and sang and told stories for the crowds. The food and ale were plentiful and free. Sydney had enjoyed the bards most of all. Edgar would leave her listening to the storytellers while he attended to his own business dealings, and she'd be in the same spot when he returned, entranced by songs and tales of faraway places, kings and queens, and dangerous adventures.

After Edgar was hanged, she stopped going to the festival.

Not all tales had happy endings. She shivered and wrapped her arms around herself.

Vadnae bent her head toward Sydney and told her, "Don't say anything unless Lord Aldric asks you a direct question. We don't want to insult him, whether it's intentional or not."

"All right, all right. Don't worry, I'll keep my mouth shut."

Several minutes passed before the sentry returned, accompanied by a man dressed in a fine silk tunic. The well-dressed man introduced himself as Marcus, Aldric's steward. "My lord wishes to see you at once. There seems to be some urgency, so you need not worry about your attire."

They passed through the second wall, another smaller courtyard, and entered the central keep. Elaborate tapestries, gilt-edged mirrors, and brass candle sconces adorned the walls. Thick rugs of orange, crimson, and russet hues covered the stone floors. Despite being one of the poorest lords in the kingdom, Aldric had certainly done well for himself. Sydney couldn't help wondering if any of the Guild's money had paid for the lavish furnishings.

In an alcove near a staircase hung a life-sized portrait of a man resplendently dressed, a hunting dog by his side. The jewels on one hand alone could have fed countless hungry people in Last Hope. She snorted in disgust. When Vadnae coughed and poked her in the ribs, Marcus glanced over his shoulder, quirking an eyebrow. Sydney mustered a polite smile. *Polite. Be polite.*

They continued to an enormous hall where a fire blazed in the hearth at one end. Two young women placed platters of bread, cheese, and meats on one of the long wooden tables arranged throughout the room.

"Please, make yourselves comfortable," Marcus said. "My lord will be with you momentarily."

Vadnae smiled. "Thank you, Marcus. You are most kind."

"We don't get many visitors in these parts, my lady. You bring news from Lord Stephan?"

"Our business is with Lord Aldric," Rolf said before anyone else could respond.

Marcus bowed, though obviously disappointed. "Of course. I'll have the maid prepare rooms for you."

They laid their wet cloaks and rucksacks around the hearth. Vadnae, Gregor, and Rolf sat at the table. Sydney ripped a large end from a loaf of bread and grabbed a wedge of cheese. She joined Erik near the fire. Despite the warmth, her clothes would need hours to dry.

Erik's head hung down, his body slumped. He had been uncharacteristically quiet all morning, speaking only to Gregor before they broke camp. If she couldn't get the images of the monks out of her mind, his sorrow surely ran much deeper. She offered him a piece of bread. "Hungry?"

He shook his head. "My appetite eludes me today, Sydney."

Yesterday Erik had called her a glutton for eating three apples at the noon meal. Sydney swallowed the rest of her cheese. Suddenly she wasn't hungry, either.

Aldric didn't keep them waiting long. A tall, thin man, he wore a simple woolen tunic, an odd contrast to the splendor displayed in his keep. Gray peppered his hair and beard, and his long face was creased with worry. After seeing his portrait, Sydney was surprised by his modest appearance.

Rolf stood and bowed. "My lord."

"It's good to see you, Rolf." Aldric crossed the room, and they clasped hands.

Rolf signaled the others to join him. "My lord, allow me to introduce my companions. Sir Gregor, Brother Erik, Lady Vadnae—"

"Lady Vadnae?" Aldric interrupted her curtsey, his face showing a glimpse of agitation. "You and your grandfather have not been guests in my hall in some time."

Vadnae curtseyed gracefully. "A lot has changed, Lord Aldric."

"Indeed it has." Aldric moved to one of the tables. "Please, sit. Tell me, Rolf, who is your other companion?"

"Sydney is one of your subjects, my lord. She's from Last Hope."

Aldric stared at her, and Sydney returned his gaze. "Then I suppose Willem intends to carry out his plan. He arrived yesterday. This morning I received word the monks who offered shelter to Willem and his soldiers were massacred."

Erik bowed his head. "We intended to seek shelter ourselves with the brothers of my order, but we were too late. Who would commit such a monstrous act?"

"I expect the church will ask me the same question, Brother Erik. Clearly, this attack was meant as a warning. I can think of no other explanation for such senseless slaughter."

Rolf leaned forward. "You think Schrammig had something to do with it?"

"Schrammig? It's been years since he's been to these parts."

Rolf glanced at Sydney. "He's come back, or so we've heard."

A muscle in Aldric's cheek twitched. "Perhaps murdering the monks is his way of announcing his return. You must realize the Guild still controls Last Hope. These are my lands, but I am lord in name alone." Aldric's voice became bitter. "The church will ask the Guild to investigate this matter, and who do you think will be implicated? They may well announce Willem was behind the attack because the church refused to support his bid for the throne."

Sydney bit her lip. The Guild was ruthless about protecting their power. Aldric's scenario was plausible.

Aldric pulled a rolled parchment from his tunic and tossed it on the table. "Are you aware of the contents of your uncle's message, Rolf?"

"Yes, he told me."

Aldric stood and paced. "Stephan confirms the council has named Lord Pendolf heir to the throne. He's asking me to join him in backing Willem." He ran a hand through his thinning hair. "I want to help, but let me tell you what I've told Willem. My men number not much more than a thousand. I must consider the welfare of my subjects. The farmers can't afford to leave their crops at harvest time. Willem thinks it should be easy to overthrow the Guild in Last Hope, but I believe they're too entrenched there."

Sydney straightened in her chair. "Not everyone in Last Hope supports the Guild."

"You remember Edgar, my lord?" Gregor asked him. "He was Sydney's guardian. There are many in Last Hope who are eager to get rid of the Guild."

"Edgar?" Aldric studied Sydney. "You're Edgar's child?"

"Not by blood." Sydney shifted uncomfortably. Was Aldric aware of Edgar's past?

"No one realized he had a child." Aldric sat and rubbed his face. "Willem would do well to learn from Edgar's mistakes. Edgar underestimated the Guild, and he overestimated the people of Last Hope."

Sydney's anger surged. "What the hell do you know about the people of Last Hope?"

"Sydney." Vadnae spoke softly and tugged on her sleeve.

She pulled her arm away. The words tumbled out before she had a chance to think. "You ain't never lifted a finger to stop the Guild in Last Hope. All the arrests. The hangings." Her voice caught in her throat. "Did they give you a seat of honor when they hanged Edgar?"

Aldric slapped the table. "You forget your place, Sydney. I am still your lord. I could have you flogged for such impudence."

The hush that followed pulsated with tension. Sydney refused to look away from Aldric's stare, even though her knees shook beneath the table. He was right. She was merely a peasant under his rule. He could have her dragged into the courtyard and flogged if he wished.

"Here now, Aldric." Rolf put a hand on his arm. "No need for such threats. Syd's one of Willem's advisors now."

Rolf gave her a sidelong glance and a wink. She mouthed a silent *Thank you,* relieved he'd spoken up on her behalf.

"If she plans to advise our future king, she should learn to think before she speaks. People have been hanged for less."

"These are difficult circumstances, Lord Aldric," Vadnae spoke up, her tone soothing. "We are all struggling to—"

"My lord?" Marcus appeared in the doorway, breathless.

"I told you we weren't to be disturbed."

"I-I know, my lord, but another guest has arrived. Schrammig. He demands to speak with you."

The blood drained from Aldric's face. "Schrammig? What does he want? How many men accompany him?"

Rolf jumped to his feet, buckling on his sword and tossing bags to Gregor and Erik. Sydney's heart hammered.

"Only four men, my lord. I dared not ask his business."

Aldric hesitated only a moment. "Show him to my study and fetch a bottle of my best wine. Quickly, man." The steward bowed and dashed off.

"Follow me." Aldric strode to a door in the far wall. "We could all hang if Schrammig finds you here."

The sounds of footsteps and voices came from the entranceway. Sydney couldn't hear the words, but she recognized the voice. She'd never forget the raspy voice, a match for the scar on his face. She had heard it on the last night she had seen Edgar alive.

"Sydney." Gregor tugged on her arm and then pried her fingers from the hilt of her knife. She hadn't even been aware of clutching it.

As if waking from a trance, she grabbed her rucksack and hurried after them. Aldric led them down a long corridor and stopped at a winding staircase. He thrust a lamp at Rolf. "There's a room at the top. Wait there. I'll send someone for you." He turned and quickly walked back the way they'd come.

Sydney shook her head, a vain attempt to clear the phantoms from her mind, and climbed the spiraling dark staircase. The night Edgar had been arrested haunted her dreams, and each time the brutal ending crushed her.

Memories flooded her mind. The tavern where she and Edgar had been staying had been crowded. She'd been late, and they had argued. Edgar's worries about the Guild overshadowed his concern regarding her actions and his distrust of Zared. He'd been too quiet, lost in his thoughts.

She recalled Edgar tossing a leather pouch on the table. The coins clinked softly. "Go buy us a pint," he said, absently looking across the room.

She hesitated. Neither of them had eaten. It wasn't like Edgar to spend all his coin on ale.

"Now, Sydney. Do as I say."

Knowing better than to question him, she grabbed their last coppers and hurried to the bar.

While she waited for the ale, the tavern door slammed open. The crowd grew still. Three men stood in the doorway, dressed in leather jerkins with swords strapped to their backs. Chains and knives hung from their belts. One of the men had a jagged scar down the center of his face.

Schrammig.

The bartender slapped down a tankard, amber ale sloshing over the brim. "You gonna pay for this?"

She ignored him, frozen. Schrammig approached the table where Edgar sat. The two other men stayed by the door. She clutched the soft leather pouch in her hand. All the money they had. The crowd blocked Edgar from her view. She started toward him.

The bartender grabbed her arm. "Let him be." When she pulled away, his hand clenched around her arm. "Don't be stupid, girl. You can't let them find you." He dragged her around the bar and shoved her down on her knees, out of sight.

She sat there, shaking, clutching her knees to her chest, gulping in the stale fumes of strong liquor and cheap ale. This wasn't supposed to happen. She wasn't supposed to do nothing. She couldn't abandon Edgar and save herself.

Heavy footsteps crossed the room. A tankard clattered to the floor, a chair or a table overturned. A fist smashing flesh. She started to get up, and the bartender shoved a knee in her chest. He reached underneath the bar for a bottle. His hands shook.

In the hushed room, a raspy voice spoke. "Where's the girl?"

She inched herself back as far as she could. Bottles pressed into her shoulders. With a trembling hand, she fingered the blade she kept hidden in her boot.

"Don't know who you're talking about. He was alone."

Coins clinked on the bar. "Be sure to send word if you ever see her in here again."

Sydney waited, her body shaking. Several minutes passed. At last, the bartender jerked her to her feet. "He was a good man, Edgar was. For his sake, don't ever come back here or I'll give you to Schrammig myself."

Her last glimpse of Schrammig had been at Edgar's execution, when he'd laughed and signaled to the hangman to begin.

Now, in one of the well-appointed rooms below, Schrammig was drinking a fine wine and rasping the same laugh.

In the room at the top of the staircase, the lamplight cast unearthly shadows on the bare walls. Compared with the ornate trappings elsewhere in the keep, the straw pallets and sparseness suggested quarters for servants, or perhaps a room not in use at all. The hearth held cold ash, and a musty odor pervaded. Mice scurried across the floor.

Rolf set the lamp on the bare mantel above the hearth. He moved to the grimy window. The rain beat a steady tattoo on the windowpane. "Hard telling if Schrammig is here searching for Willem. Or us. Or if he's merely paying a visit to Aldric as a warning."

Erik paced near the hearth. "Can we trust Lord Aldric? Why would this man who works for Pendolf arrive shortly after we did? It appears suspect to me."

"I trust Aldric." Rolf's voice was firm. "Willem trusts Aldric."

"I don't," Sydney said. "Aldric's down there drinking wine with Schrammig."

Rolf jabbed a finger at her. "You'd do well to leave the discussion for those of us who understand protocol. Insulting someone of Aldric's station is dangerous, for you and for the rest of us. If you spoke in such a manner to Stephan, he'd have you whipped without batting an eye."

She stepped toward him, balling her fists. "He insulted—"

"Sydney." Gregor touched her arm. "Don't let your feelings overshadow what we're trying to accomplish. We must work together."

"Gregor's right," Vadnae added. "We may find allies in unlikely places."

"You don't know Schrammig like I do," Sydney whispered. She hugged her arms to her chest. Along the walls, the shadows flickered in a macabre dance, as if the darkness were celebrating Schrammig's return.

Chapter Ten

Marcus soon came for them. "I'm afraid my Lord Aldric has been put in a difficult situation. Schrammig will be staying overnight before he continues on to Last Hope. So you see, your presence here is...."

"Dangerous?" Rolf finished.

"Indeed. My lord thinks it would be better if you stayed with his highness, Prince Willem. He's not far. Please, come with me."

Rolf grunted. "Wouldn't want to share dinner with Schrammig anyway."

The thought of dining with Schrammig turned Sydney's stomach.

Putting a finger to his lips, Marcus motioned them to follow him down the staircase. Sydney winced. The echoes of their footsteps had to be loud enough for Schrammig to hear. Several long hallways lacked the ornate decoration of those they had seen on their arrival. They exited a plain wooden door into a courtyard. A boy was waiting for them.

The rain had slackened to a fine mist, the clouds low and ominous.

Marcus squinted toward the sky. "Dreadful weather. We've no spare horses or carriages, otherwise I'd gladly offer them to you." He nodded to the boy. "He'll take you to the prince."

"Please tell Lord Aldric we regret putting him in an

awkward situation," Vadnae said.

He bowed. "Of course, Lady Vadnae. I only wish you could have enjoyed our hospitality. Perhaps another time."

The boy hurried across the courtyard. Sydney raised the hood of her cloak and started after her companions. A hand on her arm stopped her.

"May I ask a favor of you, milady?"

Marcus's question and respectful address threw her off guard. "What kind of favor?"

"My sister lives in Last Hope. She's never said it directly, but I'm sure her husband has helped the resistance. Lord Aldric told me who you are. You, of all people, understand the danger, especially since Schrammig has returned."

He clutched a tiny leather purse, knuckles white. "Will you take this to her? She has little ones to think of. I wish I could do more, but it would give me some comfort knowing she and her children will not starve."

Sydney stared at the purse. She expected Erik to warn the man not to give his money to a thief, but he and the others stood watching, silent. The steward should keep his coin. She had no business helping a stranger.

"Please. I would be in your debt." He held out the purse to her, eyes pleading.

He'd called her "milady." He trusted her. The purse was light. Loosening the drawstring and glancing inside, she saw the glint of silver. A fortune, and certainly more money than she'd ever had. Edgar had often helped people in need, giving food or money to women whose husbands had been imprisoned by the Guild when he could, or encouraging others to use the services of tradesmen who refused to join the Guild.

"Where do I find her?"

Marcus let out a sigh of relief. "Truly, milady, I am in your debt. Betty's her name. She works with Nala, the old herb woman. Most days you can find her in the market."

"I know Nala." The old woman's miracle cures were lauded

throughout Last Hope. Sydney fingered the soft leather purse. "I'll get this to your sister."

He bowed his head. "Thank you. Edgar was a great man. You are a credit to him."

All these years she had denied her connection to Edgar. Now his name was a badge of honor. Angrily she blinked away the tears in her eyes and carefully tucked the purse into the larger pouch she wore around her neck. She hoped she could live up to the steward's expectations.

In spite of the rain and the mud—Sydney couldn't get much wetter—the farther they got from Aldric's keep, the better she felt. The distance meant they were farther away from Schrammig.

As they crossed the neatly plowed fields, dusk descended, coloring the sky in shades of sapphire and auburn. A grove of trees towered behind a modest, thatched-roof farmhouse. Light glowed in the windows, and a plume of smoke rose from the chimney.

When a bevy of geese behind a distant hill took flight, Sydney halted and listened. An owl hooted, haunting and mournful. Tree branches creaked, and the breeze swirled the fallen leaves, a faint rustling. She scanned the forest edge. Nothing moved in the darkness. Nothing she could discern, at least.

The boy told them to wait. He ran to the farmer unhitching his horses from a wagon in front of the nearby barn. The farmer's head swiveled in their direction. The boy darted toward the house. Moments later, two soldiers emerged from inside.

"Rolf? Bloody hell, it's been a long time." Rolf stepped forward and they laughed and clapped each other on the back. "We wondered if we'd see again, you old bastard."

"For a while I wasn't sure you would, George."

"What are we standing out here for? Willem's been expecting you. You look like hell, Rolf."

The other soldier nudged him, thrusting his chin in Vadnae's direction.

George lowered his head. "Beg your pardon, my lady. His highness is used to being around ladies, but the rest of us haven't had the privilege."

"No offense taken," Vadnae said with a smile. He rubbed his neck and stared at the ground.

The soldiers led them into the farmhouse. Mud and dirt spattered the worn hardwood floors. Cloaks, bedrolls, blankets, and knapsacks were stacked near the white-washed walls. Half a dozen men sat on benches at a sturdy oak table. An iron pot hung over the fire in the hearth, and the strong odor of meat and smoke filled the room. Now that the moment had arrived, Sydney felt an anxious excitement about meeting Willem.

George thumped one of the soldiers on the back. "Time to clear out. We've got company. They've come to meet with Willem." The soldiers filed out. A few grumbled and gave them curious looks. Two remained by the door. George pulled up a chair for Vadnae. Sydney guessed the remaining chair was reserved for Willem. In an empty corner, they placed their wet cloaks and belongings, and then sat down to steaming bowls of stew.

The warmth of the fire and the hearty beef stew helped Sydney relax. She hadn't expected to meet Willem in a farmhouse. The setting was more informal than Aldric's keep and much more comfortable.

George filled their bowls a second time before he went to fetch Willem. When Vadnae asked if they could wash first, he laughed. "Don't worry. We're all worse for wear these days, Willem included."

Rolf rubbed the stubble on his chin. "Willem doesn't like people fawning over him."

"I suppose we're acceptable." Vadnae patted her hair into place and stood to shake out her skirts, now dry and not too badly wrinkled.

Sydney wiped her hands on her rain-soaked and muddy breeches. Her damp linen shirt clung to her skin. The warmth faded, and her anxiety returned.

In spite of whatever informalities Willem preferred, they all stood when he arrived. He crossed the room with long, purposeful strides. Despite his youth, his confident bearing commanded a certain respect. He wore not the finery of a nobleman, but the same clothes as his soldiers, a white tunic belted at the waist and brown pants tucked into mud-splattered boots. Of average height, he had the lean, muscled build of a soldier. A lock of the blond hair pulled back to the nape of his neck had fallen across his forehead. His handsome face and strong jaw denoted intelligence and determination.

Gregor dropped to one knee. Sydney tried to mimic Vadnae's graceful curtsy and ended up grabbing the edge of the table to keep from falling.

"Please, get up." Willem touched Gregor on the shoulder.

Stepping forward to address Vadnae, Willem slightly bowed his head. "It is an honor to see you again, Lady Vadnae," he murmured, yet his eyes focused on Sydney. The color of the sky on a cloudless summer day, his blue eyes were arresting, their intensity searing.

Rolf nudged Sydney aside. "Good to see you, Willem."

Willem's face split into a wide grin. He slapped Rolf on the back. "You, too, Rolf."

He pulled out the chair at the head of the table, and the rest of them sat. Sweeping his gaze across them, he paused on Sydney. She fidgeted on the wooden bench, wondering why he flustered her so.

Willem leaned his elbows on the table and clasped his hands. His only adornment, a gold signet ring, flashed in the lamplight. "I expected Oryn to accompany you."

Vadnae straightened in her chair. "I am here on my grandfather's behalf, your highness. I'm afraid he has been delayed."

He held up his hand. "Please, it's just Willem. For now I'm taking advantage of being without an official title."

Vadnae blushed. "Of course. Willem. Let me introduce you to my companions. We've all come to aid you at Grandfather's request." She gestured to Gregor. "This is Sir Gregor, formerly of the royal knights."

"Your deeds are well known, Gregor. I will value your counsel, and your sword."

"They are both yours, Willem."

"And Brother Erik."

Willem's face became troubled. "Brother Erik, we received word this morning of the attack on your brothers here. We will do what we can to bring justice to those who murder innocent monks."

Erik bowed his head. "Thank you, my liege."

"And Sydney. You may remember Edgar, who was executed for opposing the Guild in Last Hope. He was Sydney's guardian."

Sydney felt Willem watching her, as if taking her measure. In his stare, she sensed power simmering beneath the surface. She looked away, focusing on the table.

"I'm sure your insights on Last Hope will prove useful, Sydney."

She raised her head, shocked that Willem would want her counsel. He smiled, and she fought the insane desire to reach out and push the lock of hair from his face. *What the hell am I thinking?* She forced her mind to his statement. "Yes, of course, Willem...I mean, er...your highness...oh hell." Her voice gave way to embarrassed silence, and her face flushed.

Vadnae elbowed her, shaking her head. "Rolf, where is the message from my grandfather?"

Rolf handed Willem the scroll case from his rucksack. "I hope the old wizard's got more than advice up his sleeve. We couldn't enjoy Aldric's hospitality. Schrammig arrived shortly after we did."

Willem's lips tightened, and his hand gripped the scroll case. "Schrammig must have ordered the attack on the monks. They offered us shelter two nights ago. Schrammig is notorious for his savagery, although I doubt Lord Pendolf will condone his actions against the church."

Erik touched the cross around his neck. "There is a special place in hell for those who commit such acts."

"Indeed there is." Willem opened the scroll case and withdrew a rolled parchment. He read it, his face impassive. When finished, he laid the parchment aside and contemplated the group.

Sydney's unsettling desire was quickly tempered by the more real and immediate threat of Schrammig. She met Willem's stare and sought reassurance in his confidence. If he couldn't defeat Schrammig, all was lost.

As if answering her plea, Willem stood and paced the room, his hand resting on the long knife belted at his side. "I won't let Pendolf and the Guild take control of Thanumor. I intend to be king. In nearly every province, I've met people who have been secretly fighting the Guild for years. Now they're ready to fight for me. Pendolf's forces currently outnumber us, and he has the resources of the Guild at his disposal. But each day more are flocking to my side. A victory here, in Last Hope, will be an important rallying point for our allies."

Erik's brow furrowed. "Why Last Hope? It's a town of little consequence."

"Strategically, you're correct, Erik." Willem exchanged a glance with Rolf. "Stephan initially called it a foolish plan."

"I think he called it a 'damned fool plan' he wanted no part of."

Willem returned Rolf's grin. "Fortunately your uncle has faith in his future king, even when we disagree. Especially when we disagree. Last Hope will be a symbol of what we can accomplish throughout the kingdom, a town freed from the yoke of the Guild. But there is also another reason why Last

Hope is so important." He paused and nodded to Vadnae. "The Tuatha."

The hair rose on the back of Sydney's neck. "What do the faery folk have to do with Last Hope?"

"We are aware of two gateways to enter their realm," Vadnae said quietly. "One is in the Wastes, too dangerous for anyone to use. The other is beneath Last Hope."

"The tunnels?" The odd whispers echoed in Sydney's mind. *The Tuatha?* "I ain't-I mean I haven't ever seen any magic in the tunnels."

"It's there, and it will lead us to the Tuatha."

"I think Sydney's knowledge of the tunnels will be very useful, don't you, Vadnae?"

Vadnae bowed her head in response.

Sydney looked from the prince to the wizard. They weren't sharing some piece of information. "How d'you think I can help?"

Willem tossed the parchment into the fire. "We'll discuss your assistance later." He approached the soldiers guarding the door. "Send for the boy to take another message to Aldric. And tell the men to prepare to leave." One soldier saluted and left.

He turned back to the group. "I realize you're tired, but I hope you can manage on a few hours' sleep. It's all we can spare. I won't be caught here if Schrammig is searching for us. We're a bit short on space, but there's a loft upstairs." He waved a hand at a curtained doorway.

"I appreciate the offer of a room, but isn't it yours?" Vadnae asked.

"I'll get no sleep tonight, Vadnae. Most of my men are camped out in the barn and the forest. The rest of you can find space with them if you prefer."

"As long as it's dry, we don't care," said Gregor.

Vadnae grimaced, sending a sidelong glance at the knight. "The room upstairs will be fine for myself and Sydney."

Willem rubbed his cheek, as though trying to hide a grin. "I'll send someone to wake you when we're ready to move out."

Chapter Eleven

The sky was still dark when Vadnae shook her awake. "Willem wants to see us."

Sydney rubbed her eyes and climbed down the ladder from the loft. Her companions sat at the table with Willem and Lord Aldric. Willem's clothes were rumpled, his hair disheveled. Dark circles shadowed his eyes.

"There's a problem, Sydney," Willem said.

Her legs trembled when she slid onto the bench across from him. Had he found out about her past? "What's wrong?" she asked, trying to remain calm.

From within the folds of his tunic, Aldric pulled out a white handkerchief. He pushed it toward Sydney. "Schrammig asked me to give this to you."

She stared, first at him and then at the handkerchief. Her mouth went dry and her hand shook as she opened the handkerchief. A copper piece fell onto the table. A length of leather cord looped around the hole bored through it to make a necklace. The coin had been rubbed smooth, the leather frayed. She choked back a sob of rage. Edgar's good luck charm. He had always carried it with him.

"Damn you, Schrammig." She clutched the coin in her hand. Edgar had always said his good luck charm would offer protection. The talisman was a cruel reminder of what Schrammig had done to him. Pain and loss welled within her.

She rubbed the worn coin, wishing she could will Edgar back to life.

"Sydney, what is it?" Vadnae asked softly.

Sydney took a deep breath and tersely described the coin's significance. Her explanation didn't answer Willem's most important question, how Schrammig had learned she was there.

Willem finally addressed Aldric. "What did you tell him?"

Aldric shifted uneasily on the wooden bench. He glanced from Sydney to Willem. "I didn't tell him anything, nor did he ask me any questions."

Sydney's stomach clenched. She didn't know how Schrammig had found her, either. The only people who knew she was still alive, besides Oryn, sat at this table.

"How many men is Schrammig leading?"

Aldric rubbed his face. "Only a small force, numbering a hundred at most, with more on their way. His intentions toward Last Hope were very clear. He aims to maintain the Guild's control of the town."

Sydney clutched Edgar's good luck charm. Her heart began to pound. Clearly Schrammig had sent this to her to taunt her. *And his next move?*

Anaria.... She'd never forgive herself if Schrammig hurt Anaria. "We have to stop him," she blurted.

Vadnae squeezed her hand. "We'll do what we can."

"You don't understand. You saw what he did to the monks."

"I do understand, Sydney," Willem said, gently. "Now is not the time for hasty decisions. That would play right into Schrammig's hand."

Sydney bit her lip. In spite of his obvious fatigue, Willem projected a confidence she wished she shared. He was right. She couldn't let Schrammig get the best of her.

Willem ran a weary hand through his hair. "How long ago did he leave?"

"An hour perhaps. I got here as soon as I could. Schrammig had intended to stay the night, but he decided getting to Last Hope was more important. It's nearly a day's ride to town from here."

Willem stood, his chair scraping the floor. The rest of them also stood. "Aldric, I'm sending my men to your keep. They will be under your command until I return."

"Return from where? Surely you can't mean to go to Last Hope yourself? It's just one town, not worth risking your life over. I can't believe Stephan would support this plan."

Willem drew himself up, and his powerful body stiffened. "You speak out of turn, Aldric. Stephan supports me fully, and you would do well to remember that he answers to me, not the other way around. Can I count on your support?"

Aldric hesitated. In the hearth, the fire sparked. Finally, he bowed his head. "I am with you, my liege."

The hint of a smile crossed Willem's face. "My men will spread the word among the locals to seek shelter within your walls. Anyone Schrammig suspects of helping me may face the same fate as the monks he slaughtered. I will also dispatch a message to inform Stephan of the urgency of our situation. We will protect your lands, Aldric."

Aldric pulled on his cloak. "Thank you, Willem. By your leave, I will return to oversee to the preparations myself."

Willem inclined his head in response to Aldric's bow. "One more thing, Aldric. For weeks, my men have slept outdoors and in stables. Find them some space in your barracks or on the floor of your hall, it doesn't matter where, as long as you provide suitable accommodations."

"We'll find room for them. Good luck to you, Willem."

After Aldric had left, Willem picked up one of the bundles on the floor and a sheathed sword. "We'll leave at once for Last Hope."

Gregor held out their cloaks to Vadnae and Sydney. "Schrammig will be searching for us. It won't be easy getting into town if he's posted guards."

Sydney shrugged on her still damp cloak. "The gate is the only way into town."

"I'll show you my plan."

Willem led them outside. Lanterns bobbed in the darkness, and the wind carried the murmur of voices and the jingle of harness leather. A group of soldiers gathered in front of the farmhouse, loading provisions into a wagon.

"We're almost ready," one of the men said to Willem.

"Good. Rolf will lead you to Lord Aldric's keep, and until I return, you will all be under Lord Aldric's command."

Rolf took a step back, eyes wide. "My place is with you, Willem."

Willem gripped Rolf's shoulder. "Rolf, I need you here."

Rolf's hands clenched at his sides. Sydney was sure he didn't trust her or her companions, at least not enough to entrust them with Willem's safety. She couldn't guarantee her own safety in Last Hope.

Gregor placed a hand on his sword. "I give you my word no harm will come to Willem."

"Is it true what they're saying about Schrammig?" A young soldier stepped forward, eyes wide.

"Schrammig is not your concern. I've given you my orders. Make ready to leave."

Rolf leaned toward Gregor. "Your word is good, Gregor." He bowed to the others and told Willem, "We'll be ready. I'll expect the feast Aldric promised us earlier. It's the least he can do for our protection."

"Putting Rolf in charge is just going to go to his head," one of the men grumbled.

Willem chuckled and clapped him on the back. He spoke to his men, offering words of encouragement, touching shoulders and clasping hands. Their familiarity went beyond what Sydney expected of a man of Willem's rank. It was apparent he'd earned their loyalty.

After addressing his men, Willem took a lantern and led Sydney and the others around the farmhouse to the barn. Loose hay crunched beneath Sydney's boots, and her nose wrinkled at the overpowering scents of animal musk, urine, and freshly cut hay.

Willem held the lantern over the edge of an open wagon, illuminating the brown monk's robes piled between the low benches lining each side. "I hope you won't think us sacrilegious, Brother Erik, if we disguise ourselves as monks. Your brothers at their farm offered us these robes and a spare wagon. By the time we reach Last Hope, it will be dark. The disguise should be enough to get us inside."

Erik touched the coarse fabric, and a sorrowful expression crossed his face. "Won't Schrammig also target any monks entering town?"

"Unlikely. His attack on the farm served its purpose. His war is with me, not the church."

"The brothers at the abbey in Last Hope will keep our secret," Erik said. "Their hospitality would be better than staying at some flea-infested inn."

"I've lived in those flea-infested inns all my life," Sydney said.

Willem grinned and stowed his pack and sword under the wagon seat. "Believe me, Erik, after weeks of travel, one welcomes any sort of roof over one's head, regardless of how many vermin also live there."

"We may be safer with the monks." Gregor's brow creased, and he picked up one of the robes. He contemplated the group and paused briefly on Vadnae and Sydney. "The disguise should work, long enough to enter town. And once we are inside Last Hope? What is your plan, Willem?"

"The task of finding the Tuatha is mine alone, although I will also call upon Vadnae's expertise. The people of Last Hope will be valuable allies as well. Merchants, tradesmen, monks, and especially those who have organized to counter the

Guild in the past. We must convince them to fight. Erik, Sydney, I will count on your aid in this."

Sydney could locate Edgar's former conspirators, assuming they still lived. Her fist tightened around the coin in her pocket.

Gregor rubbed his chin thoughtfully. "Inciting a revolt within a walled town poses a great risk. We're on our own until Stephan arrives with reinforcements."

"This is where you come in, Gregor. You've fought battles before. I'm counting on you to assess the town's defenses and the resources we can use."

"I will."

"Let's prepare to leave as soon as we can. The rest of you go on ahead. I'd like to speak with Sydney alone."

The others left. Nervously she fingered Edgar's good luck charm. Willem's eyes seemed to stare into her soul, as Oryn's had done. Of course, Willem wasn't a wizard. He was just a man. But he was also a prince who would one day be king.

She leaned on the wagon, unsettled by his silence. "What d'you want?"

"I want to be able to trust you."

She stiffened. "What d'you mean? Why shouldn't you trust me?"

"You're a thief. You don't seem to care much for authority...Aldric's or mine. Furthermore, Aldric seems to think you may be in league with our enemies. The real question is...*why are you here?*"

Her fists clenched. How dare he accuse her of helping the Guild. She pulled out Edgar's coin and thrust it toward him. "Schrammig took this from Edgar before he hanged him. He destroyed my life. That's why I'm here, your highness. To fight the Guild." She didn't try to hide the bitterness in her words.

Turning her back to him, she furiously blinked away her tears.

"Here, I'm sorry." He faced her, holding out a clean, white

handkerchief. "It's clear Edgar meant a great deal to you."

She brushed his hand aside and instead wiped her face on her sleeve. Shoving the coin into her pocket, she stared at the figures moving around the farmhouse, pinpoints of light bobbing in the gloom. "D'you know what it's like to live in fear of the Guild? I was always afraid Schrammig was gonna come for me. I lived on the streets and stole to survive. How can someone like you understand?"

Willem folded his handkerchief and returned it to his pocket. "You need to understand why your response to Schrammig will undermine our mission. He sees you as our weak link. He knows how to break you. Look at your reaction every time someone mentions Edgar. Schrammig will use this against you. I can't allow your grief and your anger to get in the way."

She kicked at the hay on the floor. Willem was right. Dammit, she had tried so hard to let go. She'd dealt with her grief by being angry at Schrammig, the Guild, and the life she'd led after Edgar's death. She didn't know how to get past it. Taking up Edgar's cause might not be enough.

"You're not the only one who's lost someone dear to you." He swept the hair back from his face.

She'd no right to speak to him in such a familiar manner, but his openness encouraged it. "You mean your father? The king?"

Willem's lips pressed together. "Not the king. I care as little for him as he cared for me. His title is the only thing of his I want. I meant my mother, who risked her well-being to give me a better life and died before she was reassured her actions hadn't been in vain. Losing someone you care about is difficult, but surviving the loss makes you a stronger person. Now we're going to save lives, to put an end to the Guild. You must move on, for Edgar's sake as well as yours."

Zared had often told her she needed to forget Edgar, but he'd never spoken of letting go in such a meaningful way.

Zared's only interests were his own. The compassion in Willem's expression made her believe his words, because he believed them himself.

"Willem?" a voice called. "We're ready."

"I'll be right there." He put a hand on Sydney's shoulder, giving it a squeeze and sending her pulse racing. "Oryn told me I should trust you and that I'll need your help. I value his judgment. Remember what we're fighting for. When we win, we'll make Schrammig pay for what he's done."

His hand lingered a moment longer than necessary. He gave a quick nod and left to join his soldiers.

Willem's advice and understanding struck a chord deep within her. Sydney fingered the good luck charm. Despite his encouragement, she wasn't sure she could let go. Not yet. Not until she finished what Edgar had started. She owed it to him.

Chapter Twelve

The rain ceased, leaving behind a raw, penetrating chill. A light blush streaked the early morning darkness. Harnesses jingling, wagon wheels creaking, Willem's ragtag band of soldiers marched past the harvested fields. Sydney watched the dark assemblage fade into the landscape, and with it Last Hope's best defense against the Guild.

Pushing back the sleeves of the monk's robe, she helped load their gear in the wagon. The coarse wool retained the whiff of sweat and smoke, but at least it was dry.

Erik conceded she passed as a monk, if she kept her head down and her mouth shut. Vadnae's disguise proved more challenging.

Vadnae tied back her long tresses and raised her hood. "I'm certainly not going to cut my hair as short as Sydney's."

"It ain't your hair." At Vadnae's raised eyebrow, Sydney added, "You're not as flat-chested as I am."

Vadnae's cheeks flamed. "You needn't be so blunt, Sydney."

"It's just the truth." She found an extra blanket in their supplies and held it out to Vadnae. "Put this underneath your robe."

Vadnae frowned and shook her head. She turned her back and adjusted the blanket under her robe. Facing Sydney, she let out her belt to account for the extra girth. "Better?"

"It'll do." They climbed into the wagon and sat on one of the benches. "You shouldn't worry, Vadnae. They're a good asset."

"Surely you're not implying what I think you are."

"You're pretty. Men pay attention to you. Something to keep in mind once we get to Last Hope."

"I hope we're not going to be dealing with those sorts of men."

Sydney shrugged. Vadnae's delicate features and shapely figure would attract attention, whether she wanted it or not. She was also a wizard; her aura commanded respect. "You never know what skills might come in handy."

"What skills would those be, Sydney?" Willem settled himself on the bench across from them. Gregor and Erik had taken the seat in the front of the wagon.

Vadnae blushed and suddenly bent down to arrange their bags under the seat.

"Skills only a woman would know," Sydney said, giving Willem an airy smile.

Erik snorted in disgust. "A woman or a whore?"

"It all depends on how you get paid, doesn't it?"

"Sydney, please," Vadnae said through gritted teeth.

"Perhaps we should avoid discussions better left for the alehouse." Willem winked at Sydney, sending a rush of heat through her.

The wagon lurched forward, and Erik gripped the seat. "I can't believe you would be familiar with such discussions, Willem."

"Rolf and I once enjoyed the finest taverns in Pyredon, back in our younger days."

Gregor turned in his seat. "Ever go to the Thistle and Barley?"

Willem chuckled. "I've quite a story to tell about the Thistle and Barley. And it's not one to be told in polite company."

"I've a similar one myself." Gregor laughed and switched

the conversation to the other lords and their support of Willem's bid for the throne, and the three men soon discussed lords and provinces whose names quickly blurred together in Sydney's mind.

After a time, Vadnae nudged her and spoke softly. "Do the men in Last Hope really view women in such a manner?"

"Not all of them. A lot of the ones I've met do, though."

"What about Zared?"

"Zared?" Sydney stiffened and shifted on the uneven wooden bench. "Who told you about him?"

"You sometimes mumble things in your sleep. I heard you say his name. I figured he must be important to you."

Sydney stared at the fields of wheat stubble. "He ain't important."

"He used to be?"

"Vadnae, let's not talk about it."

"As you wish." Vadnae folded her hands in her lap.

Sydney wished she could explain what Zared had meant to her and her conflicting feelings for him now. *Vadnae has lived a comfortable life. She can't understand the choices I've made and the things I've been forced to do to survive.* She'd begun to consider Vadnae a friend. She'd had so few people she could trust in her life, especially women friends. Certainly none like Vadnae.

Putting on the monk's robe to disguise herself was easy. Changing the person she'd been these past years was much more difficult. How could Vadnae and the others understand what she'd need to overcome to become one of them?

———

The horizon blazed crimson when they approached the fifteen-foot-high wooden walls surrounding Last Hope. Sydney shuddered. She felt a lifetime had passed since she had been marched out to the forest. Now her past lay within those walls, waiting for her.

A man's body hung from a gibbet near the gate. Dressed in a guard's uniform, the body showed no signs of decay. One of his eyes had been gouged out. Sydney squinted at the man's ravaged face. With a start, she recognized the captain who had left her tied to the tree in the forest.

"Remember, say nothing," Willem told Sydney and Vadnae in a low voice.

Sydney managed a nod, a sour taste in her mouth. There could be a dozen reasons why the captain had been executed. No reason to think his death had anything to do with her. But he knew her. He'd planned to spare her, as a favor to Edgar. And Schrammig had returned to Last Hope.

The two guards hailed them. "Good evening, brothers. What brings you to Last Hope?"

Erik pushed back his cowl. "Our business is with the church. We've come to offer assistance to our brothers."

The two guards approached either side of the wagon.

Vadnae bowed her head. Sydney stared at the wooden slats and focused on taking slow breaths. The dead captain's face loomed large. *Coincidence. Nothing more.* Willem's foot nudged the bundle under the seat containing his sword.

"We've traveled a very long way today and would like to reach the abbey in time for the evening prayers," Erik said. "Surely you would not delay us?"

From the corner of her eye, Sydney noticed the other guard studying them and peering into the wagon.

"Can't be too careful about strangers these days, brother. I'm sure you understand. It's a shame those monks were killed."

"I hope the murderers will be found."

"I have faith they will, brother. There's talk anti-Guild folk were behind it, so you can imagine the Guild's taken a particular interest in seeing justice done. They've even sent their best man to investigate."

Sydney clenched her sweaty hands. Willem's eyes bored

into hers.

"I'm sure justice will be served," murmured Erik.

The second guard nodded to the first one and moved to open the gate. "You'll want to stay off the streets after curfew. Thieves and scoundrels don't abide by it."

"Thank you, good sir."

The guard waved them inside. "Follow this main road. It'll take you to the abbey. Good evening to you, brothers."

At this hour, a hush had settled over the town. The wagon rolled past the goats bleating in the pasture. With a jolt and a clip-clop of the horse's hooves, they arrived at the cobblestone street, Last Hope's main thoroughfare. A few people hurried past without giving them a second glance, intent on reaching their destinations before the final curfew bell. The breeze carried a foul stench of rotting garbage and human waste. A boy on stilts was lighting the hanging oil lamps on posts spaced along the main streets, light to provide the illusion of safety in the respectable parts of town.

"You recognized the dead man?" Willem asked Sydney.

She rubbed her palms on her knees and tried to slow the racing of her heart. "He was the captain of the guard who was supposed to carry out my death sentence. He knew me and he mentioned Edgar. If Schrammig had him killed, he might—"

"We've no reason to think Schrammig ordered his death."

Erik turned in his seat to face them. "Unless it's another warning for Sydney. Like Edgar's coin."

Willem frowned. "Don't jump to conclusions, Erik." He leaned toward Sydney, his knee brushing hers. "Think about it, Sydney. Schrammig would expect you to react this way, and he'd expect you to seek out the people closest to you. We're not going to do what he expects."

"I have to help them if they're in danger."

"Any rash actions will endanger the rest of us. Our mission must succeed, no matter what. Do not lose sight of the greater good. We will do nothing tonight. Tomorrow we will discuss our plans."

"He's right," Vadnae said. "It would be safer to wait until morning. We don't want to be out after curfew."

Sydney decided not to tell them she'd often been out after curfew.

On the main street, they passed the free-standing shops of Last Hope's wealthiest merchants, dark at this late hour save for the upper living quarters. Lights blazed in the windows of the Prancing Pig, a fine tavern catering to those wealthy merchants and Guild officials. The front window revealed the crowd inside, and Sydney couldn't help thinking of Anaria and the much more modest tavern where she worked.

She hadn't seen Anaria in a while, perhaps a year. So much had changed between them since Edgar had died. The woman who had helped raise her was not someone to hold her tongue when she had something to say, and she had plenty to say about Zared. Sydney wished she'd listened to her. Somehow, she had to warn her Schrammig had returned.

Sydney told Gregor to keep to the main street when they approached the large market square in the center of town. At one end stood the Guild Hall, a three-story, timbered building with decorative carvings on its heavy double doors, one of the most ornate structures in town. A faint light shone in one of the windows. Hidden in the darkness at the opposite side of the square stood the gallows, the symbol of the Guild's rise to power.

"Why isn't the church here in the square?" Erik asked.

Sydney shrugged. She was too tired to argue with Erik this time. "Most people here don't care much for the church. They like the old ways better."

At last, they arrived at the tall, black iron gates surrounding the quiet churchyard. The shadows deepened, and Sydney nervously eyed the darkness creeping in around them.

"It doesn't look very inviting." Vadnae tucked her hair within her cowl.

"I doubt they'd leave the gate open at all hours of the night." Erik approached the gate and rang a brass bell hanging beside it. The loud clanging made Sydney jump.

Several minutes passed. The bell echoed in Sydney's ears.

"Perhaps they're attending services," Gregor suggested.

"Someone should be watching the gate." A faint light bobbed in the churchyard. "See?"

Sydney folded her hands within the long sleeves and cast her face downward, attempting to appear humble and pious.

A robed figure approached the gate, holding up his lantern. "Who's there?"

"We seek shelter within your walls, brother. We've come to pay our respects to those who were lost. I am Brother Erik and—"

"Brother Erik? Is it really you?" Keys clinked, and the gate swung inward. The monk moved closer, peering at them in the faint light. "Remember me? Brother Francis? We met at the farm."

"Brother Francis." Erik held out his arms, and the two embraced. "I'm so glad to see you."

"And I you, Brother Erik. I've been taking the late vigil, hoping you would come and I could be of assistance."

Francis helped them unload their belongings from the wagon.

"We are grateful for your help, Brother Francis." Willem hoisted a sack over his shoulder.

The monk knelt and kissed his hand. "I will do whatever I can, your highness."

Erik grunted under his load. "Perhaps a place to sleep and something to eat?"

"Of course." Francis peered at Sydney and Vadnae, rubbing his chin. "They will be a bit of a problem."

Vadnae brushed a lock of hair from her face. "Sydney and I are not very convincing monks, are we?"

He shook his head. "I'm afraid not, dear lady. We'll manage

for the night, though. You two can take my cell. No one will disturb you there. The rest of us can sleep in the common room. Pilgrims occasionally come to visit, so you won't arouse any suspicion. If those accommodations are acceptable, your highness."

"They're much appreciated."

They crossed the courtyard to the stone church.

Gregor asked, "You don't expect any other visitors, do you?"

"I'm not aware of any. What sort of visitors?"

"Schrammig," Willem told him. "He has come to Last Hope, and he will be hunting for us."

Francis's eyes grew wide. "Schrammig has come here? He wouldn't be so bold as to search the church, would he? Father Abbot wouldn't stand for it."

"Schrammig can be very persuasive."

"Not here. Father Abbot and the Guild have been at odds for years, and not once has Father Abbot backed down. I doubt Schrammig's presence would change his mind, unless he's brought an army with him. Dear God, he hasn't brought soldiers, has he?"

"Some."

Francis stopped. "I hope you don't mean that war is coming here, to Last Hope."

"It's possible, Brother Francis."

"Then we must prepare for it. There's a good chance people may seek shelter within our walls. We must—"

Willem grabbed his arm. "People will be suspicious if you start stockpiling provisions, and you'll give us away. We don't want to incite panic when there is no need for it."

"Oh, yes…of course." Francis bowed his head. "Perhaps there are other things we can do. Forgive me, though, for beginning such a discussion before you have had time to refresh yourselves. I'll show you inside and then go wake the stable boy to tend to your horse."

He ushered them into the large stone building. Sydney hesitated before stepping across the threshold. She'd never been inside a church before. *Don't be superstitious.* Since she had met Oryn, she'd seen a lot of incredible things. No reason to feel apprehensive about finding safety in a church.

Glancing at the dark, silent streets surrounding the abbey, the specter of Schrammig's retribution lurked in the shadows, shattering the illusion of safety.

Chapter Thirteen

Sydney tossed and turned. The bodies of the monks and the hanged captain haunted her restless sleep. The anger she felt toward Schrammig consumed her, despite her efforts to let it go. Contemplating his possible actions toward the people she cared about put her in a cold sweat. Shortly before sunrise, she decided to leave to warn Anaria, now, before it was too late.

Lifting her head, she listened for Vadnae's light breathing. Certain that Vadnae still slept, she quietly pulled on her boots. Willem might be right; this might be exactly what Schrammig expected. He could be waiting for her. Sydney laced her boots with trembling fingers. She'd never forgive herself if anything happened to Anaria. The tavern where Anaria lived wasn't far. She could be there and back before anyone realized she'd been gone.

She stood and put on her cloak. Glancing at the monk's robe she'd worn earlier, she hesitated. Her plan had one flaw. She could get out of the abbey without being seen. Getting back in would be a problem. Even wearing the robe, the disguise might not fool the monks, and she certainly couldn't tell them the truth. *Damn.* She'd just have to find a way inside somehow.

"What are you doing?"

Sydney moved toward the door. "I'll be back before anyone else is awake."

"Wait." The bed creaked. Vadnae spoke softly, and the oil lamp on the floor flickered to life. She sat and rubbed her eyes. "Where are you going? You heard what Willem said. We're to wait here until they come for us. You can't just go wandering about town."

"I'm not gonna wander about town. I need to warn someone about Schrammig."

"What if he's waiting for you?"

Sydney shrugged, hoping to avoid that disastrous scenario.

"How will risking yourself help your friends, or us? We're here to work together and consider what's best for all of us. You can't go off by yourself."

"You don't understand," Sydney muttered.

"Then explain it to me."

Vadnae's face showed no hostility or condescension, but Sydney wasn't sure she could explain how she felt. "Anaria was like a mother to me. I can't lose her to Schrammig, too."

Vadnae studied her a moment, thoughtful. "Like Edgar, you mean."

Sydney nodded. "That's why I gotta do something."

"If it's a trap—"

"I'm not stupid, Vadnae. I can look after myself. I also know Last Hope a lot better than Schrammig does. I can hide."

Vadnae's delicate mouth frowned. "Going out alone isn't a good idea. Why don't you wait until we talk to the others?"

"I can't wait. I'm not going to sacrifice Anaria for the greater good."

"That's not what Willem meant."

"Isn't it? How much is Anaria's life worth to him?"

"Willem cares about the welfare of his people. He'll do whatever he can to make sure innocent people don't get hurt."

Sydney didn't want to be considered one of "Willem's people." She wasn't convinced his strategy would protect the people most vulnerable to reprisals from the Guild. Edgar would've protected them. She'd need to convince Willem to do the same.

"Willem wants to contact the resistance, and Anaria can tell me where to find them. We can't waste any time. I'll tell Willem about it first thing in the morning. Please, Vadnae. You can help me get back inside, and they'll never notice I was gone."

Vadnae sighed. "I still don't think it's a good idea. But you're right; there isn't any time to waste. Promise me you'll return by sunrise. Otherwise you can answer to Willem yourself."

"Thanks, Vadnae. I'll be back."

"Despite your familiarity with Last Hope, it's still dangerous to go alone. What if someone recognizes you? You need a disguise. Something other than as a monk." Vadnae picked up a bag resembling Oryn's magical pouch.

"Can you use your magic to make me look different?"

Vadnae shifted closer to the lamp and opened the bag.

"Changing your appearance with magic is along the lines of turning people into toads. I have a better idea."

Sydney stepped toward her. "What?"

Vadnae pulled out a plain brown, long-sleeved dress and laid it on the bed. "Do you like it?"

"You want me to wear a dress?"

"No one would recognize you, would they?" she asked with a smile. "You'll look much more respectable. Go on, see if it fits."

"I guess no one's used to seeing me respectable." Vadnae turned away while she put on the dress. Like the other clothes from Oryn, the dress fit her perfectly. She smoothed the soft muslin fabric of the fitted bodice and flared, ankle-length skirt. "What d'you think?"

Vadnae pursed her lips. "Better. What if someone recognizes your face?"

Sydney picked up her tattered, mud-splattered cloak. "I'll wear this over my head."

"Why bother wearing a nice dress if you're going to cover it with that thing?" Vadnae took the cloak and shook it, showering them with dried grime and filth.

Vadnae reached into the bag again. This time her hand emerged grasping a fine, gray hooded cloak. Sydney draped it over her shoulders. Vadnae smiled in approval and handed her a hand mirror.

The new outfit resulted in a startling transformation. Sydney pushed the hair back from her forehead, angling the mirror. *I could almost pass for a lady.* "No one will recognize me."

Vadnae peered into the bag, puzzled. "No shoes. A lady needs a proper pair of shoes."

"What exactly is in the bag, anyway?"

"It holds whatever a person needs. It can be quite useful, but apparently it doesn't think you need any shoes."

The idea that a bag might think she needed anything unsettled Sydney.

"My boots are fine. Oryn repaired them. Besides, not even you would want to ruin a proper pair of shoes on the muddy streets."

Vadnae returned the mirror to her bag. "I suppose. Now tell me, where is the marble you took from the tower?"

Sydney retrieved the marble from her rucksack. "You said I should keep it."

"Yes, you should. Take it with you. Then I can tell when you're back to open the gate for you."

"How?"

"It's magic. I told you it once belonged to the Tuatha."

Sydney curled her fingers around the smooth, iridescent marble. "What does it do?"

"Not all magic does things. I can sense the enchantment associated with this item and find you when you return."

Sydney put the marble in her neck pouch and bent down to slip her knife into the sheath in her boot.

"I won't be gone long." She raised the hood of her cloak

and opened the door to check the empty corridor.

"Be careful, Sydney."

"I will." She slipped out. Vadnae's support made her feel better about disregarding Willem's request to stay put.

———

She moved swiftly, her boots making soft footfalls on the cobblestones. Clouds obscured the moon, threatening rainfall, and the sharp bite of the wind nipped her nose and cheeks. Intermittent street lanterns still burned, casting a hazy glow in the darkness. The hush before dawn weighed on her, ominous and foreboding.

Leaving the main road to shorten her route, she passed the wealthier neighborhoods, home to merchants and Guild officials. Tall iron gates guarded the two- and three-story houses, sturdy structures built of stone and timber. Sydney stuck to the shadows, dodging the street lanterns, careful to avoid attracting the attention of the night watch's frequent patrols in those areas.

The cobblestones soon gave way to narrow, muddy lanes. Crowded tenements towered above her. Sydney spotted the familiar landmarks of her childhood, the weaver's faded blue door, the lingering fragrance of the chandler's workshop, the brick communal oven standing apart from the clustered buildings. She veered onto a side street saturated with the stink of urine, vomit, and some unidentifiable odors, and halted. Still quiet.

One block ahead, a weather-beaten tavern sign bearing the faded image of an eagle creaked in a gust of wind. Years earlier, long before Sydney was born, the Silver Eagle had been an upper-class establishment catering to the wealthy; now they feared for their safety in this neighborhood.

She ducked into the alley behind the Silver Eagle. The hearty aroma of roasted meat meant Anaria was in the kitchen, as she'd expected. Anaria often rose before dawn to start preparing the daily meals. Raising her hand to knock on the back door, Sydney hesitated. She had rarely spoken to Anaria since Edgar's death, both of them avoiding their grief. *Willem's right. I've got to put those feelings behind me.* She hoped Anaria would be willing to do the same.

She knocked, surveying the empty alley. A rat scurried past, oblivious to her presence. When there was no answer to her knock, she pounded on the door with her fist. Anaria had to be there. She was always there.

At last, the window in the door slid open. "Who is it?"

She recognized the voice. "Anaria?"

"What do you want?"

"It's Sydney."

The window slid shut, and the door opened. Sydney stared at the familiar figure in the doorway, and her heart beat anxiously. Light shadowed the lines on Anaria's face and her pinched, hollow cheeks. The wiry woman's hands shook when she tucked the stray auburn hairs into her bun.

"Syd?" Anaria's pale blue eyes widened. "It can't be!"

Sydney pulled back the hood of her cloak. Anaria caught her in a tight embrace. "I thought I'd lost you, Syd. I thought I'd lost you for good this time."

Anaria let her go, and they both eyed the shadows in the alley. She pulled Sydney into the narrow, cramped kitchen. "Come in, before someone sees you."

The blast of heat from the fire warmed Sydney's cold fingers and toes. A simmering pot brought memories of happier times, shared meals, and nighttime stories by a warm hearth. Anaria moved to the pot, stirring and adding a pinch of chopped herbs. Fidgeting from one foot to the other, Sydney waited.

Over the years, Anaria had grown accustomed to Edgar's coming and going at all hours, never to be questioned where he'd been or what he'd done. Sydney had never had such freedom while Edgar had been alive. After his death, Anaria no longer took note of her whereabouts, and finally she had stopped coming back.

Anaria tasted the meat, gave a satisfied nod, and wiped her hands on the apron she wore over her green kirtle and white tunic. "Anyone see you?"

"No, but the guard ain't looking for me."

"It's not the guard I'm worried about, Syd."

In spite of the warmth, a chill ran down Sydney's spine. "What d'you mean?"

"He came here last night." Anaria's voice grew soft. "Schrammig."

"Then I'm too late. I wanted to warn you...."

Anaria cut a slice of bread and spooned some of the meat over it. She handed Sydney the bread. "I'm sure you're hungry."

"What about Schrammig? I can't stay if he's—"

"He's not here. You'll sit and eat and we'll figure out what's to be done." Her tone left no room for argument.

They went into the main room of the tavern. Sydney tapped her fingers on the oak counter, pitted with age and wear, while Anaria poured them each a tankard. A smoky tallow candle on the bar threw shadows onto the white-washed walls and low, beamed ceiling. Mismatched tables and chairs stood ready for the crowds that often came for Anaria's cooking as well as for the cheap ale. Sydney's chest tightened when she spotted Edgar's corner table.

Anaria set the tankard in front of her. "Schrammig came to give me a warning. He said you'd be back. Told me if I helped you, more people would die, just like Edgar." Anaria's voice shook on her next words. "Told me he planned to show you how Edgar died."

Sydney's stomach lurched. She drained half the tankard.

"Easy. Eat something first."

Her appetite gone, she forced down a few bites. *He sees you as our weak link,* Willem had said. Clearly, he was right.

"What've you done? I got word you was sentenced to death, but now you're back and Schrammig's come back, too. This is bigger than picking pockets."

Sydney trusted Anaria, but she had no reason to burden her with information she didn't need. Anaria had often said she was better off not knowing the truth behind Edgar's actions.

"You don't want to know."

Anaria leaned her elbows on the bar and rubbed her temples. "No, I guess I don't."

Sydney pulled Edgar's good luck charm from her neck pouch and laid it on the bar. "Remember this?"

Anaria picked up the worn coin. The corners of her mouth turned up. "Still remember the night you gave it to Edgar, all those years ago. How'd you come by it?"

"Schrammig sent it to me. As a warning or a reminder."

Anaria's eyes widened. "You're not planning to take on the Guild, are you? Whatever you're trying to do, it's not worth risking your life. You know what Schrammig will do to you if he catches you."

"Edgar would've understood." Sydney raised the tankard to her lips. The bitter ale warmed her insides, but her sudden chill toward Anaria remained. Edgar hadn't died for nothing.

Anaria closed her hand around Sydney's, meeting her eyes. "You're so much like him. He was proud of you."

Sydney stared into the amber liquid. "I'm not like Edgar. He'd be ashamed of me if he'd known what I've done, if he'd known...." She couldn't get the words out and whispered, "Like you've been."

Anaria tensed, and she let go of Sydney's hand. "I've always cared about you. No matter what you've done. You've changed since I last saw you all those months ago. Wherever you've been, you've changed. For the better—like I hoped you would. Now you look like you could make something of yourself." She smoothed the hood of Sydney's cloak, the lines around her mouth softening. "Edgar always wanted to see you in a dress."

Sydney had to smile. She'd refused to wear dresses as a child, and Edgar had finally given up asking her to. Secretly she suspected he'd been relieved, because she'd been safer dressing as a boy.

"Did Edgar ever tell you of his past, his life before he came to last Hope?"

Anaria shifted uneasily on her stool. "Why do you ask?"

Her reaction surprised Sydney. "You knew, didn't you? That he was a nobleman."

Anaria pulled on her ale. "He had certain ways about him. He was different from the rest of us, too good for this sort of life. It was years before he admitted the truth to me."

"What did he say to you? Why didn't he ever tell me the truth? Why didn't you ever tell me?"

"The truth is Edgar didn't want to live in the past. He lost everything he had to the Guild. To Schrammig. He kept it from you because he was afraid Schrammig would find him one day. He didn't want you to get hurt."

"I wish he'd told me."

"He put his past behind him. No good in dredging it up again. This was his life, here with us. He was content with what he had."

He wasn't content with the Guild's oppression. He'd fought hard to stop the Guild. Sydney ran her finger around the rim of the tankard. "Do you ever miss him?"

Tears glistened in Anaria's eyes. "Every day. Some nights I still think he'll come walking in here."

"I keep thinking about how it used to be. I still miss him so damned much." Sydney rubbed angrily at her eyes and choked back a sob.

Anaria leaned over and put her arms around her, gently stroking her hair. "So strong, our Sydney." She drew back, sniffing and wiping her eyes. "There's no sense in mourning what can't be undone. We did all we could."

Sydney bit her lip. "I didn't. I should've done something."

"There's nothing you could have done. Don't you understand? It's been four years, Syd. Let him go. Get on with your life. Take this chance to make something of yourself now."

"How can I let go when I've failed him?"

Anaria grasped her hand and placed Edgar's coin in her palm. "The only person you can fail is yourself. You're strong, like Edgar was. He never gave up, not even at the very end. You're just like him. I was afraid you'd end up risking your life for your principles, like Edgar did."

Sydney closed her fist. "What if they're worth fighting for?"

"Are they worth dying for, too?"

Sydney considered her companions. And Willem. They were *all* taking the same risks. "Some things are worth dying for."

Anaria pursed her lips. "You don't like taking my advice, but for once, listen to me. You can't change the way things are. You can't win against Schrammig."

Sydney wanted to tell her change was possible. She believed in Willem. "I have to try. It's the only way I can let him go."

The quiet room amplified the gulf between them. "I shouldn't come back here," Sydney finally said. "It's too dangerous."

"Best you stay away, of course," Anaria said with a resigned voice. "It's not only Schrammig you need to worry about. Your friend Zared came by asking about you."

Sydney nearly choked on her ale. "Zared?"

"Twice since you were sentenced to death. Right daring of him, since I told him years ago I'd cut off his balls if I ever saw him again. He swore you were still alive. I didn't let myself believe him."

Anaria's dislike of Zared was mutual. His seeking Anaria out meant he knew she was alive and was willing to risk bodily harm to find her. Zared had contacts throughout Last Hope.

Eventually he'd catch up to her. If he told someone she was alive....

"You'll stay away from Zared, won't you?"

"You were right about a lot of things. Just took me a while to see it."

"You're a smart girl. Don't worry about me." She leaned close and clasped Sydney's hand. "Go see Jimmy at the Black Dog. You'll need all the help you can get if you plan to fight the Guild. Now go, before someone sees you here."

The information meant a lot to Sydney. She squeezed Anaria's hand. "Don't worry about me, either."

Sydney slipped out the back door and raised her hood. Pale pink streaked the sky. Movement in the shadows of the deserted streets caught her eye. She stopped and waited, silent, listening. Nothing. A cat. Nothing more.

By the time she came within sight of the churchyard, panic began to swell within her. The slightest noise made her heart jump in her chest. The iron gates stood wide. Several monks carrying lanterns moved around a gleaming black coach stopped inside the courtyard. Sydney crept closer to the gate. The coach door opened, and a man emerged. The light from the lanterns illuminated the scar dividing his face from forehead to chin. She drew in a sharp breath. He'd found them.

Chapter Fourteen

Sydney stood just outside the gate, hidden in the shadows. Schrammig spoke with one of the monks. Too far away for her to hear them, and she hoped, for them to spot her. Her hands clenched. She had no way of warning her companions the abbey was no longer secure.

Another man emerged from the carriage. He wore a dark cloak, his face hidden beneath the hood. His garb was neither that of a soldier nor the finery of a Guild official. Sydney's heart pounded. She pulled the blade from her boot, slightly comforted by the weapon in her hand. One of the monks bowed to Schrammig and hurried into the main building. Two others stayed behind with their guests. Schrammig paced while his cloaked companion stood silent and still.

What are they waiting for? The morning sky grew lighter by the minute.

Don't think about what he did to Edgar. She clutched her neck pouch containing Edgar's coin and the marble.

The cloaked man swiveled toward the open gate. She froze, afraid the slightest movement would reveal her presence. He took a step in her direction, his head turning one way and the other. Finally, he moved back to Schrammig's side. Sydney blew out a slow breath.

The other monk returned and spoke to Schrammig. Taking a few silent steps, Sydney edged closer.

"Come back later?" Schrammig's raspy voice grew louder. "Doesn't he realize who I am?"

The monk stepped back and murmured a response.

Schrammig's companion put a hand on his arm, whispering to him. Schrammig scowled. "Tell your abbot I'll be back later this morning, and I expect to be properly received." He turned on his heel and added, "Have care when you venture beyond these walls, brother. I hear the streets are no longer safe for men of the cloth."

He and his companion climbed into the carriage. Sydney darted to the wall adjacent to the gate and pressed her back to the mossy stones. A moment later the carriage passed by. The silhouette of the cloaked figure was visible in the open carriage window. The hooded man leaned his head out the window, in Sydney's direction.

The magnitude of power and the aura of hatred emanating from him swept over her like a wave, cold and penetrating. She crouched, too terrified to run. He was a wizard. There could be no other explanation. The power she'd sensed when she'd first met Oryn paled in comparison with this.

Seconds passed. The clip-clop of the horse's hooves slowed. Blood thrummed in her ears. Surely the wizard had seen her. At last, the horse picked up speed. After the carriage had faded from sight, she leaned into the wall, shuddering. She tucked the knife back in her boot and ventured toward the courtyard. Vadnae needed to be alerted to what she'd seen. Schrammig's association with a wizard increased the threat he posed.

A robed monk approached the entrance. "Be sure to lock the gate," another called to him.

The monk started to pull the gate. "Sydney? Are you there?"

Recognizing the voice of Brother Francis, she scurried forward. He urged her inside and closed and locked the iron bars behind her.

"How'd you know I was here?" She surveyed the dim recesses of the courtyard, her leg muscles tensing again.

"I went to wake you and Vadnae, and she told me you'd gone into town. I couldn't let her wait out here for you. The streets aren't safe at this hour."

"I'm not sure it's safe here, either."

"You saw Schrammig?"

"They came here searching for us, didn't they?"

Francis furrowed his brow. "They? Schrammig was alone, unless you mean his driver."

Fear coiled within her. She hadn't imagined the man. "I saw another man, with Schrammig, wearing a dark cloak."

"I saw no one else. I'm sure you're just tired, Sydney." He patted her back. "We've all endured a lot these past days."

The wizard's menacing power lingered, sending shivery pulses through her body. She wasn't going to try to explain to Francis what she had seen.

"Guild officials only come to see the abbot when they want something. Schrammig's interest is obvious, but how could he have learned you were here?"

"I wasn't followed. He was already here when I got back."

"May I ask, Sydney, what business brings a lady into town at this hour?"

"My business is my own." She crossed her arms, waiting for him to question whether she was really a lady.

His face reddened. "Yes, of course. I hope you'll at least take an escort, if you venture out at such a late hour again."

She started to say she didn't need an escort, but stopped herself. Francis clearly was concerned for her welfare, nothing more. He didn't realize she'd lived her entire life on those streets. But finding Schrammig here meant she shouldn't underestimate the danger she and her companions now faced.

"I'll keep your advice in mind."

Francis peered over his shoulder at the gate. "I'm glad Father Abbot is willing to stand up to the Guild, but I'm not sure insulting Schrammig was the best course of action. He's a dangerous man. Erik tells me Willem thinks Schrammig is responsible for murdering our brothers at the farm."

His words conjured up images of charred bodies. Sydney followed his glance toward the gate. Iron bars wouldn't be enough to protect them. Francis appeared to be seeking words of comfort. Comfort she couldn't give. "I'm sure Willem will keep us all safe."

"I have faith he will." Francis lifted his chin and strode forward. "Come, I'll take you to your friends. They must be worried."

———

Worried was not the word she would have used to describe Willem's reaction to her disappearance. She tried to avoid him by staring at the bowl of porridge Vadnae had saved for her. Anaria's food already weighed heavily in her stomach. Schrammig's threats had taken away what little appetite remained.

Willem paced, eyes narrowed to slits. "How could you do this? You directly disobeyed my order, Sydney." He stopped in front of Vadnae. "And you...you let her go."

"Vadnae wasn't involved. I snuck out on my own."

Willem looked from Sydney to Vadnae. His lips pressed tight, his face contorted by the struggle to contain his anger. "You put yourself in danger, as well as the rest of us. And the monks who've offered to help us, at great risk to themselves. I won't allow you to endanger our mission, Sydney."

Sydney peeked at Gregor across the table and saw the disappointment in his expression. At least Erik had decided to join Francis for the morning service, allowing her to evade his criticism.

Willem slid onto the bench beside Gregor. His voice was low, carefully controlled. "Your actions could have revealed our location. What was so important that it justified the risk?"

The authority in his voice made Sydney forget the rough wooden benches and tables of the monks' common area and the coarse brown robes he and Gregor still wore. She sensed the weight of the responsibilities set upon Willem from a closely guarded weariness in his eyes, and she realized how wrong she'd been. He was right; she had put them all at risk.

"I'm sorry." She stared at the table. "You need to contact the resistance. I talked to someone who told me where they are."

"It couldn't wait until morning? Or did you have another reason for going out on your own?"

Vadnae nudged her. Sydney realized she'd be better off telling Willem the truth. She wanted him to trust her. "I also had to see Anaria. She's like family. My only family now. I had to check on her."

"How is she?" Vadnae asked.

Sydney hesitated. Schrammig's visit to Anaria had no impact on Willem's mission. Best to leave out that detail. "She's fine, and like I said, she gave me a contact in the resistance." She paused. "I'm sorry. It was something I had to do."

"The next time you 'have to do something,' Sydney, you consult me first. If you can't abide by my rules, you won't be part of our efforts."

She swallowed hard. Vadnae's expression remained neutral. Willem's intense blue eyes bored into her. "I know I was wrong. Please, Willem, I really do want to be part of this. Give me another chance," she implored him.

His countenance softened a little. "Your intentions were good, but this cannot happen again, understand?" When she nodded, he said, "Is there anything else you want to tell me?"

She fingered her neck pouch, wondering how to explain the strange man so they would believe her. "There was someone with Schrammig. Only no one else could see him except me. I think he was a wizard."

"A wizard? How is that possible?"

Vadnae's hazel eyes widened, her face pale. "Why do you think he was a wizard?"

"He made me feel the same way Oryn did when I first saw him. You, too. But I felt his power even more strongly than Oryn's. One look at him and I knew. But he's different from you. He's dark. Twisted."

"You could tell just by looking at him?" Willem asked. "Why didn't you say you could do this before?"

She shrugged. "I didn't realize I could. The only wizards I've met are Vadnae and Oryn. Didn't expect to meet others."

"His name is Durok," Vadnae said, her voice soft.

"Were you aware he was helping Schrammig?" Willem asked.

"Grandfather suspected he was. He planned to confront Durok to uncover why he would aid the people who want to destroy us. If necessary, he would make sure Durok would not be a threat to us." Vadnae's voice faltered. "If Durok is here, and Grandfather is not, something has gone seriously wrong."

The faint echo of chanting reverberated throughout the abbey. The haunting tone reflected Sydney's mood. She had sensed Durok's immense power. Perhaps he'd been able to defeat Oryn.

"We must have faith in Oryn," Gregor finally said.

"Gregor's right," Willem agreed. "Oryn isn't one to be trifled with. But we must face the threat Durok poses to us now. Are you prepared to do that, Vadnae?"

Vadnae straightened on the bench. "I am. Grandfather trusts me to act in his stead. I'll need a little time alone to learn the nature of Durok's powers. We possess one important advantage. Grandfather never told the other wizards he'd taken on an apprentice, so it's unlikely Durok is aware of me. Even if he is, I'm sure he doesn't realize the extent of my abilities."

Gregor gestured to Sydney. "He may not realize Sydney can

see him. That could also be an advantage."

"It might," Vadnae said. "Sometimes people who aren't wizards are bound to magic in ways we don't understand. That is why we are all here, why Grandfather chose us for this task. Somehow, all our fates are tied to the fate of magic in this world."

"I thought his vision of the future was unclear," Gregor said.

"Nothing is ever certain. Regardless of the outcome, though, you cannot avoid your destiny."

Sydney wasn't sure she believed in destiny. She didn't feel bound to magic or anything else. Her choices, good and bad, were her own, weren't they? Yet Vadnae's words made her uneasy, for she recognized the truth in them.

The door of the common room opened, and Brother Francis stuck his head in. "We've finished matins. The abbot wants to speak with you now. Erik's waiting for you there."

Willem stood, and the rest of them trailed him to the door. "Don't say anything about Durok. The abbot may decide to stand up to the Guild, but I doubt he'll break with the church's decrees against magic."

———

"I trust you realize the delicate situation we are in," the white-haired abbot said once they had seated themselves at a table in his chamber. "The church is unwilling to recognize your claim, Willem, and thus I cannot offer you aid directly."

The abbot's comment drew Sydney's attention from the books and parchments crammed into the shelves lining the walls.

"I regret the imposition we've placed on your abbey. It was never my intention to place anyone in your order at risk."

"Whether you intended it or not, blood has been shed and innocent lives have been lost."

"They chose to follow their consciences, Father," Erik said.

"Did their consciences ask them to give up their lives, Brother Erik? Word has spread of your deeds, even here. You've dared to defy the church and speak out against the Guild. You've also spoken favorably about magic. Are you willing to face excommunication for your beliefs?"

Sydney regarded the plump monk with surprise and respect at this revelation. Erik hadn't told them anything of his past. She'd never considered asking him about it.

Erik bowed his head. "I must do what my heart tells me. We are all called to do God's work. I believe this is my path."

"God speaks in mysterious ways. Nevertheless, I cannot risk any more lives, Brother Erik. Schrammig will likely give us a warning. There will be consequences if we get involved. His threats are a serious concern."

"How dare he threaten the church," Erik sputtered. "What authority does he—"

The abbot held up his hand. "His authority is the Guild's authority, and at this moment, they are the power in this land. I cannot risk the well-being of this abbey."

"I deeply regret bringing danger into your house," said Erik. "I didn't mean to put anyone here at risk."

"Don't trouble yourself, Brother Erik. I'm glad the church can still serve as a refuge in times of need. Our need may be greater than ever before." He stood, signaling the end of their meeting. "Willem, you must be aware that there are people in Last Hope who are sympathetic to your cause. I can make some inquiries for you, if you wish."

Willem inclined his head. "I would be in your debt, Father."

The abbot smiled. "I will not forget."

Willem clasped the abbot's hand, his face placid. Sydney cringed inwardly. *Some help. Everyone wants something in return.*

In the corridor outside the abbot's office, Francis ran up to them. "He's back. Schrammig. This time he's brought soldiers."

Chapter Fifteen

The halls of the abbey echoed with heavy footsteps and voices. Sydney's fists clenched, her pulse quickening.

"Is there another way out?" Willem asked calmly.

The abbot stepped into the hall behind them. He folded his hands over his robe. "Hide them, Brother Francis. This time I will speak to Schrammig myself. He has no authority here."

Willem extended his arm to block the abbot's path. "Father, his soldiers may convince you otherwise."

"I refuse to be threatened by Schrammig." The abbot moved Willem's arm aside, gently. "Go with Brother Francis, while there is still time."

They hurried after Francis. Vadnae matched Sydney's pace. "He's here. Durok."

The echoes of footsteps grew louder. "What can we do?"

Vadnae's lips pressed together tightly. "I won't let him find us."

Francis dashed into a chapel off the main corridor. He closed the door behind them and stepped up to the altar. Putting his shoulder to it, he shoved. "Help me move this."

The heavy wooden altar grated on the stone floor. Gregor and Willem joined him, and within moments, they had moved the altar aside to reveal a trap door. Francis pulled on the iron ring. "You'll be safe here."

They descended a narrow ladder into a dark space. "I'll be

back soon," Francis said. "Don't worry. You're not the first people we've hidden within these walls. Schrammig won't find you."

The trap door thudded closed. Darkness swept around them. The altar above scraped the floor. Sydney pictured Francis struggling to push it back into place. The air was still and close, and her heart pounded in her ears.

Vadnae whispered under her breath. Sydney hoped she was invoking magic to hide them from Durok. She touched her pouch, fingering Edgar's good luck charm and the magic marble. Vadnae had been able to sense the marble. If Durok had similar abilities, the marble could lead him right to them. She dropped her hand at the thought.

"What if—" began Erik.

"Quiet," Willem replied. "We can't risk being heard."

"It's too close in here." Erik's voice rose in panic.

"Get hold of yourself, Erik," said Gregor. "We won't be in here long."

Sydney wasn't sure who stood beside her. The musty odor permeating the cramped space mingled with other odors of smoke, incense, and sweat.

A scratching interrupted Erik's whispered prayers. "Now what? Have they found us?"

"Probably a rat," Sydney said. "It won't hurt you."

"Dear God, not rats. I hate rats."

There was a scuffling, and someone elbowed Sydney's ribs.

"What are you doing?" she demanded.

Erik drew in long breaths. "I can't stay here. What if Francis doesn't come back? Let's get out while we can."

"Settle down, Erik," Gregor said in a calm voice. "No one's going anywhere."

Sydney was jostled again. Footsteps clomped on the floor above them. "Shut up, all of you." With Sydney's words, even Erik fell silent.

They waited, silent and still, listening to the footsteps pace back and forth. *As if someone thinks we're close but can't figure out where.* Vadnae's smooth, slender hand gripped hers. She imagined Durok searching the room above them, feet away from discovering them. She squeezed Vadnae's hand in return. Oryn's parting words the day of their first breakfast together in the tower suddenly came back to her. He'd said one day their lives would depend on each other. They needed to work together to survive. None of them could face the forces allied against them alone.

At last, the footsteps faded. They stayed silent. Soft footfalls and the scratching of rats echoed in Sydney's mind. Her heart raced, and she forced herself to take slow, deep breaths. *They won't find us. If they do, we'll fight.*

The footsteps grew louder. A harsh grating sounded overhead. Vadnae let go of her hand, and Sydney's fingers drifted to the knife in her boot.

Light poured into their hidden compartment. Francis peered down at them. "It's safe now. You can come out."

"Thank God." Erik pushed past the others, the first one up the ladder.

Francis helped the rest of them up. Sydney squinted in the brightness of the chapel, expecting Schrammig to be waiting for them. They were alone.

"He's gone." Tears welled in Francis's eyes. "But he arrested Father Abbot for defying the Guild."

Erik gasped and raised a hand to his mouth. "How dare he? How can he possibly get away with such a thing?"

"He had soldiers, Erik. Father Abbot agreed to go rather than risk bloodshed. What are we going to do now?"

Erik gave him a quick embrace. "Don't worry, Francis. We'll think of something."

With Erik's comment, they all faced Willem.

Francis stepped forward. "Willem, we'll give you whatever help you need. Schrammig won't intimidate us."

"I appreciate the risks you've taken on our behalf, Francis."

"I've made my peace with God. I'm not afraid of what might happen."

"What we need is somewhere to base our operations. I don't think using the abbey would be a wise choice at this point."

"Of course. Let me think." Francis paced the room, hands folded within his robe. He stopped and scanned the chapel, though they were alone, then moved to Willem. "There is an inn not far from the market called the Prancing Pig."

Sydney shook her head. "A bad idea. Merchants and Guild officials go to the Prancing Pig."

"Ah, but there is another entrance. A hidden one. Few people are aware it exists." Francis paused and studied her. "You are familiar with Last Hope, Sydney?"

"Lived here all my life."

"Have you ever been in the tunnels?"

Erik wrinkled his nose in distaste. "Not those tunnels again."

"You've heard of them, Erik?"

"I've told them about the tunnels," Sydney said quickly, before Erik had a chance to respond. Fortunately, Erik said nothing about the Tuatha. Willem gave her a brief nod.

"One tunnel leads directly underneath the Prancing Pig, to a hidden room we use as a secret meeting place. Hidden right under their noses. Do you think you can find it?"

Sydney reviewed her mental map of the tunnels. She remembered which passages ran beneath the market. Using the symbols on the tunnel walls, she could find the way. "I can get us there."

"Who else is aware of this place?" asked Willem.

"Only people who can be trusted. I assure you, Willem, they won't betray you to the Guild."

Sydney didn't share his certainty. Anyone could be bought for the right price, and Schrammig could be very persuasive.

"May I ask what you plan to do?"

"It's best not to speak of our plans." Willem put a hand on Francis's shoulder. "I'd like to ask you one more favor, Francis. Tell the townsfolk they aren't alone in their fight. Tell them there's hope, and that this town will be protected from the Guild and Schrammig."

"Of course, your highness." Francis bowed. "Whatever you ask. Should I say these things in your name?"

Willem's mouth turned up in a smile. "You should. Let's keep Schrammig guessing. Now, if you'll gather our belongings, we'll prepare to leave. We shouldn't linger here."

"I'll be right back. Good luck to all of you, wherever your path takes you."

Once he was gone, Willem said, "There are things we should keep among ourselves." He directed this to Erik. "None of us should speak of the Tuatha to anyone."

"Francis can be trusted."

"We wouldn't be here if I didn't trust him. However, we must be cautious, Erik. Our success now lies in our ability to elude Schrammig long enough to accomplish our mission. Secrecy is imperative."

Erik lowered his head. "Very well."

Willem addressed Vadnae. "How can we protect ourselves from Durok? Am I correct in assuming he can't locate us?"

"I sensed him searching, and I was able to shield us from him. He's powerful, but he doesn't seem aware of me. He didn't even try to counter my shield."

"Can you shield us if we split up?"

"No." Vadnae's forehead creased in worry. "I must see you in order to invoke the spell. But I can use my magic to distract him and throw him off our trail."

"Then do it, Vadnae. Our best approach is to split up. Will you need someplace quiet to focus your energies?"

"Yes, if possible."

"Erik, I want you and Vadnae to stay here."

"In the abbey?" Erik exhaled, his body relaxing.

"With the abbot in the gaol, someone needs to provide guidance to the other monks. Francis respects you. I'm sure others here do as well. This is where you will do us the most good. Find a place where Vadnae will not be disturbed. It's an unusual request, but I'm sure the monks will understand, considering the gravity of our situation."

"As you wish," Erik said. "There are bigger concerns than a woman in our midst. I'll also find out what resources we can use here."

"Gregor, I want you to go with Francis and scout our defenses, like we discussed. Speak with the people he suggests are willing to take action in opposition to the Guild."

Gregor nodded. "And you, Willem?"

"I'm going with Sydney. She can locate Edgar's allies. I want to speak with them myself."

Sydney stared at him in surprise. She couldn't guarantee her safety, let alone Willem's. "The Guild has informants everywhere. You'd be better off going with Gregor."

Gregor folded his arms across his broad chest. "Sydney's right. It's too risky. I promised Rolf you would come to no harm, and I intend to keep my word."

"I value your word, Gregor. I can also defend myself as well as any soldier I'd ask to fight for me."

Vadnae touched Gregor's arm. "Gregor, this is something Willem must do."

"I respectfully disagree with both of you," Gregor said. "If it's one thing I've learned, it's to speak up when I feel I have cause. I trust Sydney, but you're no match for Schrammig. Willem, if we lose you, we lose everything."

"I understand your concerns," Willem replied. "Believe me, I'm not underestimating the danger. Stephan would have my head if he knew what I planned to do. But this is a crucial piece of my campaign. Sydney will take me where I need to go. I accept the risks."

His words held an ominous note. Sydney looked from

Vadnae to Willem. Did he expect to find the Tuatha in the tunnels? If he did, why didn't he simply say so? Perhaps meeting with the resistance leaders was a ruse to cover up his true plans. Willem's expression revealed nothing.

Gregor sighed. "Very well then. Sydney, don't take any big risks."

She swallowed hard. Life in Last Hope was full of risks. "I'll do my best to keep Willem safe."

"We'll meet at the place Francis specified by sundown," Willem said. "Now let's get out of these robes. Our disguise isn't needed now."

Chapter Sixteen

Sydney and Willem exited the abbey through a back gate, near the stable where the monks often unloaded foodstuffs from their farm and other supplies. She scanned the street. No sign of Schrammig or his soldiers. Shaking the mud from the hem of her tattered cloak, she motioned Willem to follow. They'd dressed to be inconspicuous, she in her shirt and breeches and he in the homespun tunic and pants he'd worn when she first met him. He passed easily for a peasant, wearing a felt hat pulled down over his eyes, his hair hanging loose to his shoulders.

She cast a furtive glance at him, noticing he'd taken off his ring and fighting the urge to brush the hair back from his face. *Dammit, why does he make me feel like this?*

"Didn't want every pickpocket in Last Hope coming after my ring," he said, following her gaze. "Erik warned me they're everywhere."

"You didn't leave it with the monks, did you?"

He pulled out a pouch from within his shirt. "For safekeeping. I hope you'll warn me if anyone tries to pry it from my neck. Erik assured me you're an expert on thievery."

She scowled. "Erik has a big mouth."

Willem's smile sent a pleasant warmth tingling over her skin, and she quickly looked away.

When they arrived at the main street, Sydney halted. She'd

promised to ensure Willem's safety and to focus on their mission. She'd also made a promise to Aldric's steward, which possibly ran counter to Willem's goals.

She held out a hand to stop him. "What if we make a quick trip to the market first, then I'll take you to the resistance?" He frowned, waiting for her to continue. She described the request from Marcus and the money she had agreed to deliver to his sister.

Immediately he shook his head. "It's too much of a risk. Someone could recognize you."

"I'll be careful."

"Being careful isn't enough. I told you we can't jeopardize our mission. You could've given the money to Francis or Gregor to deliver."

"I gave my word. Marcus asked for my help. He trusted me. Like people trusted Edgar."

"I see. So it's not about the money. It's about Edgar."

"It won't take long. The market is on the way. Please." When he didn't respond, she reached for his arm. "Willem, please. I need to do this. I have to make up for…." She took a deep breath and turned away. "Never mind. You wouldn't understand."

"You're wrong, Sydney, I do understand." He took her arm this time and sighed. "We'll go to the market first. But before we go any further, tell me if you have any other obligations I should be aware of. I must be able to trust you, Sydney. Our lives depend on it."

She debated whether to tell him about Zared. She had no obligations to Zared. Nor did she want to discuss the matter, especially not with Willem. The possibility he'd judge her for the things she'd done disconcerted her, more than she cared to admit. Best not to bring Zared up if she could avoid doing so. She shook her head. "Nothing else."

He frowned but didn't press her. "Let's go."

She veered off the main street leading to the center of

town. They traversed the narrow side streets. Merchants setting out goods in front of their shops eyed them. An unattended basket of warm, fragrant bread caught Sydney's eye. Dangling purses and the glint of baubles tempted her. Her fingers twitched, and she stuck her hands in her pockets. No need for stealing today.

Spotting a crowd clustered ahead, voices a low, angry murmur, she moved back into the shadows of the buildings lining the street. Willem matched her quick movements and pulled down the brim of his hat. She took a closer glance and spied a group of men wearing black uniforms. Soldiers.

"Those are the Guild's soldiers," Willem said softly.

She swallowed, her mouth dry. "Let's go a different way."

They backtracked and took a shortcut Sydney often employed to get to the market, ducking through a series of little-used alleys snaking among the timber-framed buildings. Willem stayed by her side, moving as quietly as she did.

The smells of fragrant spices and herbs and freshly butchered meats heralded their arrival at the public square. Sellers lined the narrow lanes crisscrossing the large square. Some could afford to display their goods in permanent wooden stalls. Others carried their wares in baskets or crates or set them on tattered blankets. Eyeing the sparser than usual crowd, Sydney's shoulders tensed. No sign of the soldiers here. Yet. Word of Schrammig's return, or of the abbot's arrest, had likely already spread throughout town. Anyone who had a reason to hide from the Guild would be out of sight.

Willem pulled the brim of his hat lower. He leaned close. "How'd I do?" At Sydney's startled expression, the corners of his mouth twitched upward. "I'm no fool. You're still not sure if you can rely on me in your domain."

Sydney's stomach fluttered at his proximity. She took a step back, murmuring, "You did fine." In fact, he'd done better than she expected.

They slowly worked their way across the square. Sydney

made a point of stopping every so often in response to the vendors hawking their wares, examining a basket of apples, fragrant beeswax candles, a bolt of fine muslin, as if she and Willem were no different from anyone else at the market. Today, the market itself was different. An undercurrent of fear pervaded the crowd. Haggling was cut short, and money exchanged hands quickly.

Voices hummed in her ears when they moved toward the center of the square where the largest crowds gathered. A knot of anxiety formed in the pit of her stomach. In spite of herself, the wooden scaffold at the far end of the square drew her attention. She pulled her cloak close about her. Willem gently touched her hand. The compassion in his eyes surprised her, and warmth suffused her at the contact. Self-conscious of her reaction, she managed a brief smile and focused on the crowd.

Nala, the white-haired herb woman, sold her wares in this part of the market. Her back curved with age, she sat on a dusty blanket surrounded by baskets of aromatic herbs. Herbs for cooking, medicines for the body, and medicines for the soul.

The old woman's milky eyes swiveled in Sydney's direction. "What can I get for you, dearie?"

Nala was alone. Sydney's heart began to beat faster. She hoped this wasn't a mistake. She knelt near the blanket. "I'm looking for Betty."

She snorted. "So am I, dearie. Didn't show up today."

Sydney bit her lip. "Can you tell me where she lives? It's important."

"What d'you want with Betty? You here on the Guild's business?"

Sydney wondered how much Nala knew about the activities of Betty's husband. She was fairly certain the old woman didn't belong to the Guild. Years earlier, when Edgar was still alive, Anaria had occasionally sent her on errands to purchase herbs, instructing her to seek out Nala. "I don't work for the Guild."

"Who's your friend, dearie?" Nala waved a bony hand in Willem's direction. "I can't see, but I'm not stupid."

Willem crouched at Sydney's side. "We mean no harm to you."

"So they all say. Come closer, laddie." She stretched out her skeletal fingers and cackled. "Let me get a better look at you."

Willem did as she asked. Sydney fingered the hilt of the knife in her boot, keeping a watchful eye on the people passing by.

The instant Nala touched Willem's hand, Sydney stabbed the blade into the ground next to her, pinning her sleeve to the blanket. "Let him go, or you'll lose a finger in addition to your sight."

Nala released him. "Easy, dearie. Wasn't going to hurt him."

Willem sat back on his heels, eyes widening. "Release her."

Sydney pulled up the knife and tucked it back in her boot sheath.

"No harm done." Nala fingered the hole in her sleeve. She turned her head in Willem's direction once more. "I've been expecting you."

Willem drew back. "What do you mean?"

She gave him a toothless grin. "Some things I see clearly. You'll bring the end of us. And a new beginning."

People said Nala was a little funny in the head, but she could cure anything. Some people said she could see the future. While Sydney gaped at her pronouncement, Willem regarded the old woman with a curious expression, showing no surprise at her words.

"Now, tell me why you're seeking Betty."

Sydney took a breath to regain her composure. "Her brother asked me to give her a message."

Nala cocked her head. "Then it's true. Schrammig's come back."

"He has." Sydney scanned the crowd. No one paid them

any attention.

"Mmmph. I'd watch myself if I was you, dearie. I know you. You're on his list, ain't ya?"

Sydney trembled. "Guess I am."

"Old Market Street. Betty has a room. Number seven. Look for her there."

"Thanks."

Willem tossed a coin from his pouch in the tarnished cup at the edge of Nala's blanket.

"Don't mention it, dearie. Sure I can't interest you in any of these?" She tapped her baskets and gave Sydney a knowing smile. "I've got some the girls use when they're out on the job. Never can tell when you'll need them."

Willem's mouth quirked into a smile.

Her face flushed. *What must he think of me?* "I ain't got any use for them now." She glared at Nala, even though the old woman couldn't see her, and quickly moved back into the crowd with Willem following.

"You visit her often, do you?" Willem's grin was teasing.

She turned her glare on him. At least he could see it. "Yeah, I used her services a lot when I was out on the job."

His grin faded. "I'm sorry. I didn't realize...didn't mean...."

"No matter," she said, looking away. "Nala means well. Why'd she say she was expecting you? You weren't even surprised."

Willem dodged a man carrying a large goose, dressed and ready for roasting. Moving closer to Sydney, he quietly said, "My mother sometimes did the same thing. Not in those words, of course. Sometimes she'd speak as if in a dream, and her words would make no sense. Later, you'd realize she had seen things before they occurred. Some people said she was mad. Some said she'd been blessed—or cursed—by the faery folk. That their blood ran in her veins." He shrugged. "I never found out the truth."

Oryn had said she could see things most people could not. Sydney rubbed her arms against a sudden chill. "Did you believe what they said? About the faery folk."

"It's possible. The Tuatha are part of my destiny. Perhaps they're part of your destiny also, Sydney."

His words unnerved her. Surely she couldn't be connected to the Tuatha. But she was no longer certain of anything.

"Should I thank you for threatening a blind woman on my behalf?"

She started to make a retort, but he laughed softly. "Gregor wouldn't forgive me if anything happened to you," she told him. "You can't trust anyone around here, not even a blind woman."

"You weren't really planning to cut off her finger, were you?"

"Haven't cut off any fingers yet." She found herself returning his grin.

His smile suddenly faded, and he bent his head toward her. "The man by the booth across from us. He's been staring at you."

With a start, she recognized the man at once. Reynald was one of Zared's acquaintances. She'd never liked the way his beady eyes watched her whenever Zared wasn't paying attention. Now he stared at her, eyes wide.

"Dammit." Keeping her face blank, she touched Willem's elbow. "Let's go. Now."

They slipped between the lanes of the market to the empty side streets. Sydney scanned the square. No one pursued them. She swore under her breath. The guard discouraged people from openly selling fantasia in public, so Reynald rarely came to the market. He'd be sure to tell Zared he'd seen her. She swore again.

"He recognized you. Who is he?"

She continued walking. "No one. Just a friend of Zared."

"Zared?"

Sydney drew in a long breath to calm the panic within her. *I don't need him any more. I've moved on.* She clenched her trembling hands. She yearned to be free of him. Free of her old life.

"Who's Zared? Do these people pose a threat to us?"

His stare seemed to read the thoughts she struggled to hide. "Not sure. They might."

"No more lies, Sydney. I want the truth. All of it."

"It's my problem...not yours."

"You still don't understand, do you? Your problems affect the success of our mission." He moved toward her, close enough to see the blond stubble on his chin. "This isn't a jaunt around town going to the market and picking pockets. Either you tell me what I need to know now, or I can no longer trust you."

"All right." Her heart thumped in her chest. She dared not lose her chance to help Willem's cause. And she dared not lose his respect. Her feelings for Willem were becoming more than loyalty to the man who would one day be her king.

She stepped back, taking another deep breath. "I've known Zared for a while. You could say he's more than an acquaintance. At least at first. Things changed and I—"

Willem held up a hand. "No need to go into detail. Just tell me what's important to us right now."

"Zared may have turned me over to the Guild. I'm not certain."

"Why do you think it was Zared who turned you in?"

"Someone told the guards where I was. Could have been Zared. I ain't sure."

"Is he looking for you?"

"He went to Anaria," she admitted. "He shouldn't even think I'm alive."

"Why didn't you tell me this before, Sydney?"

"I didn't think it was important."

He took off his hat and kneaded his forehead. "Everything slowing us down is important. Does Zared work for the Guild?

Or for Schrammig? Your feelings for him are a dangerous distraction."

"My feelings are none of your concern." She balled her fists. "I can deal with Zared. Trust me."

"I can't trust you unless you're honest with me."

She'd told him enough. Too much perhaps. "Willem, I'm telling the whole truth this time. I swear."

"I suppose you're also going to tell me Old Market Street is on the way to our destination?"

"It's right near the Black Dog. We can give the money to Betty and still have plenty of time to meet with the resistance."

Willem adjusted his hat and pulled down the brim. "Very well. But if we run across your friend Zared, I'll handle the situation."

They continued on. Every so often, she glanced over her shoulder, afraid they were being tracked. Zared was certainly not the worst of their problems, but Willem was right. She could usually count on Zared to be a distraction, and this time he might be a dangerous one.

Chapter Seventeen

Crossing the increasingly narrow muddy lanes, Sydney and Willem approached the oldest part of town, nicknamed the Thieves' Den, home to the poorest inhabitants of Last Hope. Tenements leaned into the pathways, blocking out much of the sunlight. The ground floors were sturdy field stone chinked with wattle and daub, but additional wooden stories had been built up in haphazard fashion.

Sydney stayed close to Willem, quickening their pace. The shuffle of footsteps and murmur of voices echoed off the buildings. She couldn't shake the sensation they were being followed, despite her best efforts to hide their trail.

Old Market Street bordered a diminutive, open square, a quarter the size of the market square. A boarded-up well had been long abandoned. Poisoned, some said, when sickness had spread throughout the crowded quarters. A group of women gathered around two large rain barrels, buckets in hand. Scrawny, ragged children chased chickens scratching in the dirt nearby, and two goats bleated forlornly.

Little more than alleys, the surrounding streets wound among a maze of dilapidated structures. Within those streets lay the Broken Cask, the tavern where she'd had the ill-fated encounter with the Guild official.

"Spare a copper, miss?"

A filthy boy dressed in rags stepped out of a shadowy

alcove, hand outstretched. Sydney scowled at him, and he scurried away. *A whole cartload of coppers couldn't save him.*

"See what the Guild and the nobles have done to us?" she said to Willem. They skirted the edge of the square, dodging puddles and animal dung. Women watched them, faces wary. "People are forced to live like animals here."

He suddenly stopped. "You really think I don't understand the people of Last Hope?"

"I've seen where nobles live. You're a prince. You've never experienced this."

His mouth grew hard. "Don't presume to understand how I've lived. You've no knowledge of my experiences, Sydney."

The harshness of his tone startled her. Perhaps she'd spoken too freely. She lowered her head. "You're right. I don't know who you really are," she said. A few incongruities—his informalities, his conversation about his mother, and his ability to blend in with the people on the street—hinted at a past he kept well hidden.

"Most people don't." The line of his mouth softened. "To be a king is to be alone."

She understood being alone all too well. Whether it was something that could bring them together or drive them apart remained to be seen.

"This way." She counted the buildings until they came to number seven, a decrepit three-story rooming house. She knocked. No answer. Impatient, she pounded on the door.

The door finally opened a crack. "What d'you want?" asked a gruff voice.

"We're here to see one of your tenants."

"Who and what for?"

"Her name's Betty. And my business is my own."

"Betty, eh? You here to pay her rent, too? She owes me."

Sydney took a coin from the purse the steward had given her and held it just out of reach. "Let us in, and we'll pay in advance."

The door opened, and a wizened man snatched the coin from her hand. He gave her a toothless grin. "Third floor, last room on the right."

They climbed the stairs, and a figure scurried down the dim hallway on the first floor. A door slammed shut. Aside from their footsteps, the house was eerily quiet. Sydney began to doubt whether they would find Betty. At the last door, she knocked, softly calling, "Betty? Are you in there?" Silence. "I've got a message from your brother. Marcus. It's important."

The bolt slid back. The door opened, revealing a woman's face. "What do you want?"

Sydney didn't blame her for being suspicious. "I met Marcus at Aldric's keep. He asked me to give you something."

Betty eyed Sydney and then Willem. "How did you find me?"

"The herb woman at the market told us where you live."

"And how do you know my brother?"

"A long story. Can we come in? We don't work for the Guild."

She gestured them inside. "Come quickly."

A smoky oil lamp on a table by the door cast a yellow haze in the windowless room. Three blond-haired girls huddled on a straw pallet. The oldest was ten or eleven, the middle a few years younger, and the youngest no more than a babe. The lamp drew Sydney's attention. The silver base was etched with designs and a fancy script. Considering the room's sparseness and location, she wondered how Betty had come by such a valuable item.

Betty folded her arms across her chest and stared at Sydney and Willem. A thin woman, the dark circles under her eyes and her worn, patched dress affirmed her shabby surroundings. "Say what you've got to say."

Sydney held out the leather purse from the steward. "Your brother asked me to give this to you."

Betty hesitated. Her hand shook when she took the purse and opened it. Tears filled her eyes. "How did he know I needed this?"

"He knew Schrammig was coming to Last Hope. He said your husband might be in trouble."

"My Bill left last night." Betty clutched the purse to her chest. "Couldn't tell me when he'd be back. He even woke the children before he left." She brushed the tears from her eyes. "I was afraid to go to the market today. Schrammig comes back and people start asking questions."

"Questions about the resistance?"

Betty shrugged. "The Guild can ask me anything they want—I've got nothing to tell. But they don't care, do they?" Her voice dropped to a whisper. "People who've got nothing to tell end up just as dead."

Sydney couldn't help thinking of all the times Edgar had gone away without warning, often long after curfew, sometimes for a week or more. He'd never said where he was going; he just promised he'd be back.

"Are the rumors about Aldric true?" Betty asked. "He's decided to fight the Guild?"

"Things will be different this time. Aldric isn't alone, and neither is Last Hope," Willem said. He took in the room, focusing on the lamp. "Where did you get that?"

"The lamp's mine. I didn't steal it, if that's what you're thinking."

"Then you must be aware it bears Lord Stephan's family crest."

Betty's eyes widened. "You know it?"

"*Always vigilant.*" Willem's finger traced the designs on the lamp. "I'm very familiar with it. How did you come by this?"

"Stephan is my kinsman, distant cousin to my father. The lamp is the only thing we could save from the Guild. It's all I have left of my family."

"Your family?" Sydney asked. "But that means...."

"You're nobility," Willem finished.

Betty nodded. "My father had spoken out against the Guild. They destroyed our home, confiscated our land. Stephan could do nothing to help us. We came to Last Hope, Bill and I, thinking we'd be safe here. We'd heard other people had done the same."

"Like Edgar." How many other nobles had come to Last Hope for those reasons?

"Edgar was a good man. He did what he could for us. He treated everyone as equals. We never asked for anything more. We were glad to be alive. Edgar convinced my Bill one day we'd be able to go home. His hope kept us going all these years. Now Bill says soon we'll have a home again. He says Prince Willem can overthrow the Guild. That he'll fight for us."

Willem's voice was soft. "That's what I hear he intends to do."

"I've been praying for him. Like I've been praying for my Bill." Betty wiped her eyes. "My brother sends money when he can. He always seems to foresee when I need the coin. I appreciate what you've done, but you should go now. It won't do if someone sees you."

"Will you be safe here?"

"As safe as anywhere else." Betty waved a hand toward her children. "I'm not so worried about me, you see. It's my girls. I couldn't bear it if any harm came to them. I promised my Bill I'd be here waiting for him, though."

Footsteps pounded on the stairs. "Betty, they've come for you and Bill!"

"The Guild." For a moment Betty froze, gaping at the door. She grabbed Sydney's arm. "The back stairs. Go while you can." She glanced toward her children, then back to Sydney. "Please, take them. Keep them safe."

"We can't take them. How can we—"

"Please." Betty gripped her arm. "You must. I won't let

them hurt my babies."

The girls ran to their mother and wrapped their arms around her. The older two were in tears. "I won't leave," said the oldest girl.

"You must." Betty stroked her hair. She pressed the purse into the hand of the oldest girl. "Take this with you. Hold onto it for me."

The footsteps grew louder. "We'll do as you ask," Willem said. "But you're not staying behind, Betty. We're all going together."

"Please, just go. I'll stall them until you're gone." She held her girls tight and kissed their foreheads. Tears filled her eyes. "I'll find you. Be strong, like we've taught you." Touching Sydney's cheek, she mouthed, *Thank you,* and sprinted down the hall.

"Betty, wait!" Willem started to follow and stopped, cursing under his breath.

Sydney stared after her. Betty intended to sacrifice herself for her children. Edgar would have done no less. He had gone quietly with Schrammig the night of his arrest, hoping to keep her safe. Angrily she rubbed the tears from her eyes.

"Hurry, Sydney." Willem picked up the babe. "Let's go," he told the children. "Show us the way out." They didn't move. "Don't throw away the chance your mother has given you."

The girls looked confused. "Do as your mother said," Sydney snapped.

"This way," whispered the oldest girl, pointing toward a door at the other end of the hallway. She blinked rapidly, fighting tears.

The middle girl clung to Sydney. She put her arm around the bony shoulders shaking with silent sobs, wishing she could say something to make everything better. She had no words to take away the girl's grief.

"Be strong for her." She echoed Betty's words, the same words Edgar had always told her.

Be strong. They felt their way down the dark stairway, one step at a time. Sydney took the girl's small hand. She would be strong for all of them.

She strained to hear any sounds above them, afraid the door at the top of the stairs would open at any moment to interrupt their escape. At last, they exited into an alley behind the building. Sydney let out the breath she'd been holding. But they were far from safe.

"We have to get away from here," Willem said quietly.

"Right. Wait here a minute."

Ignoring his protest, she darted around the side of the building and inched her way toward the front, hoping Betty had been able to buy them time. She peeked around the corner. A black carriage stood in front of the building. Much like the carriage Schrammig and Durok had taken to the abbey. She crept closer for a better view.

Two men emerged from the building, dragging Betty between them. Neither of them resembled Schrammig, but she couldn't see their faces. The carriage door opened. Sydney glimpsed a cloaked figure and shrank back against the building. A wave of malevolence washed over her. Durok.

The carriage began to move. Seeing Durok made her wonder whether Vadnae had been successful in distracting him with her magic.

She hurried back to Willem. "I saw Schrammig's carriage leave. Durok was there."

"Schrammig," whispered the older girl, her eyes wide with horror. "But Mam didn't do anything. They'll put her in the gaol."

The others started to cry. Sydney grabbed the older girl and shook her, gently. "Stop. There ain't nothing you can do now."

"How could you let them take her? Why didn't you do something?"

Sydney drew back, as if she'd been slapped in the face with her own guilt.

"She trusted you. You let them take her."

"It was your mam's decision. She sacrificed herself to save you. She acted too quickly for us to stop her." Sydney fought to keep the tremor from her voice and struggled to push aside her feelings mirrored in the girl's eyes. She had to calm her enough so they could get away from this place. "She trusted us, and so should you. We have to stick together now. What're your names?"

The girl hesitated. "Janey." She jabbed a finger at her sisters. "Sara an' Frannie."

Willem shifted the child in his arms. "Janey, my name is Willem and this is Sydney. We told your mother we would keep you safe, and we will. Your parents are very brave, and you have to be brave, too, for their sake. And for your sisters."

"Even Da is afraid of Schrammig," Janey said.

"We all are, but we're not going to let him win." Willem knelt down by Janey. Frannie rested on his knee, gumming the sleeve of his shirt. "I'll tell you why he's not going to win. One day I will be your king, and I will punish Schrammig for his crimes."

"You don't look like a king." Sara wiped her nose on her sleeve.

Janey squinted at him. "She's right. You don't look like a king. Why would a king come here?"

"A king does whatever he must to protect his people."

"Uncle Bert told us he was king once," said Sara.

Janey rolled her eyes. "Uncle Bert's a drunk." She peered at Willem. "Maybe you are, too."

"Janey, you must honor your mother's word. She wants you to trust us. There's no time to argue. We must get away from here, now." Willem stood and began walking with Frannie in his arms, beckoning to Janey.

"Where are you taking us?"

Sydney and Willem exchanged a glance. They certainly couldn't keep the girls with them.

"The abbey," Willem said. "The monks will look after you."

At any other time, Sydney would have been amused by the thought of Erik looking after several children, but they had a serious problem. The abbey was on the other side of town. Sydney shaded her eyes from the sun directly overhead, thinking of their rendezvous at the Prancing Pig at sundown and their need to make contact with the resistance leaders. "We don't have enough time to go back there."

"Where else can we take them?"

The abbey was by far the safest option, but they needed someplace closer. The Silver Eagle wasn't far. It was their only option if she was to keep her promise to Betty, even if it put Anaria in further danger. She hated to do that, but they had no other choice.

"Anaria's nearby. We can take them there. I'm sure she'll help us."

Anaria didn't like getting involved. Sydney hoped seeing the children would change her mind, and if it didn't, she'd bring up Edgar and his convictions, much the way Anaria had earlier.

"We're going to take you someplace safe," Willem told the girls. "It's not far. You must do what we say and stay quiet. Can you do that?"

They nodded. "Will Da be there?" asked Sara.

Willem hesitated a moment. "No, but we'll tell him where you are."

"Because you're the king, right?"

"Right."

Telling the girls Willem's true identity had momentarily distracted them. The girls kept their pace and made no complaints. Janey and Willem took turns carrying little Frannie, who was surprisingly quiet and calm. Sydney hadn't asked to be responsible for the girls. Children were forced to fend for themselves in Last Hope all the time. But wasn't that what she was fighting against? Something inside her had changed, and it felt good. She would protect these three from Schrammig, whatever it took.

They stopped to let the girls rest, and she said quietly to Janey, "The Guild took away someone I cared about, too. I survived, and so will you."

Janey's bravado faded, and the tears ran down her cheeks. "Did you ever see them again?"

Sydney didn't answer. She simply put her arms around the girl and let her cry.

Chapter Eighteen

Sydney hesitated in the alley across the street from the Silver Eagle. Her breath caught in her throat when she spotted the shattered windows. Shards of glass glittered in the sunlight near the open tavern door.

"Sydney." Willem reached for her arm when she started forward. "Whoever's responsible could still be around."

"But Anaria might be in there. If she's hurt, or worse...."

"Let's assess the situation before we do anything."

His calm demeanor provided a counterpoint to her growing panic, but it gave her no comfort. Impatiently, she studied the street in front of the tavern. All appeared quiet.

"You stay with them," she told Willem, waving a hand toward the girls huddled together in the alley. "There's a back way. I'll go around and see if it's safe."

"No, I'll go. *You* stay with the girls, Sydney."

She caught his sleeve and lowered her voice. "Anaria doesn't know you. She has no reason to trust you. She'd probably gut you like a pig. I know how to defend myself, if that's what you're worried about."

"Did Anaria teach you how to use your knife?"

"No, Edgar did." She crossed her arms. "Anaria is the only family I've got now. I have to make sure she's all right. We're wasting time talking about it."

"You are like no woman I've ever known," he muttered,

shaking his head. "Go, but if you take too long, I'm coming after you."

"Thanks. I'll be careful."

She pulled the knife from her boot and hurried back the way they had come, taking the side streets until she reached the alley behind the tavern. She lifted the latch of the back door, surprised to find it unlocked. Peering at the upper windows, she saw nothing unusual. Cautiously, she pushed the door open and entered the kitchen. The pot on the fire still held last night's meal, and the bread cooled on the hearth. She listened. Silence. She crept toward the door to the main room, steeling herself for what lay within.

Light filtered into the tavern, casting jagged shadows across the overturned tables and chairs. Amber liquid seeped from the broken casks behind the bar, and the yeasty aroma of ale pervaded the room.

"Anaria?"

A shuffling came from behind the bar. "Who's there?"

Sydney's body relaxed slightly at the sound of Anaria's voice. "Anaria, it's Sydney."

Anaria peeked around the bar, holding a cleaver in one hand. "Syd, what are you doing here?"

At the sight of Anaria's split lip and blackened eye, Sydney's fist clenched around the knife. Schrammig was destroying the lives of everyone she came into contact with, and she couldn't do anything to stop him. *Saving the children will be a good start.*

"Did the Guild hurt you?"

Anaria touched her lip and shrugged. "It's not so bad."

"Not bad?" Sydney gestured at the room around them and at Anaria herself. "Look at what they've done. To you and the Silver Eagle."

"Could've been worse. They was trying to scare us. The owner's already gone to the Guild Hall to make a complaint. Didn't listen to me when I told him he was asking for more trouble. The Guild don't care if he's paid his fees this month."

Sydney glanced at Edgar's table, lying on its side, two of the legs broken. Edgar had always been careful to avoid the Silver Eagle when he suspected the Guild was searching for him, so Anaria couldn't be linked to his activities.

"It's my fault. I shouldn't have come last night."

"No, Syd." Anaria laid the cleaver on the bar and put her hands on Sydney's shoulders. "It's bad luck is all. The Guild's been doing this sort of thing all around town. Schrammig wasn't here. I doubt I'd be here now if he'd been with them."

Sydney bit her lip. Schrammig had already given Anaria a warning.

"Why'd you come back?"

She was loath to ask Anaria to do any more for her, but her new-found determination made her choice easy. "We're fighting back, Anaria. Some of my friends are outside. We need your help."

"You brought friends? What the hell are you thinking? I can't get involved."

"You're already involved. So is everyone in Last Hope. You can hide behind the bar with your cleaver or you can stand up and help us. Remember what you said about being true to Edgar's memory?" Sydney stuck the knife in her boot sheath and hurried to the front door. She signaled to Willem. Moments later, he led the girls inside, carefully lifting Frannie over the broken glass.

Anaria's eyes widened, looking from Willem and the children to Sydney.

Sydney put a hand on Sara's head. "They're why I need your help. Are you willing to abandon them to the streets or will you protect them the way you protected me?"

Anaria wiped her hands on her apron. A spectrum of emotions showed in her face, before her expression took on a look of determination. "First things first then. Let's find you girls a place to sit." Willem and Sydney helped her right some chairs and seated the girls around a table.

"You said we'd be safe here," Janey told Sydney. "This doesn't look safe."

Sydney took in the broken tables and chairs around them, and her hands clenched. The Silver Eagle was the closest thing she had to a home. Now the Guild had violated the only place in Last Hope she had ever felt secure.

"It's not the place, Janey. It's my friend Anaria. You'll be safe with her."

"It smells like Uncle Bert." Sara wrinkled her nose.

Anaria chuckled. "I'll bet your uncle would be put out at all this good ale going to waste. You girls hungry?"

Janey elbowed Sara, who had begun to nod. "No, thank you, ma'am."

"No? You've never had my cooking before."

Willem set another table upright. "Is there anything I can do? Can I help cleaning up?"

Anaria put her hands on her hips, studying Willem. "It's a kind offer, but there's not much to be done. I'd rather not give anyone a reason to suspect I've had visitors. You can keep an eye out for trouble for us. Syd, come give me a hand."

"We'll be right back." Sydney followed Anaria into the kitchen.

"They left my kitchen alone. That's how I know they was only trying to scare us." Anaria grabbed the warm loaf from the hearth and began to cut thick slices. "But the way they smashed up the tavern!" She stabbed the knife into the counter. "Damn them. I've been through too much to let them run me out of my home. This is all I've got left. You're right, Syd. They're not going to take it away from me now. I'll deserve to be damned if I don't stand with you."

She began spooning the meat from the pot. Her hands shook, and the food spilled over the edge.

Standing a little taller than she had a moment earlier, Sydney nudged her aside. "Here, let me help."

Anaria leaned against the counter, gingerly touching her

swollen lip. "Now, tell me what you want me to do. Who are those children?"

Sydney wasn't sure how much to tell her. The less Anaria knew, the better, for all their sakes. "Their father's involved in the resistance. The Guild arrested their mother when they came for him. I told her I'd keep them safe."

"How long do you need to leave them with me?"

"You just have to get them to our friends at the abbey. They'll look after them until things settle down."

"The abbey? Since when do you have friends in the church?" Anaria held up a hand before Sydney could reply. "Wait, don't tell me. You hear the abbot was arrested this morning?"

Sydney wasn't surprised word had traveled fast. Anaria had her sources of information. "Schrammig was there."

Anaria stacked the bread and meat on a tray. "A lot of those monks killed outside town had helped Edgar. He didn't really care for the church, but he always respected people for standing up for what's right. Like you are now."

The longer Sydney stayed in Last Hope, the more she learned about Edgar. The layers of what she'd believed to be true were being stripped away, and what she would find underneath remained a mystery. "Thanks for helping, Anaria. We can't take the girls with us."

Anaria nodded in the direction of the barroom. "Your friend's not from around here, is he?"

Sydney tensed. "Why do you say that?"

"Relax, Syd. I don't care who he is or where he's from. He seems like a decent fellow and a damned sight better than Zared. What I think doesn't matter, though. The important thing is...do *you* trust him?"

Willem sat at the table with the girls. Janey said something and he smiled, entirely at ease with them.

"I do. I have to."

She wished she could share Willem's identity with Anaria.

The more time they spent together, the more she realized he really did represent the opportunity for something better. She truly believed he could unite people to oppose the Guild.

"These days you can't be too careful who you trust." Anaria handed Sydney the tray. "Don't worry about the girls. I'll take them to the abbey."

"You'd be safe there, too."

"I've never been much of a churchgoer. Besides, I'm not going to let the Guild get the best of me. It'll take more than a few busted tables and chairs to scare me away. I'll be all right. I can—"

A wailing cry reverberated through the tavern. Sydney put down the tray and rushed into the main room. Tears streamed down Sara's face.

"You're always losing things," Janey told her, which caused her to cry harder. Frannie also began to cry, and Janey bounced the baby in her arms.

"What's this about?" Anaria asked Willem.

He'd put his arm around Sara, but stepped aside to let Anaria offer comfort. "She started crying. She seems to have lost something."

Sara threw herself into Anaria's embrace. Her sobs reduced to sniffles. "My good luck charm's gone."

"Da gave it to her before he left," Janey said, poking her sister. "I told you not to play with it."

"I just had it."

Willem shrugged. "It could be anywhere."

Sydney watched the red-faced girl. The token might be all she had left of her father. "Did you have it before we came inside?"

"I-I can't remember."

"I'll check the alley. What's it look like?"

"A white bead on a string," Janey said.

Anaria smoothed Sara's hair and seated her by herself. She steered Sydney away from the table and said in a low voice,

"You'll never find it. There's more important things to worry about."

"You, of all people, should understand. What if they never see their father again?" She moved to the door, glancing over her shoulder at Willem. "I'll be right back. Then we can leave."

Sydney paced the length of the alley twice but saw no trace of the bead. She hated to tell Sara it was gone. She touched the pouch containing Edgar's good luck charm. It wasn't the object itself that held so much meaning, but the memories associated with it.

She kicked at the dirt in frustration. Soft footfalls came from behind her. She whirled around.

"Good to see you again, Syd."

"Zared." Her hands began to tremble and her heart raced.

Zared's clothes were rumpled and his eyes bloodshot. He stepped toward her. He reeked of ale and cheap perfume, and she decided she'd rather not ask who he'd been with the previous night.

She exhaled slowly. In spite of his lies and betrayals, in spite of her realization that he'd used her and maybe he'd never really loved her, part of her still cared for him.

The rest of her wanted to hurt him as much as he had hurt her.

"What d'you want, Zared?"

"I needed to see you were all right."

"It's a little late for caring about me. Where were you when I was in the gaol?"

"Where could I get enough coin to spring you?"

"You could've found a way." She glared at him. "You say there's always ways to make money, remember?"

Having his own words thrown back had an impact. Zared winced. "I've been in the gaol before. It ain't so bad."

"A death sentence is something you walk away from?"

"You did."

"I wasn't gonna wait around for you."

"I had a plan. I wasn't gonna let you die. I found out where they'd taken you. I would've fought off the wolves to save you. But when I got there, you were gone." He quirked an eyebrow. "You must've found someone else to save you instead."

"I guess I did." She hoped he really didn't think she'd be stupid enough to fall for his story. "Was saving me part of your plan all along, or did you feel guilty after turning me in?"

"How can you think I'd turn you in?"

"I woke up and you were gone. Then the guards came to arrest me. Convenient, huh? Just tell me the truth. For once."

"I had business. I didn't want to wake you." He moved closer, reaching for her. She stepped back. He gave her an uneasy smile. "All these years, I've helped you hide from the Guild. I'd never hand you over to them."

She shrugged. "I hear Schrammig can be pretty persuasive."

Zared drew in a sharp breath, and the fear in his eyes surprised her.

"Dammit, Syd, I wouldn't turn you over to Schrammig. I'd never do that to you."

His fear of Schrammig indicated otherwise. "What d'you really want? I've gotta get back."

"Back to your new friend?" He sneered and jabbed a finger toward the tavern across the street. "Was he the one who saved you in the forest?"

"It ain't none of your damn business." She certainly wasn't going to explain Oryn or Willem or why they'd come to Last Hope. She doubted he'd believe her, anyway. "Looks like you've already got yourself a new whore."

"You can't walk away from me. You think your new friends care what happens to you? You think they can protect you from Schrammig?"

"You can?" She flinched when he grabbed her arm. "This is bigger than Schrammig, bigger than you or me. It's worth the risks."

"Going against the Guild?" He shook his head in disgust.

"Even if you win, then what? Who's going to protect people like us? The nobles? We're nothing to them. You can pretend to be one of them, but they'll never accept you. They don't care about you like I do. We're alike, Syd. We understand each other. We've got to stick together, like we've always done."

Once she would have agreed with Zared, but her recent experiences had changed many of her perceptions. Edgar was the best example of a nobleman who had been willing to risk his life for the common people.

"Let me go. It's over between us." Sydney started to pull away, but he tightened his grip on her arm.

"What do you mean, it's over? I've always looked out for you. Without me, you'd have been dead a long time ago."

His dark eyes fixed her with a "you owe me" look. In the past, that look had forced her to stay with him and do his bidding. He had saved her life, not only by hiding her from the Guild, but also from fantasia. All those nights he'd held her while she flailed at him and begged for more of the drug, forcing a watery gruel past her lips to soothe her parched throat, lulling her into a sleep where the unrelenting nightmares no longer frightened her.

Too late did she understand the price of her recovery. "I want you to stay with me. I need you. I'll look after you, I promise." He'd stroked her hair and whispered how he loved her, and how some men would pay a fortune for the way she could make them feel.

She'd struggled to leave him so many times, and something always brought her back. This time was different. She'd changed, and she wasn't going back to the way things had been.

"Zared, I don't need you any more." The strength in her voice surprised her.

A fleeting smile crossed his face. "You're wrong. I can protect you from Schrammig. I've got connections with people who can help you, people your new friends wouldn't consider."

More lies. "I don't need your help, and I don't want it. Why don't you protect yourself instead?"

For a moment, he stared at her. Then he shrugged and released her arm with a forced indifference. "I'll still be here in the end. You know where to find me."

He touched her cheek and turned to leave, adding, "I think you were looking for this."

An ivory bead on a piece of string landed at her feet. She bent down to get it, and when she stood, Zared was gone.

The touch of his hand lingered. *Don't fall for his lies again.* How many times had he convinced her she needed him? She rubbed her cheek. Not this time.

Unclenching her fist, she examined the bead tied to a dirty piece of string. The trinket shimmered when she held it up to the sunlight. Remembering the children's parents were nobility, or at least had once been nobility, she considered whether it really was a jewel. Not likely. Zared wouldn't give up an object possessing any monetary value. Sydney stuck the bead in her pocket.

A flash from the adjacent street caught her eye, the glint of the early afternoon sun striking steel. Hugging the walls of the alley, she moved toward it and stopped when she spotted three soldiers talking to a shopkeeper on the opposite side of the street. The poor fellow being questioned was on his knees, begging for his life. Three more soldiers were going door to door. Gold crests emblazoned the black shirts of their uniforms. They carried long knives in their belts and swords strapped to their backs. Schrammig's soldiers.

Chapter Nineteen

Sydney hurried into the tavern, her boots crunching on the broken glass. "Let's go. Now. Soldiers are headed this way."

Willem stood. "How many?"

"I saw six. They're just east of here."

Anaria ducked behind the bar and returned a moment later, buckling on a belt with a sheathed knife. Sydney recognized it as one of Edgar's knives.

Willem ushered the girls toward the back of the tavern. Silent and tight-lipped, they obeyed. His back ramrod straight, his voice commanding, Willem's authority showed despite his simple dress. He pushed back his hat and told Anaria, "The soldiers are hunting for us. Take the girls to the abbey and stay there with them."

Anaria hesitated only a moment and gave him a quick nod. She caught Sydney's arm. "You talk to Jimmy. After you left last night, I sent him word you'd be coming."

"Thanks. We'll find him." Sydney squeezed Anaria's hand. "When you get to the abbey, ask for Brother Erik or Brother Francis. Tell them we sent you."

Anaria grabbed her cloak from a peg on the wall in the kitchen. She wrapped a cloth around the loaf of bread and stuffed it into a sack, along with a hunk of sausage. Thrusting the sack at Janey, she swung little Frannie onto her hip. "You girls be quiet and do as I say now."

Janey took Sara's hand. "Yes, ma'am, we will."

"Good. We'll be fine, you'll see. What about you, Syd?"

"We'll take Edgar's escape route. They won't find us in the tunnels."

"Be careful. The tunnels aren't as safe as they used to be."

In response to Sara's expectant look, Sydney knelt down, pulling the ivory bead from her pocket. "I think you were looking for this."

"You found it." Sara's face broke into a smile. She threw her arms around Sydney's neck.

Sydney put her arms around the girl, briefly, before gently pushing her away. "Don't lose it again, all right?"

Sara held the bead to her chest. She squinted from Sydney to Willem and suddenly shoved the bead at Sydney, her smile replaced by a more serious expression. "You keep it. It's good luck."

The child's hand closed around Sydney's. She wished keeping someone safe from harm could be so simple. She fumbled with the pouch around her neck and handed her Edgar's coin. "This is my good luck charm. We'll trade until we see each other again."

"I promise I won't lose it."

Sydney shoved the bead in her neck pouch and blinked away tears. "Listen to Anaria. She's taking you someplace safe."

Janey shifted the sack in her arms, her face frightened but determined. "Will you find our da?"

Sydney couldn't lie to her. The odds of the girls seeing either of their parents again were slim. "I'll try."

"She'll find Da for us. She has lots of good luck now." Sara flapped her hand at Willem. "Besides, he's—"

Janey elbowed her sister before she could finish. "Hush your mouth, Sara. You're not supposed to tell anyone."

Anaria peered at Willem. "Don't tell me who you really

are." She gave Sydney a quick embrace. "You did the right thing by coming here. I'll do whatever I can to help, the Guild and Schrammig be damned. Now go, while you still can."

Anaria gathered the girls around her and hurried out the back door. Watching them leave brought tears to Sydney's eyes. She looked up to see Willem watching her, then quickly turned and led him into the storeroom adjacent to kitchen. Here was her chance to show Willem her worth. He'd never find a safe route to the resistance on his own.

The dimly lit room held the scents of dried herbs and earthy root vegetables, though a number of the shelves were bare. Anaria's frugality had often stretched the storeroom's contents, even during harvest season.

Sydney pushed aside a sack of flour hanging from a peg on the wall to reveal a trap door where the floor met the wall. She pried up an iron ring concealed in the floor to open the hidden entrance. "You go first."

Willem climbed down the narrow ladder without hesitating. She followed, pulling the trap door shut behind her, plunging them into darkness. The sack of flour slid into place on a spring-loaded hidden platform carefully designed to conceal the escape route.

"Do you have a lamp?"

"I will when we reach the tunnel." She felt beside the ladder until she located the loose panel. Sliding it up, she tugged on Willem's sleeve. "The way's narrow here. We'll have to crawl, but it's not far to the main tunnels."

"I trust you know what you're doing." His voice held a note of doubt. She caught his hand with a reassuring squeeze. He squeezed back, sending a tingle up her arm. Quickly she let go. A moment later, the sound of scuffling told her he was on his way. She followed and closed the panel behind her.

This was the hardest part. She crawled into the passage and squirmed across the packed earth.

"It's not far," Edgar had reassured her the first time he'd

brought her into the tunnels. She'd been ten years old, and he'd made a game of it, to help her overcome her fear of the dark space closing in around her. At one point, she had begged him to take her back, but he'd insisted they continue. "It'll be worth it, Sydney. Just wait."

Willem fumbled for her hand and helped her climb out of the narrow opening. She inhaled the dank, cool air. Running her fingers along the wall near the opening, she found the raised edges of a single, loose stone and pried it out. Behind the stone, a compartment held sticks, rags, flint, and a flask of oil. She wrapped an oil-soaked rag around one of the sticks and struck the flint. The torch sputtered and caught fire. Acrid smoke filled the air.

High enough for a person to walk upright and wide enough for two people to comfortably walk beside each other, the obsidian stone corridors glinted in the flickering torchlight.

"Amazing," Willem said as he placed his palm on the stone. "Vadnae was right. I'm sure the Tuatha built the tunnels. Without magic, it would have taken hundreds of years to carve them. I've never even seen stone of this fashion before."

Sydney smiled at his expression of awe. The tunnels were Last Hope's great mystery. Some people said they were older than the town itself, and many believed magic had been involved in their creation, as Vadnae had speculated. Most people avoided them. Sydney had heard stories of people who'd gone in and never come out, and magic was often blamed for the disappearances. She suspected the cause to be a simple lack of direction. Navigating the maze of passageways, each one similar to the next, was a challenge for anyone.

She started forward. "The Black Dog is this way."

"Is the Guild familiar with these tunnels?"

"Not these. Most people don't come down here. Some tunnels have collapsed or lead to dead ends. It's easy to get lost."

"You seem to know your way well enough."

"I've hidden here a few times." Her voice grew soft. "These tunnels help a lot of people escape the Guild."

She pictured Edgar standing here beside her, showing her how to count the notches carved into the stones at every turn in the passage. "You must never reveal how to get here," he'd said. "People's lives depend on secrecy. You understand, don't you, Sydney?"

Although Zared had introduced her to other sections of the tunnels, she had never told anyone about these passages. According to Edgar, only those who were so loyal they'd die before divulging the secret were entrusted with it. Sydney had never felt worthy of such knowledge, but she was determined to protect it.

Willem also said he trusted her, and with trust came an expectation of honesty and openness.

"It's not just the Guild we should be worried about," she said hesitantly. "I saw Zared outside the Silver Eagle. He's been following us."

Willem stopped. His eyes narrowed. "You waited until *now* to tell me this? He could lead Schrammig right to us."

"He won't come down here. He's never been in this section of the tunnels. He doesn't know it exists."

His face darkened. "You're sure?"

"You don't believe me?"

"Earlier you said you didn't think Zared would work for the Guild. Why else would he be following us?"

She really didn't want to discuss Zared, so she shrugged. "He wants me back. He thinks we can go back to the way we used to be. He doesn't give up easily."

She started forward, but Willem grabbed her arm. "I don't figure you, Sydney. Why do you refuse to consider that Zared might be connected to the Guild? Do you care for him that much?"

"Of course not." She pulled away and kept walking. She badly wanted to believe Zared would never betray her to

Schrammig. Part of what he'd said to her was true—on some level, they did understand each other. They'd both learned to survive as best they could. They both understood how hard it was to be alone, and that, more than anything else, had kept them together.

"You don't really know me. You wouldn't understand what I've done to survive."

"I understand a lot more than you think, Sydney. You act as though I've lived a privileged, sheltered life. You don't know *me* at all."

She turned and faced him. "So tell me who you really are, Willem, since you seem to know so much about me."

He hesitated only a moment. "Since you asked so nicely, I'll tell you." His mouth upturned slightly. "My mother was a maid in the king's household who had the misfortune of attracting his attention. After a few months, he tired of her and threw her out. She never told him she carried his child. He had a reputation for making sure none of his bastards survived, and she was afraid. For both of us.

"It was five years before she told anyone the truth, and she only did so for my sake. I haven't forgotten what it was like to be cold and hungry, to watch my mother go without."

The stark revelation shocked and touched Sydney. She'd never expected the future king would have lived on the streets the first few years of his life. "What did he do when she told him you were his child?"

"First she told a few of the nobles plotting against the king. Lord Stephan took us in. When the king learned the truth, he refused to recognize me as his son. Because my mother was a commoner." Willem's face grew hard. "Even some of the nobles who helped us treated her as if she were beneath them. I swore I'd never be like that. I'd never forget where I came from."

"But the nobles accepted you."

"Stephan treats me like a son, but many of the lords accept

me in exchange for what they hope to gain from my taking the throne. I suppose I should be grateful Stephan's influence has convinced them to back me."

"The other lords don't agree with your interest in the Tuatha, do they?"

He stiffened. "Why do you say that?"

She looked away, again wondering if she'd spoken out of turn. "Just what I thought after hearing you talk with Lord Aldric. And it sounded like Lord Stephan didn't think you should come to Last Hope, either."

"You're partly right," he said, much to her surprise. "Stephan didn't agree about coming here, but he's always been a supporter of magic. Not all of the lords are as willing to accept it as he is, though. I've had to prove myself every step of the way. Sometimes I think...I think it might be easier to forget the whole thing, to instead live a normal, simple life. But I can't. It's not who I'm meant to be."

His willingness to share his doubts startled her, and his expression displayed a flash of vulnerability that sent her pulse racing.

"My mother sometimes likened being king to being a whore," he said in a quiet voice. "You keep selling a piece of yourself until finally there's nothing left."

Willem's words resonated within her. How much of herself remained after what she'd had to do to survive these past four years? Clearly, he understood more about her than she'd revealed outright, and he didn't think any less of her for it. But there was a world of difference between them. Willem's destiny was to be king. Hers remained a mystery.

She matched his soft tone. "A king never has to sell his body to eat. That's the difference, Willem. Zared and I—we ain't so different."

He shook his head. "I don't believe that. You are what you make of yourself. What you've done in the past doesn't determine your future. Oryn didn't ask you to be involved in this because he needed a pickpocket. He needed someone who would recognize what's right and stand up for it."

"I grew up on the streets of Last Hope. Picking pockets is what I do best. Edgar gave his life for what he believed in. All I ever did was survive."

Willem's gaze searched her face. "No, Sydney, you've changed. You made a choice, like Edgar did. You decided what we're doing is worth fighting for. You wouldn't be here if you hadn't." He took a step closer and then hesitated. "In spite of what you think, it's you and I who aren't so different. We're both trapped by how other people see us."

Warmth flowed through her. She started to reach out to touch his face and stopped herself, instead backing away.

They fell silent and continued on. Willem had missed another important element they had in common. They had both built emotional walls to protect themselves, and she wasn't sure either of them would ever be willing or able to take those walls down.

Not far from their destination, the tunnel split in three directions. Sydney stopped and considered each option. She hadn't been this far into the passage in some time. Willem waited quietly while she reviewed her mental map of the tunnels. Finally, she took the right-hand fork. "It has to be this one. I'm sure of it."

The tunnel began a gradual upward slope, convincing her that she'd made the correct choice. When footsteps echoed ahead of them, she put her arm out to stop Willem and quickly stubbed out the torch. The footsteps grew louder. Whoever was there must have already seen them. She grasped Willem's sleeve and inched backward.

"Sydney, run." Willem's warning was truncated by a muffled grunt.

Before she could take two steps, someone grabbed her from behind, pinning her arms behind her back. She cursed and kicked at her attacker. Her satisfaction at the resulting groan was short-lived.

The panel of a dark lantern opened in front of her face, momentarily blinding her. Her attacker shoved her to her knees and bound her hands. "We've been expecting you."

Chapter Twenty

Sydney struggled to work loose the knots in the leather cord binding her wrists behind her back. A blindfold covered her eyes. The stale odors of ale and hearth smoke led her to believe they'd taken her to a tavern, albeit an empty one. A door opened, followed by footsteps crossing the creaky floorboards.

"Here she is, like you wanted."

"You bloody fool. Don't you recognize her?"

The footsteps drew closer, and Sydney tensed. A hand brushed her forehead, pulling away the blindfold, and she jerked back. Blinking, she focused on the man staring down at her. At once she recognized him. He'd been the bartender at the tavern on the night of Edgar's arrest, the man who had hidden her and then said he'd give her to Schrammig if he ever saw her again.

The four years since their last encounter had aged him. His hair had thinned and turned gray, and his face held the same haunted expression she had often seen in Edgar.

"Get up, Sydney." He pulled her up and untied her wrists. Putting a firm hand on her shoulder, he guided her to a table near the bar. "She's Edgar's kid," he said to the man watching them from his stool.

"She's supposed to be dead," the other man said.

"I told you she wasn't dead. Anaria said she'd be here."

The realization of who he was jolted her. "You're Jimmy? This is the Black Dog?"

Jimmy nodded. He sat and motioned to his friend. "This here's Devon. Now take a seat and tell us why you're here."

She remained standing. Thin slivers of daylight slipped between the boarded-up windows. The sputtering candles along the bar failed to dispel the gloom and unease lingering in the air. "Why don't you start by telling me what the hell you're doing and where my friend is? I thought we were on the same side."

Devon leaned his hands on his knees. "Since when are you taking sides? You never helped us before."

His accusation had gnawed at her conscience for years. "I never helped the Guild, either. I couldn't help anyone as long as I had to struggle just to survive."

"I heard different. I heard you made a deal with the Guild so they'd leave you alone."

Sydney balled her fists and lunged toward him. "Lies. You don't know a damned thing about me."

Jimmy jumped to his feet and grabbed her arm, holding her back. "That's enough." He narrowed his eyes at Devon. The other man simply shrugged. Jimmy turned back to Sydney. "His brother disappeared about the same time we lost Edgar. He took it hard."

"How d'you think I felt after losing Edgar?" She yanked her arm from his grasp and sat on the edge of the chair. "The Guild's made my life a living hell."

Devon pulled a knife from his belt and began to clean his grimy fingernails.

"Arguing among ourselves isn't going to solve anything." Jimmy eased into the chair across from her, running a hand through his hair. "What concerns us, Sydney, is the stranger you've brought here. There's a reason the Guild's never discovered these sections of the tunnels."

Tendrils of apprehension climbed her spine. They didn't

trust her. "I've never told anyone about the tunnels."

"Who's your friend?"

She hesitated, suddenly unsure whether she should reveal Willem's identity. But Anaria trusted Jimmy, and her trust did not come lightly. Sydney wiped her perspiring palms on her knees and straightened in the chair, considering her words. "What would you say if I told you I've joined the supporters of Willem, the bastard prince? And they sent me to find out if he can rely on your help?"

Jimmy and Devon stared at her, eyes wide.

"Willem? The man who's challenging Pendolf's claim to the throne?"

Devon snorted. "A prince? Likely story. Why should we believe her?"

"Why would I lie?"

"I think she's telling the truth, Devon. This could be the chance we've been waiting for."

"This time we can defeat the Guild," she said with confidence. "My *friend* is Willem, and he's come here to ask for your help. Personally."

Jimmy blanched. "Willem? Go get him, Devon. Now. If you hurt him...."

Devon stared at them for a minute before shoving the knife into his belt and sliding off his stool. He stalked to a door behind the bar. "He's fine. We only roughed him up a bit."

"Get Bill while you're at it."

Sydney's stomach fluttered. Maybe Bill was Betty's husband. She hadn't expected to find him.

Jimmy got to his feet, grabbed a bundle from the corner of the bar, and set her things in front of her. "Willem, huh? Guess you really are picking up where Edgar left off. It's about time you did."

A quick glance accounted for her belongings. Her knife and the glass bead lay on top of her neck pouch, with the marble from Oryn's tower. She picked up the bead, shifting it from one hand to the other. "You don't seem surprised I'm alive."

He shrugged. "I've kept track of you as best I could. Hoped one day you'd come back to us."

"Why?"

Jimmy spoke so softly, she had to lean forward to hear him. "So help me, I made a promise to a friend. He made me promise that if anything happened to him, I'd look after his kid."

Sydney clutched the bead, her heart racing. Edgar had never mentioned Jimmy to her. The people he'd enlisted to watch over her had all failed. Could things have been different if he hadn't kept all of this information from her, if he'd somehow let her know she wasn't alone?

"Why did you tell me you'd give me to Schrammig if you ever saw me again?"

Jimmy gave her a blank look. "When did I say that?"

"That night...." She didn't need to explain which night; Jimmy's pained expression told her he remembered it as well as she did. "After Schrammig left. After he gave you money to tell him if you ever saw me."

He jerked back in his chair. "You believed me?"

"Why wouldn't I? I didn't know you. You just stood there and let them take Edgar away. Why wouldn't I believe you'd do the same to me?"

A long sigh escaped his lips, and he ran a hand across his face. "Of course I wouldn't. In one moment, I watched Schrammig destroy what we'd worked so hard to accomplish. We couldn't keep up the fight without Edgar. But Edgar made the choice himself. He would've done anything to protect you from Schrammig, even give up his life."

Hearing someone else speak those words wrenched her heart. She bit her lip, blinking back tears. "Damn him. He should've thought about himself instead of me."

"He cared more about you than himself. I understand now. My boy's about ten, and I haven't seen him in four years. We do whatever we can to keep our children safe."

Jimmy stood and paced. "When I met Edgar, you was about seven or eight. At first, I thought him daft to be challenging the Guild and trying to raise you. That's no life for a child." He coughed out a bitter laugh. "What sort of a life can any of us give our children? Edgar wasn't daft at all. You gave him hope for the future. That's why we believed him when he said we were fighting for a better life."

Warm tears slid down her cheeks. She should have appreciated Edgar when she'd had the chance.

Jimmy returned to his seat, and his body sagged. "I'm sorry I failed him. I should've looked after you, like I promised. But you disappeared. Anaria didn't even know where you went."

"I had to disappear. I was fifteen, dammit. And scared. Schrammig found Edgar. I thought I'd be next."

"And after he left?"

She looked away. "I was scared for a long time. I just tried to survive."

The door opened. She hastily wiped her eyes and set the marble on the pouch. At once, she realized the man named Bill had to be Betty's husband and the girls' father. Their eyes, their noses, even their cheekbones reflected in his features. She dreaded telling him of his wife's fate, but he deserved to hear the truth. She'd rather wait for Willem, so he could help soften the blow.

Bill approached them. "Devon said you wanted to see me about something important, but he wouldn't say what."

"Bill, this is Sydney. She's Edgar's—"

"Where did you get this?" Bill snatched the glass bead from the table.

"I got it from—"

"Did you steal it? Tell me where you got it!" He thrust the bead at her.

Sydney jumped to her feet and stepped back. "Your daughter gave it to me."

"Sara? Impossible. Tell me the truth! Where's my daughter? You stole it from her, didn't you?"

"I didn't steal anything," Sydney snapped. "Sara gave it to me. We saved her life. We saved your children from the Guild."

The blood drained from Bill's face. "The Guild?" His hand dropped to his side. "My girls.... Where are they?"

"They're fine." Sydney struggled for the right words. "Your wife...."

"Betty?" His voice made a strangled croak.

"The Guild arrested her."

"No." He sank into a chair and buried his face in his hands. His shoulders shook. In a muffled voice, he said, "I thought she'd be safer if I wasn't there."

"I'm sorry, Bill," Jimmy said.

Sydney explained the request from Aldric's steward, the money for Betty, and how they had taken the girls to safety, but Bill wasn't listening.

Bill raised his head to Jimmy. "We can't leave her there. She'll be hanged."

"Bill, there's nothing we can do. We can't get her out of the gaol. Just be thankful your children are safe."

"Thankful?" Bill stood, his fists clenching and unclenching. "Dammit, my wife's done nothing wrong. It's my fault they went after her, and now she'll pay for it with her life. You think I should be thankful?"

"We're all aware of the risks. Betty, too. She's a smart woman. She wouldn't want you to do anything rash for her sake. Think of your children. Do you want them to lose both their parents?"

Parents struggling to protect their children. Jimmy's promise to Edgar and the son he hadn't seen in several years. Countless others who had lost loved ones to the Guild—especially to Schrammig. Sydney fought against the anger churning inside her. A victory over the Guild couldn't take away the depth of their pain.

She took a step forward. "Betty asked us to take the girls. We promised them we'd find their father if we could."

"Who's 'we'?"

"Sydney's Edgar's kid. She came here with Prince Willem."

"Willem?" Bill glanced around the room. "He's here?"

Sydney nodded, wishing Willem stood beside her to offer words of encouragement.

Bill clapped Jimmy on the back, a hopeful smile spreading across his face. "This is good. Schrammig is no match for Willem's forces. This means Betty has a chance, a good chance." He handed Sydney his daughter's trinket. "Sara is particular about her things. You keep this for her. It's too dangerous for me to see them now, but they understand. Once this is over, we can all go home, like Edgar said we'd be able to do." He turned back to Jimmy. His words came fast, tumbling one after the other. "Did I tell you how Willem's forces defeated an enemy twice their size? Without losing a single man?"

Sydney winced at Bill's jumbled words. He paced back and forth, arms wrapped around himself. Not a good idea to tell him or Jimmy that Willem's closest force consisted of barely a hundred men holed up in Lord Aldric's keep, nearly a day's journey from Last Hope.

Jimmy stood, cutting off Bill's rambling. "Devon should've been back by now. Where the hell did he take Willem? You stay here, Bill. The last thing we need is for Devon to cause more trouble."

"I'll come," Sydney said.

"No. Wait here." He left through the door near the bar.

Knots spiraled in her stomach. Surely the delay meant trouble.

Bill sank into the chair, his brief burst of optimism gone. There wasn't much hope for his wife, and Sydney wasn't going to lie to him and pretend otherwise. She had no words of comfort to offer. After returning her knife to the sheath in her boot, she grasped the glass bead.

"You should keep this."

His chin jerked up. He shook his head sadly. "No, you give it back to her. My poor girls. My poor wife. I told Betty no harm would come to us here. I should have kept to my business and let the Guild keep to theirs."

"They would've arrested someone else's wife. Nothing will change if we don't stand up to the Guild."

"You're Edgar's child, all right. You sound just like him."

Edgar had often said similar things. Now she understood how powerful those words could be.

"The rest of us haven't been as successful as Edgar was. Jimmy's tried, but most people are too afraid. Your coming here and bringing Willem will give them hope again." Bill surveyed the room. "Willem brought his wizards with him, didn't he?"

Sydney choked back her surprise. "You expected wizards?"

A brief smile crossed Bill's face. "Willem's always supported them. Never hurts to have a little magic on your side, does it? Edgar often said we'd need them in the end, whether we liked the idea or not."

"Why would Edgar say that?"

"Surely he told you." Bill sat back in his chair, frowning. "Didn't he?"

"No, he didn't. There's a hell of a lot he didn't tell me."

"Oh. Perhaps I shouldn't have brought it up then."

"You've gotta tell me. How else will I find out the truth?" He hesitated, and she added softly, "Please. Tell me."

Bill rubbed the back of his neck. "I'd want someone to tell my children about their father, if the worst happened to me. I can never repay you for what you've done for my girls." He drew in a long breath and leaned closer. "Edgar's family had long advocated for magic and wizards, despite the edicts outlawing them."

"His family." Of course, he would have had family. Titles, land, wealth—all those things passed from one generation to the next. "Are any of them still alive?"

"Not likely. When the Guild became powerful enough, they started eliminating the nobles who posed a threat. They destroyed Edgar's family. He was the only one who escaped. I think for a long time he blamed the wizards for not acting to save those who had supported them."

Sydney recalled her anger toward Oryn when she realized he could have done something to save Edgar. Edgar's resentment must have run much deeper. "Then why did he change his mind? What made him think the wizards would help?"

Bill shrugged. "I'm not sure. He seemed certain they would help us fight the Guild, though. He worried that ordinary people, like Jimmy and Devon, wouldn't understand."

A movement in the shadows caught her eye. Bill's words faded. A shadowy figure of a man watched them, and though she could only see his outline, his eyes gleamed silver. Sydney dared not take her eyes from him, but she also feared he'd glimpse her staring at him. She sensed none of the menace she associated with Durok. In fact, she didn't feel any sort of power at all, good or evil. Rather, a sense of calm enveloped her. For a moment, the room around them disappeared, and she stood alone with the man and his bright silver eyes.

"Sydney." A hand touched her arm.

The man vanished, along with the serenity he'd brought her. The knots returned to her stomach.

"Are you all right?"

She started to motion to the spot where the strange man had been, but stopped herself. "You ever seen a wizard?"

"Not me. But I always wanted to meet one someday."

She kept her attention on the shadows. "Did Edgar ever say anything about the Tuatha? The faery folk?"

Bill drew in a sharp breath. "No, he didn't. You'd best not

think about them. From what I've heard, they're a dangerous lot."

Dangerous indeed. And somehow her fate was tied to them.

Chapter Twenty-One

"They should've been back by now."

Sydney paced the length of the bar, fingers drumming against her thigh. Her skin tingled, as if charged with an unseen energy. She glanced from the wax pooling around the bases of the candles to the shadowy corner where she had seen the silver-eyed man. He hadn't reappeared, but she couldn't shake the feeling that someone—*or something*—was watching them.

Bill had long since lapsed into silence. He seemed content to sit and wait for Jimmy's return.

"Something must be wrong." She rubbed her arms. The shadows loomed, menacing, as if fighting to leap from the walls and take on more substantial shapes.

"Jimmy said to wait for him. I'm sure there's no cause for worry." Bill's hesitant voice and creased forehead belied his confident words.

"Where's Willem? Did they tell you?"

"There aren't many places they would take him."

"Let's go find him. I can't stay here."

Bill didn't move. "Jimmy told us to wait. He'll be back."

"What if he doesn't come back?" Her voice grew shrill, her rising panic a reflection of her fear rather than concern for Willem. "What if they don't believe Willem's who he says is?"

"Of course they believe it. This is what we've been waiting for."

She had told Willem that people in Last Hope didn't have much use for kings or the nobility. "Devon doesn't think so."

"Devon's a hothead, but he listens to Jimmy. We all do. Even if we don't always agree...."

Sydney slapped the table. "We're wasting time. Willem needs your help to fight the Guild. Our help. If we don't work together, Schrammig will win."

"Willem isn't the only one we need," Bill said, rising to his feet. "We also need someone who can convince people that this is their fight, too. Someone like you."

Staring at the weariness etched into his face and the spark of hope in his eyes, Sydney wished Edgar could have showed the sort of faith in her that she felt from Bill. *If only he could see how much I've changed.*

"Let's go." Bill grabbed a lantern. In the empty tavern, the shadows fluttered. Sydney hurried after him, through the same door Jimmy had used.

They soon descended a narrow staircase. The air grew cooler, and the dampness and stone indicated they were entering the tunnels.

Not far from the staircase, the tunnel branched in two directions. Bill headed to the right. Faint, unearthly whispers echoed from the other tunnel. Peering into the darkness, Sydney glimpsed a shimmering glow farther ahead.

"Something's down there. A light."

Bill's brow furrowed. "I don't see anything. That's a dead end."

The whispers grew louder. "Don't you hear it?"

He didn't hear anything, and he didn't see any light. *I'm not daft.* People told of seeing strange things in the tunnels. Staring into the passage, a tremor swept through her. Follow the voices and the light, and she'd never come back.

"There's nothing down there." Bill put a hand on her back,

guiding her into the other passage. "That tunnel collapsed a long time ago."

Despite the calmness of his tone, a shadow crossed his face. "It's easy to get confused," he added. "It's not natural, being stuck underground like this. I try to avoid it, but sometimes there's no other place to hide." He forced a laugh. "People stay here long enough, they start to see all kinds of things."

Sydney stepped away from him. "What kinds of things?"

"Nothing." He shook his head. "Just crazy talk."

"Is it magic they see?"

Bill shuddered. "If it is, it's dangerous magic. That's what Edgar said."

Edgar's knowledge of wizards and magic was much greater than she had suspected. Maybe he'd believed the Tuatha were dangerous. She needed answers to her questions. She worried that only the Tuatha themselves could provide those answers.

The murmurs of voices reverberated when they turned a corner. Human voices.

"That's Jimmy." Bill quickened his pace.

Other passageways branched from the main corridor. The soft glow of lamplight illuminated the entrance of one of them.

"Jimmy?" Bill called.

"In here."

Bill allowed Sydney to enter first. The narrow corridor opened into a room, carved from the same smooth rock as the tunnels.

Devon stood in the entrance, blocking her path. "What're you doing here?"

"Where the hell is Willem?"

"Sydney?"

Relief flooded through her at the sound of Willem's voice. She pushed past Devon, who made no move to stop her. Willem and Jimmy rose from their seats on wooden crates on the floor. Willem's expression mirrored her relief. Moving closer, she was alarmed by the cut above his left eye and an ugly bruise along his jaw.

"Are you all right?" she asked.

He gingerly touched his jaw. "It probably looks worse than it feels. I was more concerned about you."

Sydney whirled on Jimmy. "I told you who he was. Why'd you do this to him?"

"We got a report of someone in the tunnels nearby." Devon said. "Might be the Guild. How else would they know where we are? Someone told them."

"I told you, it wasn't us," she insisted, returning his stare. Schrammig's soldiers couldn't have tracked them without revealing themselves. She doubted they'd have found the secret entrance in the Silver Eagle if they searched the tavern.

"That's enough, both of you." Jimmy stepped between Sydney and Devon.

"She told you the truth." Bill approached Willem and dropped to one knee. "My liege. I'd recognize you anywhere. It is an honor to finally meet you."

Jimmy and Devon watched silently. Jimmy's eyes widened, but the scowl didn't leave Devon's face.

Willem put a hand on Bill's shoulder. "Please, get up. I am not yet your king." Bill stood, and Willem gave him a smile. "You must be Bill."

Bill bowed his head. "I saw you once before, many years ago. It was at a banquet in Lord Stephan's honor."

"Lord Stephan never passed up an opportunity for a feast." Willem said with a chuckle. "I can't tell you how many banquets I attended while I was a part of his household. Have we ever met, Bill?"

"We were never formally introduced. It was a long time ago. You weren't much more than a lad then. Even so, all the nobles had really come to see you, the boy who would one day be king and rid us of the Guild. It was a moment I never forgot. Neither did anyone else who was there." He paused, and added, "I can see your father in you. I only met him a few times, but anyone who had seen him would pick up the resemblance."

Willem's face hardened. "I might resemble him, but we couldn't be more different. He was nothing more than a greedy tyrant."

Bill lowered his head. "I meant no disrespect. You are the king we've been waiting for. Sydney told me what you did for my girls. I am in your debt."

Willem removed his gold signet ring from the pouch around his neck. "If there are still doubts, perhaps this will convince you."

He held out the ring to Jimmy, who peered at it but seemed loath to touch it. The ring was probably worth more money than any of Last Hope's inhabitants had ever seen.

"That's the king's seal," Bill said. "Remember the notice we saw in the square last month? It bore this very seal upon it."

"My mother took it from the king years ago as proof of my parentage."

"Then it's true." Jimmy's tone was hushed, and he bowed his head to Willem. "You're really the heir to the throne. Forgive us for your ill treatment, but you must realize how cautious we've become."

Willem returned the ring to the pouch. "I'm sure I would have done the same thing if I'd been in your place. But we have more important concerns. Now, while there's still time, I need your supporters firmly behind me so we can defeat the Guild here. Let's discuss what you can offer us."

Sydney paced, examining the stacks of crates and barrels, while Jimmy and Bill dragged more empty crates into the room. Smells of tallow, leather, and salted meat permeated the room. The wooden containers threw oddly shaped shadows across the walls in the flickering lamplight.

She studied the shadowy recesses to reassure herself the silver-eyed man hadn't followed them. She needed to tell Willem about him privately, to warn him. The strange man might be a Tuatha.

"What's so important about Last Hope?" Jimmy asked once they seated themselves on the crates. "No one has ever cared about this place before."

Willem glanced at each of them before speaking. "A victory over the Guild here will ignite my fight throughout the kingdom. It's not just a military victory. I want the people of Thanumor on my side. By fighting for me, you will also be fighting to reclaim your lives from the Guild."

"The king's never done anything for us before." Devon had declined to sit, and instead leaned his lanky frame against one of the barrels, arms folded across his chest. "No one cares what happens to people like us."

Sydney understood why Devon felt the way he did. Now the test would be whether Willem could convince someone like Devon that he'd act in the people's best interests.

"I understand how you feel—"

"No, you don't." Devon took a step forward "How the hell can you understand me? You can dress like one of us, but that doesn't change who you are." He turned to Bill, who shifted uncomfortably on his crate. "When all this is over, we'll still be here in this hellhole and you'll be gone. So don't pretend to understand who we are. You'll never be one of us."

Willem glanced at Sydney for a moment.

"No, we aren't the same, Devon," he said. "There will always be some with privileges and others without. I cannot change that. But I can tell you that I'm fighting for a better life for all of us, nobles and commoners. Those who rule, whether they are kings or nobles, bear a responsibility to their people. The king who sits in his castle while his people starve, while honest men steal to feed their families and their wives and daughters are forced to sell their bodies on the street, is no ruler. He is a tyrant. We need no more of those. Fight for me, and I will pledge my life to serving you as your king."

"You expect us to risk our lives for you?"

"We all face the same risks. Schrammig wants me dead. His soldiers are hunting for me."

"Schrammig has everyone running scared," Jimmy said, shaking his head. "Us included. People who stand up to Schrammig end up dead."

"He hasn't scared everyone," Willem said. "Lord Aldric is prepared to defend his lands. As we speak, my men are on their way to support him."

"What about Schrammig's army? How d'you plan to handle that?"

"What do you know about his army? How did you get this information?"

Jimmy and Devon exchanged a glance. "We have a contact in the Guild," Jimmy finally said. "Before Schrammig arrived, Celena told us the Guild's forces were moving in this direction. She figured they'd be here in less than a week."

"You're sure of this?"

"She's always given us reliable information."

"How large a force does Schrammig have? It would be useful to compare her information with my own intelligence. It would also be helpful to know what route they're taking. That was the one thing we couldn't plan for."

"We'd hoped to get more specifics, but she's one of the Guild's top officials here. Since Schrammig arrived, we've had no contact with her."

"The Guild has more men and resources than we do at this time, so any inside information you can obtain is vital. However, we do have one advantage." Willem paused, as if considering his words. "We have wizards on our side."

Devon drew in a sharp breath, and Jimmy's eyes widened. Only Bill didn't seem surprised by Willem's revelation. Sydney wondered if Willem also planned to tell them about Durok and his support of Schrammig.

"I thought they were all long dead," Jimmy said in a hushed tone.

"A few still exist, and they have pledged their support to me."

Sydney caught herself before she questioned him. *A few wizards? More than two?* She knew only of Vadnae and Oryn. Willem was stretching the truth, unless there was something he hadn't told her. She didn't think he should count the Tuatha as being on his side, at least not yet.

"You trust them?" Devon scoffed. "Magic was outlawed for a good reason. Wizards just want to rule the rest of us. Next thing, they'll be taking over the kingdom."

"Have you any firsthand knowledge of wizards, Devon?" Devon didn't reply, and Willem continued, "If you did, you would understand why I want them on my side. They've helped us win battles in the past; they will help us again. It's true, some wizards sought power above all else, just as some men desired the same thing. I think you'd find most wizards simply want to live their lives and not be persecuted."

"That's all we want, too," Devon said, his face taut. "We don't need a bloody lord telling us what to do. Aldric knows nothing of Last Hope. He'll just pick up where the Guild left off. Why should we help you if that's all we've got to look forward to?"

"I assure you Aldric will treat his subjects fairly."

"Devon's right," Jimmy said. "Aldric's taxes were higher than the Guild's. Why should we go back to his rule? You said yourself we don't need any more tyrants."

"Aldric is your lord and that fact is not up for discussion," Willem said, his voice rising in anger. "He's hardly a tyrant." Then he paused to collect himself. "I'm not offering to do away with the nobility simply because it's inconvenient for you. But perhaps there are other solutions. Have you any suggestions?"

"You want to know what we think?" At Willem's nod, Jimmy rubbed his chin thoughtfully. "What if we rule ourselves, here in Last Hope? Let the town answer to the king alone."

"Then who speaks for the people of Last Hope?" asked Bill. "You and Devon?"

"We know the people a lot better than you do," Devon retorted. "Besides, you said you weren't staying here, remember? You've got a title to reclaim."

"Enough," Jimmy cut them off. "Shut up, Devon, unless you've got something useful to say." To Willem, he said, "I don't speak for no one but myself, but why can't we decide our fate? Give the people control over their lives, and you really give them something to fight for."

A dangerous choice, Sydney thought. The five of them in this room couldn't even come to an agreement.

"I think we're jumping ahead of ourselves, Jimmy. First we free Last Hope from the Guild. Then we can discuss what should be done next. I give you my pledge that the townsfolk will be involved in those discussions."

"That's not good enough," Devon said.

"I have nothing to offer you right now except my word."

"Then write it down," Jimmy suggested. "Write down your pledge to Last Hope so we have a record of it."

An amused smile crossed Willem's face. "Very well. Have you any writing instruments?"

In one of the crates, Jimmy found a quill pen, an inkwell, and a scrap of parchment. After Willem wrote a few lines, he held the parchment out to Jimmy. "Shall I read it to you?"

"I can read it myself," Jimmy said, a note of pride in his voice. He took the parchment and squinted at it a moment. "It says 'I, Willem, King of Thanumor, do hereby pledge to grant the town of Last Hope a charter.' And he's signed it."

Sydney moved closer for a better look at the neat lettering and sprawling signature beneath it.

Jimmy then procured a bit of wax, and Willem sealed the note with his ring. "Keep it safe," he told Jimmy as he handed it to him. Jimmy carefully tucked it into his shirt, and then

Willem held out his hand. "My word is good. I swear to you I will protect the people of Last Hope. I won't let the town fall under the rule of any who would exploit her people, noblemen or commoner."

"Thank you," Jimmy said, clasping his hand. "Devon?"

"What do you want us to do?" Devon asked as he also took Willem's outstretched hand.

"I want you to tell people to prepare themselves for the fight to come, to be ready when we send word. Tell them to send their families to the abbey, where they'll be protected. You're no match for Schrammig's soldiers, so we will wait until my reinforcements arrive before making our move."

"Celena has said half the Guild officials are loyal to her," mused Jimmy. "If she could turn the Guild itself against Schrammig...." He shook his head. "We can't contact her safely."

In the pause the followed, Sydney felt Devon's gaze on her. "I'd wager Sydney has some friends in the Guild."

Her jaw clenched. "I don't."

However, one person with contacts in the Guild came immediately to mind. Zared. Doubtful he was acquainted with someone as powerful as Celena. But he'd hinted he had contacts who could help protect her from Schrammig. Clearly he had some useful knowledge.

She hesitated, and then said, "But I know someone who's got connections in the Guild."

"You expect us to trust your friends?"

She looked from Devon to Jimmy. "I hope you'll trust me."

Jimmy studied her, and she felt as though he were dissecting her with his eyes. Finally, he nodded. "I trust you, Sydney. If anyone here has a problem with that, tell me now."

Devon shrugged. "You're in charge. If you want to rely on her friends—"

Footsteps pounded in the corridor.

A man burst into the room. Gasping, he paused to catch his

breath. "Jimmy, they found soldiers in the tunnels."

Everyone stood at once. "How many? Where are they?"

"Couldn't tell how many. They're far enough away, but they're headed in our direction."

Devon threw an accusing glance at Sydney. "Someone followed you."

"Shut up, Devon. Or you'll stay here to wait for them." Devon paled. Jimmy nodded to Bill. "Bill, get them out of here. We can't risk Schrammig discovering them. Or us."

"What about you?" Willem asked.

"We'll stop them from getting any closer. We'll do what we can, Willem. You have my word. We won't let Schrammig win this time."

Sydney checked the knife in her boot. She hurried after Bill and Willem, hoping Willem's promises could generate the level of trust necessary to unite the people and win. And that he'd keep those promises once he became king.

Chapter Twenty-Two

Bill's lantern cast a feeble glow in the dimly lit tunnel. The air felt heavier here, the darkness more oppressive. The maze of corridors curved in all directions. After a while, Sydney stopped trying to figure out whether these tunnels, of which she had no knowledge, connected with the familiar ones. Bill kept glancing over his shoulder, his gaze pausing on Sydney and Willem and then the darkness behind them. She wondered if the urgency in his furtive movements was more than a desire to avoid Schrammig's soldiers. She sensed other sinister things lurking within these passages.

Only once did Bill hesitate. They stood at an intersection, where the corridors branched out like the spokes of a wheel. Sydney's attention was drawn to one of them, from whose gloomy depths the same unearthly voices she'd noted earlier swirled toward her, drifting on a cool breeze.

"You hear them, don't you?" Willem moved to her side, speaking softly.

For an instant, his blue eyes flashed in the lantern light, a reminder of the strange silver-eyed man. The light shifted, and he was simply Willem once more.

"I heard them earlier," she said. "In the tavern, I saw a strange man in the shadows. I think he's...." She hesitated, reluctant to speak the words aloud. "He may be a Tuatha."

Willem turned to the passage from which the voices had

come. "Perhaps he is. They're here, Sydney. It's only a matter of time before we find them."

What do we do then?

Bill had continued on to an adjoining passage and called to them to hurry. She exchanged a glance with Willem, and in unspoken agreement, they said nothing to Bill of the strange whispery voices.

They finally arrived at a section of the tunnels Sydney recognized. When they rounded a bend, she spotted the familiar notches on the wall. It took but a moment to place this tunnel in her mental map of the underground passages.

"You can find your way now, Sydney?" At her nod, Bill said, "There's another meeting place nearby. You should be safe there."

"Thanks, but our friends are expecting us."

"Schrammig's soldiers will be searching for you."

"We'll be fine. They can't track us down here."

"Bill, we appreciate what you've done for us," Willem said. "Jimmy needs your help more than we do."

"Of course." Bill quickly masked a frown. "We have a great deal of work to do. I just assumed you'd be helping us."

"We are. However, other tasks must be accomplished first."

"If you plan to contact Celena—"

"It's best not to speak of our plans," Willem cautioned him.

"Of course. I don't want to jeopardize your actions. Whatever you do, stay away from the Black Dog. It's not safe any more. Should you need refuge, there are places you can go, people who often help us when they can."

He rattled off several names and addresses, and a street located in the merchant district. Sydney carefully committed them to memory.

Willem put a hand on his shoulder. "Thank you, Bill. When I am king, I will restore your lands and title. I give you my word."

"I am your servant, my liege. All I want is to provide for my family. Tell my girls...." His voice broke, and he drew in a long breath. "Tell them I'll come for them when I can."

"They're at the abbey. The monks will look after them," Sydney said. She hoped Anaria had delivered the girls safely and stayed there herself.

Bill wiped a hand across his eyes. "I won't give up on Betty, either."

Willem squeezed his shoulder. "We'll do whatever we can to find her."

Bill lowered his head in response, and Sydney recognized his resignation. She had seen a similar expression on Anaria's face during their first conversation after Edgar had been arrested. At least Anaria had prepared herself for Edgar's death long before it occurred. Sydney doubted Bill had ever expected his wife would face such a fate.

"You can count on us," Bill said, standing a little taller.

Willem smiled, and they clasped hands. "I intend to."

Bill held out his hand to Sydney. "I'm glad you've come back to us. Edgar would've been proud of you."

She shook his hand, quickly blinking back the tears. "Thanks. I hope he would."

Handing the lantern to Sydney, Bill uncovered a hidden compartment like the one she had used earlier and lit a torch. He nodded to them and started back the way they had come. His footsteps grew fainter, and the light faded from view. Sydney moved down the corridor. "Let's hurry. This will take us toward the Prancing Pig."

They passed several exits to the town above. Sydney decided they would be safer underground. Here they had more places to hide.

"Have you ever seen the Tuatha here before?" Willem asked in a low voice.

She shook her head. "I'd never thought much of them at all until I met Oryn. I'd heard of them in tales mostly. I didn't think magic still existed, either."

"Didn't Edgar tell you of his dealings with the wizards?"

"Edgar never told me anything about his life before he came here." She immediately regretted her harsh tone and added, more softly, "Bill told me more than Edgar ever did."

"I assumed you were aware of his past."

"He probably had his reasons for not telling me." Reasons she'd never understand. "I guess he wanted to forget his past. Sounds like he didn't want anything more to do with wizards."

"By coming to Last Hope, Edgar became more involved in opposing the Guild than he might have been elsewhere in the kingdom. You can't hide from your destiny. Fate catches up with you."

Sydney didn't want to believe an outside force had controlled Edgar's life or hers. Willem and Vadnae appeared to think otherwise.

"I believe things happen for a reason," Willem continued. "There's a reason we're here in Last Hope. This is a unique place. People here are different from the rest of the kingdom. More independent. Even so, I never expected Jimmy would suggest the town rule itself."

"Why not? You can't expect a nobleman who's never lived here to understand us and know what's best for us."

"Those are dangerous words, Sydney. The Guild's supporters have used similar words to turn people against the nobility. I'm going to be king. I'm not planning to dismantle the structure of our society. The people can't rule themselves. Asking someone like Aldric to fight for me and then telling him he has to give up a portion of his lands will set a dangerous precedent." He shook his head with a sigh. "Still, I'll keep my word to Jimmy and the people of Last Hope. There must be a way to balance the needs of both the commoners and the nobility. I will make it my goal to find a solution and ensure that the people are cared for."

Convincing the other lords to consider the welfare of the people under their rule would be a daunting task. Even for

Willem.

"The friend you spoke of who knows people in the Guild," Willem suddenly said. "It's Zared, isn't it?"

She could have lied. But she wanted to be honest with him. He had been honest and open with her concerning a number of things she had never expected to discuss with the future king. She longed to maintain their familiarity. So she simply nodded.

His face tightened, and he swore under his breath. "It's a big risk. It's not worth it."

The lantern light sent shadows dancing across the smooth stone walls. "Ain't it worth it? Celena's information is important. That's all there is to it. I can handle Zared." At the quick shake of his head, she added, "You talk about trust. Trust me on this."

"Zared concerns me. Do you honestly think you can trust him? If anyone were to betray Celena's role to Schrammig, she'd be hanged and we would lose a valuable ally."

"She's not much of an ally if we can't contact her."

"Jimmy will find a way."

Jimmy would have his hands full convincing people to work together to fight the Guild, especially if others felt as Devon did.

"What if he can't?"

Willem sighed and adjusted the brim of his hat. "Just don't let whatever you feel for Zared cloud your judgment. Don't compromise yourself."

Willem's words were the same ones she had been telling herself. She hoped the next time she and Zared met, she'd keep her emotions under control.

They halted at an intersection. Sydney nodded toward the correct path and continued walking, but stopped when she didn't hear Willem behind her. He stood staring at another passage she didn't remember seeing.

"Sydney, come look at this."

Twenty feet ahead, a soft glow illuminated the passage. The light emanated from stones spaced evenly along the tunnel walls.

"Magic." She could think of no other explanation for the strange light. Standing together in awe, they heard whispers echo once more, louder this time, coming from within the tunnel. The elusive tones ebbed and flowed, in the pattern of words and phrases. None of them made any sense.

"I've seen this place before," he said.

"That ain't possible. We haven't been this way before."

"I've seen this tunnel in a dream." Willem stepped forward and put a hand on the wall, as if to reassure himself it was real.

"How can you dream of a place you've never seen?"

"Sometimes I dream things, and later they prove to be true. I dreamed about this tunnel, the light, the sounds." His brow creased. "Vadnae said the gateway to the realm of the Tuatha is within the tunnels. Maybe this is it."

Her legs trembled. Like the tunnel Bill had led her away from, the certainty they wouldn't be able to return if they entered sent shivers through her. "We should tell Vadnae and bring her back here. I can remember where the tunnel is."

"We can't go back. There was someone else in my dream." Willem turned to her. "Until now, I never realized who it was. Now I'm sure; it was you, Sydney. We must go in together."

She backed away. It was one thing for Willem to dream of a place he'd never been, but another thing entirely for him to dream about her. Before they'd even met. "That's daft, Willem. We ain't-we aren't wizards. What if the Tuatha are really as dangerous as people say? What if we don't come back? No point making you king if they trap you in the faery realm."

Willem reached for her hand. "Sydney. The message Oryn sent me said that I should trust you, that you would be the one to help me find the faery realm. This is something we're meant to do."

Before she could ask why Oryn would say such a thing, her neck pouch grew warm. She backed away from Willem and set the lantern on the ground. With shaking hands, she pulled the leather cord over her head and loosened the drawstring. The marble glowed, like the stones in the passage ahead of them. She shook it into her palm.

"What's that?"

"Picked it up in Oryn's tower." The glowing orb reflected the light from the lantern and the stones.

"It's magic, isn't it?"

The glow changed from a soft yellow to orange to red—and then to black. Suddenly Durok's power assailed her. His hatred and malice chilled her to the core. Blackness engulfed her.

Two gleaming eyes gazed out of the void. They probed her innermost thoughts, her fears, her desires. She sought to cry out, but no sound escaped her lips.

"Sydney!"

Willem's voice sounded faint. Unseen hands clawed at her. Blindly, she struck back. Her mind reeled, and she relived every painful moment in her life, every loss, every hurt, every betrayal. Unbearable pain. No way to fight back.

"You are strong, Sydney," a voice murmured. "Don't let him defeat you."

The voice reminded her of Edgar, bringing with it memories, not of Edgar on the scaffold, but of him tucking her into bed when she was a child and telling her he'd keep her safe. "You're safe now, Sydney. Give me your hand and you'll be free of him."

She let him take her hand. His fingers pried open her fist. The darkness lifted.

"Sydney, can you hear me?"

She forced her eyes open. Willem's stricken face hovered

above her. With a steady arm around her, he helped her sit. Her heart thudded in her chest. She made an effort to stand, but the ground spun and pain stabbed behind her eyes.

"Easy." Willem's arm rested on her waist. "Just sit here for a minute."

"The marble...."

He held up her neck pouch. "Safely put away. I took the marble from you without being affected myself."

Her hand ached. Opening her fist, she gasped. The middle of her palm was red and blistered.

"Let me see."

"It's all right." She clutched her hand to her chest.

"Here, let me help. Please." He pulled his handkerchief from his pocket. Gently, he took her hand and wrapped the soft fabric around her palm. "We'll deal with your wound later, when someone can tend to it properly. Vadnae or one of the monks, perhaps. We're lucky you weren't more seriously hurt."

"What happened?"

"I was hoping you could tell me."

He still held her hand. The lantern light softened his expression, and for an instant she glimpsed something more than compassion.

Then the image of the probing eyes flashed before her. Shuddering, she shifted away from Willem and gulped a deep breath. "It was Durok. He saw me. We have to get away from here." She struggled to get to her feet. Willem helped her up, steadying her, his strong hands gripping her waist.

"We can't go back the way we came." He inclined his head to the wall blocking the end of the tunnel. "It closed up when you touched the marble."

Sydney stumbled forward and ran her fingers over the wall. "There's gotta be a way out." She started when Willem touched her arm.

"There is a way." He put his hands on her shoulders and turned her to face the tunnel with the glowing stones. "We can keep moving forward. This is our path, I'm sure of it. Together we'll face whatever comes."

His mouth set in a determined line. So many people depended on them to succeed. She made a fist, wincing at the pain. She wasn't going to let Durok get the best of her. Willem wasn't giving up, and neither was she.

Reaching up, she brushed her thumb across his cheek. He drew in an uneven breath, and she smiled shyly. "Let's go in."

Chapter Twenty-Three

The glowing stones, no larger than Sydney's palm, illuminated their path, emitting an amber-tinged light. She caught glimpses of peculiar shadows and couldn't be sure whether they were shadows of substantial things or something ethereal. The whispered voices came and went, sometimes louder, sometimes so faint they seemed but a memory deep within her soul.

A cloyingly sweet, floral bouquet wafted on a light breeze. Sydney's stomach turned, and her thrumming pulse warned of danger.

Willem quickened his pace. "This is it. I'm certain. Don't you feel it? We're so close."

The memories Durok had dredged from the depths of her mind lingered near the surface, blocking Willem's words. More painful than any physical wound, the emotions she'd long suppressed gripped her. She blinked, and instead of in the tunnel found herself back in Zared's tiny, filthy room, begging him for any news of Edgar.

"They're gonna hang him," Zared finally told her. "Tomorrow. In the square."

Zared's arms wrapped around her waist. A child wailed in the street below. Her tears wouldn't come. His embrace couldn't fill her emptiness.

"Sydney?"

Willem's voice shattered the memory, jerking her back to the present. Recalling the comfort she'd felt at his touch, she realized how easy it would be to succumb to the unspoken feelings between them. For a moment, she wished they had met under different circumstances, that he was just a man and not a king.

She stepped away from his outstretched hand, overwhelmed by the intensity of her emotions. "I'll be fine."

Willem moved to the shadows between the glowing stones, and his eyes flashed in the light. His image appeared to fade, as if he were becoming one of the shadows himself. Like the silver-eyed man.

"Willem?"

He stepped forward. "What is it?"

Hesitantly, she touched his arm to reassure herself he was really there. "Nothing. Thought I saw something odd." She continued walking, ignoring his puzzled expression. "What if Durok comes after us? Did your dream tell you how we're supposed to get out of here?"

"Well, no," he admitted. "I've had a few such dreams, but I never see the outcome. Somehow they relate to important events in my life. I still think we're safer here than we were in the other tunnels."

"Why?" The blocked tunnel would deter Schrammig's soldiers, but she wasn't confident a mere wall could stop Durok.

"The Tuatha are protecting us. I can feel it."

She waved a hand at the tunnel. "I don't feel any safer here. I've seen things—shadows of things. You can hear those voices as well as I can. And just now...." She wondered if he'd think Durok was driving her mad.

"What is it? Tell me, Sydney."

"You started to look like one of the shadows."

He scanned the tunnel around them. "Are you sure? I didn't feel anything."

She attempted to describe his resemblance to the silver-eyed man. Her concern sounded foolish when she voiced it aloud. Of course, Willem wasn't a shade. He was as real as she was. But Sydney wasn't sure of anything any more. "What the hell does all this mean?"

The ground shifted. Willem disappeared. A gray haze enveloped her, and within it, shadowy figures approached her, arms outstretched.

"Sydney!"

The shadows drew closer, surrounding her in an icy embrace. Suddenly she couldn't move. Her fingers and toes became numb. Darkness crept across her mind, blotting out all thoughts and feelings, except the horror engulfing her. *I can't let them defeat me.* She shouted the words into the gray void. Her voice came out as a whisper.

"Edgar," she cried, calling on the memories the shadows couldn't overtake. "Help me, Edgar."

She kept calling Edgar's name. His name was the only word retaining any meaning in the fog overtaking her mind. A brilliant light flared. The shadows shrank from it. The light grew, driving away the haze and darkness. The icy fingers released her, and Sydney was left shaken, but free.

A hand gripped hers, and she held tight. "Willem?"

He squeezed her hand. His face came into focus, his eyes concentrating with their searing intensity, his strong jaw clenched in concern. The ground beneath her feet became firm, the tunnel walls solid. The glowing stones bathed her with their light. She shivered, rubbing her arms. Warmth began to return.

"You almost became one of them," he whispered. "You started to fade before my eyes."

"It was the shadows. You helped bring me back."

He was staring at something behind her. "It wasn't me. It was him."

The hair prickled on the back of her neck. She turned.

Standing behind her, only feet away, was the silver-eyed man.

At first glance, the tall, slender figure's entire appearance was gray, from his hair to his nearly translucent skin, to his clothes. Yet, unlike the shadows, which had absorbed the light, he reflected it. His eyes flashed silver, and his hair was both golden and copper. Even the fibers in his otherwise simple clothes contained a multitude of colors.

"You are one of the faery folk? The Tuatha?" Willem asked him.

"Some call us that. You are not the first to venture where you do not belong, and I doubt you will be the last." His voice had a lilting, musical quality. "Why did you take such a path?"

"We had no choice," Willem said.

The silver-eyed man smiled. "There are always choices, your highness," he said with a bow. "Nothing is foretold that cannot be changed, and often we don't comprehend the truth until we see it. You would do well to remember such things." He turned back the way they had come. "Quickly now. We shouldn't tarry here."

He took one step and then whirled around and approached Sydney. She sensed the power emanating from him. More powerful than any of the wizards she had encountered, including Durok, his was a different sort of power. It was part of him, and it also extended beyond him. Seeing him calmed her, easing her apprehension, just as when she had glimpsed him in the tavern.

He held out his hand. "Give me your magic, since you do not seem capable of using it yourself."

She stared at him in surprise. He gestured to her pouch. "It ain't my magic," she said, defensive at his pronouncement. She handed him the pouch. "I don't know how to use it. I don't even know what it's supposed to do."

He pulled out the marble. His lips pressed together in concentration. "Your wizard means well, but there is much she does not yet understand. She must learn quickly if she is to defeat her enemy."

He closed his hand around the marble, tossed it into the air, and caught it in one swift motion. "Those who misuse our gifts must be taught a lesson." Returning the marble to the pouch, he held it out to Sydney. "You may keep this now."

Sydney put the pouch around her neck. "You mean Durok can't use it against me any more?"

"Not any longer. His powers are adequate, but my manner of enchantment is beyond his understanding. Now follow me. You may not be able to return if you linger in the borderlands. I won't go in to fetch you twice."

"Let's do as he says," Willem murmured.

Willem's initial awe was turning to puzzlement, as was hers. She wasn't sure what to make of the Tuatha. They hurried to match their guide's pace.

The silver-eyed man hummed a little tune, sometimes skipping ahead and waiting for them to catch up.

She leaned close to Willem. "Are they always like this?"

He shrugged. "I couldn't say. I've never met them before, either."

Sydney had pictured the Tuatha being more dignified, in keeping with their power. This one appeared to possess the attitude and attention span of a child. Several times, he became distracted by a sound they couldn't hear or an unusual pattern on the tunnel wall.

"Don't rush me," he said while they waited, patiently, for him to return to the task at hand.

Finally, he stopped in front of an opening that neither of them had noticed when they'd passed that way earlier. "This is where you were meant to go, your highness."

"We didn't see this before."

Willem's words held an uncharacteristic note of doubt. He had been so certain of his dream and the path they were to take. Perhaps the shadows had deceived them.

"You are correct." The silver-eyed man answered her

thoughts. "The Shadow Folk use the illusion of safety to lure their victims. Very effective, as you nearly discovered."

Sydney noticed Willem's frown. He'd insisted they were safe within this passage.

Willem gestured toward the opening. "Will this take us into your realm?"

"It will. We have been expecting you. It has been many years since one of your kings has been an honored guest." Motioning to Sydney, he added, "However, you must enter alone."

"You want him to go in there by himself?"

"This time there are no other choices. Follow him, and you will suffer consequences."

Willem moved closer to her. "What consequences?"

"Those who enter our realm uninvited are punished. That punishment is often imprisonment. Sometimes death." He inclined his head toward Willem. "Are you coming? We haven't much time."

"Give us a moment." Willem beckoned Sydney farther down the corridor, although she was certain the silver-eyed man could hear their every word.

"Your king will be quite safe with us," he called. "You need not worry about him. Also, he may return whenever he wishes."

"You believe him?" Sydney asked.

"I must believe him. This is what I came here to do, so I'm asking you not to follow me. Go meet the others. I'll return as soon as I can."

She stiffened. "I can't leave you here. I gave Gregor my word. I gave them all my word you'd be safe."

When he spoke, the authority returned to his voice. "I will be safe. You can leave me, and you will. This is my decision. That's all there is to it."

"What if you don't come back?" She relaxed her stance, hoping her eyes held a stronger plea than her words. "We need you, Willem. We can't win without you."

"I'll be back. Go finish what Edgar started. Help the people of Last Hope challenge Schrammig."

Finish what Edgar started. She breathed in slowly and managed a brief nod. "I'll do my part."

Willem bent his head toward her and touched her cheek.

On impulse, she leaned close and kissed him, barely brushing her lips to his and pulling away before he could respond.

He held her gaze for a long moment. Her cheeks flamed. What was she thinking? Lusting after the future king was definitely not part of the mission. Nor were her other feelings, which went far beyond lust.

"Sydney." He took her hand and squeezed it. "I'll come back. That's a promise." He straightened his shoulders and faced the Tuatha. "I'm ready now."

The silver-eyed man gestured to the tunnel. A bright light filled the opening. He gave Willem a flourishing bow. "The Tuatha welcome you."

Willem stepped into the light without a backward glance.

The silver-eyed man stared at Sydney. She cast her eyes downward, realizing he'd seen her impulsive kiss.

"I assure you, we will let no harm come to him while he is within our realm. You'll see him again soon. Now you travel your own path, and like your king, you must travel it alone. But there are some dangers you cannot face without aid. The fate of our realm is tied to yours. We won't let either be destroyed. When you need me, you can call upon me."

A dozen questions flooded her mind, and she hadn't the courage to ask any of them. "How can I call on you? I don't even know your name."

His eyes flashed in the light. He uttered several words she couldn't understand. "Names can be powerful, Sydney, if they are used properly. Mine will be revealed when your need is greatest. Until then, farewell."

He stepped into the opening. Another bright light flashed, this one blinding. Sydney covered her eyes. When she removed her hands, the opening had disappeared, along with the glowing stones. The lantern light cast unnatural shadows. She was alone.

Chapter Twenty-Four

Rounding a corner, Sydney stopped mid-stride when she spotted a faint light ahead. She shifted the lantern to her left hand, using her right hand to pull the knife from her boot. As she curled her injured palm around the hilt, she winced. Her limited familiarity with this section of the tunnels made her reluctant to backtrack to find another route, if one even existed.

She crept ahead. The tunnel was silent, save for her muffled footsteps. Glancing over her shoulder, she started at the shadows moving on the walls behind her. The lantern flickered, and a cool, stale breeze blew across her face. She shivered. The silver-eyed man had called them the Shadow Folk. The breeze died as quickly as it had come, and the lantern flared back to full strength. The shadows were simply shadows once more. She let out a shaky breath and continued.

The shuffle of footsteps and a single voice echoed. Sydney flattened herself against the wall, gripping the blade in one hand and the lantern in the other.

The footsteps drew nearer, and a familiar voice called, "Who's there?"

She took a cautious step forward.

"Sydney, are you there?"

"Francis." She sheathed her knife and hurried to him. "It's me, Brother Francis."

"Sydney." The brown-robed monk clasped her hand in his. The subtle aroma of incense on his robe was oddly comforting after the cloying scent in the strange tunnel. "We've been looking for you." He stepped to the side, squinting into the dark passage behind her. "Where's Prince Willem?"

"He's—" Sydney stopped herself. "He's safe, he just ain't here."

"Not here? Then how can he be safe? Schrammig's soldiers are everywhere."

"I've seen the soldiers. Believe me, Willem's probably safer than the rest of us. Where's Gregor?"

Francis studied her, as if trying to determine her truthfulness. He bowed his head. "I'm sorry. It's not my place to ask you such questions. I suppose we are all anxious, considering the day's events."

"What else happened?"

He folded his hands within his robe. "Father Abbot wasn't the only one arrested today. The Guild has been tracking down anyone suspected of helping the resistance. People are scared. They're afraid for their families and their livelihoods. Some are taking refuge in the church."

"Did any children come to the church? Three girls together?"

"More children than I could keep track of, I'm afraid. We're doing our best to care for all of them. As a result of Father Abbot's arrest and Brother Erik's persuasiveness, most of the other monks have vowed to do what they can to deter the Guild. We don't condone violence, but we can offer shelter to those in need, and, if necessary, we will defend ourselves and those under our protection. Schrammig or any agent of the Guild will find it difficult to enter our sanctuary now."

That piece of news surprised her. In spite of her earlier misgivings about seeking refuge and assistance from the church, Sydney now realized the monks were important allies. Once people had secured the safety of their children, they'd be more likely to fight. She touched the pouch, clutching the round bead. Betty's girls—and Anaria—had to be safe.

"The other monks agreed you could use the abbey as a refuge and plan your attack from there. Gregor and I came to meet you."

The light she had seen came from a room off the main passage. Francis put a hand on Sydney's shoulder when they stopped in the entrance. "Gregor, I've found her at last."

Gregor emerged, relief flooding his face at the sight of Sydney. "I'm so glad you've returned. But you're alone. Where's Willem?"

She rubbed the back of her neck. "It's a long story. Don't know for certain where he is now, but he's safe." She hoped the silver-eyed man would ensure Willem's safety and his return to Last Hope.

"Safe? Are you sure?"

"I'll tell you more when we get back to the abbey." She inclined her head slightly toward Francis, hoping Gregor would realize what she meant. "I'll explain all of it then. Willem is safe, I promise."

A frown replaced his expression of relief. "Very well, I'm eager to hear your explanation."

She doubted he believed her.

⸻

Francis opened a side door into the quiet corridors of the monk's dormitory. "I'll take you to one of the smaller common rooms. It should be empty at this late hour. Are you hungry, Sydney? Can I get you something from the kitchen?"

Her stomach contracted with hunger. She hadn't eaten since breakfast. "I'd like some food," she said.

He left them in a room much like the one where they had gathered that morning, saying he would send Vadnae and Erik to join them. Sydney sat across from Gregor at one of the long tables. She leaned her elbows on the wooden surface, pitted with age and use, resting her chin on her hands. Her limbs felt heavy, her muscles tight.

"You're hurt?"

She closed her other hand over Willem's handkerchief. "I'll be fine." She could handle the physical pain. The emotional pain—the fear and doubt and loneliness lurking in her mind—was much harder to face.

"We'll get through this together, Sydney." The lines on Gregor's weathered face reflected her weariness, yet he sat straight, radiating a sense of calm.

Gregor's confidence in Oryn, in Willem, and in their efforts against the Guild had continually boosted her spirits, despite the trials they'd faced along the way. She was certain they were doing the right thing. Whether they would all succeed, let alone survive, was not so clear.

The door swung open on rusty hinges, and Vadnae and Francis entered.

Francis set the tray he carried in front of Sydney, giving her an apologetic smile. "I hope this will be sufficient. It was all I could find."

Sydney breathed in the hearty aroma of the potato pie. "Just what I need, thanks."

"Please call for me if I can be of further service. Erik will be here shortly." Francis bowed and left the room.

Vadnae sank into the chair beside Sydney and touched her arm. "I'm so relieved you're back. I was worried. We all were."

"I'm here." Sydney picked up the pie and began eating while she waited for Vadnae to ask about Willem's whereabouts.

After a short silence, Gregor said, "You knew Willem wasn't coming back, didn't you, Vadnae?"

Sydney's head snapped up. She had never considered that possibility.

"I suspected he wouldn't return."

"Why didn't you share this with the rest of us? Where is he?" Gregor glanced from Vadnae to Sydney.

Sydney drew in a long breath. "With the Tuatha."

"The Tuatha? How? Why?"

"You've seen them?" Vadnae asked. "In the tunnels?"

Sydney nodded. She felt guilty admitting it. Vadnae should have been the one to encounter the faery folk.

"As Grandfather expected. And Willem has gone with them. Please, tell me what you saw, Sydney. Every detail."

One of the wall lanterns sputtered. Shadows seemed to coalesce and hover around the light, like moths to a flame. Once Sydney would have said shadows couldn't hurt her; now she believed otherwise.

She set the remainder of the pie on the tray, no longer hungry. As she spoke, her attention was drawn to the shadows flickering across the wall. They became more animated now, elongating and contracting, but never fully forming. She described the recent events, from her first glimpse of the silver-eyed man in the tavern to her last glimpse of Willem when he passed through the light into the faery realm. Her words felt inadequate. When she finished, Gregor's stunned expression was a sharp contrast to Vadnae's thoughtful one. A shuffled footstep drew her attention to the figure in the doorway.

Erik joined them at the table. "I heard what she said. I can't believe it." He exchanged a glance with Gregor, who simply shrugged.

"You saw the Shadow Folk," Vadnae said softly.

"That's what the silver-eyed man called them. You've heard of them?"

"Grandfather and I talked about them. They're mentioned in the texts I've read on the Tuatha, but there isn't much agreement about who or what they really are. They may be guardians of the realm of the Tuatha, or they may be those who were banished from their realm and forced to live between our worlds, never allowed to be truly part of either."

Sydney drew her arms close against a sudden chill. "Why do I keep seeing them? How can they be following me?"

"You've seen them again? Are you sure?"

"I didn't imagine them."

"I will consider this further," Vadnae assured her, "so I can help you understand."

Sydney picked at the remainder of the pie before her. In addition to food, she needed a strong drink. "There's one more thing." She pulled the pouch from around her neck and set it in front of Vadnae. "I think Durok was watching us. The marble from Oryn's tower started to glow and change colors, and when I touched it...." She shuddered. "Then I saw him. His eyes, at least. I'm sure it was him."

"The marble? When I attempted to locate you earlier, I couldn't detect the marble at all."

"Did Durok hurt you?" Gregor asked.

She unwrapped Willem's handkerchief and held out her hand, gingerly flexing her fingers. The burn on her palm still flamed an ugly bright red. "It ain't so bad. What's worse, he made me remember things from my life. Painful things. Like I was living them again."

Vadnae sighed. "It's my fault. I'm sorry, Sydney. I underestimated him. I never should have let you take the marble with you. I didn't think he could use it to find you."

Sydney pushed the pouch toward her. "The silver-eyed man asked for the marble. He knew what Durok had done. He said...." She struggled to remember his exact words. "After he held it, he said I could keep it and that anyone who misused it would be taught a lesson."

Vadnae took the pouch and dumped the marble and glass bead into her hand. She held up the bead. "Where did you get this?"

"Remember the money Aldric's steward gave me for his sister?" Sydney described meeting Betty and her children. "Sara gave it to me. She said it was her good luck charm."

Erik squinted at the objects in Vadnae's hand. "If the marble is magic, what does it do?"

Vadnae smiled. This time Sydney anticipated the answer, although she didn't fully understand it.

"The marble doesn't do anything by itself. Magic simply exists. It's a wizard—or the Tuatha—who makes use of it." Vadnae touched the marble. "I told Sydney to keep this with her. By locating the marble, I would find her. Durok must have discovered she had it, the same way I planned to locate it. Only he went a step further and used the object to channel his magic against her."

Erik drew back, and Vadnae quickly added, "There's no need to worry. The Tuatha has placed a powerful enchantment of protection on the marble so a wizard can no longer use it. That explains why I couldn't detect it." She returned the marble and bead to the pouch and handed it back to Sydney.

"I still don't understand why Willem chose to go alone," Gregor said. "You said yourself the Tuatha are unpredictable, Vadnae. Willem understood this. Why would he take such a risk? Surely he would ask for your counsel before making such an important decision."

Sydney debated mentioning Willem's dream of the tunnel with the glowing stones. She doubted she could convey the level of certainty he seemed to feel about it.

"He did ask for my counsel," Vadnae responded. "And I advised him accordingly."

"Are you saying Willem planned to go with the Tuatha?" Sydney whispered. "He'd planned it from the start?"

Vadnae nodded. Sydney slumped on the bench. There was no good reason that should feel like a personal betrayal, but it did. He should have told her. They'd shared a connection, she was sure of it, something deeper than their common goal of defeating Schrammig and the Guild. But all along he'd planned to leave her behind, once she'd taken him where he needed to go.

"Why didn't he tell any of us?" demanded Erik. "A king can't go running off with some magical beings. What are we supposed to do without him? When will he return? What if he doesn't come back?"

Vadnae pushed the hair back from her face. "He'll be back. Centuries ago, when the Tuatha still lived in our world, they required a new king to undergo certain rituals, to ensure he was worthy of the knowledge they'd share with him. That's why Willem went with them. Grandfather helped prepare him, but he must face the challenge alone."

Considering Willem's determination to succeed, Sydney couldn't imagine him failing. Especially if Oryn had prepared him for such a task.

"We can't sit here and wait for him to come back," said Erik. "We have to stop Schrammig, but he has us cornered." With a shudder, he added, "Like rats."

"We also met with the leaders of the resistance today," Sydney told them. "They're not gonna give up and hide while Schrammig takes control of the town. They've gathered weapons and supplies, and they plan to fight."

Gregor nodded his approval. "That's what we hoped. Francis and I talked with some merchants and other tradesmen in town today. They didn't seem pleased with the Guild, especially not with Schrammig. We can defend the town, if we need to. A number of the Guild officials may also decide to turn against Schrammig. Francis said one of the monks who died at the farm had a contact in the Guild. I'm not sure there's another means of getting inside information, though."

Sydney's stomach dropped. That contact in the Guild was important. She would have to use Zared's connections to get the information they needed.

"We must continue our efforts until Willem returns," Gregor said. "He'd expect no less from us."

"Gregor, we're not soldiers," Erik complained. "We can't

face the Guild's army. We can't do this without Willem."

"First, we're not going to panic." Gregor glanced over the group, pausing on each of them. "We each possess strengths to help us in this fight. I am yet a knight, and in Willem's absence, I will organize our defense. Perhaps even our offense."

"What about Durok?"

Vadnae folded her hands. "I'll handle Durok. That is my task."

"I know someone who's got connections in the Guild," Sydney said. Zared had been right. She still needed him after all.

"Excellent, Sydney. How soon can you contact him?"

"Tonight." She hoped Zared wouldn't let her down this time.

Vadnae's delicate brow creased. "Who is your friend? Someone in the resistance?" Sydney didn't respond. "Or is it Zared?"

Sydney returned her stare. "He'll get the information we need."

A knock at the door provided Sydney with a means to avoid further questions. Francis stuck his head in. "Sydney? Those children you asked me about earlier?" He stood aside to reveal Janey. "The others were asleep, but this one insisted on seeing you."

Sydney hurried to the door. "You didn't have to wait up for me."

"I had to make sure you'd come."

"I saw your da." The expression of gratitude and relief on Janey's face brought tears to Sydney's eyes.

"Where? Is he coming to get us?"

"He's fine." Sydney stepped into the hallway. Her companions spoke softly. Vadnae was probably telling them about Zared. She focused on Janey. "Your da said he'd be here when he could, but he's going to be busy for a while."

Janey's smile faded. "Because of the Guild?"

"He said he'd come for you." Sydney sought to infuse confidence in her voice. "He also said to tell you he loves you."

Janey pressed her lips together, fighting tears. After a moment, she rubbed her sleeve across her face. She stuck her hand in her pocket and pulled out Edgar's coin. "I made sure Sara didn't lose it."

Sydney held out her hand, curling her fingers around the coin. She grasped her neck pouch. "Hers is right here."

"Sara said to keep it. For extra luck. You need it more than we do."

"Thanks." Sydney put her arm around Janey, feeling the warmth of the girl's small body. She'd felt the same fears and loneliness. "Did Anaria stay here with you?"

Janey drew back, shaking her head. "She said she wasn't going to hide. She said you'd understand."

Sydney hadn't expected Anaria to stay, but she wished she had. Now wasn't the time to be a hero. Anaria had said the same thing to her. But heroes were needed more than ever.

Francis held his hand out to Janey. "Come, child. You should be in bed."

Janey leaned toward Sydney and whispered, "Anaria made me promise to tell you she loves you." She flashed a knowing smile and turned to follow Francis.

Chapter Twenty-Five

"Sydney, we should talk before you leave." Vadnae stood silhouetted in the doorway of the monks' dormitory.

She feigned confidence. "I'll be fine. I can deal with Zared."

"I hope so. I'm afraid I can't help you there. But I want to talk about Durok."

Sydney shuddered, and her hand went to her pouch. "You said I'd be safe from him now."

Vadnae leaned against the doorframe, her face pinched with worry. "He can't hurt you by using the marble now. But I've been wondering if there's another reason why he could find you. I told you Grandfather sees possibilities in people. You're connected to the Tuatha, although I'm not sure how. What do you know about your parents? Your birth parents, I mean."

Edgar had told Sydney the story of how he'd found her, a babe abandoned on the streets, and then he refused to answer any of her questions or repeat the tale. "Sometimes you're better off not knowing the truth," he'd said. "Only thing that matters is the person you become."

She shrugged. "Never knew anything about them. Babies are left to die in Last Hope all the time. Why does it matter?"

"Did you ever see anything unusual when you were a child? Like the shadows you glimpsed in the tunnels?"

"Not until I met Oryn."

"Until you came to the tower in the Wastes." Vadnae stared

thoughtfully at a point in the distance. Looking back at Sydney, she said, "I've found a way to defeat Durok. When the time comes, I'll need you to follow my instructions."

"Me? I'm not a wizard. What can I do?"

Vadnae's face softened. "A lot more than you think, Sydney. You must trust me when the time comes."

"I will. But what should I—"

"I cannot tell you anything more now." Her words echoed Oryn's. "Just trust that we will defeat him."

"Got a plan for defeating Schrammig, too?"

"I wish I did. I'll leave Schrammig to the rest of you. Now go find Zared. We need all the allies we can get."

"I'll be back as soon as I can."

Vadnae caught her hand and gave it a comforting squeeze. "Be careful, Sydney. Please."

Sydney nodded, touched by her concern. This time she hoped she'd return with good news.

———

At the edge of the Thieves' Den, in a part of town where the guard rarely patrolled and the Guild had no interests, Sydney hesitated in front of the door to a decrepit, thatch-roofed two-story building, its walls soot-blackened by a fire of years past. Traces of light escaped boarded-up windows, and laughter echoed in the quiet street. Perhaps it had once been a proper tavern, with a proper name. Now it provided a haven for those who had a reason to hide or a vice to indulge. Steeling herself, she entered.

The large room on the ground floor functioned as a tavern, but ale and liquor weren't the only commodities; tobacco and fantasia and a host of other drugs were available, some of which Sydney had sampled and many of which she didn't recognize. Women and girls in various states of undress offered other amusements, plying their trade in the dimly lit corners or upstairs in private rooms.

Sydney drew her cloak close and moved into the crowd. The air reeked of ale and sweat and pungent herbs. Hazy smoke stung her eyes. She scanned the crowd, searching for Zared, careful not to linger near familiar faces. After circling the room once, she saw no sign of him. Dammit, he had to be here somewhere. She was certain he expected her to look for him here.

She paused near the bar on the far side of the room to scan the crowd again. A hand plucked at her sleeve.

"Syd? Never expected to see you here again." Kat flung an arm around Sydney's shoulders and teetered against her. She stank of ale.

Kat wore the same form-fitting dress she had worn last time Sydney saw her, bringing back painful memories. The Guild official. Her arrest. She stepped back and removed Kat's arm.

"You getting too good for the likes of us?"

"I've been busy lately."

"Oh yeah." Kat lowered her voice. "Weren't you arrested? That can cut into a girl's social life."

Sydney leaned in close. "Someone must've told the guard where to find me."

"Not me. I swear, I'd never rat on you."

Kat could have been so strung out on fantasia she didn't remember who she'd told what. "You think Zared turned me in?"

"Zared? After what he's done for you?" Kat shook her head. "Not him."

Sydney doubted she'd find out the truth from either Kat or Zared. "You seen Zared tonight?"

Kat pursed her dark red lips. "Not tonight. Not for a couple days." She elbowed Sydney and grinned. "He'll be glad to see you, won't he? He's been in a bad way since you've been gone."

"In what way?" Her conflicted feelings for Zared came rushing back, and she struggled to keep her voice calm.

"Uneasy like. Drinking too much, screwing whoever takes his fancy. I bet he's been missing you, eh?"

Sydney doubted missing her was the reason. She forced a smile. "You think so?"

"Don't be stupid, Syd. You was always his favorite. Never understood why, mind you. There's not much to you. You tell him to come to me once he's tired of you." She gave Sydney a grin and pushed her shoulders back so her ample breasts strained against the thin fabric of her dress. "When he's ready for a real woman."

"Sure, Kat." Sydney followed Kat's gaze to two men at a nearby table. One of them winked at her.

"Think they got any money?"

Sydney studied them. Flashes of silver from beneath their worn cloaks and the bulge of a purse told her they weren't the tavern's usual clientele. Likely merchants. Or Guild officials.

"They've got money. I'd stay away from them if I was you."

"Me, I don't care who they are, as long as I get paid. Need a bit of easy coin in case you don't find Zared?"

"No thanks. They're all yours."

"Suit yourself."

"Kat." Sydney caught her arm. "Be careful of the fantasia, will you?"

Kat flashed a gap-toothed smile. "Always am, luv. That reminds me, when you find Zared, tell him Reynald wants to see him."

Sydney glanced over the crowd without spotting the man she and Willem had seen earlier at the market. Zared's motives could be questionable, but Reynald's only interest was profit, often at the expense of anyone who got in his way.

Her stomach knotted. She needed a drink to calm her nerves while she decided what to do if Zared didn't show, but she had no money. Folding her arms across her chest, she paced near the bar, keeping an eye on the crowd. Sweat beaded on her forehead. This was a bad idea.

"Need a drink?"

Sydney froze when Zared tossed a silver coin onto the bar. "Two ales." He sat and gave her his most charming smile. "I figured you'd come."

She stared at his dark eyes, trying to slow her racing heart. "This is business, Zared. I need information. You can give it to me. That's why I'm here. Nothing more."

The bartender slapped down two tankards, and Zared pushed one in her direction. "Business it is then. What do you want?"

She slid onto the stool beside him and gulped the ale. She kept her voice low. "You've got connections in the Guild. Use them, so I can talk with one of the Guild officials."

"Not an easy thing to do these days, especially for someone who's on Schrammig's wanted list. I've been trying to stay clear of the Guild myself."

"Either you'll help me or you won't. I can't play games. Not this time."

"That information don't come cheap."

"You said you'd protect me from Schrammig. This is the help I need. I don't have any money, and I ain't offering anything else." She started to get up, and he grabbed her wrist.

"Sit down. I'll help. First you gotta tell me who this Guild official is."

She jerked her arm from his grasp. After glancing at the crowd to see if anyone was paying particular attention to them, she said quietly, "Her name is Celena."

"I know her." He raised the tankard to his lips and swallowed.

"I need to see her. It's important."

"Why?"

"That's my business."

He bent his head toward her, speaking softly. "Your

business is obvious. Schrammig's here, you come back, and people are planning to rise up against the Guild. There's talk a certain Guild official has plans to act against Schrammig. So I'm guessing that's why you want to see Celena, and it's my bloody business, too, if I'm putting myself at risk to help you."

She inhaled sharply, surprised Celena would be so open concerning her loyalties. "How do you know so much about Celena?"

"I've got connections, remember? She happens to be one of them."

The idea that Zared personally had a connection to a Guild official was hard to believe. "You sleeping with her?"

"Would you be jealous if I was?"

She snorted. "From what Kat says, you ain't too picky who you screw these days."

"Kat can't keep her mouth shut. She's better off sticking to what she does best."

Sydney glimpsed Kat straddled across the lap of one of the men who had shown an interest. "You gonna help me or not?" she asked Zared.

"You're lucky I look out for my business partners." He jabbed his thumb toward the door. "See those men? They work for the Guild."

Two men stood near the doorway, a cloaked figure between them. Her breath caught in her throat. This time she didn't need to see his eyes to feel his menacing power. Hatred and terror cascaded over her. The room whirled.

"Syd?"

Ale sloshed over the rim of the tankard. She clenched her hands. Staring at the tankard, she desperately hoped Durok hadn't sensed her presence, if he could do such a thing. "The man in the black cloak. What's he doing now?"

"What the hell are you talking about? I don't see anyone dressed like that."

Only she could see him, like in the courtyard at the abbey.

She downed the rest of the ale. "Are you planning to turn me in, or can we get outta here?"

Zared held her wrist again, and his eyes flashed a warning. "I said I wouldn't give you to the Guild, Syd. Maybe this time you'll believe me." Releasing her, he hopped off his stool and motioned for her to follow.

The other men remained by the door, but she didn't see the cloaked figure. Scanning the crowd, she saw no sign of him.

"What are you waiting for?"

She drew in a shaky breath and hurried after Zared.

"You taking more of those drugs again?" he asked with a frown. They exited a back door and entered a long hallway.

"If you knew—" She stopped herself. Zared wouldn't understand if she told him the truth. "Let's just go."

The first hallway led to a second, narrower one, down a couple rickety steps, and finally out into the cool night air. She peered into the darkness around them, seeing nothing, hearing only the distant voices from within the tavern. She no longer sensed Durok's power.

"This way." Zared indicated the street behind the tavern.

"Stop where you are," a voice called. The panel of a dark lantern slid open. Sydney squinted in the light but discerned a figure blocking their escape route.

"Didn't expect to see you here, Reynald." Zared's hand moved to the razor-sharp weapon at his belt.

Reynald spoke to Zared, his beady eyes fixed on Sydney. "I just want Syd. Leave now, and I'll pretend you wasn't here."

Zared's expression was void of emotion. "You know what Schrammig will do to her. He'll kill her."

"I don't give a damn what happens to her. You'd better start thinking of yourself, Zared. You gonna throw away your life for this whore?" Reynald took a step forward. Two of Schrammig's soldiers moved to stand beside him, swords drawn.

The soldiers started toward them. Zared drew his blade,

and Sydney bent down to grasp the knife in her boot. Her neck pouch grew warm. *Not again.* Both Vadnae and the silver-eyed man said the marble could no longer be used to harm her.

"What the hell are you doing?" whispered Zared.

"I don't know." She fought the panic in her voice, but tendrils of dread encircled her. The pouch glowed brighter. She couldn't face Durok now, while the soldiers approached. She jerked the pouch from around her neck and tossed it on the ground. The outline of the glowing marble shone from within it. The two soldiers had stopped and stared at her, their eyes wide.

Someone spoke, but she stared at the pouch, unable to look away. The marble called to her, in the same whispered voices she had heard in the tunnels.

"Run, Syd." Zared shoved her, nearly knocking her off her feet.

The whispers roared in her ears and drowned out Zared's fleeing footsteps. The world spun around her. She could only focus on the glowing marble. On instinct, she stooped to grab the pouch. Part of her mind screamed a silent warning, but an unknown force compelled her to act. Her hands shook, and she fumbled to loosen the drawstring. The glow became a blinding light. Suddenly the whispers silenced, and the screams began.

Inhuman cries of pain jerked the world back into focus. The bodies of Reynald and the soldiers crumpled, convulsing. Finally, they lay still. The marble ceased to glow.

A sharp intake of breath made her look up. Zared stood nearby. He looked from her to the three men. After a moment's hesitation, he hurried to Reynald's contorted form and knelt beside him. He put a hand on Reynald's chest and leaned his head close. "He ain't breathing." He checked the two soldiers, and his expression turned to wild-eyed terror and awe. "They're all bloody dead. What the hell did you do?"

She couldn't speak. Her hands shook so hard she could

barely shove the marble into the pouch. Her stomach heaved. She stumbled to the side of the building and retched. *This isn't my fault. It can't be. What kind of power can kill three men without a mark?*

Voices echoed in the street.

"Let's go. Now, Syd."

She wiped her mouth on her sleeve, unable to erase the sour taste. Still trembling, she slipped the pouch over her head. "I didn't do it. Zared, I swear, it ain't my fault."

Zared didn't answer. She reached for his arm, but he stepped back and turned away. He picked up Reynald's lantern and closed the panel, plunging them into merciful darkness, banishing the shadows lurking at the edge of her vision. "Are you coming or not?"

Chapter Twenty-Six

Zared easily navigated the maze of streets and alleys, often cross-tracking their trail. Concentrating on her surroundings helped Sydney push aside the images of the three convulsing bodies, but their screams still sounded in her head. The pouch containing the marble weighed heavily around her neck. Within it was a power she didn't understand and couldn't control. She shivered and pulled her cloak tighter.

Their quiet footfalls on the dirt paths grew louder when they arrived at the cobblestone streets. Zared gripped her arm and guided her into an alley to avoid a street lantern. In the waning moonlight, she could barely see his shadowed figure.

"Before we go any farther, you gotta tell me what's going on."

She tried to pull away, but he held tight. "Let me go. I can't tell you what happened. I don't know."

"C'mon, Syd. D'you think I'm stupid? Whatever you're carrying did something."

"Let me go." Her hand went to the pouch.

He dropped her arm and stepped back. "You gonna use it on me next?" His voice shook.

"I wouldn't." In spite of how much he'd hurt her in the past, she'd never wish such a fate on Zared. She hadn't planned to tell him anything about magic or wizards or the Tuatha, but he'd seen what the marble had done. She had to tell him something. "It's magic. That's all I can say."

"Magic?" Despite the scorn in his voice, Sydney detected an undercurrent of fear. "First you're trying to fight the Guild, and now you're using outlawed magic? I doubt anyone will miss Reynald, but you can sure as hell bet Schrammig will miss two of his soldiers. How many reasons do you want to give them to hang you?"

Sydney would rather be hanged than find out if the stories of Schrammig's methods of torture were true. "You said you could protect me from Schrammig."

"That was before you started killing people."

Her fury rose, and she spoke through clenched teeth. "I didn't kill anyone."

He regarded her a long moment. "I don't know who you are any more, Syd." He pushed the hair back from his face and tilted his head at her. "Even with Celena's help, what makes you think you can win?"

A typical response from Zared. Avoiding trouble was his key to survival. "You do whatever you want, Zared, just take me to Celena first. When are we going to see her?"

"You realize how late it is? I'm not gonna wake her now."

"You said you knew her."

"Not well enough to disturb her in the middle of the night. The way I see it, you've got two options. Go back to wherever you and your friends are hiding and meet me in a couple hours, or come with me and we'll go find Celena first thing in the morning." A grin slowly spread across his face. "I've got a nice room this time. Your choice."

Some choice. Every instinct told her that going with Zared was a bad idea. But the option of returning to the abbey was not appealing, either. Traveling these streets alone, exhausted, and being hunted by Schrammig's soldiers and possibly Durok, was too risky.

She folded her arms. "I'll go with you, but I meant it when I said it was over between us."

He chuckled under his breath and put his arm around her. "That's what I like about you. You always tell me where I stand. Don't worry, I promise I'll be a gentleman. It's just business, right?"

"Just business." She moved away from him, hoping they'd both stick to that.

Zared stopped at an intersection of cobblestone streets. He indicated the two-story inn across from them. Two roses entwining a fancy script graced the sign above the door.

"Not bad, huh? No one will find us there."

People like them weren't welcome in a fine establishment such as this. "You expect them to let us in?"

He grinned and pulled a key from his pocket. "I told you I had a room. I've paid a couple days in advance."

"Where'd you get enough coin to pay for it? The Guild?"

His smile faded. "Of course not. I've got a connection here. Figured this would be a good place to stay. Come on, let's go inside. The guard has regular patrols in this part of town. Wouldn't want to be caught outside after curfew, would we?"

They went around the building to a side door. Zared knocked, and soon the door opened. The young woman who stood in the doorway wore a white apron over a simple gray kirtle, a matching handkerchief covering her hair. Her face broke into a wide smile, and she ushered Zared inside. When Sydney brushed past, the maid gave her an unwelcoming stare.

"Wait here." He followed the maid farther down the hallway.

He'd probably slept with her and made a deal to get a room. She was his type, young and pretty. Her muffled giggle carried down the hall.

Zared soon returned carrying a lamp and led Sydney up a staircase. He unlocked the door at the end of a hallway. In one corner of the room stood a washstand and basin. The thick blankets on the four poster bed were turned down. After several days of sleeping on the ground and the cold floor of

Francis's room, Sydney hadn't anticipated how inviting a real bed would be. She sat on the soft feather mattress and ran her hands over the blankets and pillows, thinking of Vadnae's bedroom in the tower. Zared set the lamp on the bedside table and tossed his cloak over the armchair in front of the hearth, where embers still glowed.

"We'll leave in a couple hours. Rest if you want." He picked up a flask from the table. He shook it, took a long swallow, and offered the flask to her. "You look like you need a drink."

Sydney needed a lot more than the contents of the flask to calm her nerves. She took only one sip of the strong liquor. Her eyes watered, and a warmth spread within her. She returned the flask to him, piled her cloak and boots on the floor by the bed, and crawled under the blankets. Long shadows flickered across the wall. She touched her neck pouch, shutting her eyes to block out her vision of the dead men.

She was starting to drift off when Zared's voice jolted her awake.

"There's something I gotta tell you, Syd."

She opened her eyes. He sat in the chair, elbows on his knees and his chin resting on his hands. His dark hair fell across his face. "It's about Schrammig."

Her breath hitched in her throat. She sat up. "What about him?" Glancing at the door, she half-expected Schrammig to be waiting outside.

Zared stood and began to pace. "I thought I'd never have to tell you. After a while, I figured it didn't matter. Now...."

"Zared, just tell me."

He hesitated, and when he finally spoke, his voice was soft. "It was right after Edgar was hanged. Schrammig came to me. Said he knew I'd helped you hide. He knew about us. Said he could hang us both. Instead he offered me a deal."

Her gut twisted. "You made a deal with Schrammig?"

"I didn't have a choice. You don't say no to Schrammig."

"There's always a choice."

"You didn't think so back then. Staying alive was more important, remember?"

His words raised the guilt that had haunted her after Edgar's death. Zared was right—she had wanted to stay alive, more than anything. "What kind of deal was it?"

Zared stared at the floor. "He wanted me to keep an eye on you, make sure you stayed in Last Hope. He said as long as you didn't make any trouble for the Guild, he'd leave you alone. That's all it was, I swear. When he never came back, I figured it was for the best. You'd forget about the Guild, and we could go on with our lives."

"I've spent the past four years trying to forget. Nothing can take away the pain." Sydney rubbed at the angry tears on her cheeks. "How could you make a deal with Schrammig if you felt anything for me?"

"I did it to save your life. If I'd said no, he would have killed you."

"D'you expect me to feel grateful? You didn't do it 'cause you cared about me, you did it to save yourself." She drew her knees to her chest and wrapped her arms around them. She'd held onto the belief that they had loved each other, at least in the beginning. Now she wondered if he'd stayed with her only because he was afraid Schrammig would come back to check on him.

Zared sat on the bed. "I did it to protect you. Schrammig won't give up until he finds you. You can only hide for so long. He found Edgar, didn't he?"

Her hands balled to fists. "Don't even mention Edgar's name. Why tell me this now? You gonna feel guilty when you hand me over to Schrammig? That's part of the deal, ain't it?"

"Don't you understand? The deal's over. You were sentenced to death. When Schrammig got here, I didn't know where you were or if you were alive. He'll kill us both if he finds us. This is our chance, Syd. I have enough coin to last us a little while. Let's get out of here and go someplace where

Schrammig will never find us."

When she first met Zared, they had talked about leaving town and making a new start. Edgar had tried to do the same thing by coming to Last Hope. He had wanted to make a new life here, and still the Guild had caught up to him.

She wiped her eyes on her sleeve. "Don't you think Schrammig's soldiers will be guarding the town gate? The Guild is everywhere. You can't escape them. Even if we could, I'm not running away this time."

"You really think you can win? With what? Magic?" He eyed the pouch resting between her breasts over her heart. "This is the beginning of a war. You'd better decide whose side you want to be on."

Sydney shook her head. "I've already made my choice. Take me to Celena. I can't keep being afraid of Schrammig." She lay down, putting her back to him.

"You should be afraid of him." He got up and turned down the lamp.

———

She dreamed Willem stood in a green field under a deep blue sky. The sun warmed her face, and she squinted in the bright light. She had never seen such vivid colors. The beauty was marred only by the dark shadows circling Willem. His body writhed in pain. He held out a hand, calling her name. She stepped forward to take his hand, to protect him like he had protected her from Durok. An invisible wall stopped her. Inches away. She placed her palms on the unseen barrier, searching in vain for an opening. She pounded on the wall and rammed her shoulder against it. No matter how hard she pushed, she couldn't pass through. Willem stumbled to his knees. The shadows swooped down on him. Her heart wrenched. He couldn't see her, didn't realize how desperately she was trying to help him. She screamed his name. In an instant, the shadows turned on her, surrounding her in a suffocating embrace.

She woke up, gasping, in a cold sweat.

"Syd, what's wrong?" Zared scrambled beside her, his arms enfolding her.

She sat up and drew in a shaky breath. "Just a dream." She didn't know what tasks the Tuatha had planned for Willem. Even if he needed help, she could do nothing.

She leaned against Zared's chest while he stroked her hair. "I'm sorry," he whispered. "I've always cared about you. I never meant to hurt you. You've gotta believe me."

I don't know what to believe.

She was tired of the shadows and things she didn't understand. Tired of not knowing the truth. Tired of the fear and the aching loneliness. Dammit, she longed to feel good, at least for a little while.

"Do you really care?" She stared into his dark eyes smoldering with desire.

He exhaled slowly at her touch. "Of course I do. You're all I've got."

Drawing him close, her lips sought his. His mouth possessed her, and they shed their clothes. Their need grew fierce, greedy, consuming. She straddled his lap, the heat of their bodies fueling her desire. They wrapped their arms around each other, their joining a familiar refuge from the hellhole of their lives.

This time, she wanted so much more than he could give. She wanted Willem. A man who would be king. A man who had touched her soul and who was now completely beyond her reach.

The door creaked open. Sydney jerked awake. Sunlight streaming between the wooden shutters showed Zared's shadowed figure slipping into the room. "Where were you?"

"Couldn't sleep, so I went to give a message to Celena."

"We were supposed to see her together. Why didn't you wake me?" She grabbed her clothes.

He shrugged. "I figured you could use the extra sleep. Celena's here. She's waiting for you downstairs."

"Here?" Sydney quickly dressed in her shirt and breeches and pulled on her boots. "Is it safe for her to be here?"

"Safer than having you go to her, is what she said." When she started to move to the door, Zared stood in front of her. He reached for her but stopped, uncharacteristically hesitant. "You sure you want to do this? We can still leave."

She stared at the dark circles under his eyes and his haunted expression. "You don't trust Celena?"

"I never said I trusted her. Even though she doesn't like Schrammig, she's still one of the top officials in the Guild. There'll be a price if she helps you."

Zared's words made her question what she was doing, but she'd already made up her mind.

"Whatever the price, it's worth it if she can help."

"I hope you're right, Syd."

They descended the stairs and entered a sitting room. Sconces along the walls cast a cheery light. Two armchairs sat before a fire crackling in the hearth, and a polished oak side table held a silver tea service and a plate of biscuits. *Too comfortable.*

A woman sitting in one of the armchairs stood. Tall and striking, she wore an elegant velvet blue dress, its fitted bodice emphasizing her narrow waist. Long, dark tresses coiled on top of her head and curled against her slender neck. Her dark eyes took in Sydney.

"You must be Sydney. Please, sit." She waved her hand at the other chair. To Zared, she said, "You may leave us now," addressing him as if he were a servant.

"Remember what I said," Zared murmured. He brushed his

lips across her cheek and left, closing the door behind him.

Sydney tried unsuccessfully to smooth the wrinkles from her clothes before she crossed the room and sat in the other chair.

"Would you care for tea or a biscuit?" Celena moved to the side table, hand poised above the teapot. A ruby ring glittered on her forefinger, and a silver pendant sparkled at her throat.

The absurdity of a Guild official asking if she wanted tea warned Sydney of the wrongness of this situation. "No, thanks. I'm not really hungry." Her stomach flip flopped. Eating was out of the question.

Celena poured herself a cup and returned to her seat. The scent of fresh powder wafted from her. She leaned forward, her voice quiet. "We don't have much time, Sydney. I know who you are and why you wanted to speak with me. Only a select few are privy to my opinions of the Guild."

Sydney nodded. "Jimmy, one of the resistance leaders, said you've helped them before."

"I don't recognize the name, but names are not important. What he told you is true."

"He also said you had information on Schrammig's army, but he hadn't heard from you in a while. That's why I needed to see you. Willem needs your information."

"Then the rumors are true? Willem has come to Last Hope?"

Sydney hesitated. *I've revealed too much.* Unlike her immediate connection with Jimmy, her sense of wrongness warned her not to trust Celena, even if she claimed to be on their side.

"I can contact his allies," she said, avoiding Celena's question. "Willem swore he would protect the town."

Celena sipped her tea. "Many of the Guild members are loyal to me, not to Schrammig. I'll do what I can to help." She stood and set her teacup and saucer on the side table. Her eyes flickered toward the door, and she beckoned to Sydney, a quick, urgent motion.

Sydney glanced at the door and hurried to Celena's side. Warnings echoed in her head.

Celena slipped an arm around her waist and guided her toward the window. Daylight showed beneath the heavy draperies. "You remind me of Edgar. He excelled at earning people's trust and convincing them to follow him. But don't underestimate the Guild. Especially Schrammig. He won't kill you, not yet, but he'll torment you until you break."

Sydney's mouth went dry. "What're you saying?"

Footsteps sounded in the hallway. Celena swiftly crossed the room, smoothing her hair. Her hand rested on the latch. She flipped Sydney a glance, mouthing, *I'm sorry,* before she opened the door and stepped aside.

A man entered. A jagged scar split his face from forehead to chin. Sydney drew her knife and crouched near the chair.

"That won't do you any good, Sydney." His raspy voice sliced through her. The same voice that had haunted her since Edgar's death. He stepped into the room and crooked a finger behind him. One of his soldiers entered, pushing Zared before him. Zared's hands were tied behind his back, his face bruised and one eye swollen shut.

Celena stood silent and expressionless. She was supposed to be an ally. Sydney gripped her knife and clutched her neck pouch with the other hand. She didn't hear any voices. Dammit, she needed the marble to work.

Schrammig put a hand on Zared's shoulder and forced him to his knees.

"Please don't do this." Zared's eyes were wide, and his body shook. "I don't want to die. Not like this."

Schrammig looked at Celena, then Sydney. He grabbed Zared's hair and pulled his head back. With the other hand, he drew the knife in his belt. "This is how we deal with traitors."

He slit Zared's throat with one swift motion. Blood sprayed the rug. Sydney choked back a scream. She pulled her stare away from the blood spurting from the wound to look at

Zared's face. His eyes met hers, pleading. His mouth opened, but he couldn't speak. His body crumpled to the floor. A spreading red stain seeped into the rug around him. Schrammig bent to wipe his blade on Zared's shirt and moved toward Sydney, a smug smile on his face.

She had often imagined the moment when she'd confront Schrammig and demand justice for what he'd done. Rage and loss constricted her throat. She didn't trust herself to speak. She gripped the knife so tightly her palm began to ache. Jamming the blade into his throat would be satisfying.

She willed herself to be calm and focused, like Edgar had taught her. Schrammig was bigger, stronger, and more experienced. Sometimes being small and quick—and underestimated—provided an advantage.

"You gonna teach me how to fight, Sydney?" He shoved the chair aside, smirking.

Her rage exploded, and she lunged at him, her knife arcing toward his chest. He easily blocked her. The force of his blow reverberated up her arm. Schrammig waited for her to attack. Again, he blocked her, driving her back into the table holding the tea service. His smile twisted. He was enjoying their fight, as if it were a game. His boot slammed into her wrist, sending her weapon skittering across the floor. She grabbed her wrist, clenching her teeth.

Reaching behind her, she grasped the handle of the silver teapot. She swung it at his head, but he ducked. The lid flew off, and tea splashed onto the rug. He slashed at her arm holding the teapot, slicing her sleeve and drawing blood. Staggering away from the table, she dropped the teapot and clutched her arm. He ducked behind her, clamped his hand on her arm, and bent it behind her back, almost to the breaking point. Pain shot to her shoulder. Schrammig forced her to her knees. He grabbed a fistful of her hair and pulled her head back, as he had done to Zared.

His blade pressed against her throat. She drew in a slow

breath, hoping she could at least die well. "Do it."

"I won't make it that easy on you." Schrammig grabbed her shirt and jerked her to her feet. "Time to go, Sydney." He wrenched her arms behind her and dragged her to the door. In the doorway, he said to Celena, "It's always nice to see where your loyalties really lie."

Sydney spied a flicker of emotion in Celena's eyes. Celena simply nodded to Schrammig without saying a word.

The maid who'd let them in the night before stood beyond the door, eyes wide. After they passed her, she peered into the room and began to scream.

Chapter Twenty-Seven

A sliver of light from beneath the door provided the only illumination in Sydney's windowless cell. The fetid odor of musty stone mingled with the metallic scent of blood. She ran her fingers over the corners and cracks of the rough stone floor and walls, searching for a loose stone, anything to use as a weapon. Palms scraped and knees bruised, she found nothing.

She'd managed to tear off part of her sleeve and bind the wound she'd received from Schrammig. Blood quickly soaked the fabric, but the wound didn't seem deep.

The scene in the cozy sitting room replayed in her mind again and again. Each time she sought to imagine a different outcome—to will her actions to change and react quicker or fight harder—and each time Zared's pleading stare met hers as the silver blade slit his throat.

There was nothing she could have done.

Tears blurred her vision. "I'm sorry, Zared," she whispered. Sorry for his senseless death. Sorry she'd ignored his warning about Celena. Even though he couldn't give her the kind of love she really wanted, he'd given her everything he could.

She hugged her knees to her chest. She could still feel his mouth on hers, his caress, the warmth of his body. Now he was gone. So often they'd been drawn together by the fear of being alone.

Now, here in this dark cell, she really was alone.

The darkness brought forth the inner demons she'd banished to the recesses of her mind. They fed on her anger and her despair. Her racing heart thumped in her ears. For the first time in a long while, she desperately wished for one of the multicolored pills to take away all her pain.

She didn't know how to fight Schrammig. She couldn't do this on her own.

You must have the strength to do what is right, rather than what is easy. Oryn's words. She wished she could believe in herself like Oryn did. He'd given her a second chance, a chance to redeem herself. She had failed him. She had also failed Vadnae and Willem and the resistance. Worse, she had failed to live up to Edgar's expectations a second time.

But I'm not like Edgar.

She no longer knew who Edgar really was. The image she'd carried of the man who'd raised her and loved her like she'd been a child of his own blood didn't appear to reflect the real man at all. She could only be certain he'd loved her. Edgar had loved her unconditionally, and he would have been proud of her.

That was why she couldn't give up. Edgar never gave up, not even at the end, and neither would she.

"I hope you haven't been waiting long."

The voice snapped her out of a fitful sleep. Hatred and anger overwhelmed her. *Durok.* She jumped to her feet, straining for a glimpse of him in the darkness.

Two wall torches flickered to life, revealing a man who stood ten feet away on the opposite side of the cell. He wore the same black cloak she'd seen earlier. For the first time, she glimpsed his face, surprised to find an ordinary man. Dark hair framed a pale face, and the lines around his eyes belied his youthful appearance. His eyes, however, were anything but ordinary. At first glance, they were nearly black, but colors spiraled within them. The room spun around her, and she forced herself to look away from his hypnotic stare.

She'd felt a similar power within Oryn, but this man's stare violated her, as if stripping her naked, body and soul, all her innermost fears and desires spread out before him.

His thin lips curled back from his teeth. "This time your friends are not here to protect you. Would you rather use this?" He held out his hand, revealing the marble. Its soft glow illuminated his face.

Sydney averted her eyes, afraid the marble would change colors, like it had done in the tunnel.

"Perhaps you'd like to use it against me, as you used it to take the lives of those soldiers last night." He took a step toward her, hand outstretched. "Here, take it."

The screams of the three dead men echoed in her head. But the whispered voices remained silent, and the wavering shadows on the walls had no more life than the torches provided.

He closed his fist around the marble and drew his hand within the folds of his cloak. "There is so much you don't understand, Sydney. I can give you the answers you seek. Unlike some, I believe knowledge should be shared and not locked away by those who are afraid to use it. The old man was a fool to think he could stop me."

"Oryn?" she gasped. "Where is he? What've you done to him?"

"He's in a place where he can no longer interfere. You needn't worry, he hasn't been harmed. There are rules even I must obey. You, however, don't seem to be bound by them."

"What rules?" Sydney moved to the side, the wall at her back.

He continued toward her. "I wouldn't expect Oryn to explain the rules of magic to you. You're not a wizard, so why should he tell you such things? But you've accomplished something I've only dreamed of doing. No wizard can break our most sacred law. Magic cannot be used to take the life of a living creature. To do so causes one's death. You, however, have achieved this and lived."

The image of the three dead men seared her mind. This time, she not only saw them, but she also felt their horror. This time, she viewed the scene as if seeing it through their eyes. Reynald and the two soldiers had seen the shadows, the same ones that had nearly overtaken her in the tunnels, the ones she had seen circling Willem in her dream. The Shadow Folk. They had surrounded the three men, drawing out their memories, until nothing remained. The shadows enveloped her, and a crushing emptiness pressed against her.

"Make it stop!"

"As you wish."

The pressure lifted. Air rushed into her lungs. She was on her knees. Durok's mouth arched in a sneer. His voracious need for this power coiled around them, ensnaring her. The thought of what he'd do if he gained it terrified her.

"I didn't do it." Her voice shook. She stood and backed away from him.

He laughed, a guttural sound. "Of course you didn't. Only the Tuatha—and the Shadow Folk—can wield such magic. Now you have seen it yourself. They used it on your behalf."

"I didn't ask them to."

"That makes no difference. You are bound to them now, more strongly than before. You cannot escape them. They haunt your dreams, don't they? They even haunt your waking hours."

One of the torches flickered. The shadows danced across the walls. She shuddered. "No, they don't," she lied.

He fixed her with a piercing stare. "Don't they? Most who encounter them do not survive. They desire life more than anything, the life denied them since being banished by the

Tuatha to their shadowy world. Theirs is a tormented fate, for they cannot die and have no hope of recovering the lives stolen from them."

He seemed to possess more insight into the Shadow Folk than Vadnae, and his explanation fit with what she had seen and experienced. Oryn should have told Vadnae and the rest of them about this threat.

"This is where the old man made his biggest mistake," Durok continued, as if reading her mind. "He planned for you to lead Willem to the Tuatha, but he obviously didn't realize to what extent someone who is bound to the Tuatha is also connected to the Shadow Folk. They are two sides of the same coin. You cannot bring one back into our world without the other. I made sure the Shadow Folk would be drawn to the darkness within you. You are more kin to them than to the Tuatha. The old man never told you that, did he? He was afraid of what you might do if you could access such power."

Surely Oryn would have told her if she was remotely related to the Tuatha. He'd neglected to share so many things. Sydney didn't know who or what to believe any more. Durok's dark eyes offered her a glimpse into the vast abyss of the knowledge she craved—and feared.

"Think, Sydney. You can call on the Shadow Folk to use their power. Wouldn't you like to use it against Schrammig?"

Sydney drew in a sharp breath.

"You've dreamed of getting justice for all the lives he has taken. Why not make those dreams come true?"

Her hands balled into fists. The same helplessness she'd felt when she had watched Zared die welled within her. "It didn't work on Schrammig."

"The Tuatha will do what they can to make sure their magic isn't misused again. I can stop them. I can help you, Sydney. I can help you use the magic. You want to hurt Schrammig for all he has taken from you. Think of how satisfying tormenting him would be."

She wanted Schrammig to suffer, to watch him gasp in terror when the Shadow Folk tore the life from his body. That would be justice. And it would give Durok exactly what he wanted. His words were a trap. What he offered was only a means to further his own desires. The darkness within her was nothing compared with what lay within his soul.

Her nails dug into her palms. "I don't need your help to defeat Schrammig."

He laughed softly. "Very well. You may reconsider when you realize what Schrammig has planned for you." He grabbed her arm. His icy touch was so cold it burned. She jerked away, but his grip tightened, and his eyes bored into hers. "Schrammig's methods are much cruder than mine and quite effective. Now let's not keep him waiting."

With a wave of his hand, the cell door swung open silently. Following a long hallway, they passed several other doors. Their footsteps echoed on the uneven stone floor. Durok held her in a firm grip.

At the end of the corridor, they stopped at another door. Durok knocked once and entered. Schrammig sat behind a desk, ledgers and parchments spread out before him. On one corner a silver tray contained bread, cheese, and a bottle of wine. Sydney's stomach rumbled. She hadn't eaten in a long time.

A smile played across Schrammig's lips. "Hungry? Help yourself. A shame we had to interrupt your tea." He picked up a piece of bread and tossed it at her.

She stepped to the side and let the bread fall to the floor.

"Suit yourself." Schrammig ran his fingers over a scroll case. "News from Pendolf, our new king. Willem's allies are stirring up trouble all over the kingdom. A pity he won't live long enough to see the rest of his supporters crushed."

He stood, circling to the front of the desk. "Your friends in Last Hope are keeping me busy. Our latest hanging hasn't deterred them, but once they witness more, I think they'll start to realize the futility of their actions."

Durok's hand rested on her back, pushing her forward, close enough to see the puckered skin around Schrammig's scarred face. Her voice quavered. "They won't give up. Your hangings ain't gonna scare them this time."

Schrammig leaned his muscular frame against the desk. "They'll think differently when their families, even their wives, swing from the end of a rope. I made sure your friend Betty was the first to go this morning."

Sydney trembled. She and Willem had probably led the Guild right to Betty. *Don't think about Betty.* Not about Bill mourning for his wife. Or Janey, Sara, and little Frannie, now without a mother.

"Everyone has a breaking point, Sydney. Some people will do whatever it takes to save their lives. Selfish cowards like Zared are very predictable, although he surprised me at the end. Apparently, he cared more about you than I anticipated."

"You bastard." She spat at him.

He wiped his sleeve across his face and moved closer. "You should thank me for giving him a merciful death. You won't be so lucky."

He shoved her to the floor. His heavy boot kicked her side. She gasped in pain, clutching her stomach, and tried to crawl away.

"You're pitiful. I wish Edgar could've seen you like this. It took a while to break him, but in the end, you were the key." He pushed aside a roll of parchment on the desk and picked up a coin on a leather cord—Edgar's good luck charm. He dangled the coin in front of Sydney. "I'm glad you received my little gift. It seemed to be one of Edgar's most prized possessions. He didn't think I'd find out about you."

Sydney resisted the urge to snatch the coin away from him.

"Edgar was so self-righteous, claiming to be fighting on behalf of the people. Willing to die to prove his point. Until he realized I'd hunt you down, too." Schrammig closed his fist around the coin. The scar on his face split his smile. "He wasn't willing to beg for his life, but yours was another matter."

She didn't want to imagine Edgar begging for anything. Schrammig had used Edgar's love for her to break his will.

He knows how to break you.

You're right, Willem. So how can I fight him?

Schrammig shifted the coin from one hand to the other. "At first, I wondered if letting you live was a wise choice. I wondered if your hatred of me and the Guild would eventually drive you to rally the people of Last Hope and continue Edgar's fight.

"But I know you, Sydney. I don't need magic to understand you and predict your actions and reactions. Edgar was your world, wasn't he? When I killed him, I destroyed your life. You disappeared with Zared. People probably thought you'd also been killed. I think you wished you had been."

Sydney staggered to her feet, gripping the desk for support. "You don't know me. I will finish what Edgar started. Willem will win, and the Guild will be defeated."

"Willem will never win. You believe he's a champion of the people? What do you think his supporters among the nobility would say if they discovered he was consorting with whores and pickpockets? He can't afford to alienate the only people besides the Guild who have money and power." He leaned closer to her. "Do you really think he cares about someone like you?"

Of course he does, she wanted to say. She kept silent, trying to control her emotions and hide her feelings for Willem.

"Willem's a fool if he thinks the people are going to help him win this war. The people of Last Hope aren't going to rise up against the Guild, especially not when the rest of our forces arrive tomorrow. Last Hope will be an example of what happens to those who think they can defy the Guild. Do you think Willem will defend the town? A good leader knows when to cut his losses."

Schrammig had already butchered the monks at their farm outside town. The people of Last Hope were next. She drew in a shaky breath. "Willem swore he'd fight for us—for the people. He won't let you destroy Last Hope."

Schrammig laughed. "Only the Guild represents the interests of the people. Not the nobles. Not the king's bastard son. Even Edgar was biding his time until he could reclaim his lands and title. The commoners meant nothing to him."

"You lie. Edgar fought to make sure people had better lives. All the Guild bloody cares about is power and lining their pockets. At the people's expense."

"Sometimes the truth can surprise you. Take Edgar. His life among the people of Last Hope hardly makes up for his past actions. I'm sure he never told you how they treated those who worked on his family's lands." Schrammig paced around the desk.

He clenched Edgar's coin in his fist. "Sometimes we'd see them riding in the distance, dressed in their finest clothes, heading for the grand manor on the hill where they never wanted for anything. We spent our days tending their crops and animals, and we were lucky if we had four walls and a roof over our heads. A poor harvest, and we'd be reduced to begging for scraps from their table. Those damned nobles cared more for their pigs and their sheep than the people who worked their land."

The hate in his eyes made her shiver. "The Guild had enough power to make them pay for what they'd done. The Guild is the only way people like us can rise to the same level as the nobility. At last, the nobles fear us."

"Edgar never would've done that," she whispered. So many times he had gone without, helping those less fortunate. Some of Schrammig's story rang true, but she refused to believe Edgar had allowed such treatment to occur. Not Edgar.

"It doesn't matter if you believe me. Edgar isn't here to

defend himself, is he? Nor is he here to defend you. Before he died, he claimed you were under the protection of a wizard." Schrammig gestured to Durok. "As you can see, I have a wizard, too. Magic won't help you now, Sydney."

He walked across the room and lit a lamp on the wall. A rack displayed sharp metal spikes, chains, restraints, wooden rods, and pincers. Sydney's muscles tensed, and her breath grew shallow. Durok moved to her side. His hand clenched her shoulder. A burning pain shot through her arm.

"I suggest you reconsider my offer," he murmured in her ear. "While you still can."

Schrammig ran his hands over his instruments of torture, almost lovingly. "Don't worry, Sydney, I won't kill you. At least not yet. Durok has assured me you'll take us to Willem, so I need you alive. I want to know where he is and where the rest of your friends in the resistance are hiding. I hear you're familiar with those damn tunnels."

Edgar had surely faced a similar torture. He would have been strong. He wouldn't have given in.

She thrust her chin at Schrammig, despite the hammering of her heart in her ears and the shivers of terror writhing across her skin. "I've got nothing to say to you."

Schrammig picked up a wooden rod from a brazier in the corner. The metal tip glowed red. "We'll see."

Durok dragged her toward Schrammig, and she kicked at him. The more she struggled, the more the pain in her arm intensified. He couldn't kill her using magic, but he could hurt her. The room spun. He stopped in front of a pair of manacles hanging on a chain attached to the ceiling and clamped the cold, iron bands around her wrists. He stepped back. With a wave of his hand, the manacles started to grow warm.

The Shadow Folk hovered at the edge of the light on the far wall.

"You can make this easy on yourself," Schrammig said. "Tell me where Willem is. Edgar gave in pretty quickly."

She focused on the soft glow of the lamp. With a tearing sound, he split her shirt from the back. Burning metal seared her skin. The screams coming from her lips didn't seem to be hers.

The Shadow Folk surrounded her. *Let us help you,* they seemed to say. Suddenly she felt nothing, only cold, only darkness.

In the darkness, the lush green field of her dreams appeared. Willem smiled and held her hand and led her into a field of red and orange flowers, colors brighter than any she had ever seen. Their cloying scent filled the air. She wanted to warn Willem of Durok and Schrammig and the Shadow Folk, but before she could speak, he took her face in his hands and kissed her. He tasted of the sweet flowers in the field.

"Fight them, Sydney. Don't give in. Don't let them defeat you."

"How?" She grasped his hand. "How do I fight them?"

Pain tugged at the edge of her senses. Willem's fingers slipped away. "Come back," she cried, but he was gone, and the darkness surrounded her. Her blood pumped like icy slush, turning every part of her body frigid. The shadows moved toward her, more substantial than before, their voices swelling. They promised to make her dreams real. They promised vengeance. They would make Schrammig pay for what he'd done, for all the lives he'd destroyed.

"Use the magic," Durok's voice thundered in her ears. "Call them, and save yourself while you still can."

Agony exploded. Dark waves of power engulfed her. She couldn't let Durok have that power, even if it meant sacrificing herself.

"I won't do it." Her voice came through clenched teeth. The darkness lifted, and the room came into sharp focus. Flickering lamplight. Blistering steel around her wrists. Sticky wetness dripping down her arms. The reek of burning flesh. Her flesh. Pain beyond bearing.

"You can't defeat me," she gasped, echoing Willem's words. "I have nothing to tell you."

Before the merciful darkness overtook her, she remembered something the silver-eyed man had said to her. *Names can be powerful. You will know mine when your need is greatest.* Now would be a damn good time to remember his name.

Chapter Twenty-Eight

"Sydney? Can you hear me?"

The faraway voice beckoned her to escape the nightmares tormenting her sleep, nightmares of Schrammig's torture room.

"Sydney, try to drink this."

A woman's voice grew louder. Sydney fought the turmoil in her mind and struggled to open her eyes. Her vision blurred. A sharp pain stabbed through her head. She closed her eyes. She could still feel the iron clamps around her wrists and the burning rod lashing her back. Pain meant she still lived.

Gentle hands lifted her head, and a cup pressed against her lips. She swallowed. The cool liquid soothed her parched throat, though her stomach churned at its foul taste.

"Rest now."

Sydney lay back on the bed, a soft pillow cradling her head. For a moment, she thought she was in Zared's bed at the inn. But Zared was dead. She squeezed her eyes tight, trying to shut out memories of Zared and Betty and Edgar, and all the others Schrammig had hurt or killed.

Footsteps moved away from the bed. Clenching her jaw against the pain, Sydney forced her eyes open, and they began to focus. With a start, she recognized the woman standing next to the bed, although her appearance was quite different from the woman who had offered her tea in the sitting room at the inn. Celena had traded her blue velvet dress for a fitted gray tunic and trousers, and her hair now hung in a single braid down her back. Her brow creased in worry.

Celena placed the cup she'd been holding on a table near the bed. "How do you feel?"

"How d'you think I feel?" Her voice was a haggard whisper. Celena was a traitor. Whether she'd betrayed the Guild or the resistance no longer mattered. Sydney pushed herself into a sitting position. The blanket fell away, revealing her raw and blistered wrists.

She started to swing her legs over the edge of the bed and realized she was wearing a tattered tunic and pants that were not hers. The room spun. She drew in long, slow breaths until the lightheadedness stopped.

Celena motioned to the cup containing the foul-tasting brew. "It will help ease the pain, but give it time to work."

"What is it? A drug?"

"An herbal remedy. Very effective. The old woman who sold it to me swears by it."

The room tilted again, and Sydney gripped the edge of the bed to steady herself. One herbalist in Last Hope was known for her remedies and miracle cures. "From Nala, at the market?"

At Celena's nod, a shiver ran down her spine. The herb woman had recognized Willem. Were the threads of fate weaving tighter and tighter around her? Could she free herself from them?

"You're lucky Schrammig wants to keep you alive. You wouldn't have lasted long in your cell. He's put you under my care. We're both his prisoners now."

Celena's expression was as placid as it had been when Schrammig slit Zared's throat. Zared had warned her there was always a price to pay where Celena was concerned. "After what you've done, why should I trust you?"

"I'm sorry about what happened, Sydney. I had no choice."

"You gave me to Schrammig to be tortured." Sydney pulled up her sleeve and thrust out her arm, gritting her teeth. "This is only part of what he did to me. And Zared...." She shut her eyes a moment, taking a deep breath. "You didn't do a damn thing to save him."

Celena's mouth tightened. The line of her full, red lips appeared harsh, almost cruel. "I had no choice," she repeated. "Zared was stupid. Why come to me when he knew damn well Schrammig has been watching me? Zared led him right to you. I went along with Schrammig's plan to buy myself—buy us—some time."

"At Zared's expense. He didn't deserve to die."

"Zared had outlived his usefulness. Schrammig would have killed him regardless of what you or I did. Since Schrammig has been occupied with you, I was able to get a message to your friends. He'll be surprised by the power I still wield here."

Celena moved closer, squatting beside the bed. "That Jimmy you mentioned has been rallying people around town in your name. Edgar's legacy is proving to be a powerful force. Schrammig is so concerned, he's ordered more soldiers into town. Our more immediate problem, Sydney, yours and mine, is how to survive and escape before Schrammig and his bloody wizard kill us both."

Sydney managed to get her feet on the floor. She didn't trust her shaky legs enough to try to stand. "Why should I believe anything you say? Whose side are you really on?"

A fist pounded on the door. Celena gripped Sydney's arm. "Say nothing." She stood, straightened her tunic, and tucked a tendril of hair behind her ear before she hurried to the door and opened it.

Celena blocked her view of the doorway. She exchanged quiet words and closed the door.

"He's on his way here now, so listen to what I'm going to say."

Sydney started to ask who, but Celena held up a hand to

silence her.

"Listen to me, Sydney. I don't care if you hate me for what I've done, but we must work together if we're going to survive." She lowered her voice and added, "I also received a message from your friend Vadnae today."

"Vadnae?" Sydney's mind raced. Why would Vadnae risk contacting Celena when Schrammig and especially Durok could be watching?

"Somehow she managed to get past Schrammig's guards. Either she's very brave and resourceful or very stupid. Or she's a wizard. Like Durok." Celena paused, but Sydney said nothing. "She said to tell you to find the glowing tunnel. 'Bring him there,' were her exact words. She'll be waiting for you. In case you doubt me, Vadnae also said to tell you sometimes you could trust a wolf. I suppose I've been called worse, if that's what she meant."

The wolf in the forest when she'd first met Oryn and the toy wolf in Vadnae's bedroom entered Sydney's thoughts. Celena couldn't have known about those things. Vadnae's message meant she had a plan to defeat Durok. They still had a chance.

"This is about magic, isn't it?"

Sydney nodded, and footsteps echoed outside the room. The door was flung open. Schrammig stood in the doorway. "Is she ready?"

Celena folded her arms across her chest. "She's still alive."

He scowled. "How fortunate you were available to play nursemaid." He strode across the room and grabbed Sydney's arm, pulling her to her feet. "Get up."

Agony spiraled up her arm. She bit her lip, tasting blood, steeling herself, refusing to show Schrammig how much he'd hurt her. She stood, and the throbbing lessened. She hoped the medicine was working.

"Glad you've recovered so quickly." He kept a tight grip on her arm and moved toward the door. Two of his soldiers waited in the hallway. Schrammig turned back to Celena. "Once I'm back, you'll be hanged for treason."

Celena's only reaction was a sharp intake of breath. In a calm voice, she said, "Call it what you will. The only treason I've committed is against people like you who've warped the Guild for their own gain."

"The Guild doesn't need people like you who would rather sit back and play nice with the nobility who've kept us down."

She gave a little shrug and deliberately turned her back on him and sat on the bed, hands folded in her lap. "You'll be surprised when the Guild finally turns on you, Schrammig. With all the enemies you've made, someone is bound to catch you off guard. I suggest you keep a close eye on Sydney while you're in the tunnels. She hates you a great deal more than I do."

Schrammig took a step toward Celena, his hand clenched on the hilt of his sword. "I'd kill you now, but I'm going to enjoy watching you hang, along with the rest of your supporters." He dragged Sydney outside, leaving the soldiers to guard the door.

Schrammig's carriage waited in front of the Guild Hall. Sydney looked up at the night sky. Surely she hadn't been a prisoner for more than a day, although she felt like a lifetime had passed since she'd gone to the tavern to meet Zared.

"No one goes in or out until I return," Schrammig told his captain. "Certain Guild members are secretly helping the resistance. Do whatever is necessary to root them out. Send for reinforcements if you need them."

The captain saluted and returned to the building. One soldier positioned himself in front of the entrance.

Schrammig opened the carriage door and shoved Sydney in the seat opposite Durok and sat next to her. "You can hate me all you want, Sydney, but you're going to take me to Willem. Your friends are hiding him somewhere in those tunnels."

She swallowed hard. "If I refuse?"

"There are many unpleasant ways to die. Do you think so much of Willem that you'd give your life for him?"

She couldn't answer his question. She leaned her head on the glass windowpane and closed her eyes. The pain had subsided, but a fog clouded her mind. The gentle rocking of the carriage lulled her toward sleep.

Vadnae has a plan, she repeated silently. She assumed Vadnae could find the tunnel with the glowing stones by using her magic and hoped her powers were greater than Durok's. Whose side the Tuatha and Shadow Folk were on, if any, remained unclear. Nor was she convinced the silver-eyed man would be an ally, even if she could remember his name.

Fighting the fatigue threatening to overtake her, Sydney jolted against the carriage window when they turned from the main road onto unpaved streets. She recognized the dilapidated tenements. These were her neighborhoods.

Ahead, lanterns bobbed. Groups of soldiers were pounding on doors. The light revealed shattered windows, doors pulled off their hinges, and people's belongings strewn across the street. The farther they went, the more soldiers gathered. No sign of any residents, and no groups of prisoners waiting to be marched to the gallows.

She turned her attention to Schrammig. The light from the carriage lantern fell across him, illuminating his scar.

He leaned toward her. "Worried? This time there's no escape for your friends. It's only a matter of time before I find them. Someone is always willing to talk."

At last the carriage stopped. Her heart sank. The wooden slats across the door to the Black Dog had been pried off and lay scattered on the ground. Schrammig kicked one out of his path, and they entered the tavern. Four soldiers sat at the table where Sydney and Jimmy had talked about the night Edgar had been arrested. The soldiers saw Schrammig and scrambled to their feet.

"What's your report?"

"We found supplies, sir, but no sign of any people."

"It would be impossible to search all of the tunnels without knowing where they lead."

"Here's our guide." Schrammig picked up a lantern and thrust it at Sydney. "Let's go."

Edgar's voice suddenly sounded in her head: "No one else must ever learn about these tunnels. People's lives depend on it."

Schrammig had already discovered their hiding places. Leading him into the tunnels was her only option.

She gripped the lantern and crossed the room. Schrammig, Durok, and the soldiers trailed her. They went down the narrow stairs and entered the dark passages.

Schrammig put a hand on her shoulder and pulled her to him. "Don't try anything stupid, Sydney. If you run, we'll find you. Now take us to Willem."

Sydney could navigate these tunnels, but there was no telling how long the drug Celena had given her would last. Escape was not possible. She held onto the hope that Vadnae would be waiting for her.

They continued on, the lantern illuminating a short distance ahead. This time, there was no sign of the Shadow Folk. No strange flickering shapes, no voices whispering in her ears. The silence felt as if someone had drawn a great breath in anticipation of something even greater to come.

At each intersection, Sydney held up the lantern, pretending to consider the adjoining passages while she quickly checked the notches on the walls to make sure she was going the right way. Schrammig and Durok didn't appear to notice. That secret was more important than the location of the tunnels, and Sydney intended to keep it from Schrammig.

She easily found the tunnels where Bill had taken her and Willem. At last, she arrived at the intersection where Willem had first seen the tunnel with the glowing stones. The opening had disappeared.

"Send them back," Durok said to Schrammig, motioning to the soldiers behind them.

"Why?" Schrammig eyed the tunnel and put a hand on his sword hilt. "Is there magic here?"

"I must deal with this. Do as I ask, if you want Willem."

Schrammig scowled and ordered his men to move back to wait for his signal.

"We are very close," Durok said softly. "I can sense them. This is where you found them, isn't it?"

Sydney said nothing.

Durok walked ahead, running his hands over the smooth walls. "They expected Willem, so they would've shown him the way. I doubt we will receive such a welcome."

He pulled an object from within the folds of his cloak. Sydney's pouch. "We must make ourselves welcome. Hold out your hand, Sydney."

She started to back away.

Schrammig's knife pressed against the back of her neck. "Do it."

The blade bit into her flesh. She took slow, deliberate breaths, trying to calm her racing heart. "All right." Schrammig removed his blade and took the lantern from her. She held out her hand to Durok. The red burn from the marble no longer hurt. Durok placed the marble in her palm.

Sydney stood transfixed by the object in her hand. The marble glowed, illuminating the tunnel around them.

Durok began chanting. Whatever magic he invoked, his voice was suddenly drowned out by the voices of the Shadow Folk echoing in her head. The shadows flew at her, surrounding her, like they had in her dream. She couldn't speak or move. The tunnel, Durok, Schrammig—all of it vanished before her. The world became gray. Her teeth chattered, and she shivered. Enveloping her, the shadows whispered, "You are one of us. You belong with us."

I'm not, she tried to shout, but the words didn't come.

"No, she is not." A human voice rang out clear and strong.

The shadows moved back, hovering in a ring around Sydney, as if uncertain.

"You cannot have her. She has already been spoken for."

At those words, the shadows fled. The light and warmth returned. Sydney found herself back in the tunnel, on the ground, her hand clenching the marble. Still shivering, she gasped, deep shuddering breaths.

"How is this possible? There were no others!"

Sydney's head jerked up. Vadnae stood in the adjoining passage. Relief flooded through her. She let go of the marble, and it tumbled to the ground.

"You were mistaken, Durok. My grandfather, Oryn, whom I think you've already met, taught me well." Vadnae held out her hand. The marble rose into the air and flew to her.

"Did Oryn teach you magic for children and naught else?"

A smile crossed Vadnae's lips. "You might be surprised at what I can do."

Her slender hand gestured to the wall across from Sydney. The wall grated open, revealing a new passageway. Glowing stones provided a diffuse light. "I think this is what you were seeking."

"Thank you. But I'm not going in there alone." Durok moved toward Sydney.

Schrammig approached them, turning from Durok to Vadnae. "What the hell is this? Where's Willem? In there?"

"Stay out of this, Schrammig. This is beyond your comprehension." Durok pulled Sydney to her feet. His touch burned. All the pain she'd experienced before from the torture exploded within her. She clawed and kicked at him.

The shadows returned. They brushed against her, penetrating the agonizing pain. More substantial than before, they glided past her and Durok. He dragged her into the glowing tunnel with them.

"Vadnae, do something!" She craned her neck, unable to

see Vadnae or Schrammig.

"She can't help you. You've all failed. Now use the magic. Give the Shadow Folk what they want. This time, if you don't, you will die."

The gray haze surrounded her. Durok fought her, again using her painful memories against her. Fear. Despair. Loneliness. The Shadow Folk were drawn to those feelings, and she felt herself being drawn to the Shadow Folk.

Desperately she searched for memories to save her. She focused on Vadnae's strength, Gregor's honor, Erik's faith, and Willem's conviction, and above all, Edgar's love.

I am myself. No one can take that from me.

The name she knew then, with every fiber of her being, was the one she called on for help. The world spun into darkness, and she beseeched *Llyr*, the silver-eyed man, to answer her call.

Chapter Twenty-Nine

The tunnels vanished. Sydney stood on a barren plain. Pockets of mist hovered near the ground and clung to her hair and clothes. The desolate terrain extended in all directions, much like the Wastes surrounding Oryn's tower. Shivering, she took a hesitant step. A dark silhouette lurked nearby. Durok.

Vadnae and Schrammig were gone, and there was no sign of Llyr.

Durok's guttural laugh broke the silence. "Never trust the Tuatha, Sydney. They can't offer the help you seek. There is no reason why they would help someone like you."

Someone like you.

Someone who was a thief and a whore, an orphaned street urchin with no prospects for the future. Someone who'd never considered the notion that her insignificant life might involve kings or princes. Someone who hadn't believed magic really existed.

Now she'd become much more. She was no longer the child hiding in Edgar's shadow. Now she could step out from behind Edgar's legacy and fight for what was right, not because someone told her she should, but because she believed in it herself. She had something worth fighting for, and people dear to her were counting on her.

She was no wizard, but whatever, whoever she was, here in this place, she had power.

That possibility surprised, even frightened her. The magic here was greater than any she had felt before, an undercurrent flowing around and within her, with the potential to lead to a raging torrent. The magic was different from Llyr's—more uncontrolled, more dangerous. Perhaps more powerful. The kind of magic Durok sought. The kind of magic she had sensed within the Shadow Folk.

"Did you think your friends could defeat me?" Durok's eyes became dark slits. "Once I'm finished with you, I'll deal with your wizard. She will be sorry she crossed my path."

"Are you certain, Durok?"

Sydney whirled around. Vadnae stepped out of the mist. Her gown appeared white, but when she moved, the iridescent threads reflected a light emanating from within her, giving her a radiant glow. Like Llyr. Sydney didn't know how Vadnae had followed them. Durok's hand clamped around her wrist, burning like the manacles had earlier. Fiery tendrils of pain writhed up her arm. She gritted her teeth and struggled to pull away. The landscape spun.

"Let her go."

"Or what? Your powers are pitiful. You will be even easier to defeat than Oryn."

Durok dug his fingers into Sydney's arm. Black spots appeared before her eyes.

"Do you really think it was easy to defeat Oryn?" Vadnae spoke calmly. "Would it surprise you to learn your confrontation with Oryn was carefully planned? You were so concerned with him, you never stopped to consider a greater threat to you."

He snorted. "A greater threat? Unlikely. The Tuatha don't scare me."

"No, not the Tuatha. We're only in the borderlands. I'm the one you should be afraid of, Durok. By distracting you, Grandfather gave me enough time to prepare for this moment. It's one you will never forget." Vadnae's quiet voice carried a simmering power.

The hand around Sydney's wrist flinched. She jerked free from Durok's grasp and stumbled away. Though still reeling from the pain, serenity pooled within her, flowing from the ground into her body. Around her, the mists shifted, like flitting shadows on a wall.

Durok's hate-filled stare paused on her only a moment. He whirled toward Vadnae. "You are nothing more than an apprentice. Your powers are no match for mine." His hand balled to a fist. Wisps of mist coalesced into the shape of a whip. It twined around Vadnae's waist, pulling her off her feet.

Vadnae simply smiled. A wind gusted around her, swirling her hair, and the mist-whip dissipated. She stood, brushing dirt from her dress. "Magic holds so little meaning for you, Durok. Is it naught more than to be used for your personal gain? To cause pain to others?"

"You'd rather I support the people who've condemned us for who we are? Who've burned us alive?" Durok flung a hand toward Sydney. "I'd rather be powerful. By bringing me here, you've given me the means to destroy you. Both of you. I will start with Sydney, so you can witness what real magic can do."

He can't use magic to kill me. It's against the rules. Isn't it?

Durok's enchantment drew power from the pool of energy surrounding her. The air crackled. Her skin tingled. The pressure began to build, forcing the air from her lungs. She fell to her knees and gasped for breath.

"Fight him, Sydney." Vadnae's voice resonated in her mind. "We can fight him together. Call on the Shadow Folk. They won't hurt you this time. Here I can control them."

The mist coalesced into shadowy, human figures. They gathered around Vadnae, hundreds of them, slowly gliding forward, Vadnae a pillar of light in their midst. She chanted, her eyes closed, arms upraised.

"You're too late." Durok's voice cracked like his enchanted whip.

The pressure increased. Sydney focused on the light, fighting to remain conscious. "Help me," she called to the shadowy figures, putting all of her strength into those words. "Help us."

The whispers came, gentle and soothing, taking away the pain.

"I'm sorry it has to end this way," Vadnae said. "This power does not belong in our world. I cannot allow you to use it."

"How are you going to stop me?"

Vadnae stepped back, and the Shadow Folk surged forward.

Durok's triumphant smile faded. His eyes bulged, and his mouth opened. The shadows surrounded him. He spun around to flee, but it was too late. Sydney turned from the dark figure clawing at the insubstantial creatures. She couldn't block his shrill screams. Moments later, he was silenced.

She dared to look then, expecting to see Durok's body on the ground, as she had seen Reynald and the soldiers after the Shadow Folk had killed them. There was no body. One of the shadows stood apart from the others. This one had a face, Durok's face.

The shadow that had once been Durok moved toward her, the others following. His eyes met hers, filling her with the despair of a life now condemned to darkness.

This time she wasn't afraid. In fact, what she felt was pity, not for Durok, who surely deserved this fate, but for the other Shadow Folk, whose despair and desperation were far greater than hers had ever been. They had no hope of escape. Several of the shadowy figures hesitated, and others continued to approach her, arms outstretched, as if asking for her help.

"Sydney, get away from them! Llyr, don't let them take her!"

Llyr, the silver-eyed man, appeared before Sydney, his hand outstretched. "Take my hand. You must come with me now."

His hand clasped hers, enveloping her in a sense of peace and security.

———

"You should not have brought her here."

"I couldn't leave her."

"You've broken one too many of our rules. This time the others may not be willing to overlook your transgression."

"The rules are antiquated. Once we pledge our support to the new king, our realm will change. The old ways must adapt."

Sydney recognized the second voice as Llyr's. The first, a woman's voice with the same lilting quality as his, was not familiar. Opening her eyes, she blinked in the bright sunlight. She lay in a field of soft grass. All her pain was gone. She sat and took a few slow breaths. This was the field she had dreamed of, where she had seen Willem.

Not far away, Llyr sat cross-legged on the ground next to a woman. On her head she wore a garland of flowers, and her hair was the color of the setting sun, amber and gold and copper. Her dress, the rich blue of a cloudless summer day, fluttered in the breeze. Bracelets resembling green vines wound around her bare arms.

The woman's gaze fixed on Sydney. The immense power emanating from her made her beauty awesome and terrifying.

"You've been offered temporary sanctuary," she said. "Nothing more."

Sydney blinked, and the woman disappeared with the breeze.

"You must be hungry." Llyr now sat beside her. He unwrapped a cloth containing several miniature cakes.

Her stomach rumbled. She picked up one of the cakes, but stopped before tasting it, suspicious after having unknowingly taken Celena's drug. "What happens if I eat it?"

He laughed. "Are you afraid I'll put you under an

enchantment?"

"Will you?"

"Please, Sydney, eat. Our food will satisfy your hunger, nothing more. You must believe me when I say that I offer it with only the best of intentions."

She took a bite of the cake. Sweet and savory and filled with a fruit like none she'd ever tasted. Llyr smiled. She devoured it, wiping away crumbs with her sleeve, and ate a second cake. Llyr handed her a glass bottle containing a sweet, heady drink.

"It's my own honeysuckle wine. The finest in the land, or so I've been told."

She drank a small sip of the strong wine. The sun warmed her face, and her eyes began to close. The brilliant red and purple flowers in the field swayed gently in the breeze. Llyr touched her arm and handed her another cake. Eating it renewed her energy.

"Where are we? Where's Vadnae? Is she all right?"

"Vadnae is fine. You will see her again soon. What she did was dangerous, but necessary. She impressed many of us. As for you...." He sighed. "Perhaps I was wrong to bring you here, but I did what I thought best."

"Why shouldn't I be here? I'm not even sure where here is." Once she spoke, however, she realized this place must be the faery realm.

"You are correct, you are in our realm. You're one of the few outsiders to venture here in hundreds of years."

Llyr had read her mind. As he'd done when she first met him in the tunnels. She remembered what he'd said to her about his realm. The breeze shifted, and a chill invaded her. "You said I couldn't come here. You said I'd die if I did."

"Most do not survive the borderlands. You needn't worry, though. You are here under my protection." He smiled at the sky. "None of the others will harm you."

The woman's face, now frowning, entered Sydney's mind.

She shuddered. "Why would they want to? I ain't-I mean, I haven't done anything." Nothing except kill three people using magic she didn't understand and couldn't control.

Llyr's silver eyes focused on her. "Unknowingly using the powers of the Shadow Folk once is forgivable. Had you done it again, you would not be here now. Durok wanted their power for himself, and thus he has faced the harshest of punishments."

Thinking of Durok and his fate made the burn on her palm twinge. She glanced at the blistered flesh, and at the wounds on her wrists. "He's not the only one who deserves that kind of punishment."

"Never say that." Llyr stabbed a finger at her. "Never. Durok was a wizard, so he fell under our jurisdiction. Your kind, Sydney, have no business in the Shadow realm, regardless of their crimes. To suggest such a thing is precisely the reason we left your world. Magic should never be used for such ends."

Chastened, she looked away. "I didn't mean—"

"The intent is what matters most where magic is concerned. Durok sought to use your desperation and hatred to tempt you into using the Shadow Folk. A wizard can learn, as Vadnae did, how to enter our world. Durok wasn't able to do so. He instead decided to use someone like you, someone who has some Tuatha blood, to do what he could not."

She stared at Llyr. "Tuatha blood? But I'm not...." She stopped. Her past contained too many possibilities. Unknown parents. The ability to sense things—sense magic—where other people could not. Both Vadnae and Durok said she was connected to the Tuatha. To be related to them by blood was something she had never considered. "Are you saying I'm kin to the Tuatha?"

At his nod, her mind reeled. "How? How can that be?"

Llyr shifted uneasily. He grasped the bottle of wine and took a long drink.

When he finished, she snatched the bottle from him,

although she resisted drinking more herself. Her hands shook. "Dammit, tell me, Llyr. How can I have Tuatha blood? I'm from Last Hope. Edgar found me when I was a baby." Or so he had said. Surely Edgar hadn't been aware of the truth behind her birth, whatever it was. Surely he wouldn't have hidden such a thing from her.

Llyr rested his elbows on his knees, hands clasped in his lap. "I'll tell you how such a thing is possible. I've already broken our rules by giving you my true name and bringing you here. Breaking one or two more won't matter."

When a breeze gusted across the field, he frowned, but continued, "Many years ago, when we were free to roam as we pleased in your world, your kind welcomed us in their halls. Some even welcomed us into their lives. Over time, a number of your nobility came to share our bloodline. In fact, in Willem, our lineage is stronger than we've seen in a long time. That is one of the reasons why he is the first of your kings in nigh a hundred years to whom we will pledge our support."

"What about me? I'm not nobility."

"I'm afraid your existence is a harsh reminder to us. Much has changed since the Lady closed our realm. One of our most important rules forbids contact with your world, but some Tuatha refuse to obey it. If they are caught, they face the same fate as Durok. You have experienced the Shadow realm, so you understand what a terrible price they must pay for their curiosity, should they choose to return to our world." He shook his head sadly and sighed. "Often the Tuatha who leave our realm never return, for fear of the consequences. But to live in the human realm also comes at a high price for us."

She had felt the despair of the Shadow Folk, and she had almost become part of their cold, lifeless world. Turning to the fields around them, sadness swept over her. In spite of the vibrant colors, intense fragrances, and exquisite tastes, a deep undercurrent of longing flowed within this world, a longing for something the Tuatha could never re-create.

"You didn't answer my question. How can I be kin to the Tuatha?"

"I've told you how it is possible, how some of our kind ventured into your world and broke our rules." He paused and raised an eyebrow. "I trust you are familiar with what is required to conceive a child?"

She snorted. "Yeah, that's something I understand. But why—"

"Then the answer to *how* you can be our kin should be clear. Anything more, I am forbidden to speak of, and even I dare not do so."

His response wasn't satisfying, but Sydney doubted she could get him to tell her any more. Llyr was frightened of his own kind. And yet Willem sought them as allies. "Why did the Shadow Folk say I was one of them?"

"The Shadow Folk are part of us, and we are also part of them. The light cannot exist without the darkness, you see. We do our best to keep the two in balance. Durok tried to upset that balance by offering the Shadow Folk a way to escape their imprisonment—by using you." Llyr hesitated, and then shifted closer to her, speaking softly. "My kind cannot free the Shadow Folk, but it has been said that someone like you—someone who can walk in both worlds—could accomplish this. Fortunately, you were strong enough to resist them, as Oryn said you would be. The old wizard is rather pleased by your actions. In fact, I would say you exceeded our expectations."

"Durok said he defeated Oryn."

"Oryn is here and very much alive and well."

Sydney exhaled, relieved. "Can I see him? And Vadnae?"

A cloud passed in front of the sun. Llyr peered at the sky. "Perhaps later. First, there is someone who needs your assistance to complete his final task."

"Willem?" Her heart beat a little faster.

Llyr nodded. "One task remains, and this is the most

difficult. The kings of old were permitted to bring one reminder of the past when they arrived in our realm to complete their tasks. We neglected to give Willem the opportunity to do so. Instead, I am giving you the chance to play that role. Will you accept it?"

"What do I have to do?"

"You will find out soon enough." Llyr leaned close, covering her eyes with his hand. "Breathe, Sydney, and count to three." His breath was warm on her face. It flowed into her, and a tingling spread throughout her body.

When she opened her eyes, the field was filled with the same brilliant red and purple flowers, but Llyr was gone and Willem stood beside her.

"Sydney?" Willem's eyes grew wide.

She remembered the kiss she'd given him, and her face flushed.

"Is it really you?" He touched her arm, as if reassuring himself she was real. "I dreamed of this place, dreamed we were here together." He took her hand, helping her to her feet and sending a shiver through her. "This can't be a dream. This is real."

Perhaps they'd shared the same dream. Anything seemed possible here. A gentle breeze brushed her face, carrying the sweet fragrance of the flowers at their feet. Willem's eyes were bluer than she remembered, the color of the brilliant sky above. They pulled her in, filling the emptiness inside her with the love she saw within them.

"I hoped you would find your way here, Sydney."

A thought tugged at the edge of her mind. She couldn't recall how she got here and why she'd come. The answer floated away on the breeze. Willem drew her close. She pressed her head to his chest, listening to the steady beat of his heart. Willem was right; this had to be real. She'd never felt so alive, so aware of every sensation, from the longing and desire pulsing in her blood, to the intoxicating scent of the exotic flowers, to the curve of her body against his.

"I hoped I'd find you." The words came out before Sydney realized she'd spoken aloud.

He cupped her face in his hands and tilted her head toward him. "You feel it, don't you? Here we can have everything we want."

Everything we want. His mouth sought hers, and she pulled him close. She desired him, as a man and not a king. Here, in this beautiful place, she could have him. With each caress, the barriers they had built between them came down.

"I want you to stay here with me. Please say you will."

His words jolted a memory deep within her. *I want you to stay with me.* Zared's words. They let loose a flood of memories. Blood dripping from a silver blade. A red stain spreading across a colorful rug. Bodies swinging from the gallows. Hot iron burning her flesh.

"I can't do this." She untangled herself from Willem's embrace and backed away. "We can't stay here. What about Last Hope?"

"Last Hope?" He shook his head. "What's Last Hope?"

"What is it?" Her chest tightened. "Last Hope is the town you promised to protect. Don't you remember?"

He stared at a distant spot on the horizon. "All I remember is the dream, this place...." He met her gaze. "And you."

He reached for her. Her body ached to stay here with him, to feel his mouth and hands on her skin.

When he touched her this time, his body tensed.

Willem drew back, a horrified expression on his face. Reflected in his eyes, the scene from the tapestry in Oryn's tower came alive. Hundreds, perhaps thousands of men fighting and dying on blood-soaked fields, towns burning, skies filled with thick black smoke, women and children starving in barren fields.

"You see it, too." His voice came out a hoarse whisper. "Now I remember. That is a glimpse of my future. I am to be a king. I've spent my entire life preparing to be king."

She shuddered, trying to shake off the frightening vision. "The future?"

His mouth pressed into a grim smile, and his eyes darkened, blue once more. He stepped back, hands clenched at his sides. "What kind of king would I be if I allow my people to suffer in such a manner?"

"They're already suffering. You said you'd fight for a better life for all of us."

"You've never experienced war." He paced, shaking his head. "I can't simply go back and take the crown and lead the kingdom to peace and prosperity. The Guild isn't going to give up. The lords who oppose me aren't going to give up. My vision will occur throughout the kingdom."

He gripped her arms. "People could lose their homes, their families, their lives, if they choose to follow me. What if I'm not the one? They all expect me to be the king who will oust the Guild and set things right. What if they're wrong? What if I convince them to support me and believe in me, and we don't win?"

His doubt frightened her. This was not the Willem who had helped change her opinion of herself, or the man who had promised to return before he stepped into the glowing portal with Llyr, the man who had promised to protect the people of Last Hope. Somehow she had to find the Willem she believed in—the one she loved—just as she'd been able to find herself.

Ignoring the hands clenching her arms, she said, "We've got nothing to lose. The Guild's ruined our lives. You've given us hope, and we're ready to fight. Even if we fail, we're willing to take the risk." He didn't respond, so she jerked out of his grasp and pushed back her sleeves, thrusting her blistered wrists at him. "You told me to fight Schrammig. That was part of my dream. You said I shouldn't let him defeat me. You gave me the strength to resist. I didn't let him break me."

His shoulders slumped. "Oh, Sydney," he murmured,

taking her hand, touching her wrist gently with his fingertips. "I'm sorry."

She snatched her arm away. "I don't want your pity. I want you to finish what you've started. You gave your word to protect the people of Last Hope. Being king is your destiny, remember?"

"I never asked to be a king. You don't understand what it means, the expectations I must live up to every day." He brushed the lock of hair from his face, his expression haggard, dark smudges beneath his eyes.

"You once said we weren't so different. That we're both trapped by how other people see us." She placed her hand on his chest. "Willem, I know how you feel."

Willem's pulse quickened. He covered her hand with his own. "I'd forgotten. You do understand, more than most people would. The Tuatha said I could stay here if I wanted. I could live a simple life. *We* could live a simple life." He bent his head toward her. "It's tempting, isn't it?"

For several moments, they stared at each other. Sydney's heart pounded. *If you go back, you lose this chance. He won't feel this way about you again.* Turning toward the field, she sensed the same longing and sadness, only this time those feelings came from her heart. She looked away. This wasn't about her. The resistance needed Willem. The kingdom needed him. More than she did.

Clouds hid the sun, throwing them into shadow. Willem drew in a long breath and let go of her hand. "This kind of life is not for us."

She bowed her head, afraid to speak.

He stepped back, squaring his shoulders. "It's my destiny to be king. I must also accept the consequences. I swore an oath to you, and to the people of Last Hope. I will keep my word. I will fight for my people, no matter what the cost."

"You said you wanted to be king so you could change things. You made me believe it. That's the sort of king people will follow."

"Sydney." Willem's fingers caressed her cheek. "Thank you. For believing in me."

The heat burned within her at his touch. She moved out of his reach, hoping he couldn't see her trembling. "I knew you wouldn't give up."

"Let's get out of here while we can." They began to run toward a glowing doorway in the base of an ancient oak tree on the other side of the field.

They neared the tree. A strong breeze blew across the field. Behind it, the flowers drooped and the grass withered. The field became a barren plain, and the mist drew in around them, obscuring their view.

Sydney stopped. "How did we get back here? This is where the Shadow Folk live."

"You must pass through the borderlands in order to return home." Llyr stepped out of the mists. The woman he had spoken to in the field joined him.

"You did well, your highness." She inclined her head to Willem. From within the shimmering green cloak she wore over her gown, she withdrew a sheathed sword and knife and handed them to Willem. Intertwining vines etched in the hilt matched her bracelets. "May these protect you on your journeys."

Willem bowed. "Thank you, my lady. You are very generous." He buckled on the sword and slid the knife into his belt.

"We look forward to being guests at your coronation."

"I look forward to extending you an invitation, although it may be some time before I can plan for such an event."

"Time holds little meaning for us here. The day will come when the time is right. When it does, I will keep my promise, and you will keep yours." She held out her hand, and Willem brought it to his lips.

"I give you my word, my lady. I will be a champion for your

return."

The woman's mouth pressed together in a smile offering little warmth.

She then moved toward Sydney, who fought the urge to step back and clasped her hands to keep them steady, although surely the woman knew what she was thinking and feeling.

"Sydney, your courage and determination surprise me. Be careful of the path you choose. Certain paths are more difficult than others."

She waved her hand, and the glowing doorway appeared out of the mist. "Now you must return to your world. Vadnae will rejoin you once she has learned what we must teach her. It is only fitting for a king to be advised by a powerful wizard."

Willem bowed his head to her and took Sydney's arm. Together, they entered the blinding light, to return and save what remained of Last Hope.

Chapter Thirty

Sydney and Willem emerged from the tunnels without encountering any of Schrammig's soldiers. They hurried toward the abbey, where they planned to join Gregor and Erik and perhaps other members of the resistance. Sydney quickly became unnerved by the silent, empty streets. Nearing the center of town, she led Willem down a side street behind the market square. The market should have been teeming with people at mid-day, the air filled with the aromas of roasted meats and pungent spices and the shouts of merchants hawking their wares. Instead, the square was deserted. The permanent wooden stalls had been burned to the ground, blackened boards still smoldering. The harsh odor of smoke tinged with burnt wool lingered.

Sydney edged forward, staring at the four ropes—and four bodies—on the wooden scaffold at the far end of the square. She imagined the wooden beam creaking as the ropes strained against the weight. One of the bodies resembled a woman's. From this distance, she couldn't be sure. Skirting the edge of the square would take her close enough to determine whether any of the faces were familiar. She took another step forward, scanning the streets bordering the empty marketplace, searching for soldiers.

"Sydney, don't." Willem grabbed her arm, pulling her back and turning her to face him. "Schrammig's soldiers will be watching this place. Don't make it any easier for him."

He followed her gaze to the gallows. "I see it, too. But those poor souls are dead. There's nothing we can do for them. Schrammig will pay for his crimes, I promise you. Saving ourselves must be our first priority now."

Living on the streets, Sydney had excelled at saving herself. Willem was right. This was no time to agonize about Schrammig's victims.

"One of them could be Betty. Schrammig said he hanged her."

Willem's jaw clenched. "I'm sorry, Sydney. The girls—are they safe?"

"Saw them at the abbey. This time I'll listen to you. Let's get out of here, before someone sees us."

He handed her the knife from his belt. "You might need this."

"Thanks." She took the knife, and their fingertips touched. Her hand tingled. She quickly knelt to secure the blade in her boot sheath. They hadn't spoken of what had passed between them in the field. They were back in the real world now, not a magical fantasy. A dangerous world.

"Sydney." His voice was low, his blue eyes fixed on her.

Heat rushed to her face, and her body trembled. "We should keep moving," she whispered.

"Of course, you're right." He drew in a long breath and motioned for her to lead the way.

Sydney avoided the main thoroughfare and zigzagged from one cobblestone side street to the next. Blocks from the market, the smoke still lingered in the air.

The pale afternoon sunlight held a hazy glow, perhaps from the smoke of a distant fire. Sydney squinted. Not just the fire. Everything now, from the sun to the sky to the dusty streets and dingy buildings, appeared drab and dull after being in the faery realm.

They spotted groups of soldiers patrolling the main streets, but not enough to indicate that Schrammig's reinforcements had entered Last Hope.

Not far from the abbey, shouting shattered the illusion of calm. The smoky haze was stronger here, and the air thick. Sydney's stomach churned. In a town like Last Hope, flames could rapidly engulf an entire block of wooden buildings clustered together. As a child, she'd once seen a fire burn for days, destroying entire streets in her neighborhood.

Willem drew his sword, and they slowly proceeded. She recalled the blackened bodies at the monk's farm and the hate in Schrammig's eyes when he'd spoken of Edgar. Schrammig didn't value the lives of others. He wouldn't make a distinction between the Guild's enemies and innocent bystanders.

At the next corner, they came upon two men, armed with clubs and long knives, facing down four soldiers. In horror, Sydney watched one of the men stumble to his knees. The soldier's sword went through his abdomen and out his back, and jerked him forward when the blade exited, leaving him crumpled on the ground, blood pooling beneath him. The other man cried out when a soldier slammed into him and sent him sprawling. He crawled away, fumbling for his knife. The soldiers surrounded him.

"Sydney, stay here."

Willem ran toward them. He swung at one of the soldiers, severing the man's sword arm. The other three turned on him.

Sydney had never seen anyone move so fast. Willem's thrusts and parries anticipated the moves of his attackers, and he held off all three at once. But he was only defending himself, not gaining any ground.

Dammit, I can't just stand here. She pulled out the knife and targeted the soldier hanging back waiting to catch Willem off guard. Her knife was no match for their swords, but the soldier's attention was focused on Willem. That gave her an advantage.

When she neared him, he spun to face her. Her blade

nicked his arm, and he jumped back. Frantically she ducked a blow aimed at her throat. His elbow jabbed her stomach, knocking the wind out of her. She doubled over. He relaxed his stance before he swung hastily. Sydney sprang up inside his swing and thrust the knife into his throat. Blood sprayed her face and sleeve. He staggered back, dropping his sword and clawing at the knife, then fell to his knees.

Sydney whirled around. Another soldier sprawled at Willem's feet. The last one tried to run, but the injured man grabbed a sword and plunged it through his back. Willem was breathing hard, sweat pouring down his face. His left sleeve was torn below his shoulder, the fabric blood-soaked.

"Are you all right?"

She nodded and wiped the dead man's blood from her face with her sleeve. "How's your arm?"

He winced as he flexed his arm and rolled up his sleeve. "I've had worse. Hand me the knife."

Grimacing, she pulled the knife from the soldier's throat. She cleaned the blade on the dead man's uniform and handed it to Willem.

"Got scratched up, too, eh?" The man who had killed the fleeing soldier came over to them. He walked around the dead soldiers, kicking each of the bodies. "Not bad work. Never seen anyone use a sword like you did."

"I've had practice." Willem used the blade to cut off the rest of his sleeve. He fumbled to bind the material around his arm but couldn't manage using one hand.

"Here." Sydney took the strip of cloth from him. The wound, though not deep, still bled freely. She tied the makeshift bandage as he instructed, wondering what kinds of battles he had been in.

"Thanks," he said with a clenched smile when she finished. "Don't worry, I'll be fine." He cut an arc with his sword, using his wounded arm.

"Four less of them bastards, thanks to you." The man

studied Sydney first, then Willem. "What're the two of you doing out here?"

His clothes were simple and worn. Sydney guessed he was part of the resistance, or someone who was tired of being pushed around by the soldiers. Either way, he clearly wasn't on Schrammig's side.

"We're meeting friends at the abbey," she said when Willem seemed to be waiting for her lead.

The man smiled, revealing yellowed teeth. "You must be one of them important types what's been meeting there to figure how to get rid of Schrammig before he kills us all."

"Have you been there?" Willem asked.

"Naw. I got my duties, same as they do. Tom here," he pointed to the body of his friend, "Tom said they wanted people to stand guard and keep out the soldiers. These streets," now he waved a hand around them, "was our watch. We done a good job, too, until four of 'em jumped us."

"Are people doing this elsewhere in Last Hope?"

He shrugged. "Dunno for sure, but I guess so. I only got these streets—not sure about the others. Think they must be doing the same thing, don't you?"

"I hope so," Willem said.

Sydney glanced at the dead soldiers. Without Willem's help, the soldiers would easily have overpowered the two men. Not a good omen for the resistance.

"I ain't such a bad fighter," he said. "Four on two's not good odds. Even worse when they got better weapons."

Willem wiped his sword on one of the dead soldier's tunics. "You did well. I'm sorry about your friend, though."

"Nothing for it," he said with a sigh. "Tom always said he aimed to go down for a good cause. This would be one, eh?"

"Indeed it would."

They gathered the swords and found more knives on the bodies of the soldiers. Then they dragged the bodies into a nearby alley. The man searched the soldiers' pockets and took a handful of coins. He sat back on his heels. "Gotta find someone to help get Tom home. You get on to the abbey. Next patrol shouldn't be by for a while."

Willem put a hand on the man's shoulder. "You're a good man. Be well."

Sydney and Willem continued on, and he said quietly, "That was nice work, Sydney. Did Edgar teach you to fight like that?"

"Yeah, but I've never had to kill anyone before."

The three men in the alley who had been killed by the Shadow Folk on her behalf screamed in her mind. She'd seen plenty of death, but she had never taken another life. Now she'd killed a man without thinking. Blood streaked her hands and shirt. She took in Willem's blood-spattered clothes and the fatigue reflected in his face.

Willem put his arm around her waist, and she leaned against him. "There will be a lot more killing before we're done," he said softly.

At last, they arrived at the gates of the churchyard. The courtyard inside the gate was quiet. Willem rang the bell.

No one came to let them in. Sydney paced, anxious. "What's taking so long?"

"They'll come."

She let out a sigh of relief when a brown-robed monk hurried across the courtyard. His gait was unsteady. Studying him closer, she realized that she was swaying on her feet. She held one of the iron bars to steady herself. The burns on her wrists and back throbbed, and the cobblestones spun toward her.

"Sydney?" Willem's voice faded, and the soothing darkness surrounded her.

———————

Sydney's eyes opened to the sound of chanting. She felt oddly comforted by the rise and fall of the low, harmonic strains. The candle flickered, and shadows bounded across the walls. Only shadows, nothing more. She was in the abbey, and she was safe.

She sat up slowly. The pain had lessened. What remained was bearable. Touching the bandages on her wrists, she wondered how long it would take her wounds to heal.

"I'm glad you're finally awake, my dear." A figure stepped forward.

Sydney gasped at the familiar unkempt white hair and beard and disheveled blue cloak. "Oryn?"

"It is good to see you, Sydney." Oryn's face crinkled into a smile. He sat on the bed and patted her hand.

She blinked back tears. In spite of Llyr's assurance that he lived, she had doubted she'd ever see Oryn again. Their first encounter in the forest outside Last Hope, when he had saved her life and thrust her upon this strange and unknown path, seemed so long ago. So much had changed.

"Are you really here, or is this a dream?"

He squeezed her hand. Solid, reassuring. "It's no dream, although I cannot stay long. Llyr owed me a favor and helped me come here. I need to speak with you. There are things I should have told you sooner. I never meant to keep the truth from you."

She tensed. He'd kept so much from her. "You didn't tell me or any of the others the truth, not about the Tuatha or Durok or the Shadow Folk."

"There are many things I would do differently, had I the power to do them again. Now you understand the threat Durok posed. Any knowledge I shared with you could have also fallen into his hands. I couldn't let such a thing happen."

"You knew he'd come after me. You knew all along what he planned to do, didn't you?"

"Predicting future events is never precise. I could anticipate his actions, and I acted to counter them as best I could."

She scooted away from him, drawing her knees to her

chest. "I've been a pawn in this whole thing. You only saved my life 'cause you needed me, 'cause I'm a part-Tuatha freak. I never asked for any of this. None of this bloody magic and wizards."

Oryn's blue eyes stared at her, and the lines on his face softened. "Edgar once said something similar to me. His fate was bound to magic, as is yours, dear Sydney. Edgar attempted to live a different life, but ultimately he could not escape his destiny."

"I don't believe in fate. My life is what I make of it."

"Some of us have no choice in the matter. I suppose you will learn that in time. In fact, what I've come to tell you concerns these things. It concerns who you are."

Suddenly afraid to breathe, she whispered, "My parents?"

Oryn nodded.

"You know who they are?"

"I wish I'd told you years ago. Some secrets are difficult to share. I lied to Edgar, you see. I knew you were his child, and I never told him. He went to his grave without knowing the truth."

Her throat constricted. "I was left to die as a babe. Edgar found me—he can't be my father. He can't!"

"He found you, yes, but months earlier he had met a woman in the tunnels. She was a Tuatha. They only saw each other once. She died not long after you were born, but she made sure Edgar would be the one to raise you."

Sydney shrank away from him. She refused to believe it. Finally, someone was telling her the truth, but it was something she didn't want to hear. "Edgar and Anaria loved each other. I'm certain they did. He was faithful to her."

Oryn fidgeted on the bed, tugging at his beard. "It's not that simple, not where the Tuatha are concerned. I believe she seduced Edgar, for her own reasons. What those were, I'm not entirely sure. She made a choice to bear his child, regardless of the consequences she would face from her kind. I assume she saw something in the future, perhaps something I haven't seen myself. Whatever it was compelled her to do such a thing."

The more Sydney fought to ignore and deny this thing called *fate*, the more it pulled her toward an unknown future.

"What did she see?"

"In you, Sydney, I see potential. You will help shape the fate of our kingdom. But the future depends on the choices we make. Your choices are based on the foundation Edgar gave you. This woman would have seen that, as clearly as I. Perhaps that is why she chose Edgar. She sensed he was an honorable man in his heart."

Edgar had taught her well. If only she'd appreciated it while he was still alive. "How could you not tell him the truth?"

"Would he have loved you any differently if he had learned you were his child? He treated you as if you were. Nothing would have changed that."

Tears filled her eyes.

"Sometimes I wish I had told him the truth when I had the chance. Even wizards make mistakes. I wish I'd been able to protect you from the pain you endured after losing Edgar. I regret failing to shield you very much. But your experiences made you strong. In you, I see Edgar's strength."

The candle flickered. Oryn rose and took her hands in his gnarled ones. "Perhaps we will meet again, dear Sydney. I hope you will forgive me one day. More importantly, I hope you forgive yourself. Edgar would have been proud of your accomplishments. Never doubt that. Willem and the others will need your strength. There is still much to be done."

He stepped back. "Farewell."

She held out her hand, but his outline began to fade, until only a shadowy form remained.

"Farewell, Oryn."

The candle flickered again, and he was gone.

Chapter Thirty-One

Unwilling to ponder Oryn's revelations alone, Sydney decided she felt well enough to venture out of her room. Her footsteps echoed in the flagstone corridors, and she saw no one in the dimly lit hallways and side chapels. A rectangular window showed moonlight illuminating the courtyard.

Her energy quickly faded, and the pain returned. She leaned against the wall, closing her eyes until the lightheadedness passed. *I'm not going to let Schrammig win.* She forced herself to continue, even though she had to pause every few steps to stop the hallway from spinning.

Oryn's words continued to spin in her mind, weaving the threads of truth about her. Her mother was a Tuatha. Impossible, but true. *Sometimes you're better off not knowing the truth,* Edgar had often said. She wanted to think Oryn's revelation didn't change who she was. She'd already changed.

"Sydney?"

The child's voice joined the echoes in her mind. It called her name once more. Sydney rubbed her eyes and turned. Janey stood behind her, her face creased with worry.

"Ain't you supposed to be in bed? It's near midnight. I got lectured last time I walked around by myself at night. Brother Erik likes to lecture."

Sydney had to smile at the idea of Erik lecturing the children who had come under the monks' care. "Why aren't you in bed?"

"I'm looking for you. I wanted to sit with you, in case you woke up."

"Was I asleep a long time?"

"Yeah. Everyone's been worried. Are you better now?"

"I'm fine. I think." Sydney took a tentative step away from the wall. The floor felt solid beneath her now. She forced a smile to reassure the girl. "See? Much better now."

Janey squinted. "You don't look so good. They said you got hurt bad." Her voice dropped to a whisper. "They said Schrammig hurt you." She moved closer to Sydney, and her wide-eyed gaze darted around the corridor, as if she'd conjure him by speaking his name.

"He did. He's hurt a lot of people."

"Like my mam? He hurt her, didn't he?"

A rope creaking. Bodies hanging from the gallows. Sydney shuddered. She shouldn't be the one to tell Janey her mother had been hanged.

"Da was here." Janey's voice shook. "Said he'd find Mam and bring her home. Told me to take care of Sara and Frannie. He scared me." Tears streamed down her cheeks, although her voice was flat, emotionless. "She's dead, ain't she?"

Sydney simply nodded and put her arms around Janey. The girl's bony shoulders shook with sobs.

"Why didn't he tell me? Sara's too little. She'd be too scared. He could've told me. Why did he pretend she'd be all right?"

Sydney stroked her hair. "To protect you from it as long as he could."

Like Edgar sought to protect her. She blinked back tears.

"He can't protect any of us from Schrammig." Janey pulled away, wiping her eyes. She fixed Sydney with a stare. "He did it. Schrammig."

Sydney gave another nod. No sense in shielding her. "Schrammig's killed a lot of good people in Last Hope, like your mother. He's killed people I cared about, too."

Janey hunched her shoulders and clenched her fists. "I hate him. I'd kill him if I could."

Her words thrust Sydney back to the day she had learned of Edgar's death. The grief and anger she had felt coursed through her. That day she'd truly started hating the Guild and Schrammig. Sydney gripped the girl's arm. "It's not worth hating him. I already hate him enough for both of us. D'you hear me? Think about your sisters, like your da said. Be strong for them and for your da."

Janey regarded her a moment. She moved away and stood straighter, head up, shoulders back. "I'll try. That's what Willem said. That I should be strong for Sara and Frannie."

"You've seen Willem? Where is he?"

"He's gone now."

"Gone? How can he be gone?" Another wave of vertigo assaulted her. Sydney leaned against the wall.

"He came to see you. Brother Erik said not to let anyone in, but...." Janey shrugged. "I figured you'd want to see Willem."

"Did he say where he went?"

"Someplace dangerous. He left with Da's friends."

Sydney's fists opened and closed helplessly. Willem should have awakened her. "Janey, where's Brother Erik?"

She bobbed her head toward the long hallway. "Saw him in the sanctuary." She brushed the tears from her face and threw her arms around Sydney's waist. "Willem said he'd be back."

"He will." Sydney tried to sound confident. She pressed her lips to the top of Janey's head and sent her to bed.

Willem will be back. She wished she could believe her words.

———————

Sydney pushed open the heavy wooden door to the church sanctuary. Candles glowed on the altar, and lamps hung from the beams running the length of the room. The dim light cast shadows across the sleeping figures crammed into the church pews and huddled in the aisles. Some people talked quietly, clustered together in the corners, and some knelt before the altar near the front, praying with the monks. The sweet, earthy aroma of incense, combined with the reek of unwashed bodies, overpowered the enclosed space, making Sydney's stomach churn.

She moved around the perimeter. Most of the people huddled on the floor were women and children. Some stared at her with vacant eyes, arms cradling their sleeping babes. She remembered Willem's vision of the future, people forced out of their homes, seeking shelter wherever they could. An icy lump grew in her chest.

"Please, miss."

A girl only a year or two younger than herself tugged on the hem of Sydney's breeches. The girl sat away from the others. One small boy curled in her lap and another's head rested on her leg.

"Please, we haven't eaten in two days. They said there'd be food here, but no one will help me. It ain't for me. For my boys."

"I'm sure the monks will help...." Sydney stopped herself when the girl shifted the boy on her lap. Candlelight fell on her painted cheeks and lips, accentuating the hollows in her face and the dark circles beneath her eyes.

She met Sydney's stare, her face hard. An emaciated hand pulled a thin blanket across her tattered, low-cut dress. "Said they won't help the likes of me. All I want is some food for my boys."

Sydney could imagine what the monks had said to the girl and what the people around her had said. She stepped toward her. The girl gave her a fierce stare and clutched her children.

"Don't go anywhere. I'll bring food. For all of you."

The girl's body relaxed. She bent her head over the sleeping boys and softly hummed a wordless tune, one Sydney remembered Anaria humming to her years earlier. A faery tune, an old song meant to offer protection to children.

Often mothers like this one prayed for help from whatever gods they believed in, only to find none of them ever answered. What might Llyr think of this world, so different from his? Sydney clenched her hands. The ugliness and the pain gave her world an authenticity that had been missing in the faery realm. Their world was too beautiful, too perfect.

She approached the monks kneeling near the altar, heads bowed, and waited a minute. Impatient, she scuffed her boots on the stone floor.

One of them pivoted toward her. Erik's plump face peered at her from beneath his cowl. "Sydney?"

The monk beside him lifted his head. Erik whispered to him, then rose and hurried to Sydney. He clasped her hands and embraced her, a much warmer welcome than she expected from him.

He ushered her to an empty corner. His face fell when he glanced at her bandaged wrists. "I'm sorry, Sydney. We shouldn't have let you go. Gregor was beside himself."

"I'm all right. I will be, anyway. Where's Willem? Janey said he left. We just got here."

"This is the second night you've been here."

"I missed a whole day?"

Erik nodded toward the sanctuary. "You see what's happened. The Guild has been burning people out of their homes. Others are scared, with nowhere else to go. I'm not sure we can care for all of them if they keep coming. How can we keep them safe? The streets are filled with soldiers now. Schrammig sent us a message, saying if we don't hand over all the members of the resistance hiding here, he'll take them by force. He's given us until noon tomorrow."

The room started to spin. Erik put a hand on her back, steadying her. "You don't look well. You should be in bed."

She brushed away his arm. "You still didn't tell me where Willem went."

Erik slumped. "I wish he'd stayed. We need him. He met with your friends Jimmy and Celena. They brought information about Willem's allies converging on Last Hope. They also said they had a plan to take control of the Guild Hall, tonight. Willem and Gregor went with them, along with Brother Francis and a good many of the other monks."

Erik started babbling about tunnels and soldiers, but she wasn't really listening. She'd been left behind. She didn't want to accept that she barely had the strength to walk the length of the abbey. Anger overshadowed her pain. Schrammig's torture had stolen her chance to fight alongside Willem.

She became aware of Erik holding her arm.

"Sydney? What are we going to do? What if Willem doesn't come back or if the soldiers get here first? What do we do?"

For the first time, Erik was seeking her guidance. "He'll be back. Until then....." She surveyed the people huddled in the sanctuary. They'd come here hoping they'd be safe. Willem had promised he'd protect the people of Last Hope—but he couldn't do it alone.

"We should be ready, for whatever happens. We should find a way to defend ourselves."

He paled. "Defend the abbey? Against those soldiers? We're monks. We have no weapons. All we can do is pray."

"Pray? Don't be stupid, Erik. How the hell is prayer going to help?"

One of the monks near the altar glowered at her.

"Our prayers saved your life, Sydney."

She didn't believe him, but this was not the time to argue with Erik about his beliefs. She lowered her voice. "Sitting around praying ain't enough. We can't give up. There's gotta be something we can do."

"I know. But how—"

"Brother Erik, if I may interrupt?" One of the other monks

approached them. "I didn't mean to eavesdrop, but we can protect ourselves. We've been discussing what we would do ever since Father Abbot's arrest. We owe it to him to do whatever we can. God will provide."

Erik glanced around the room. "I suppose many things here in the abbey could be used for our defense."

Prayer might soothe their souls, but Sydney doubted it would provide swords or real weapons. Or the knowledge of how to use them. "What about hiding places? Is there somewhere these people can hide?"

The other monk nodded. "Brother Erik, you and Brother Francis spoke of the tunnels beneath the town. We have catacombs that run beneath the abbey. Many people could hide down there."

Erik clapped him on the back. "Excellent, Brother Thomas. We should make plans. Gather as many of the other brothers as you can."

"But it's nearly midnight. Most of them are asleep."

"Then wake them. We've no time to waste."

Sydney touched Erik's arm. "First, there's a woman and her children who need food." She nodded to where the young whore sat alone with her boys. "She said no one here will help her."

Brother Thomas turned in the direction Sydney had indicated. "Some people aren't deserving of help," he said with a condescending sniff.

Sydney glared at him. "Her children are hungry. You ain't gonna help her because she's a whore? D'you think she likes selling her body on the streets? Sometimes it's the only way to get food and shelter."

"There are always alternatives—"

"Dammit, Erik, there aren't. Not for people like us. I've been there, too. So you feed her and her children and anyone else who needs it."

Erik shifted uneasily. "Brother Thomas, go wake the

others. Sydney and I will fetch food from the kitchen."

Brother Thomas nodded and hurried to the remaining monks kneeling at the altar. Townspeople began to rouse their neighbors from slumber. Soon the monks began recruiting teams of volunteers to patrol the streets around the abbey and ready makeshift barricades.

"Come with me, Sydney," Erik said. "I think there's bread, perhaps stew. And some potatoes."

Sydney followed him, her dizziness and pain lessening. "We should get all the food we can find. We'll likely need it later."

Erik wiped the sweat from his forehead with a handkerchief. "You know we can't fight Schrammig. Even if we hide people, he might still find them. How much of a chance do you think we have of surviving this?"

"Erik, we have to try." She touched her bandaged wrists. "We can't let Schrammig win. We owe it to Willem. And to ourselves."

Chapter Thirty-Two

Sydney jerked up when the door to the sanctuary opened. Erik stood in the doorway. He scanned the room and beckoned urgently to her. She went to him, her stomach churning.

His face pinched and drawn, Erik stepped back into the hallway and closed the door. "Schrammig is on his way here."

At least the lookouts had bought them a little time. "How many soldiers?"

"There are soldiers everywhere now." He steered her to one of the windows. His voice quavered. "Look outside."

An orange glow on the horizon overshadowed the pink hues of dawn. Last Hope was burning. Her jaw clenched. She'd reassured the monks that Willem's plan, whatever it was, would succeed. If he had failed, no one remained to stop Schrammig from burning Last Hope to the ground. "What if they burn the church?"

Erik's expression showed determination mingled with dismay and fear. "Let's pray they don't. We'll do our best to slow them down until everyone is in the catacombs."

Slowing down the soldiers was a death sentence. She and Erik knew that, as did the monks who had volunteered for the task. She tried to dispel the image of the blackened bodies from the monks' farm and the lingering reek of burning flesh.

Focus on surviving. People are counting on us.

"I must go back to help reinforce the barricades. We'll give you as much time as we can." Erik looked out the window, and a long sigh escaped his lips. "Brother Jerome still thinks we can negotiate. He insists on waiting in the courtyard so he can speak with Schrammig personally."

"Schrammig ain't coming here to negotiate. He'll kill whoever he finds."

"I told Brother Jerome about Schrammig. He won't listen. There's nothing we can do to stop him."

Some monks were as opinionated as Erik. Brother Jerome, one of the older monks, insisted on adhering to church policy. He didn't believe they should challenge the Guild's authority. Perhaps he felt secure in the church's promise of an afterlife and wasn't afraid to die.

Sydney studied Erik's plump face, so critical when they'd first met, now lined with the weight of the horrors they'd experienced and those to come. "Be careful."

Erik put a hand on her shoulder. "You, too. You should be well hidden in the catacombs. Hurry." He squeezed her shoulder. After taking a few steps, he stopped and faced her. "Sydney, I wanted to say—that is, I want to apologize. For judging you so harshly when we first met. I shouldn't have treated you, or anyone else, that way." He turned and hurried away.

His compassion eased her tension for a moment. "Thanks, Erik," she called. He glanced back briefly to give her a genuine smile.

Sydney returned to the sanctuary. The first rays of dawn gleamed through the stained glass window above the altar. She and Brother Thomas had already relocated many of the refugees to the hidden catacombs beneath the church. More people had arrived from the town to fill the empty spaces in the sanctuary—many more than she expected.

A handful of the remaining townsfolk watched her with anxious faces. She rubbed her eyes, trying to quell her fatigue and her rising panic. Scanning the faces of the children, she didn't see Janey, Sara, and Frannie, but they must be already hidden.

Brother Thomas sat near the altar, keeping a silent vigil. Neither of them had really slept. "The soldiers are coming," she said quietly. "Help me get everyone up."

People nudged their neighbors and woke their children. Brother Thomas guided the crowd to the curtained doorway beyond the altar. The hidden door led to a hallway, a narrow stair, and into the cellar. There they would find the warrens where the monks buried their dead, where they would join the others already hiding and hope to stay alive. Whether Schrammig would find them and how long they might be able to last was a question Sydney couldn't answer.

Sydney bent to help a woman pick up a heavy sack containing her belongings. "Make sure you don't leave anything behind."

The woman pulled the sack away from her, muttering, "Don't need your help. It's the likes of you brought them soldiers here."

"Don't pay her no mind." The man beside her raised a hand to the mass of scar tissue in his right eye socket. "Courtesy of the Guild." He hobbled ahead, leaning on a wooden crutch. "Someone's gotta stand up to them. Why shouldn't Edgar's kid be the one to do it?"

The woman in front of him grumbled a curse.

"Some people don't understand how we've suffered." Another woman who cradled an infant touched Sydney's arm and gave her a grateful smile. "You do."

A distant, rhythmic thudding seemed to echo Sydney's pounding heart. "Hurry," she urged the stragglers, sensing the fear rippling from one to the next.

A hand tugged at her sleeve. "Sydney!"

The sight of Sara's tear-streaked face jolted her. "Sara, what's wrong? Why aren't you with your sisters?"

Tears streamed down Sara's face. "Janey's gone."

"Gone where?"

Sara was crying too hard to answer.

Sydney guided her away from the crowd. She knelt down and put her hands on Sara's shoulders. "Calm down," she said in a soothing voice. "Where's Janey?"

Sara gulped in deep breaths, choking back her sobs. "I-I saw her leave. She said...she said, she was gonna hurt them." Her bottom lip trembled. "She said not to tell anyone."

Sydney swore softly. Janey wanted revenge, and it was going to get her killed. Sydney drew in a long breath to calm herself. "You go with the others. I'll find your sister."

"I wanna come with you."

"No." Sydney shook her head. "Go back to Frannie. Look after her. Follow the others. They'll keep you safe. I'll be back as soon as I can."

Sydney didn't see Brother Thomas. There was no time to tell him where she was going. She made sure Sara rejoined the crowd and slipped out of the sanctuary, cursing Janey under her breath. She didn't blame the girl for being angry, but this was not the way to resolve her rage.

In the hallway, the pounding grew louder, now accompanied by cracking and splintering. The barricade wasn't going to hold much longer. Sydney quickened her pace, fighting the dizziness threatening to return.

She went into the first chapel she found. A candle glowed on the wooden altar, and a brazier in the corner gave off a sweet aroma. She had encouraged the monks to keep the chapels lit as a distraction. The last thing she wanted was for her and Janey to become the distraction.

"Janey? Are you in here?"

She heard a shuffling sound behind the altar.

"Janey, you can't stay here. It ain't safe."

"Leave me alone."

Relieved to hear Janey's voice, Sydney resisted the urge to

haul her out and shake some sense into her. "Don't be stupid. The soldiers are coming. I wouldn't try to face Schrammig on my own. How can you? Think about your sisters. Sara's worried sick."

"She said she wouldn't tell."

"She doesn't want anything to happen to you. Neither do I. I promised Bill—your da—I'd look after you. So did Willem."

Janey's head poked around the side of the altar. "Willem did, too?"

"'Course he did. We said we'd watch out for you."

"Willem's not back yet."

"Not yet." The shadows flickering on the chapel walls suddenly loomed large and menacing. *Only shadows*. She hoped. "Willem ain't here, but I am." She fought to keep her voice calm. "Now let's get the hell out, while we still can."

After a moment, Janey scrambled from behind the altar. In one hand she clutched a kitchen knife. She stared at the floor, scuffing her feet. "I'm sorry."

"Apologize later."

Sydney peeked out of the chapel. A smoky haze filled the corridor. She raised a hand to wave Janey forward but stopped when voices and footsteps sounded in the hallway.

Heavy, booted footsteps.

"Dammit." She ducked back into the chapel and grabbed Janey's arm. "Hurry, go hide."

This time Janey obeyed without question. Eyes wide, lips pinched tight, she scurried behind the altar.

Sydney drew her knife and gripped one of the empty candlesticks in her other hand. She crouched beside the altar, allowing herself a view of the entrance. "Keep still, Janey. Don't move, don't make a sound."

Seconds passed. Her body trembled, from fear and exhaustion. She struggled to keep the unsteadiness at bay. The footsteps and voices grew louder.

"There's a light. Check in there."

"You'd think they'd all be in there praying for their lives."

Harsh laughter. "Didn't help that monk outside, did it?"

Sydney gripped her knife. Glancing at Janey's frightened face, she understood exactly how Edgar had felt the night Schrammig had arrested him. He hadn't been thinking about himself. He'd been thinking about her. If the soldiers searched the room, they'd find Janey. Sydney couldn't let anything happen to her.

Two soldiers entered the chapel. Sydney jumped up. She hurled the candlestick at one man. He ducked. The candlestick clanged on the floor. The two soldiers exchanged smiles and moved in Sydney's direction, blocking her path to the door. She brandished her knife.

"Looks like this one wants to fight. Drop the knife, girl. It'll be easier on you."

Sydney avoided looking at the altar. *Let them think I'm alone in here.* She held out the blade. "All right, I give up."

The soldier closest to her took a step forward. "That's better. Now drop your weapon." He took another step.

"Not a chance." Sydney lunged for him. Her knife glanced off the sword he raised to block her. The blow sent her weapon flying across the floor. His fist slammed into her side, knocking her down. Pain exploded. Tears filled her eyes, and she gasped for air. The room started to spin.

"Get up," snarled the soldier. He jerked her to her feet and dragged her into the hallway.

"Schrammig wants all the prisoners. You take her outside. I'll keep searching."

The soldier gripped Sydney's arm as she stumbled down the hallway. She took deep breaths, trying to regain her focus. Slowly the corridor came into sharp relief. Turning a corner, they approached the exit to the courtyard. The benches and barrels the monks had used to brace the heavy wooden door were scattered on the floor. The door itself had been torn from its hinges and shattered into pieces.

"Schrammig usually doesn't take prisoners. Start thinking about how you're going to beg for your life."

Begging would never work with Schrammig, especially where she was concerned. Nor did she plan to give him such satisfaction.

They left the abbey and entered the courtyard. Her captor hesitated beyond the door. The glow on the horizon washed the courtyard in an eerie haze. Smoke hung like fog, stinging Sydney's eyes. The harsh odors of burnt wool, timber, and thatch assailed her lungs. Many of the uniformed men swarming the courtyard gathered near the abbey gates. Too many soldiers to count.

"You there! Why are you standing there?"

The raspy voice sent a stab of fear through Sydney. One figure detached from the group. The light caught his jagged scar.

"Sir, here's a prisoner for you. We found her hiding inside."

Schrammig strode forward. He rested one hand on the hilt of the sword belted at his side. "No prisoners."

"But I thought—that is, you said—"

"I've changed my mind. How many men are still in there?"

"About twenty? We're searching, sir, as you ordered."

"I've changed my orders. I want every man out here, now. Go get them. If you find anyone inside, kill them. Then burn the damn church. We're moving out."

"Yes, sir. Right away." The soldier took a few steps and then stopped. He nodded to Sydney. "What about her?"

Schrammig swiveled toward Sydney. A smile crossed his lips. "I'll deal with this one."

The soldier gave a curt bow and hurried back inside.

Schrammig clamped a hand on her shoulder and steered her away from the gathering soldiers.

"Sir?"

He stopped. "Now what?"

"Sir, one of the scouts just reported in. He says the enemy

is headed this way. We don't have much time."

"That's why I gave the order to regroup. Is there a problem? Or are you afraid of these pitiful mobs armed with sticks?"

"No, sir, of course not. But these aren't townspeople. They're soldiers, carrying Lord Stephan's banner."

Schrammig's hand tightened on Sydney's shoulder. "You're sure of this?"

"It's what the scout reported, sir. They broke through our outer defenses. They came out of nowhere." The man hesitated. "Some are saying the enemy is using magic to hide from us."

"Magic," Schrammig spat. "Anyone who speaks of magic in my presence won't live to repeat it. Willem and Stephan bleed the same as the rest of us. Now move out. I'll be right there."

"Yes, sir."

Schrammig dragged Sydney into the waning shadows at the edge of the building. He twisted her arm, bringing tears to her eyes. "Magic doesn't scare me, Sydney. Durok claimed to be the most powerful wizard alive, but you're here and he's not. I don't care how you defeated him. You saved me the trouble. In the end, wizards can never be trusted."

"There's a lot you don't know about wizards."

"Is there?" He leaned closer. He reeked of blood, sweat, and smoke. "There are no wizards here to save you now. I intended to hang you, but there's no time. Besides, I'd much rather kill you myself. I didn't have that pleasure with Edgar."

"No!" A small figure hurtled toward them and threw herself on Schrammig. "Leave her alone!" Janey shrieked.

"Janey, no!"

Janey's knife struck Schrammig's shoulder. Snarling, he whirled around. He grabbed the girl and threw her on the ground. The blade clattered on the cobblestones. He clutched his shoulder. Blood oozed between his fingers. "You little bitch."

"Janey, get up! Run!"

Janey whimpered, her body still.

Schrammig drew his sword. "Too bad she couldn't save you. She dies first." He stepped toward Janey's unmoving body.

Freed from his grasp, Sydney dived for the knife. Schrammig plunged his sword into Janey's chest. Sydney's scream was drowned out by shouting and the clash of steel. Outside the courtyard, the street erupted in a writhing sea of bodies.

Schrammig faced her. Blood stained the end of his sword. Her legs shook, and helpless rage immobilized her. He raised his weapon. Sydney scrambled to her feet and backed away, but he was quicker. He smacked her across the face. She stumbled against the building. Her vision blurred, and the blood pounded in her ears.

His arm pressed against her neck, forcing her back to the mossy wall. His blade was cold against her throat, and the knife slipped from her injured hand. The shouts and cries of the dying men in the courtyard became an incoherent din.

Pain consumed her body. Hate filled her mind. Dark shapes appeared at the edges of her vision. The Shadow Folk. Somehow she'd called them back. They promised vengeance and retribution. From the corner of her eye, she glimpsed Janey's body, a red stain blossoming on the front of her dress.

She summoned her last reserves of strength. "You ain't gonna win this time."

Her vision cleared. She stared into Schrammig's eyes. The Shadow Folk swarmed around him. For the first time, his eyes grew wide with fear. He lowered his sword and moved back. An image of a boy she didn't recognize appeared in her mind. A group of older boys taunted him, one of whom, she realized with a start, was a much younger version of Edgar. She felt the younger boy's terror and anger and helplessness. The others threw mud, then stones, and then they beat him with their fists.

His hands covered his head, but he never cried out and never begged for mercy.

She didn't want to believe the vision, although she knew it to be true. "Leave me alone!" she shouted at the shadowy figures. "I don't want your help!"

The vision disappeared. The shadows fled. But they had done enough.

Seeing Schrammig crouched on the ground, still cowering, as he'd once done so long ago, inflamed her rage. She needed to hurt him the way he'd hurt so many others.

She kicked him in the groin. His body doubled, his face warped in pain. "This is for Edgar." She kicked him again, this time in the stomach. "This is for Janey and Zared and Betty and all the other lives you've destroyed." She struck him repeatedly with her boot, until she felt his ribs crack and saw flecks of blood upon his lips. She could never hurt him as much as he had hurt her.

Finally, she staggered back, shocked by her fury. Schrammig gasped, his breath rattling. Her legs buckled, and she crumpled to the ground.

"Milady? Are you all right?"

She raised her head. Several soldiers stood over her. Her hand fumbled for Janey's knife.

"We're not going to hurt you."

Their red uniforms were similar to the one Rolf had worn when she had first met him. Lord Stephan's soldiers.

One of them bent to examine Schrammig. "Quick, go get Willem."

Sydney crawled to Janey. She lifted the girl's body and cradled her to her chest. "I'm sorry, Janey. I'm so sorry."

Heedless of the soldiers standing watch, Sydney let the tears stream down her face, clutching the girl she'd tried so desperately to save. A girl too much like herself.

"Where is he?"

Sydney looked up at the sound of Willem's voice. He strode

in her direction, and she almost didn't recognize him. His blue eyes gleamed in a face smudged with soot, and blood and gore streaked his leather jerkin. For a moment, he stared at Schrammig, silent. Then he turned to Sydney. His eyes grew wide.

"Sydney?" In a moment, he was kneeling beside her. He touched her face. "Are you hurt?" he whispered.

She shook her head and looked down at Janey.

Willem gently took Janey from her. Brushing a lock of hair from the girl's face, he laid her on the ground.

"I couldn't save her." Sydney's voice was hoarse. "I promised I'd protect her, but I couldn't."

"I'm sorry, Sydney." Willem sat and put his arm around her. "You're safe now. He can't hurt you any more." He raised his head to speak to one of the soldiers. "Get him out of here. Keep him alive. I intend to see him hang."

Two men stepped forward and dragged Schrammig's battered body away.

Willem's strong arms drew her in, enfolding her in a sense of peace and security. Together, they sat on the bloodstained cobblestones, and he held her while she cried.

Chapter Thirty-Three

Sydney stood near the front of the somber crowd gathered in the market square. The wooden scaffold loomed before them. A single rope swayed in the gusty breeze. Shivering, she hugged her arms to her chest.

Anaria put an arm around her. "We'll see the bastard dead soon enough, but it's not over then. It won't bring any of them back. Not Edgar. Not Janey. Not any of them that's dead 'cause of him. It's over when you accept they're dead and get on with your life."

The images of Janey's body crumpled on the ground and Zared's pleading stare as the blade slit his throat still haunted her. But Anaria was right. She needed to move on.

"I should've listened to you a long time ago," she told Anaria.

"High time I hear those words from you," Anaria said with a snort. "You always was a stubborn girl. Had to find your own way. Like Edgar, I suppose."

Sydney bit her lip. She'd debated whether to tell Anaria the truth about Edgar being her father and finally decided to let Anaria believe the same thing Edgar had believed. Revealing that Edgar had not been completely faithful to her would be more painful, and Sydney couldn't bear to cause her any more pain.

"I'm not one to give you advice, Syd, but it's time you start thinking about your future. Something besides Last Hope." Anaria inclined her head toward the area near the scaffold usually reserved for Guild officials. Today, Willem, Lord Aldric, and Lord Stephan, who had arrived with Willem's reinforcements, were the guests of honor. A number of well-dressed merchants, including Celena and Jimmy, stood alongside them. Jimmy shifted from one foot to another, twisting the cap in his hands.

"I'm not too familiar with kings," Anaria continued, "but Willem seems like a decent, honorable man. Someone who cares about other people—especially his friends."

Sydney turned from her stare. She wasn't sure what to think about Willem now. People in Last Hope considered him a hero. Some claimed he'd used magic to defeat Schrammig, feeding rumors he could call upon wizards and the faery folk for aid. His efforts to reestablish order and begin the rebuilding had earned him the respect of the townsfolk. Sydney's feelings for him hadn't changed, but with each passing day, Willem the future king moved beyond her reach.

A murmur rippled through the crowd. Willem had stepped onto the platform. The other nobles were dressed in their finest clothes and furs; Willem wore a simple tunic and trousers. His only adornment was his gold signet ring, which flashed in the sunlight when he held up his hands to silence the crowd.

"People of Last Hope, you have suffered much over the years at the hands of the Guild. You have suffered even more these past days. I pledge to you that I will see Last Hope restored. You are now free of the Guild. A new day is dawning, not only here, but throughout Thanumor. We will soon overthrow the Guild in every city and town. Last Hope is just the beginning. You are an example of what is possible. As a testament to what you have accomplished here, I'm granting the town a charter."

He beckoned to Jimmy, whose face reddened as he

reluctantly joined him. Willem put a hand on his shoulder. "This charter means the town is now autonomous. I am appointing Jimmy, proprietor of the Black Dog and a leader in your fight against the Guild, as mayor. He will choose a town council to assist him, and together they will govern Last Hope. You will still pay Lord Aldric for the use of his lands, and he will be given a seat on the council, but you will not be beholden to any lord. You will only be beholden to your king."

The crowd erupted in thunderous applause. Jimmy beamed. He started to hug Willem, but stopped himself, and clasped Willem's hand instead. Sydney cheered along with the rest of the crowd and shouted Willem's name.

Willem again raised his hands for silence. "First, we must all bear witness to the sentence of one who has caused this town much pain. The names of his victims are too many to repeat here, but they will never be forgotten. Schrammig has been accused of many crimes and many deaths, and he has been found guilty. I hereby order him to be hanged until dead."

The crowd was silent. Willem and Jimmy returned to their places. Anaria gripped Sydney's hand. The black-hooded hangman inspected the rope. When he finished, two red-coated soldiers, Lord Stephan's men, escorted Schrammig in front of the crowd to the steps leading to the platform.

The crowd jeered and shouted at him.

"Murderer!"

"Hanging's too good for him!"

A stone flew past Schrammig's head, barely missing him. Someone hurled another stone, which struck him in the arm. The two soldiers escorting Schrammig faced the crowd and drew their swords, putting themselves between the mob and their prisoner. Sydney sensed the explosive anger in the people around her. More people threw stones; some hit Schrammig, some hit the soldiers. The crowd began to surge forward.

"Don't let him get away!"

"Let's kill him now!"

The crowd pushed them forward, and Sydney grabbed Anaria's arm. *They'll tear him to pieces.* Part of her wanted to join them. And part of her was sickened by the idea. The shouts around her built to a crescendo.

A hollow stomping cut through the din. "Stop! Don't do this!" Jimmy had leaped onto the platform. He stamped his feet and waved his arms to get their attention.

The crowd quieted to a spattering of taunts and insults.

"This isn't justice," Jimmy said. "I understand how you feel. I've lost good friends, same as you. Friends, family, even our children. But we can't stoop to his level. He deserves much worse than this," Jimmy jabbed his thumb at the noose behind him, "but that's what the Guild would do. We're better than they are. We need to see justice done here today, so we can find a way to move on with our lives." He glanced at Willem, who had also approached the crowd. Willem gave a brief nod.

Jimmy motioned to the soldiers and moved to the other side of the platform.

Schrammig limped up the steps and stood before the noose. Blood matted one side of his head. His white shirt was torn and blood-spattered. "This is what I think of your sentence," he said. He spat in Willem's direction and stared defiantly at the crowd. "These nobles don't care about your interests. Only the Guild does. One day you'll realize I'm right."

The hangman placed the noose around his neck and tightened the rope.

Schrammig's gaze sought Sydney's. His eyes blazed the same defiance she had seen in the young boy who had been beaten by Edgar and the others. She refused to look away, and finally, it was he who turned.

The hangman glanced at Willem, who nodded. He pulled the lever. The trapdoor banged open, and the rope stretched taut.

Weeping broke the stillness. Anaria wiped the tears from

her eyes. Sydney didn't cry. Numbness enveloped her. She watched the body jerking, legs kicking, until finally, it swayed gently back and forth.

The crowd cheered. Sydney put her arm around Anaria, who drew in a ragged breath. "Let's go," Sydney said. She needed to get away from the crush of people celebrating Schrammig's death. They made their way toward the edge of the square.

"Anaria! Sydney!" Jimmy waved at them. Every few feet someone stopped him to shake his hand or slap him on the back.

"Congratulations are in order, eh?" Anaria said when he finally caught up with them. She jabbed his chest playfully. "Drink's on me next time you come in, unless the mayor of Last Hope's too high and mighty to visit the likes of us now."

Jimmy grinned. "Not if you're offering free ale." He touched Anaria's hand, his smile fading. "Never expected to live to see this day, did we?"

Anaria gripped his hand, and a tear slid down her cheek. Jimmy wiped it away with his thumb, his hand resting on her face for a moment. The glance passing between them startled Sydney. *Affection?* Then it was gone, and Anaria grinned and swatted Jimmy's hand away.

He faced Sydney. "About this new town council. 'Course the merchants will be part of it, but I figured we outta ask some ordinary folks to join, too. Represent the interests of the people. Celena recommended you."

"Me?" She stared at him in shock.

"She speaks highly of you. So do a lot of others around here. You're a natural leader. You could do a lot of good for Last Hope. Help us make a new start."

She couldn't picture herself discussing important town issues with merchants like Celena. What the hell did she know about those things? As much as she did about magic or anything else she'd been caught up in since she met Oryn.

"You could use a new start, too, Syd," Anaria added.

"Just think on it, won't you?"

A new start. Anaria was right. She needed that. "I'll think on it."

"Great." Jimmy squeezed her shoulder. He winked at Anaria. "Have to go, but I'll be by soon for the ale."

He headed back into the crowd. Sydney glanced at the body hanging from the gallows. She drew in a long breath. "I could use a drink now. Think there are any taverns open?"

Anaria's arm encircled Sydney's waist. "I know just the place."

———————

"Sydney?" Gregor's tall frame filled the doorway of the abbey kitchen. "Erik said I'd find you here. I haven't seen you in days."

"I'm keeping busy." Sydney swept a handful of peelings into a bucket and plucked another potato from a sack on the floor. The kitchen was empty at mid-morning, and she relished the quiet. The mundane tasks of peeling potatoes, chopping vegetables, even washing dishes, offered a respite from the draining efforts of reuniting families and finding food and shelter for the many people displaced by the battle to save Last Hope from the Guild.

Gregor sat across from her. "You've done a lot of good here. But you're hiding."

She focused on the short, even strokes of her knife. "I ain't hiding."

"Why haven't you spoken to Sara?"

She tensed. The knife slipped, barely missing her thumb. "I've been busy. You've seen how many people are still staying here. I'm helping the monks—"

"You're helping everyone but a little girl who really needs a friend right now." Gregor placed his hand over her fingers, removing the knife from her grasp. "Willem's forces are moving out in three days. I'm leaving for Aldric's keep on the morrow to join him. I offered to escort Sara and Frannie there, to the care of their uncle. Aldric's steward is their only relative. He and his wife will take them in."

Sydney nodded, her throat tight. Bill had been missing since the day she and Willem had returned to the abbey; at last, his body had been found. Two more orphans. The girls had lost not only their parents, but also their sister.

"I was hoping you could tell Sara she'll be living with her uncle. I figured you could come with us, help ease the transition. The monks can spare you."

"I don't know."

"Sydney, I can imagine what you must be feeling." Gregor's blue-gray eyes showed compassion. "Janey's death isn't your fault. You keep blaming yourself for things beyond your control. Let them go. Sara needs you, too."

Sydney pictured Sara's trusting face, felt the small arms around her neck. She'd let Sara down. "I don't know if I'm the sort of friend she needs."

"You are exactly what she needs. Now come." Gregor gently took her arm and marched her down the hallway toward the common room where Sara and her sister were staying with the other townsfolk who had lost their homes. "She's in there alone. Go talk to her."

Sara sat on one of the straw pallets. She tossed a glittering object from one hand to the other. Her face lit up when Sydney approached. She held out her hand, revealing a yellow glass bead. "Look. Willem gave it to me. It's a new good luck charm."

Sydney touched the shiny bead with her finger. "When did you see Willem?"

"He came after breakfast. But you haven't been here at all."

"I'm sorry. It's just...." She took a deep breath and sat beside the girl. "It's Janey."

Sara's eyes filled with tears. "I miss her. You said you'd find her. You said you'd keep her safe."

"Oh, Sara. I'm so sorry." Sydney put her arms around the girl and blinked back tears. "I tried to save her, but I couldn't."

"I was mad at you, but I'm not any more. Brother Erik says we should forgive the people we're mad at." Sara pulled away, frowning. "I don't want to forgive Schrammig. He's dead now, isn't he?"

"Yes, he's dead. And he doesn't need to be forgiven."

"Good. That's what Willem said, too. He said we're going to live with Uncle Marcus. Why can't me and Frannie stay with you? You and Willem can look after us. We'll go wherever you go."

Sydney had considered asking Anaria to allow her and the girls to live at the Silver Eagle, but quickly dismissed the idea. She could barely support herself. Living at Aldric's keep would provide the girls with the opportunities their parents would have wanted for them.

"You can't stay with me or Willem. I wish you could, but it's not possible."

"We don't eat much. We can be really quiet."

Sydney patted Sara's leg. "Your uncle's a good man. He'll give you a decent home."

Sara's lip quivered. "Will you come visit?"

"Of course. Every chance I get."

Sara threw her arms around Sydney's waist. "Promise?"

"I promise." This one she intended to keep. "Now let's go find your sister and pack your things."

Gregor waited for her. He put a comforting arm around her shoulders. "I heard what you said. I'm impressed, Sydney. You've changed a great deal since we've met."

She smiled. "Thanks. A lot has happened since then. To all of us. Even Erik's changed. Hard to believe he's decided to stay here a while. In a town full of thieves and pickpockets."

Gregor chuckled. "Each trial we endure shapes us and gives

us strength. We can see those changes even in Erik. I'm certain we'll face more challenges to come, but I hope none as difficult as those we have already survived."

During these recent days, Sydney had sensed a measure of contentment in Gregor. Perhaps serving Willem would help him regain the honor that had been unjustly taken from him.

"We're survivors, ain't we?"

The lines around his eyes crinkled in a smile. "That we are, Sydney."

Chapter Thirty-Four

The wagon threaded among the tents, wagons, carts, horses, and host of men encamped on the fields around Lord Aldric's keep. Sydney's thoughts returned to the tapestry from Oryn's tower and the vision she and Willem had shared in the faery realm. She shuddered. Sara leaned against her, clutching little Frannie, and Sydney gave the girl a comforting hug.

"Wait here while I find the steward," Gregor said when they entered the bustling outer courtyard. He jumped from the wagon and hurried through the crowd of soldiers. Voices and laughter were accompanied by the clanging of a blacksmith's hammer. A dog barked in the distance. The late afternoon sun burnished the walls of the stone keep, and the smell of cooking fires, leather, and animal musk filled the crowded space.

"You'll be safe here," she assured Sara. "You'll see."

Moments later, Marcus and a stout woman approached the wagon. "Sara? Frannie?" The woman's voice caught in her throat. "Oh, my dear girls!"

"Auntie Pricilla!"

Sydney helped Sara down and handed Frannie to Pricilla.

"Thank you, Sydney." Marcus embraced her. "I heard what you did for my family. We are in your debt."

"I wish I'd—"

"Hush now." Pricilla held Frannie in one arm and with the other pressed Sara to her skirts. Her eyes glistened. "You did what you could. We could ask no more than that."

"She says she's going to visit whenever she can," Sara piped up.

Sydney smiled, despite the catch in her throat. "I'll try."

"You are always welcome here," Marcus said. He turned to his wife and reached down to tousle Sara's hair. "You should get them inside, my dear. This is no place for children."

Sara gave a little wave, and Pricilla took her hand and ushered her into the inner courtyard.

Sydney blinked away a tear. *It's for the best. The girls deserve this kind of life.*

"Sydney!" Rolf's voice shouted across the courtyard.

She nodded to Marcus and made her way to Rolf and Gregor. Rolf slapped her on the back. She flinched. Her wounds from the torture she'd endured were still healing.

Rolf didn't appear to notice. "So good to see you again, Syd," he said with a grin. "Can't believe I missed all the excitement. I've heard all kinds of stories. You've gotta tell me all about it."

He guided them around the clusters of soldiers and horses and barrels of supplies. "Willem asked me to show you to your rooms. You're lucky you're not sleeping in the barracks like the rest of us."

"I don't mind—" Gregor began.

"Willem's orders." Rolf shrugged. "Wouldn't want to go against those. I'll meet you for dinner, and we can swap stories. You met Stephan yet? I'll introduce you. My uncle's a good man. You'll like him."

"Dinner?" Sydney pictured Aldric's grand hall. Her mouth went dry.

"In Willem's honor, of course. More food than I'll wager you've ever seen. I tried to get us seats at the head table, but Stephan commandeered them for more important folks, the other nobles and such."

Sydney narrowed her eyes at Gregor. "You didn't tell me

there'd be a fancy dinner."

"Don't worry, you'll be fine."

Rolf looked her over and shook his head. "You didn't bring anything suitable to wear, did you?"

Her face grew warm. She scuffed the mud from her boots, wishing she still had the dress Vadnae had given her, but it had been lost somewhere in Last Hope. "Not really. I can wash these."

"Definitely not. Willem would have me flogged if I let you show up looking like a vagabond. We'll find something for you, Syd. Something more appropriate. Like a dress." Rolf winked at her.

The maid Rolf sent to her brought an armful of gowns for Sydney to try. They were attractive, but the layers of skirts and petticoats weighed her down, and the fine-boned corsets, meant to accentuate her narrow waist, dug into her ribs.

"How am I supposed to breathe? Or eat?" Sydney turned from the floor-length mirror to the maid arranging the other dresses on the bed.

"Sparingly, miss."

Willem has never seen me in a gown like this. Looking like a lady. But she wasn't willing to torment herself to meet whatever standards of beauty the noblewomen adhered to, not even for Willem. She gestured to the maid to help her out of the gown. Ignoring the maid's disapproving stare, she frowned and examined the options spread out on the bed. At last, she chose a simple, burgundy velvet dress, which, the maid informed her with a sniff, had been borrowed from one of the steward's daughters.

"I hope it suits you, miss." The maid thrust the dress into Sydney's arms, her eyebrows raised in a haughty expression. "I expect you can manage this one. I must go. A few of the ladies have requested my services."

Sydney watched her march down the lavishly furnished hallway of the guest wing. She certainly didn't need any help getting dressed, but the implied insult still stung. *Even the maid can see I'm not one of them.*

She took in the room where she was to sleep. A cheery fire burned in the hearth, and soft blankets and pillows mounded on the four-poster bed. For days she'd been sleeping on a straw pallet on the floor of a room packed with people.

Tittering voices and laughter sounded in the hallway outside her room. Sydney laid the dress she'd chosen across the bed and stared at it. *I don't even know how to act at a banquet.* She took a deep breath and began to dress. Lacing up the bodice took more time and concentration than she expected. When she finished, she washed her face using the basin of water provided and finger combed her hair. The dirt beneath her fingernails wouldn't wash away. She paced nervously and then practiced walking with her head held high, as if she belonged. Her pacing led her to the mirror, and peering at herself, she was amazed at the transformation. The dress was simple but still elegant. Ladylike. Luckily, the long sleeves covered the wounds on her wrists, and the ankle-length skirt hid her boots. She smiled, thinking of how horrified Vadnae would be that she didn't have a proper pair of shoes to wear to the banquet.

If only she felt like she belonged.

Aldric's great hall was filled with tables, finely dressed nobles, servants, and—Rolf was right—more food than she'd ever seen. Servants moved from table to table, carrying silver trays displaying several kinds of roasted game, a suckling pig, winter vegetables, and savory tarts.

The wine was as plentiful as the food. The other women seated at their table merely sipped from their silver goblets. Despite their disapproving glances, Sydney had her goblet refilled a second and a third time. The wine didn't take away her discomfort at the obscene abundance, but it helped soothe some of her anxiety when she watched the elegantly dressed women who seemed perfectly at ease in this setting, especially the women who spoke to Willem in his place of honor at the head table.

A servant helpfully refilled her goblet a fourth time, and Rolf suggested a toast. "Before Syd finishes all the wine, let's drink to those who aren't with us tonight."

Gregor raised his goblet. "Hear, hear. Let's also drink to Vadnae, may she return to us soon."

"And Erik," Sydney added, thinking how much the plump monk would have enjoyed the feast.

Rolf grimaced. "I'll need another refill for Erik."

"Rolf, my boy, you aren't embarrassing me again, are you?" Lord Stephan's voice boomed as he approached their table. He slapped Rolf on the back. "You must forgive my nephew's manners. He's become accustomed to eating in the barracks."

A broad-shouldered man whose auburn hair was flecked with gray, Stephan smiled and greeted everyone by name. He stopped beside Sydney. "We've not been formally introduced, although I've heard a great deal about you. Perhaps you would care to take a walk with me, Sydney."

She clutched the silver wine goblet. Gregor elbowed her. The women across the table were whispering again. "Uh, all right."

She accepted his hand, and he led her around the tables to a more secluded corner. She craned her neck for a view of the head table. Aldric and another nobleman blocked Willem from view.

Stephan followed her gaze. "Willem speaks highly of you."

Her cheeks glowed. Too much wine. She wished her head were a little clearer. "I'm glad I had the chance to help him in Last Hope."

"Have you always lived there?"

Aldric had once asked her a similar question, as if living in Last Hope was something to be ashamed of. She looked Stephan in the eye. "I have. I bet you already know that."

He returned her stare and frowned. "Yes, I do. I also know Edgar was your father. It's a pity there is nothing left of his lands for you to claim. I hope you realize that there are some things even noble blood cannot overcome. Do you understand what I'm saying, Sydney?"

She folded her arms across her chest. "No, I don't."

His frown deepened. "Willem is like a son to me. I've put a great deal of time and effort into ensuring that his birthright is restored. I won't let anything—or anyone—stand in his way."

"You think I—"

He cut her off with a wave of his hand. "I think you're a distraction, whatever your intentions may be." From within his fur-lined tunic, he withdrew a leather purse. "Please, take this."

"You're giving me money? To stay away from Willem? Does he know this?"

Stephan held out the purse. "Willem would want you to be compensated for your service to the crown."

She stared at him, shocked. With a swift motion, she knocked the purse to the floor. "Keep your damn money. You can't buy me off. Let Willem make his own choices." She turned on her heel and left, her heart pounding in her ears.

———

Sydney paced her room, unable to sleep. She'd believed Willem was different from the other nobles, but doubt crept into her mind. Maybe she was wrong. Maybe that was why he'd been avoiding her.

She bit her lip. She cared what Willem thought. She cared too damn much.

The burgundy dress was draped over the chair, a shell of someone she could never be. She stroked the velvety material, imagining Willem, as king, presiding over an even more decadent banquet. He'd need a woman by his side who was acquainted with protocol, accepted by the nobles. *I can't be the woman he needs. Am I even the woman he wants?*

A tapping on the door made her jump. She glanced at the

window. Late, probably past midnight. She went to the door and said softly, "Who's there?"

"Open the door. Please."

Willem. She fumbled with the latch, her pulse quickening. Willem stood in the hallway, still wearing his gold-trimmed, red silk tunic and white linen trousers. The lamplight caught the deep blue of his eyes.

He glanced over his shoulder at the empty corridor. Quickly entering, he closed and locked the door behind him and leaned against it. "I haven't had a moment's peace in days. I've wanted to see you, Sydney, but—"

"You couldn't speak to me at dinner? Coming to my room at this late hour is the best you can do?"

He winced. "I'm sorry. I didn't mean for it to look improper."

She searched his face for a spark of emotion. None. Was she mistaken in thinking he shared her feelings? Why else had he come to her room? She swallowed hard. "To hell with what's proper. I'll wager someone saw you sneaking in here. It'll be the talk of the keep tomorrow morning."

A flush crept up his neck. "If you'd rather I leave—"

"No, don't go. Stay here. I mean…oh hell…."

His mouth twitched into a smile. "Let them gossip all they want. I don't care what they think."

Maybe you should. She dared not speak the words aloud. Dressed in his finest attire, Willem carried himself with the confidence of a man accustomed to wealth and power. She brushed flecks of dried mud from her woolen shirt. For a moment, she wished she hadn't taken off the dress. "What about your friend Lord Stephan? D'you care what he thinks? He tried to give me money so I'd stay away from you."

"Stephan offered you money?"

"For my services to the crown," she added with a bitter laugh.

"He actually *said* that?"

The incredulous expression on Willem's face, which quickly flared to anger at her nod, told her that Stephan had indeed acted on his own.

Willem's face darkened. "I'll deal with Stephan first thing in the morning. He has no cause to speak on my behalf, much less to insult you."

"Damn right he doesn't." She walked to the window, crossing her arms. "He treated me like a whore. Is that what they all think of me?"

In a few strides, Willem caught up with her. Taking her arm, he gently turned her to face him. "Sydney, I would never think that of you."

The tenderness in his expression banished her doubt. Willem would never judge her, but his words didn't change how other people viewed her.

"Don't think badly of Stephan. He's a decent man. Sometimes a little too focused on the welfare of the kingdom. What did you say to him? I hope you didn't throw the money at him."

She forced a smile. "No, I threw it on the floor."

Willem chuckled. "You've never been afraid to speak your mind—or show your feelings. It's admirable. You're not like anyone I've ever met. You're not afraid to live by your principles."

"I've survived."

"You've gone far beyond just surviving, Sydney."

They stood, silent. Sydney's heart pounded. If they'd stayed with the Tuatha, none of these things would matter.

He took her hand. "I have something of yours. I wanted to return it to you myself."

Guiding her toward the hearth, his hand rested on her back. They sat on a soft fur pelt. Embers still glowed in the banked fire. Their knees touched. She longed to kiss him, to run her hands through his hair and press her body to his.

"I've never seen you in a dress like that." His voice was

low. "You were beautiful."

His words ignited the flame within her. She tensed, fighting to control her emotions. Willem wasn't like the other men she'd been with. She didn't know what to expect from him. It frightened and thrilled her at the same time.

"You came here because of the dress? Because I looked respectable?"

"No. Well, not exactly. I mean…you've always been beautiful.…" He rubbed the back of his neck, flustered in a way she'd never seen him before. He hurried to pull something from his pocket. "I came to give this to you. Found it in the Guild Hall, in Schrammig's room."

Edgar's coin. Tears filled her eyes. Sydney took the worn copper piece and curled her hand around it. "Thank you. I didn't expect to get it back."

"I know how much it means to you."

She ran her finger along the worn edges of the coin. "Schrammig did, too. You were right. He knew how to break me." She hadn't told anyone about her encounters with Schrammig. She doubted Willem was aware of the extent of her wounds.

She pushed back her sleeves, revealing the still-healing burns on her wrists. "He tortured me. The bastard.…" She gave a little shrug. "Pain doesn't bother me too much. What he said about Edgar hurt more. He grew up on Edgar's lands. The peasants who lived there—Schrammig—he said they were mistreated by Edgar and his family. Likely it's true."

Willem took her hand and squeezed it. "That was a long time ago. People make mistakes. I think Edgar more than atoned for whatever he did in the past."

She remained unsure whether *she'd* atoned for her past. She'd nearly fallen on the wrong side of the knife's edge Oryn had spoken of during her first day in the tower. Staring into the red and orange embers in the hearth, she said softly, "There's something more," and then paused. The kindness she saw in

Willem's face gave her the courage to continue. "I saw the Shadow Folk. That night at the abbey. Llyr said using their powers would be unforgivable. I wanted to hurt Schrammig. I wanted him to suffer." She closed her eyes to block the image of Janey's broken body. "I wanted the Shadow Folk to tear him to pieces, but I stopped myself."

Willem touched her cheek, bushing away a tear with his thumb. "You did the right thing. You're strong enough to resist the Shadow Folk. Oryn knew you would be."

She clenched her fists. The all too familiar tightening in her chest made her draw in a sharp breath. "Oryn said my mother was a Tuatha, and Edgar was my father. What the hell am I supposed to believe? I don't even know what I am."

In the dim light, flecks of silver reflected in Willem's eyes. He was of royal lineage. Some Tuatha blood ran in his veins, too.

"We'll find the answers. Our lives are bound together, Sydney. I don't understand why or how, but they are. I'm certain of it."

Bound together. That was how she felt. A mysterious force drawing them toward each other, no matter how impossible their relationship might be. That force pulled her toward him. His mouth sought hers. Her desire surged. Drawing her close, his fingers caressed her neck. She savored his kiss, letting it ease the hunger she'd felt.

At last, he moved back, breathless, his face flushed. "I've wanted to kiss you ever since we left the faery realm."

"So why didn't you?"

A smile played around his mouth. He laced his fingers through hers. "I didn't want to be distracted. Being this close to you is so damn distracting."

He trembled when she ran her fingertips over the calluses on his fingers and palm. A soldier's hand. Willem had his destiny to fulfill. He had a kingdom to claim. She was a distraction. Willem's world was one she didn't understand and didn't want to be a part of.

She placed her hand on his chest, feeling his heartbeat quicken. "Or is it because *we* aren't possible?"

"Anything is possible. If I asked you to come with me...." He drew back slightly, his gaze searching her face.

An ember sparked in the hearth. She lowered her head, her voice a whisper. "Willem, you know I can't."

Placing a hand under her chin, he raised her face to meet his. "I've a war to fight and a crown to claim. That would be no life for you. But things will be different once I'm king. When this war is over, I'll send word to you and—"

She put a finger to his lips. "Please. Don't make me any promises. You don't know what might happen next week or even tomorrow morning." She traced his mouth, feeling a tremor pass through him. "All we have is right now."

He took her hand and kissed her palm. "You've been hurt before. I don't want to cause you any more pain."

His gentle touch and the emotion in his eyes freed her from the grief, fear, and betrayal that had long been her companions.

"I know." She wrapped her arms tightly around his neck, trailing kisses across his cheek. She released the leather thong binding his hair and brushed back the blond locks falling about his face. His mouth captured hers, exploring, teasing. Her hands moved to his belt. She hesitated, afraid he might want her to stop. Their eyes met, his need mirroring hers. She undid the buckle.

Willem's sigh was like a long, slow groan. He stood, pulling her to her feet. In one motion, he drew the tunic over his head. Several wounds, including the one in his left shoulder, had been sutured, and a purple bruise marked his right side. She kissed the bruise, his skin warm against her mouth. His arms encircled her, pressing her to his bare chest. Her wounds, not yet healed, sent pain lancing through her back at the contact.

He relaxed his hold when she winced. Taking her hands, he led her to the bed. The lamplight flickered, throwing shadows across his face. He gently removed her clothes, mindful of her injuries. "We'll be careful," he whispered, shrugging out of his trousers.

His eyes took in every inch of her. No man had ever regarded her with a combination of intense longing and love before, like she was someone to be cherished, desired, and loved, body and soul. Suddenly shy, she crossed her arms, embarrassed by her bruises.

"Sydney." His voice was low. "You're beautiful. And strong. Don't ever be ashamed of who you are."

Willem kissed her wrists. His mouth trailed upwards, and shivers of pleasure centered within her. He took her in his arms, laying her down on the bed. His warmth flowed into her, and his feather-light caresses ignited her desire in ways she'd never experienced. She ran her hands over his chiseled body, aroused by his response to her touch.

Her need became overwhelming. She wrapped her legs around him and drew him into her. They moved slowly, a rhythm pulsing within her. The pleasure reflected in his eyes filled hers with tears. Together, they crested to new heights of ecstasy. They held onto each other, shuddering, until their passion was spent.

She nestled beside him, secure in the curve of her body against his. He stroked her hair, his breath warm on the back of her neck. Lying in his arms, her heart ached for what she might never truly have. She brought his hand to her lips and kissed it. *Bound together.* This pain she would gladly bear, knowing their love filled the void inside her.

Willem left before dawn. Neither of them spoke. He simply touched her face, kissed her, and quietly closed the door behind him.

Sydney pressed her face to the pillow they'd shared,

inhaling his scent, trying to capture his face and the contours of his body in her mind. Thinking of the brief night they'd shared, his body enfolding hers, rekindled her desire, and she longed for him with more intensity than she'd ever felt for a man.

Now he was gone. She brushed away her tears, steeling her heart.

The lush hues of dawn saturated the room, soothing her to sleep. In her dreams, she found herself on a misty, barren plain. Llyr had called this place the borderlands. She walked and walked until she approached a massive oak tree. Vadnae waited for her. She held out her hands to Sydney and embraced her.

"Is this real or a dream?"

"Both." Vadnae smiled. "I haven't yet finished my training, but I wanted to see you. They didn't give me a chance to say goodbye."

"Will you come back?"

"Soon, perhaps. Willem may need me more than he anticipates." Vadnae led her away from the tree. "There is something I want to tell you. What you did to Schrammig was very dangerous."

"I didn't ask the Shadow Folk to do anything for me."

"They are unpredictable and difficult to control. Sometimes the line between good and evil can be blurred. I don't believe they are evil, as the Tuatha seem to think. You must be careful, Sydney. Remember, though magic is not evil in itself, it can be misused. If you ever need me, I'll give you whatever help I can."

"How can I find you?"

Vadnae's image began to fade. "You will." She placed the glowing marble in Sydney's hand. "Grandfather asked me to give this to you. Don't forget, you possess your own magic. Goodbye, Sydney. We will meet again soon."

The landscape shifted into darkness. Sydney felt as if she

were falling. She jolted up in bed. Sunlight streamed between the gap in the heavy draperies. She drew in a shaky breath. Vadnae's friendship was more valuable than her guidance.

Opening her fist, she found she still held the marble, which had stopped glowing. She felt the power within it, a soft vibration resonating within her soul.

She got up, dressed in her old clothes, and packed her belongings. Edgar's coin still lay on a table near the hearth. Picking up an iron poker, she stoked the fire until the embers began to glow.

"I'm ready to move on, Edgar," she said aloud. "I know you'd understand."

She tossed the coin into the hearth. The leather cord sizzled and smoked, and the flames crackled.

She was ready to return to Last Hope.

Acknowledgments

Thanks to all of the members of my critique groups, the Novel Experience and the Maryland Dream Weavers, who have supported me during this long journey and never let me give up. Over the years we have grown as writers and friends. I can't thank you enough for your help.

Special thanks to Taria for the gorgeous cover.

A heartfelt thank you to Jenny and Vic for their editing services.

And thanks to my friends and family, who have always believed in me, and especially to my husband, who helped me follow my dream.

About the Author

Cindy Young-Turner has been writing for most of her life. At age twelve, she won her first writing contest, a local contest in her small hometown in Massachusetts calling for stories written in the style of Edgar Allan Poe. Thus began her love of stories that are dark and fantastical. She believes genre fiction can be just as well written and valuable as literature. The universal themes of love, hate, revenge, and redemption are present regardless of whether characters live in the distant future, on other planets, or in fantastical realms. By day she edits and does business development for international development projects. In her free time, she works on inspiring her characters to fight for change and justice in their imaginary worlds.

Please visit her website at http://cindyyoungturner.com for more information.